QUEEN OF THE SHADOW WOODS

THE SHADOWBLOOD DUET
VAL E. LANE

WAVE SONG PUBLISHING

TRIGGER WARNINGS

QOTSW is considered a New Adult fantasy and intended for readers
18+

Please Note that this list is not exhaustive.

Graphic violence and combat

Death of loved ones

Torture and physical abuse

Child abuse and neglect

Emotional and psychological abuse

Imprisonment and captivity

Self-harm

Suicidal thoughts

PTSD, trauma, and nightmares

Depression and hopelessness

Persecution for identity

Discrimination and xenophobia

Animal death

Fire and arson

War and mass death

Body horror

Forced marriage

Sexual assault and sexual situations

Substance/alcohol use

PLAYLIST

Queen of the Shadow Woods

Joel Sunny - Into the Woods

Astyria - Just a Girl

Ruelle - Game of Survival

RAIGN - Who Are You

Lord Huron - Meet Me in the Woods

Freya Ridings - Ultraviolet

LEVV - Arrow

Sam Tinnesz - Far From Home (The Raven)

LULLANAS - Queen of Disaster

Ruelle - War of Hearts

Dark Mage,JB RICKY,EYLA - Eyes Don't Lie

Luke Sital-Singh - Dark

Faouzia - UNETHICAL

Florence + The Machine - Howl

Tommee Profitt,Fleurie - Tragic

Krigarè - Never Alone

QUEEN OF THE SHADOW WOODS

Sam Tinnesz,Zayde Wølf - Man or a Monster (feat. Zayde Wølf)

Faouzia - Porcelain

The Weeknd,Lana Del Rey - The Abyss (feat. Lana Del Rey)

Ruelle,AG - Head And My Heart

mehro - chance with you

Madalen Duke - How Villains Are Made

Steelfeather - Heart of Darkness

Lana Del Rey - Cinnamon Girl

Tommee Profitt,Stephen Stanley - I'll Carry You

Taylor Swift - invisible string

The EverLove - Make Me Believe

Phillip Phillips - Dancing With Your Shadows

Astyria - Darkness Inside

Taylor Swift - The Fate of Ophelia

das - tired

Beth Crowley - I Didn't Ask For This

Sam Tinnesz,UNSECRET - Something I Can Never Have

MARINA - HOW TO SAY GOODBYE

MIIA - Dynasty

Lord Huron - The Yawning Grave

Katie Hargrove,Sarah deCourcy,Fired Earth Music - Find My Way Home

Christian Reindl,Atrel - Nobody Wants to Be Alone (feat. Atrel)

Saint Mesa - Wolf

Alexa Ray,Randall Jermaine - Fearless

Billie Eilish - No Time To Die

MØØNWATER,NOCTURN - Darkside

Egzod,Maestro Chives - Royalty

Florence + The Machine - Cosmic Love

Elley Duhé - MIDDLE OF THE NIGHT

Zayde Wølf - Not Scared of the Dark

Ghostly Kisses - Blackbirds

Susie Suh,Robot Koch - Here with Me

Taylor Swift - Out Of The Woods (Taylor's Version)

Rumi,Jinu,KPop Demon Hunters Cast,EJAE,Andrew Choi - Free

RAIGN - Empire Of Our Own (Orchestral Mix)

Ciara - Paint It, Black

Madeline Megery - Where You Roam

Isak Danielson - Power

PHILDEL - Into the Woods

Annaca - Wicked Thoughts

Sam Tinnesz - Even If It Hurts

Hozier - In the Woods Somewhere

Klergy,Mindy Jones - Hide and Seek

Joseph William Morgan - Memory

Taylor Swift - I Can Do It With a Broken Heart

ANA X,T.H.O.R.,Sybrid,Kat Meoz - It's In My Blood

Chord Overstreet - Hold On

Tommee Profitt,Sam Tinnesz - Heart Of The Darkness

Hozier - Empire Now

Ursine Vulpine,Annaca - Without You

Power-Haus,Tom Evans,Dramatic Violin - Middle Of The Night

+ Additional Bonus Songs on Spotify

*To the ones without a village, feeling like you're fighting through every day
alone.
You are not alone.
And you WILL find your way out of the woods.*

PROLOGUE

"You're certain you want me to try this?" The withering old woman clasped her wrinkle-etched hands together. "If her heart has already stopped, even magic won't save her."

The young woman at her doorstep placed a gentle hand across her barely bulging stomach. "I know. But I have to try. I can't lose her. I've already lost her father."

"You're so sure it's a girl?" The elder witch's eyes twinkled for just a mere moment with a revived vibrance.

The young mother nodded with confidence. Through pursed lips that had long ago shriveled into thin lines, the old woman let out a heavy sigh.

"I'll do what I can, Dyanna," she said. "Come forward."

Dyanna, unnerved at the mention of her name when she hadn't yet revealed it, stepped towards the figure in the middle of the dim cottage, surrounded by overflowing shelves of tomes, liquid vials, and jars of luminescent powders.

"One thing you should know." The witch began pacing around her, eyeing the bump of her belly. "*If* the spell works, and the child lives, she will be marked by the truth. You won't be able to hide this from her—or anyone else."

"I'll make sure she is protected. I'll keep her hidden."

"Your confidence blinds you to reality, my dear. This won't be easy. For you or the child. Things could become dangerous quickly. I myself fear I may not be safe even here much longer."

"I'll take care of her. I'll do what her father failed to do." Dyanna's heart quickened at the thought of him, how he'd vanished without so much as a goodbye, knowing she was carrying his sickly child.

"And when you no longer can?" The woman glowered. "Then what? Who will protect her?"

A breath caught in Dyanna's chest, doubt flaring for a heartbeat. But then she pushed it down and gathered the courage to answer.

"The truth," she said simply.

"Very well, then." The old woman nodded and held out her hand. "Just leave my name out of it if things don't go as planned."

Dyanna straightened her shoulders and placed a coin purse in the woman's crinkled palm. "You have my word."

PART I

1

THE WITCH

Caramyn

Twenty years later...

If she didn't kill them, the Shadows would. It was much quicker that way. And much more merciful.

It didn't matter where they came from or why. She'd learned by now that innocence was never called to these Woods. If they were here, they were a threat.

Nocking a feather-fletched arrow, Caramyn held her breath as she watched the three intruders below whispering around their fire. She was surprised they'd made it this long. Most were dead in less than an hour.

"We shouldn't be in these Woods." One of the men leaned forward, checking over his shoulder both directions. "What if the Witch knows we're here?"

"Calm down." The man next to him sneered. "We're at least safer with her than in the Felhold prisons. Robbing that royal gravesite was the best idea you've had in ages, but we can't spend the spoil until we've laid low for a while. Believe me, no one will look for us here."

Another man tossed a twig into the fire. "He's right. There's no Witch anyway. It's all made up horseshit to keep people scared. Witches, Shadows, those abominations with the haunted eyes—they're all long gone with the last of the magic scum. And there's probably such a spoil left behind at the Veil from the battle. Mark my words, they just don't want us common folk knowing what treasures they're hiding in these Woods."

Caramyn pressed her lips together. It was almost comical what these people thought up. There was no treasure within these trees. Only an ominous force that loomed beyond where even she dared to venture. A great void of black mist where the forest abruptly ended and a wall of darkness began—the Veil. A barrier of Shadow where the last Shadowblood took his final stand against the Lightborn, banishing them into the abyss, and where the remnants of his dark power lingered over the Woods like a suffocating cloak. And now, Shadows haunted the forest as prowling wraiths, emitting ghostly whispers and deathly curses that would chill even the bravest warrior's blood. And they certainly knew these intruders were here.

These fools were right about one thing, though. She was no witch. At least not the sort that once freely thrived in Evylere before it was a crime punishable by death.

No. Not a witch. She was something so wretched that only darkness defended her, and the Shadows were as real the cursed mark on her arm that bound her to them—that pattern of black, inky branch-like veins beneath pale skin that clustered in the hollow of her elbow and spread down her forearm in three delicate tendrils that all too strongly resembled roots.

The mark of a Shadowblood—though her half-Lightborn mother always swore it was anything but, that it wasn't possible. But she'd heard the stories. She knew the horrifying truth of the marks that betrayed cursed blood darkened by Shadows.

And she might've been able to hide it, if that had been the only mark she'd been cursed with. But her eyes betrayed her impossible heritage wherever she went, like all Lightborn, whose striking, unnatural eye colors served as visible proof of what stirred beneath the skin. But instead of the molten copper of a fire mage or the tide-washed topaz of a water witch, hers were moonlit amethysts that rivaled the hues of dusk. Ethereal purple that represented...nothing. No power. No magic. Only an anomaly that's cause had yet to be explained.

And though she always carried some hope with her that maybe she was wrong, that perhaps, like her mother said, it might just be a strange birthmark—a co-incidence—and nothing more, the night she came to the Woods had confirmed everything she feared. When she crossed the boundary of this cursed forest, the three rootlike veins lengthened, crawling farther down her forearm toward her wrist, branching as they grew, as if awakened by something ancient and watchful. A sigil. A claim. A permanent reminder that there was no redemption for those called to the Shadows.

And yet, the Shadows welcomed her when the world did not. They did not require long sleeves and hooded cloaks in their presence. They did not glance away when her mystic eyes suddenly met theirs. They accepted her wholly, and she existed in peace among them, driven by some strange instinct to guard the Veil alongside them in exchange for their protection.

And whenever she hesitated to kill an intruder—as she did now—her eyes would drift to that mark to remind her that perhaps she was meant for this darkness, and the darkness for her. And that's what she always told herself before she shot arrows through their hearts.

From her silent perch in the treetops, she released her breath and bowstring together. The arrow struck her target, and he crumpled without a sound. His two startled companions leapt to their feet, too slow, too late, to change their fate.

"It's the king's men!" One shouted, his gaze flickering across the trees.

They reached for their weapons, but then the Shadows coiled around them, writhing in patterns like vipers at their feet of the two men standing.

"No, it's the Witch!" One of them choked out as Shadows closed in around them and Caramyn leapt down from a gnarled tree branch without so much as the crunch of a leaf. She watched as the wraiths hissed, encompassing their victims before they ripped the essence of life from their bodies. No time for a scream, barely even a breath.

When all fell quiet, she retrieved her arrow and searched all three bodies, taking whatever treasures she could find. The tattoos etched onto their right arms confirmed they were just the type she suspected—prisoners, probably escaped, as these markings indicated serious crimes.

She searched satchels, pockets, and even their shoes. If they'd truly robbed a royal grave, the loot could sustain her for months, maybe years. She pocketed a wealth of gold, jewels, and a peculiar signet ring with a royal crest she didn't recognize. A thick golden band framed by intricate etchings of the moon phases on either side, until they met in the center to converge into a full moon. It could fetch a decent price at the market in Havenswood—if she ever felt safe enough to go back.

Rumors had been stirring about her presence in the superstitious hub of Havenswood, a mountain town cut off by rivers and terrain from the rest of the mortal lands. Their isolation made them hostile to anything that they suspected might've crossed from the witchlands or escaped from the Veil, or whatever scary bedtime stories they told their children.

Her cloaked disguise did little to make her forgettable when someone managed to catch a glimpse beneath her hood of her ethereal violet eyes or the marks that crept along her right arm like a blooming vine—the marks she bore that let the world know she was an enemy of the crown and the Order. The marks that would get her sent straight to Felhold to have her eyes plucked out and be torn limb from limb by the executioner prince of Blackwynd at the feet of his father. Even just a mark that hinted at magic was something sinister, dangerous, a rot in the veins, as they called it.

She would have to let the gossip die down for a while before returning. A long while. And that meant winter would be very, very difficult.

She thought to wear the ring on the walk home for safekeeping. After all, it might compliment her earthy brown locks nicely. She slipped the ring onto her finger, the campfire's glow illuminating it against her skin like warm amber.

She hated fire. The flames tugged at painful memories of the day she fled to this forest prison from the only home she ever knew, though it had sometimes felt like a prison itself. The accusations echoed in her mind just as clear as the day she left her world burning behind her.

Cursed. Tainted. Mistake. Monster.

Monster.

A monster not even a father could stick around for. A monster they thought her, so a monster she had become.

And so the monster beat out every last dying ember of the fire, unstrung her bow, and began her trek back to her small cottage nestled in the heart of the forest, halfway to the Veil. She knew every branch, every tree's crooked silhouette, and every call of the crows that flocked above. The deep forest roots twisting through the earth might've been a network of veins connected straight to her hidden heart, for in each nimble step of her bare feet, she walked and breathed in time with the pulse of the Woods. But her pace quickened as the sky darkened. She didn't like being out after nightfall if she could help it.

Her cottage entrance rarely looked more inviting than it did just before the last bit of sunlight faded in the Woods. Once inside, she placed her bow in the corner, then carved three notches into the wall with her dagger. Ninety-nine—the number of men who'd met their end at the tip of her arrow, or the blade of her dagger, or the wrath of the Shadows since she'd been here. Ninety-nine men. Only men.

She'd never seen a woman in the Woods. And the truth was, she hardly felt guilty anymore for the men. She hadn't always been this way, so numb to it all. In the beginning, she hid, letting trespassers wander until the forest claimed them. But the day came when a man finally found her and tried to force himself on her.

The Shadows intervened, and she understood—it was not mercy, but permission to pass her own sentence. She'd just returned from skinning a rabbit for supper, and her knife was still sharp. That was the first time she killed, and the moment she learned hiding would never be enough, not from those who came only to take. The Shadows would always find them eventually, but sometimes she was meant to find them first. And she had learned to harden herself to it. To hunt back, and to take no chances with men.

Men started the war on magic. Men created the Order to rid the world of it. Men had chased her to the edge of these Woods. And men had shown her there was nowhere else safe to go.

Trust no one...flee to where shadows hide the light...and when you find it, guard it with your life.

She shook away the echo of her mother's words and phantoms of the past she dared not invite in, despite their constant knocking. She sometimes dreamed of the freedom she might have had if not for the Blackwynd King—of a world where she wasn't bound to these Woods by duty and survival. But she couldn't risk an existence outside this forest, even if she often yearned to know what the world beyond these gnarled, twisting trees was like. Beyond the Bleak Wilderness that isolated this barren corner of the kingdom from the rest of the human lands and the witchlands.

A shiver tickled her spine. The lengthening starry nights carried the promise of late autumn on crisp, chilly air that leaked in through the space beneath the door. She dreaded the turning of the seasons. There was hardly enough prey in the Woods during summer, let alone when the frost came.

She stoked the fire that had been crackling long before she left. A raven crowed in the corner of the room. She stroked the bird's midnight feathers. "Don't worry, Nocthar. Of course I brought something for you." She opened her palm to reveal some cornmeal leftovers she had kept from the men's camp. The bird pecked the crumbs with a gratuitous chirp.

With that, Caramyn turned and sprawled across her fur-lined cot. Staring up at the tally marks, she touched a hand to her chest, just to be sure there was still a heart in there.

Is this how she would spend the rest of her days? Alone. Banished. Forever paying her debt to the Shadows for their sanctuary. Not living. Just enduring.

She supposed she had no other choice. There could be nothing more. Because she was the impossible daughter of a Shadowblood. And running from it had only led her here. Even closer to whatever dark destiny bound her to these Woods.

She closed her eyes, wondering when she would meet the next condemned soul who would bring the total on her wall to one hundred. It could be days, weeks, or even months. Or it could be tomorrow.

2
STRANGER IN THE WOODS

Caramyn

A glow of misty white light poured in from the single window, falling on Caramyn's face as she stirred with the dawn. Sunlight didn't reach the forest floor often, and there was always a grey haze overhead. The chill of morning seeped into her bones like a damp cloth. She stoked the dying fire to revive the barely glowing embers, then placed a kettle of porridge over it as the flames flickered back to life.

As she fetched cinnamon bark and dried berries from her cabinets, it was hard to ignore the unusual pounding in her forehead, but she disregarded it as no more than a bad night's rest. She hadn't slept well, and her dreams had been strange, with broken images of a bloody woman, a weeping child, and a shattered crown.

In hopes to forget the visions as her meal warmed, she sorted through her collection of books piled on the wooden wall of shelves. Most were old tomes and spellbooks that were already here when she found the abandoned cottage the day she ran to the Woods, though many pages were missing or burned, and she could hardly make sense of the ones that were intact. She'd tried her hand at some Spellbound magic from the bits and pieces she could put together, but despite the legend that anyone—even humans—could learn simple rune and relic-based magic, she never could quite grasp it, and thought it probably for the better.

She pulled a pile of her own books closer to her and traced her finger down their spines, grazing it over a range of fiction and nonfiction works. Some she'd stolen from intruders, and others she'd bought in Havenswood. She had read all of them, but she hoped that perhaps a title would jump out to her a second time. Anything to pass the hours and distract her from the aching in her head.

Herbal Remedies Every Healer Should Know

Dragon's Breath and Blood Rites

Hunter's Recipes

The list went on.

Nocthar squawked. She took a bite of porridge straight from the kettle, sweetened with a handful of berries, and then put a hand to her throbbing forehead. She rarely got headaches, so when she checked her apothecary table for the herbs needed to soothe it, she realized it was lacking one needed for that purpose. The best remedy she knew would require some Pheonix Tail root, which grew close to the edge of the Woods.

"Come on, Nocthar." She sighed. "I have to take care of this before it kills me."

Opening the moss-covered door, she stepped out, letting the black bird fly out in front of her. With each step, the pounding in her head worsened. She pressed on, desperate to reach the edge of the Woods before the pain became unbearable. But the farther she went, the more ill she fell. Her body numbed with cold. Her joints ached. The outlines of tree branches against the sky twisted into curling, sloshing tentacles as the earth tilted, and she staggered. Distorted shapes and shadows pulsed in her mind as the pain reverberated like a drum between her ears. She could no longer tell how many paces she'd gone, or how long it had been since she left the cottage. The drumming was deafening, and darkness blotted her mind's eye, visions of the strange woman from her dream flashing in between. And then the voice came.

"Of Vaerwynd blood you are not.
Suffer the death of a flesh-cursed rot.
If worthy to live, you should somehow prove.
The ring only Vaerwynd can remove."

The forest blurred as Caramyn clutched her hand with a sickening revelation. The ring she'd taken from the men—it was a magic relic. A cursed one. How could she have been so damn foolish?

Stumbling, she tried to use her last bit of strength to remove the ring, but it was sealed to her finger like bone and skin. Drained of her strength, her body went limp and paralyzed. The bleak, nearly barren treetops above her swirled against a white sky, and she could do nothing but watch as her raven circled her cawing, helpless. She was falling down a tunnel, watching the opening above her grow smaller and smaller until empty darkness was all that was left.

Caramyn awoke to needle-like talons scratching against her hand, and the thumping of flapping wings. Nocthar was frantic, pulling at her hair and nipping her fingertips with his beak. She fluttered her eyelids and found that it was all she could manage. Her limbs were still useless and weak, and the forest continued to spin. But at least she wasn't dead.

With a grunt, she tried to stand, to roll over, to even just sit up. But her body refused to obey. She hadn't even brought her bow. Only the hunting knife that never left her side.

Shattered gods. I'm an idiot.

She lay there, fighting to stay awake, studying the trees. She traced the outlines of the gnarled branches with her eyes, noticing the faintest cracks of sunlight fighting their way through the great boughs and tree limbs that cracked like veins against the skyline. And she realized...she was lying at the very edge of the Shadow Woods, just a few footfalls away from the tree line that marked the edge of the forest—the edge of her protection.

Nocthar's cries alerted her to something approaching. He took flight to investigate, a rush of wind from his wings stirring the leaves on the ground.

Caramyn tried once again to rise to her feet, digging her fingernails into the dirt as she pushed to no avail, her body cold and paralyzed with weakness. In the half decade spent in these woods, she had always been so calculating, so easily adept at recognizing a trap. And yet she had failed this time.

She turned her head to see silhouettes of riders along the outside of the tree line. "What's that over there in the woods?" A male voice broke through the border of the forest. The thought of someone—a man—being here with her in this state pricked her spine like a dagger to the back.

The solid crunch of hooves and creaking of leather drew near. There were at least four, no—five. Caramyn wiggled her hand towards her belt to clutch the hilt of her dagger, but her grip was weak. She pulled it loose from her belt with two fingers curled around the handle but her feeble strength wasn't enough to keep it from plopping into the dirt beside her.

As fast as he had flown away, her raven returned and snatched the knife up off the ground in his talons, only to disappear into the sky as the strangers neared.

Nocthar, what the hell? That knife was my only defense!

"It...it looks to be a young woman, Sire." This voice was different. And as gritty as sand against cobblestone, followed by the sound of someone else dismounting. Heavy footsteps, unhurried, grew closer and closer. Let him come near. Let him cross a single step over the line into the Woods. Let the Shadows come for him. For all of them.

But what if they didn't?

Her mind raced through possible maneuvers she might use to escape when he reached her if the Shadows didn't get to him fast enough. The feeling in her arms was faintly coming back. If she had been able to grip her hunting knife, she could wait until the damned fool leaned over her, then plunge it through his shoulder. Or she could kick him off balance and swipe her blade across his throat before he could catch himself. If only her muscles didn't feel like jelly...and if she only still had her knife. But there was certainly more than one of them. She didn't stand a chance like this. Not unless the Shadows intervened. She was surprised they hadn't already.

Was it a Blackwynd soldier? An Inquisitor of the Order? She didn't hear armor. But only someone of high rank would be addressed in the manner she'd heard. *Sire.* Surely the king himself had no business here. And if he did—well, she would relish the opportunity to end him and his reign right here. That is, if she wasn't too weak and delirious to move.

Desperate, and curious to see if she could stall long enough to get them talking more, she closed her eyes and played the part to survive—for now.

"She's unconscious." The man's voice lowered, and she could feel him kneeling beside her. Blood rushed through Caramyn at his nearness, her heart pounding wildly at the threat so close. She risked a peek out of desperation. His positioning was obviously strategic, crouched at her side from a safe enough distance. He was no ordinary damned fool.

"It's a miracle she's even alive out here. No place for a lady," the cobblestone voice replied from the back of his horse on the other side of the forest. "No place for anyone with a sense of self preservation, actually."

The kneeling man beside her said nothing, but Caramyn could feel his eyes searching her. She wanted to vault up and over, leaving her dagger buried in him, and disappear between the trees. She felt some parts of her body returning to her now with each pump of her racing heart. But her legs still refused to cooperate. And she still felt feverishly ill. Where were the Shadows?

The man spoke again, startling her as his smooth voice became sharp. "But the perfect place for a fugitive."

She felt a breeze of wind graze her skin as he reached for her. Her eyes flew open, and she found just enough strength to strike out and block his hand with hers.

Drawn crossbows clicked in the same fraction of a second she had moved. The mounted guard would surely fire if she so much as flinched from here. The man smirked at her as though she was as pathetic as a child caught in a prank. But it faded quickly into a face void of emotion. A handsome face that wore the strength of battle beneath the refinement of royalty. By instinct, she turned her head when his silvery eyes met her gaze, looking away.

He had the eyes of a Lightborn. At least one of them. The right eye was a soft grey. Human. And the other—metallic silver. A steel singer.

He pulled his arm from her feeble grasp and stilled her hand with his. Each motion was like swimming through molasses in a dream. Her chest tightened as she held her breath. She would not show fear.

She refused to look at him, but she felt his gaze on her. At least the Shadow-blood marking was covered by her sleeves, but she couldn't hide her face. "Look at me." He spoke gently as he turned her head with a finger under her chin. His stare met hers, and she waited for his reaction to her potent violet eyes. But none ever came.

The nobleman addressed the riders but continued looking at her. "Put the crossbows down. She's not armed." Then she understood why Nocthar had flown away with her dagger—to keep this bastard from taking it. "She is no threat here."

His words stung. If only he knew. Were she not under this spell, she would have already taken out all five of them from the treetops. They lowered their weapons as the tension in their bows eased out like a sigh. One of the horses snorted and stomped.

"Just because she's not armed doesn't mean she isn't dangerous. Caution's saved me more than kindness ever has. Look at those eyes. Those aren't ordinary Lightborn eyes. Who knows what strange magic conjured her up." Cobblestone raised a thick reddish eyebrow at her. Even from afar, Caramyn could tell he was the oldest of the group, and the venom in his voice made her feel like she was a poisonous insect beneath his lifted boot.

"Magic or not, Wyran, she's half-conscious on the border of the Shadow Woods. Something's wrong." The handsome man beside her said, strangely fixated on her hands.   He looked at her again. "Can you speak?"

Caramyn's stomach turned. She couldn't find the coordination to form a sentence. Her tongue felt heavy. So she just blinked, silently begging the Shadows to help her. As her vision steadied, she inspected the broad-shouldered stranger looming over her. He reeked of royal blood, undeniably by the Blackwynd Crest he wore. He was far too young to be King Daemar, but he was certainly nobility. His midnight hair brushed a bit down over his eyebrows, turning in subtle waves just barely framing his prominent cheekbones, where the faintest scar curved upwards if she looked closely enough. He peered down through those steely grey eyes that emphasized the contrast of his black overcoat and cloak draped over his tall, broad form. "I can't tell if she's sick or drunk. She can't even answer me."

"Such a wasted journey." Wyran groaned. "A damn shame we came all this way for nothing."

"Perhaps it wasn't wasted. Not now." The princely man lifted her hand, his face swiftly hardening from pity to concern as he eyed the signet ring on her finger. Then he slipped it off with ease before tucking it away into his pocket. The sound of wailing Shadows groaned in the distance, approaching, and a twinge of relief hit Caramyn. But the prince stood to his feet, clearly aware of his looming fate if he lingered. "We can't stay here. But we're bringing her with us. I must know who she is, and why she has my mother's ring."

Caramyn's breath hitched in her chest. If the ring was Vaerwynd, and it really was his mother's, then that would mean he was the son of the dethroned Lightborn queen. A magic queen. And yet on the clasp of his cloak he wore the crest of the Blackwynd throne—the throne that sought to eradicate magic like a plague. He bore claim to two conflicting identities. One that should have died with the Lightborn Court, and one that would have been its executioner.

But as long as he had anything to do with the Blackwynd Court, Caramyn was determined not to let him ever step foot in the Shadow Woods again. And she'd do whatever she had to do—play along with whatever game he was about to drag her into—if it meant keeping him as far away as possible from the refuge of her Woods.

Trust no one...Guard it with your life.

3

A FORGOTTEN NAME

Caramyn

Calloused hands pulled Caramyn to her feet, careful, but firm. She stumbled as her knees buckled, but the nobleman steadied her. Caramyn recoiled at his touch, and couldn't help but shoot him a scathing look, but his scent of leather, cedar, and crisp night air revived her senses.

The moment the man removed the ring, she could feel her the flesh of her lips again, and some sensation and warmth crept back into her body. She couldn't decide if she should try to speak or continue to let them think her mute, as she thought through every plan of escape possible. She could try to break free later when her strength fully returned...but only if she could get them to let their guard down.

She sighed to herself, trying to remember to breathe. Maybe the Shadows had a different plan. Maybe they wanted to have a little fun with this one, like they did with Number Seventy-Three, the only trespasser who'd ever tried to capture her and almost lived to accomplish his mission. Almost. It'd almost become a game, how the Shadows disoriented him as he tracked her in the Woods, and Caramyn was able to use that to her advantage to win.

But then the man dragged her across the forest's edge, just as the Shadows hissed on the other side. They were too late. But she would find her way out of this, with or without them. She had to. When she regained her strength, somewhere along the way, she'd figure it out. She had survived this long. She would survive again.

"Shall I offer my horse, Prince Asterious?" One of the other soldiers chimed up.

Asterious. The Blackwynd Prince. The man who tore those with magic to pieces for the fun of it.

Once more, Caramyn's thoughts roiled with confusion.

"She's not strong enough to hold herself up." The prince said. "She'll have to ride with me for now."

Caramyn swallowed, her mind racing. Asterious was the King's son. His reputation was built on the death he brought. She'd heard the rumors that had even manage to reach the heart of Havenswood—how he ruled the Felhold Prisons, never leaving the dungeons where he delighted in serving as his father's brutal executioner. He cherished the bloodshed of his father's enemies—of those with magic. Perhaps that was why his own magic was tolerated. As a steel singer, he was lethal. A weapon to the crown. She was sure that if he didn't need her for information about the ring, she would've been dead already.

It seemed unlikely that the cruel prince would be lurking around in this gods-forsaken corner of the kingdom unless the King sent him to find her. But it hardly seemed sensible that he'd send his very own son across the kingdom just to kill off rumors of a haunted forest. Unless there really was something worth protecting within it...Something she must keep him from at all costs.

Asterious guided Caramyn to his horse, a regal black beast. She tried to hoist herself into the saddle, but her grip on the cantle was as solid as water. Her foot half in the stirrup, she lost her balance and teetered backward, knocking into a firmly planted Asterious. He didn't budge.

"Shattered gods, you're worse than I thought." The slightest chuckle slipped through his words. "You could almost rival Wyran at the tavern on Frostlight."

Frostlight. Caramyn hung onto the word. She hadn't been part of a Frostlight celebration since she was a child. A handful of times, she'd wandered to the edge of Havenswood on the eve of Frostlight and watched the festivals from afar, drawn in by the glow of the lights so bright they radiated over the city wall like an aurora over fresh snow. She'd listen to the feasting, and dancing, and the music—oh, the music, so joyful and sweet that it soothed her aching soul just for a night...and she'd spend the day and night's journey back swaying to the memory of it.

The men snickered at the comment, especially the gruff, auburn-haired Wyran, but Asterious was stone-faced. Without warning, he scooped Caramyn up and placed her up onto the horse with one swift, effortless movement.

"I hope you can ride better than you can walk right now." His smooth voice tickled her ears like velvet night and satin, but there was something hurried in it, and she noticed how the men glanced back at the depths of the Woods every so often.

Caramyn shuddered as Asterious' touch lingered on her skin from where he'd swept her off her feet. She'd never been pressed against a man's body like that, never felt so weightless in someone's arms. The strength of his hands had made her recoil and flush with emotion all at the same time. A flutter of heat had swept through her at the sensation of his palms against her waist and thigh.

But she shook away the feeling once she was settled in the saddle, peering through the ears of the great animal. The last time she'd been on a horse, she was running for her life as her home went up in smoke behind her, until it stumbled and threw her, and she was left with only her two feet.

"What is your name?" Asterious looked up at her through a silver gaze like thunder, soft but intimidating all at once.

She thought for a moment. She could give him a false name. But would it really matter? He clearly didn't know she was the Witch. If he did, he would've killed her by now. There were few things Lightborn, Spellbounds, and humans all agreed on, except that anyone involved with Shadow magic was an enemy. It was the reason Shadowbloods were hunted by Lightborn long before the human crown decided to destroy them both.

Her name would be long forgotten by the small village of so few people that ever knew it. She was born hiding from the world. And still hiding twenty years later. Her name would be nothing to a stranger.

Straightening her spine in the saddle as much as her sore joints would allow, she focused on the space between the horse's perked ears and the stretch of land ahead, refusing to meet the prince's eye. "Caramyn."

Without a response, the prince swung up into the saddle behind her, and commanded his men onward. She sensed Nocthar following them discreetly, his caws breaking the silence every now and then. She still felt weak and feverish, but with the ring removed, her body ached less. She wondered how long it would take to feel like herself again and be able to trust her own instincts once more. For now, the world still felt too muddled to make sense of anything.

But she listened to the men chatter amongst each other and slowly figured out each of their names. Aside from Wyran, Tyrios talked the most, and rode closest to Asterious, a hardened look on his face but something tame within his green eyes. He was respectful, and Caramyn almost thought he might've made a better prince with his mannerly nature. The younger pair, Riven and Gariel, kept silent much of the time, but they were always watching the surroundings, flanking the group at the rear.

After they'd been riding a while, traversing the withering open terrain of the Bleak Wilderness, the prince's voice startled her from behind. It was low. Quiet, as though he preferred that she was the only one to hear him clearly.

"Caramyn...was it?"

She nodded slowly, feeling his breath on her neck.

"Do you feel recovered enough now to tell me how you came across the ring?"

He would have no reason to keep her alive if she told him the truth. She would be sealing her fate if he knew the Shadows were on her side. And if he ever saw the Shadow marking on her arm...

So she feigned weakness far greater than what she really felt, letting her head loll back with a pained moan. She drooped against him and closed her eyes, giving a feeble shake of her head. So as long as she kept quiet, she could use his desperation to her advantage. She could lead him on, let him distract himself by believing he'd saved her from the Shadow Woods.

She thought of the ninety-nine marks on her wall and considered that maybe this was why the Shadows didn't help her as he loomed over her in the Woods. Perhaps she needed to see him for what he was. He was no ordinary intruder. He was a prince of two courts that would both hate every part of her, from her corrupted Lightborn eyes to her Shadow markings. Regardless of which one was his true identity, she was an enemy regardless.

And that made him the next target, the next threat to her haven of Shadows. She had to find out what he wanted with her Shadow Woods. Because there was clearly a reason he'd come to them in the first place. And if he was a Blackwynd, the reason couldn't be good. Perhaps these past five years spent as a fugitive was all to prepare her for this. To harden her enough to face her enemies. To make King Daemar suffer as she'd suffered from his rule. By making his half-breed Lightborn son her one-hundredth.

4

THE GIRL FROM THE WOODS

Asterious

A whole day had passed and all he knew was her name. It brought the prince no further understanding of the strange young woman with eyes like blooming orchids in the moonlight who possessed the Vaerwynd signet ring. He sat behind her, forced to keep himself distracted from the feeling of a woman's warmth pressed against him by counting the horse's footfalls, even as he secretly savored her scent of spices threaded with honey, and fresh rain on leaves. He should've let her ride with Tyrios or Riven, but whatever connection she had to his family secrets made him want to keep her close. He had to get her talking eventually. But for now, she could hardly keep herself in the saddle as the horses ambled onward.

He couldn't quench his growing curiosity as he focused on the curving locks of her unruly bark-brown hair, barely bound in a loose braid. She looked worn, her eyes tired and her body thin, even for someone of her smaller frame. But she was fit. Certainly not too delicate. Despite her wild look, there was still something lovely and soft about her. And he still wasn't quite sure what to make of those eyes like gleaming amethysts. Of all the Lightborn he'd killed, he'd never seen eyes like those. His father would've ordered her dead on sight for them, regardless. But she was far more useful to him alive right now. A clue about his mother was the last thing he expected to find at the edge of the Shadow Woods, and he wasn't going to waste it, magic or not.

They rode in silence, except for the occasional caw of a single raven circling above. Color had returned to her skin, a stark contrast from the ghostly pallor that had consumed her when he found her. But she still seemed far too exhausted and feeble to hold a conversation, as his earlier attempt had proven.

"She seems to be recovering." Tyrios spoke up from his left.

"What did she say her name was?" Wyran asked.

"Carmen, or something." Gariel carelessly waved a hand.

"It's Caramyn." There was a sharpness in the girl's voice, even as she weakly corrected my soldier. "Ka-ruh-min." She enunciated each syllable through short, labored breaths.

"Caramyn," Asterious ensured he said the name correctly, trying to keep his tone as neutral as possible. If she felt well enough to correct her name, perhaps she could answer him now. "What you had in your possession was...is very important to me. And if you tell me where your home lies, I can take you there. First, however, I want to know how you found the ring." He drew a breath, knowing his next sentence could come across as a subtle threat, but said it anyway. "And how much you truly know."

Caramyn turned slightly in the saddle, cocking her head. "And if I tell you I don't remember?"

Something sinister sparked in Asterious. Whether it was the truth or not, it wasn't good enough. He'd already failed at what he came all this way to do. He wouldn't let this all come to nothing. Not when it was the only hope he had left.

"Then...you have a long ride ahead of you. Because I'm not letting you go until you do."

He felt the girl tense against him. "You're taking me to your father? To Felhold?" She uttered, her voice frail but full of disdain.

"No."

"Then where?"

"When you answer my questions, then I'll answer yours. But until then, you're my captive, and I owe you no response."

Caramyn grimaced. "How noble a prince to save the injured young maiden in the woods and then turn on her like a wolf. I suppose you really are as cruel as they say."

Her words prodded at something deep inside him, something he'd rather not unleash. He didn't want it to be this way. But if she was going to think she could fool him by lying, he had all the more reason not to let her go. She knew something. She *was* something. And they were each other's problems now.

He urged his horse onward to pick up the pace. The sooner they reached the witchlands, the better.

5

CRUEL AND RECKLESS

Caramyn

This wretched asshole, pretending to be the honorable one here, while spewing his threats like an entitled, petulant child. She would expect nothing less. But let him throw his tantrum. He was only confirming to her that he needed her information more than he needed her dead. At least for now. At least until she could get close enough to find out what he wanted from the Shadow Woods and kill him first.

He startled her when he spoke again, as though he'd been stewing on their last exchange.

"You think me cruel? If I were cruel I would have left you to die in those Woods. You were barely breathing. It's a miracle the Shadows hadn't already finished the job."

"Ah, so you rescued me, all for merely the price of my blind obedience. And to be punished for not responding not to your liking. For simply not remembering what you want to know." Caramyn spat.

"If you truly don't remember, then it shouldn't matter where I take you, should it? You have no home awaiting you. No family missing you. At least none that you know of, so you say."

He wasn't wrong. There was no town she could tell him to take her that wouldn't turn her right back in. And anywhere beyond the Havenspeak mountains would be unfamiliar territory that she couldn't risk crossing weaponless. If she told him to leave her in the Bleak Wilderness, he'd be even more suspicious...and she'd never learn what he wanted from her Woods to begin with.

She reached to pet the horse's neck, desperate for something to distract herself from the painful sting of his mention of home and family. Just as she moved, Asterious grabbed her arm and whispered against her ear, his breath warm along her neck. "Don't think you can make him run away or whatever else you're plotting in your pretty head. He'll only listen to me." She ignored the tingle that fluttered down her back.

She peered down at the mighty black stallion below her, his hooves nearly the size of dinner chargers, and his ebony mane reaching past his chest in flowing waves. It was said the Blackwynds were known for their superior horsemanship, and perhaps that proved to be true by the loyalty of this stunning animal. What a shame for it to be at the command of this bastard, thought Caramyn.

"What's his name?" she asked.

"Alofreise." She was surprised he answered, and even more surprised when he halted the animal with a cue she couldn't detect and dismounted.

"What are you doing, Your Highness?" Riven asked, the riders slowing their horses.

"Securing her," he mumbled, taking out a rope from his saddle bag.

"Excellent call, Asterious," Wyran barked, his hollow hazel eyes gliding over her in a way that made her want to shrink. "Best not to take chances with these kind."

The prince had told her not to try to take control of the horse, but she tried anyway. For all she knew he was lying, and she wanted to test him, if anything just to piss him off. She kicked with her heels as hard as she could, but the stallion stood in place like a statue, his ears pinned. Asterious laughed. "Don't say I didn't warn you. Alofreise wouldn't dream of betraying me."

She rolled her eyes as the prince reached up and slid the rope around her wrists, binding them up so that she had no choice but to keep them clasped together in front of her. She tried to focus on the horse as Asterious mounted back up and settled behind her. With her hands so tightly bound, it was all the more difficult to scoot her body away from his.

"What are you so afraid of, Prince? Am I that much of a threat to you that you must tie me up?" she sneered.

Asterious chuckled low, the sound vibrating through her spine. "If I were afraid, you would already know. Fear has a way of making the best of us cruel. Reckless." He leaned in, voice dropping. "And you haven't seen me cruel and reckless. Not yet."

They continued without further exchange. Her backside grazed his crotch with every stride, and it disgusted her that she blushed at the feeling. But as the hours passed she forgot about the sensation as the ropes irritated her skin, scratching and leaving her wrists red the more she maneuvered.

After a while, she found the warmth of the prince's chest against her back almost pleasant. He was secure, like a wall holding her steady as the horse's body swayed underneath them. And every so often she could feel his breath on her neck as he exhaled, which made her skin fizzle in a way that was unfamiliar to her. But she reminded herself that it was normal for her body to react this way. She'd never known the touch of a man, and despite the ferocity of her natural desires, she wouldn't let her body's physical reaction change what she thought of this selfish prince. Or what she planned to do to him.

As day slipped into night, the lights of Havenswood shimmered in the distance, a solitary beacon of civilization in the wilderness. It was a large city, surrounded by towering stone walls that followed the curves of the mountains. She expected they would pass through, as the main road went right through the center. Which is why it surprised Caramyn when the prince commanded his men otherwise.

"We'll go around the city. Soldiers will be patrolling the borders by now and we can't risk being seen."

"Aren't you the Blackwynd Prince?" Caramyn raised an eyebrow.

"I am. But I no longer wear the Blackwynd chains."

She twisted her face into a sneer at his cryptic answer. "Why go around? That'll take half a day, if not more."

His knuckles tightened on the reins. "Remember our agreement? You don't get answers until I do. And as such you are in no place to question my decisions."

"And you are in no place to be such an ass," she replied boldly.

"Best watch your words before you find out what the prince is capable of." Wryan spouted off. Caramyn rolled her eyes.

"He's right. It's best not to provoke him." It was Tyrios who spoke this time, to her surprise, and something in his voice almost seemed pleading. She wondered what cruelty the prince must have shown them to make them bleat these warnings. But she refused to show any sign of fear. She would not be silent to make any of these men comfortable.

She was glad they would stay out of the city. The last thing she wanted was to bring more attention to herself and potentially have someone accuse her of being the Witch of the Woods in front of the witch-killer prince. The fewer who saw her, the better. She knew why she had to hide. But why did Prince Asterious seem to be traveling in secrecy through his own kingdom?

6

COWARD

Caramyn

The mist crept along the landscape in the quiet hours of dusk. They urged the horses forward, keeping at a distance when they neared Havenswood's entrance. The unmarked mountain passes around the city wound through the terrain in tangled paths. Low branches, rocky hills, and uneven footing hidden beneath freshly fallen leaves created an ever-changing ride for Caramyn, and she struggled to adjust in the saddle, leaving her no choice but to rely on Asterious to keep her steady. Her legs and abdomen ached from straining to stay centered, unable to use her hands for balance.

"Keep your shoulders back a bit more." Asterious' words rumbled against her back. "It will help you balance easier."

She did as he suggested, but not without a defiant tilt of her chin. "Untying my wrists would also help me keep my balance easier."

Caramyn felt the hum of Asterious' deep chuckle as she leaned into him further.

"I'm not sure why that's funny." Caramyn raised an eyebrow. "You're kidnapping me. All because I can't tell you something I don't even understand."

"Don't take me for a fool, Caramyn. You were in possession of a relic that has only ever passed through the hands of High Lightborn royalty. Something that should have never even crossed this wretched side of the kingdom. You look at me through eyes marked with unfamiliar magic and you were found at the edge of death, quite literally and figuratively. I fail to believe you can't explain any of it, but rather that you *won't.*"

"And I was at the edge of death because of that relic. The only thing I remember is that I felt like I was dying after I touched that thing. I don't find it hard to believe that it could have erased my memory as well. So, since you know so much about it, perhaps you can explain why it almost killed me." Caramyn's words were riddled with venom, but secretly she hoped he really could explain it.

"Because you deserved it. Only a Vaerwynd can wear that ring. And only a Vaerwynd can remove it."

Then it hit her. The Shadows must have known he was the only one who could save her, even if it meant he would take her. If he hadn't removed the ring—if he'd never found her—she would have died. But of course, she'd never show a hint of appreciation to this arrogant, entitled asshole, because it was clear he hadn't done it out of any shred of kindness in his heart.

"So, I should've died simply for wearing it?"

"You should've died for stealing it."

"I didn't steal that stupid ring."

"Then how the hell did you get it?" The question flew out of his mouth, rushed, impatient, and flustered. He was desperate...for something.

Caramyn opened her mouth to speak, though she hadn't planned what to say, but before a sound escaped her lips, Nocthar's warning call screeched through the skies.

An arrow flew swiftly from the right and buried itself into Tyrios' arm. He plucked it out with a groan and drew his sword. The others unhooked their crossbows from their saddlebags and took aim.

"Bandits," Asterious muttered with an eye roll, sounding more annoyed than concerned. "How inconvenient."

Sure enough, shrouded in the evening fog, a small camp lay in the distance through the trees, with tents of hide and cots on the ground. A handful of men clad in pelts and masks, emerged from the mist, as two others peeked out from behind a boulder and fired another arrow. It whizzed past them as the prince ducked. He reached around Caramyn before she could blink, shielding her with his arm.

She noted how he hesitated, as if holding himself back from riding straight into the fray, his horse equally tense, snorting and prancing. Riven rode past them with a pleading look in his eyes. "Get out of here, Asterious. Just protect her and stay back. For all our sakes."

Asterious grimaced and bared his teeth as he swore under his breath. With a nudge of his legs, he sent Alofreise surging forward into a gallop, plowing into one of the bandits on the way and wrapping an arm around her to keep her from falling.

Caramyn clung to the saddle, jostled as wind-stung tears blurred the world around her. She craned her neck around Asterious' shoulder to witness Tyrios and Wryan effortlessly swiping the rogues down with their swords, and the other two launching arrows with fluid, tireless movements.

"You left your men to fight them alone?" She was still catching her breath as the prince pulled the horse to a halt, but she couldn't help herself or her confusion.

"My priority is to get you away from the danger. You were almost shot. My men know the plan. They can easily handle a few backwoods bandits." Asterious said coldly.

"You have a sword at your hilt, and you didn't even draw it. You're a coward." Caramyn saw how her words made the corner of his mouth twitch. The way his eyes locked onto nothing in the distance and his jaw clenched, as if enduring her words like a pelting hailstorm. "So much for the cruel Prince Asterious, the executioner, the killer, the bloodthirsty, merciless—"

"That's enough." Asterious' muscles tightened, his arms closing in like a cage as he leaned forward. He hissed the words, the heat of his anger smoldering like hot cinders in his voice against her ear. "You don't have the slightest idea of what you say. You don't *want* to see me bloodthirsty and merciless. And Shattered gods know my men don't want to see it. I could kill them all *and* you as well before you could even think to stop me. And you're quickly fraying the thin thread that keeps me from doing it."

Caramyn's heart raced. She had never been threatened in this manner. No one had ever been able to put her in this position until now. It was easy to laugh off her fear when she knew she was unbound and free to play the predator. But here in this helpless position, without a weapon, restrained in the grasp of this monstrous man, no matter how much she wanted to deny it, she felt very much like the prey.

The prince's men came trotting up before long, seemingly unbothered by what had just occurred, as if they had merely just returned from a friendly hunt.

She didn't dare voice her thoughts, but she silently hoped he could feel the way she abhorred his closeness, his vile arrogance and threats. Her burning hatred toward him and her disgust with every part of who he was. But he didn't seem to notice her any longer as he addressed the others.

"We should pick up the pace through here. It's likely more bandits will be scouting the wall's edges waiting for their next easy target. If we're already moving quickly, they won't have time to attack. No need to draw out this journey with more...interruptions. We need to get back soon as possible." Asterious nodded towards the mountain pass ahead and leaned forward, his voice low enough for only her ears. "And as for you, don't bother talking to me again unless you're going to explain yourself."

Caramyn shuddered, no longer sure of herself and the fate that lay before her, especially as Riven's words echoed in her head.

Protect her and stay back...for all our sakes...

7

STILL MINE

Asterious

Asterious wasn't worried about the bandits. They were mere child's play to his men. Tyrios and Wryan had been two of the fiercest warriors in his father's army, and Riven and Gariel were lethal spies. They could handle themselves with their eyes closed and one hand behind their backs. But something far more deadly lurked in their midst, and his only option was to protect her—to protect them all from something far more tragic occurring. If that made him look like a coward, so be it.

It didn't matter, he reminded himself. Whatever this woman thought of him was irrelevant. It only mattered that he didn't let her words seep into his mind, and that he got the truth out of her eventually. But her insults and accusations ignited something in him that he hadn't felt in a long time. She stirred up unchecked emotion that he thought by now he'd learn to suppress, and her body scraping against him all day didn't make it any easier. He considered making her ride with Tyrios, but for some damn reason he didn't like the thought of her being pressed up against him the same way.

There were still a few days left until they reached the old Vaerwynd lands. The second night they made camp and rested, something was particularly intriguing about Caramyn as she sat staring into the dying fire. Gariel kept watch in the distance while the others slept, silent as a statue like always. Asterious found sleep evaded him, and he stood up, walking over to join her. "You should eat that," he gestured to the half-eaten leg of freshly hunted rabbit at her side. "You'll need strength for the rest of the journey."

Caramyn sat with her arms in her lap, hunched over, drawing Asterious' attention to her bound hands. By the fire's dim light, he could see the reddened, irritated flesh around her wrists. "Why do you care?" she mumbled.

"I don't." He grunted. "But you're more valuable to me not starved to death."

"Then I'll make sure I don't eat another bite tonight. Try not to lose sleep over it." She looked away with a shrug.

Why did she infuriate him so? She had every right to hate him, to be so callous toward him. Anyone in her position would. Yet her remarks left him scathing for reasons he couldn't explain.

He should've walked away. Should've gone back to lie down and tried to get some sleep despite the nightmares. Let her be hungry and stubborn and alone. But he couldn't stop thinking about her hands, damn it. He stepped away without a word, over to the horses, and reached into Tyrios' saddle bag, only to make his way back to her, much to her displeasure. Like a very stupid moth to a flame.

"Here," He sat down beside her and opened the tiny jar of salve in his hand. "For the rope burns."

To his surprise, she said nothing, only sighed and offered him her hands with a small movement. But when he started to roll back the edge of her sleeve past her wrist, she yanked them away. "That's far enough." She hissed.

He nodded and dipped a thumb into the salve, the icy healing balm cool on his fingertip. "Of course. Whatever you'll allow. Nothing more." Taking her hands in his, he rubbed the salve over the marks on her wrist. She kept her gaze fixed on the embers of the fire, but he couldn't tear his away from her. He studied those ethereal eyes that spoke of something otherworldly. He'd never seen or heard of—or killed—anything like her. Sapphire, red, emerald, white, gold, and silver. Those were the only eye colors a Lightborn could possess. Spellbounds were harder to identify unless they'd carved their runes into their flesh. And Shadowbloods were unmistakable, their eyes black as voids, dark veins lacing their skin as proof of the blood that ran within. But she was none of these. Her magic was new, unnamed, if it was even magic at all.

What was he doing? What the hell was he doing? She was a potential source of information. Nothing more. He quickly put the salve away and stood up.

"Gariel." He motioned for the spy on night watch, who came to his side without a sound. "Unbind her."

"You want to let her go, Sire?" Gariel scratched at the nape of his cropped dark hair, an eyebrow raised.

"No, she's still mine." Asterious spoke under his breath while looking at the strange girl crouched by the fire. "But just look at her. She's still weak. She won't get far if she tries anything. No need for the rope."

Before Gariel could protest, the prince walked on, back to the simple blanket spread on the ground and lay down. He pressed his head against the cold ground, facing away from the fire, and away from the girl beside it.

8

A LIFE WORTH FIGHTING FOR

Caramyn

That night Caramyn would've liked to believe she could've killed them all and made her escape in the darkness without a trace. But for the first time in a very long time, she began to doubt herself. This was not the Shadow Woods, and these were no ordinary men. They were trained warriors. She'd seen them take down the bandits in seconds, with the ease of crushing cockroaches. She was not foolish enough to think she could outrun them or overpower them on her own, with no weapon, and no knowledge of where she was.

When Gariel cut the rope around her wrist, he warned her that this didn't mean anything had changed before going back to his post, his eyes never leaving her. She rubbed the place where the ropes had been, working the salve deeper into the raw flesh as she remembered the prince's thumb across her skin, and how she'd flinched at the thought he might see her markings in the faint edges of those dark veins if she'd let him pull her sleeve any higher. She didn't understand him. She didn't want to. He must've been toying with her mind for whatever it benefited him. Nocthar had been quiet, as though even he didn't see a way out of this.

She closed her eyes, the fire's warmth embracing her. She would kill him when the time was right, when she could get him alone and make her escape. The opportunity would come. It always did. And then she could return to the Shadow Woods. She could run back and continue hiding...alone. Back to her life...a life she sometimes wondered if was worth fighting for.

9

THE FORBIDDEN COURT

Caramyn

The rest of the journey was long, and much the same. But the prince never came to her at night again, and when it was his turn to keep watch through the night, he stood as far as possible from her. They'd bind her hands whenever she had to piss, or anytime she couldn't be watched closely, and she thanked the Shattered gods that she didn't have her monthly bleeding during this time.

During the long, quiet stretches of riding, she tracked their path, recalling maps from her cottage to better understand her location and plan her eventual route back home. She collected maps whenever she came across them in the markets, because up until now they were the only way she could explore the world outside the wilderness. She knew Evylere well, and she pictured it now—a vast kingdom once ruled by the Lightborn court and human courts, split into three regions by great rivers that met in the center like main arteries. The lower east region beyond Havenswood was a long-shunned place. Before the Order's purge, it had been the unofficial Shadowblood domain, where they sealed away their secrets and dark power throughout The Bleak Wilderness and the Woods long before the Veil existed. The human court lay North in Felhold, and the old Vaerwynd lands made up the West—now affectionately known as the witchlands—where remnants of the ancient gods' powers were said to have fallen in the Great Shattering and created the Lightborn race.

After passing Havenswood and crossing the great river splitting East from West, her suspicions began to form. They were long past any chance of going to Felhold, and she knew that on the other side of the river, tucked away near the coast facing the Shattered Sea lay the old Vaerwynd Court—the ruling place of the Lightborn king and queen before the downfall of their magic at the hands of the humans and the Shadowbloods.

Caramyn thought back to the newest map she'd bought from the town cartographer with some Lily's Claw and a few stolen coins back in Havenswood. It was the only map that labeled the old Vaerwynd Castle as 'forbidden ruins,' and she wondered what King Daemar feared so much that he couldn't even permit people to visit the lands he claimed to have defeated. But more than that, she wondered why his son seemed to be taking her there now.

Though she'd memorized the geography, she'd never dreamed of how beautiful Evylere truly was, and each day of travel brought with it something more breathtaking than the next. Her maps could've never prepared her for the crystal flowing streams, the vibrant hues of the changing trees and wildflowers that peppered the landscapes. The far-off snow-capped mountains to the north took her breath away, and she wondered how she'd ever get used to the ever grey bleakness of the Shadow Woods again after this.

On the last day traveling, Caramyn was exhausted, her body still yet to fully recover from the ring's ailment. She yearned for a break from the confines of the saddle, her backside and spine aching with every stride. And something deep in her conscious ached as well. As the distance grew between her and the Shadow Woods, the stronger she felt something was amiss. She wondered if she'd made a mistake, if she should have tried escaping by now. It deeply troubled her that whatever she was meant to be guarding there was now left unprotected. But she reassured herself that the Shadows didn't need her the way she needed them. The Woods had stood on its own long before she ever came to them. And perhaps this was how she was meant to protect it this time—by uncovering this mysterious prince's plans and destroying him in the silence of his own shadows.

As their mounts passed through the heart of the empty witchlands, she forgot her soreness and worry for a moment as she looked on in awe at the sight ahead. A forest full of trees far different from the gnarled, claw-like brambles of her Woods. These were lush and full of color. And in the midst of them, white spires reaching up, gleaming in the last rays of sunlight like diamonds. Beyond the forest and trees lied a horizon of blue, spanning the dusk skyline in gentle ripples—Mistwake Bay, of the Shattered Sea—if her memory of the maps served her correctly.

Why would the Blackwynd prince bring her here? To the abandoned castle of the Lightborn his father betrayed decades ago—the forbidden ruins of the fallen Vaerwynd Court.

Up until now, Havenswood's stone wall had been the mightiest structure she'd ever laid eyes on. But this onyx and ivory stone palace before her stalled her breath. Stretching to the clouds, serrated battlements lined the top edges of each of the four corner towers. Time had ravaged the castle with a dark covering of moss and vines creeping up along the sides. The walls still bore the scars of seige, crumbling where flaming boulders had pierced its wards, their magic nullified by distant iron bells. But even in its battle-worn state, it boasted a beauty no human structure could ever hope to match.

Grand silver gates guarded the entrance, and a small stone wall skirted the outside of the castle, but it seemed more for decoration than protection. As they neared, a soldier or servant of some sort rushed out from the castle entrance to open the gates.

Nocthar had trailed them the entire way. She watched him perch gracefully atop one of the castle towers. With his help, she knew she could find a way out of here—when the time came.

"The Forbidden Ruins," Caramyn muttered under her breath, recalling the mark on the map.

"Ruins not so much anymore." Asterious purred with a razor-edged chuckle. "But I like that first part. The Forbidden Court...hmm. I think I'll keep that."

Caramyn rolled her eyes beneath her lids. "I don't understand. Why—*how* have you revived this place? Shouldn't you be at Blackwynd Castle in Felhold slaughtering anyone who opposes your father?" At this point, asking questions was more a tactic to annoy Asterious than to seek answers she knew he would not give.

"Blackwynd has enough monsters without me. And I thought I told you not to ask any more questions until you're ready to give me real answers to mine." He spoke as he dismounted in the middle of the courtyard, and someone led his horse away. The surface was cobbled of some type of gleaming stone flecked with shimmers of light that brightened with the weight of their footsteps. Caramyn was almost too distracted by their beauty to respond. Almost.

"That's not how it seemed when you were tending to my wounds around the fire." She puckered her face and raised an eyebrow, expecting the prince to ignore her as they passed through the doors of the castle. He led her down the halls, Wryan flanking the other side of her, and she took note of Wyran's disdainful expression at her comment.

"As I said before, you're no use to me if you're not physically well. We must do everything we can to help heal that delicate memory of yours." The prince narrowed his eyes at her, tugging gently on the rope Wyran insisted they bound around her wrists again as he guided her through the twisting corridors of the palace.

The inside of the castle was in better shape than the outside, and she understood why King Daemar would've wanted to keep people from coming here, because he clearly hadn't managed to breach the interior for whatever reason. The inside was untouched, all its records likely still preserved, all its treasures still in place. The iridescent white floor sparkled beneath fine rugs that blanketed the walkways, and bright glowing torchlight kept the stone halls illuminated and warm. They spiraled up a long flight of stairs, which seemed to never end. When they reached the top of the tower, Asterious produced a metal key from his coat and inserted it into the lock. With a turn of the key, the heavy gold-inlaid door creaked on its hinges and Asterious clicked his tongue. "You'll stay here, and only here while you let that memory rest."

Caramyn had expected a dungeon or a dirty, damp room with a pile of soiled straw for a bed, but to her surprise, the room was grand and inviting. She might even dare say it was fit for royalty. There was a large bed with creamy silk cushions and luxurious fur blankets. By a bright stained-glass window stood a gold-trimmed vanity with a mirror and a matching armoire. To the right, in the far corner of the room, a divider separated a charming claw foot tub and a dressing area. There was even a cozy fireplace, though it obviously hadn't been used in ages.

"I'll have some torches and some supper brought up." Asterious gestured for her to step into the room.

Caramyn scanned the room once more, "What a nice prison cell. Was this the queen's room?" she asked mockingly.

"Yes." His voice flattened. "It was."

He turned to go, without looking back, in a way that chilled Caramyn's blood. "Anyway, I'll make sure you're taken care of, but you may not leave this room until I've spoken further with you."

Caramyn crossed her arms, desperate to get in one more jab. "Are you going to put that lovely Wyran in charge of guarding my door?"

"I wouldn't dream of punishing him like that. I'll find some other poor soul to burden with that task." The prince's face curled into a look of disdain as he pulled the door shut behind him, and it clicked in place. Caramyn wiggled the doorknob the second he was gone, but the lock was solid.

The tiredness in her bones returned all at once and demanded her attention. All she wanted to do was lie down and figure out the rest later. But instead she remained standing, observing her surroundings as a small voice startled her at the door followed by the lock turning.

The shortest woman Caramyn had ever seen fumbled through the door carrying a bundle of unlit torches tucked beneath her arm. She was a small lady, squirrel-like, perhaps in her forties or fifties, bright-eyed, with a dark bun tied at the nape of her neck.

"Caramyn, was it? The prince asked me to bring you these," she said, hanging more torches along the hooks in the wall. "And this, for your sore muscles."

Azell handed her a vial of something. It smelled light and airy, but Caramyn didn't trust it. She placed it on the dresser as the sprightly woman placed the last torch. "Thank you. What's your name?"

"I'm Azell, the maid of this castle...for the time being."

"You make it sound as though you're the only maid here." Caramyn said, prodding for information without being too obvious.

"I might as well be." The lady laughed, but then a sense of seriousness befell her wispy voice. "There are a small few of us who chose loyalty to the prince. But I was tasked with tending to you..." Azell grinned with a laugh that crinkled the corners of her eyes.

"What do you mean 'chose loyalty to the prince?'"

"Oh, never mind all that for now. It's a long story and I've already said too much. And if he hasn't explained it to you by now, there must be a reason," she said with a mischievous smile, lighting the torches one by one. "But don't fret about it. Just clean up and get some rest, dear girl. I'm sure it will all make more sense soon."

Caramyn shook her head. "Are you Lightborn or Spellbound?" she blurted out.

Azell blushed, slapping a hand to her chest. "Me? Magic? Shattered gods, no. Not even a half-breed. Just a human who knew something had to change." She darted toward the door before Caramyn could ask anything else.

"Anyway, I'll be back in a bit with some supper. I'm sure you must be starving." And with that, she disappeared and locked the door behind her but was right back in a few more minutes with a steaming bowl of venison stew and maple-glazed sprouts.

Caramyn thanked her and scarfed down the food once she was gone, savoring the warm broth and crispy vegetables after so many days of dried meat and hard bread. It was one of the most delicious meals she'd had in a while, but half of the delicacy seemed to have come from the idea that it had been made for her, despite the circumstances. She hadn't eaten a meal prepared by someone else in half a decade.

With her belly full, she could focus, though exhaustion still gnawed at her bones. Nocthar still hadn't returned with her dagger. Before she could allow herself to rest, she had to have something in her hand...something to defend herself with in this strange place. She searched beneath the bed and rummaged through the drawers, finding nothing with potential. Then as she eyed the vanity, she noticed a hairbrush made of ivory with a bone handle. She cracked the brush against the wall, splintering the bone into shards. One was particularly large enough to suffice as a makeshift dagger for now. She didn't know what came next, and she refused to be vulnerable. To feel as helpless as she had felt the night around the campfire with the prince, or when he picked her up off the forest floor.

Once she'd crafted the knife, through heavy eyelids threatening to close the entire time she worked, she dragged herself over to the edge of the bed, clutching the weapon and sitting cross-legged facing the door, her feet finally relieved of their aching. She planned to sit there and watch the door through the night...just in case. It was still unclear what the prince wanted, and for all she knew this fancy room could be a trap. And she already disliked the dark, but the dark in an unfamiliar place was an entirely worse kind of unsettling.

But after an hour or of fighting back yawns, staring in the silence at an unmoving door, she was already fading. She couldn't help but lie down...just for a few minutes. The security of the Shadow Woods was all too far away, and the prince she hated was all too near in this castle somewhere, but for now, she didn't care. She just needed a few moments of sleep.

10
INTERROGATION

Caramyn

When she woke, it was late morning, and she'd managed to come to her senses just as Azell tiptoed in with breakfast—two eggs and fresh berries on toast. Caramyn hurried to hide the bone shard dagger away under the pillow as she sat up.

"Good morning. I hope you rested well. The prince is planning to question you today, just so you're aware. You might want to wash up."

"I—I meant to last night. But I was so tired…" Caramyn watched Azell as she flitted to the door, still rubbing sleep from her eyes. She glanced over at the tub, and the hearth to see if there was enough wood to heat some water.

"Check the bathtub. There's a handle that draws up warm water. Some type of Spellbound magic I believe. No one in their right mind would be hauling buckets of water up these stairs." She laughed, and Caramyn wondered if she'd read her mind or just got the hint from her rank appearance.

Azell closed the door, leaving her standing in front of the massive mirror of the vanity. Caramyn examined herself from top to bottom, pondering whatever questions the prince might ask her, and what she might give for answers. How much could she say without risking her own neck? And how much could she get out of the prince in return.

It had been too long since she'd last been able to see herself this clearly. Her small handheld mirror back at the cottage couldn't capture the way she had blossomed from a clumsy fifteen-year-old into a graceful woman with petal-shaped lips, fierce eyes beneath strong brows, softened by a delicate chin and neck, and a healthy sun-kissed glow on her skin.

She touched a finger to her matted hair and pictured how wonderful it would feel to scrub all this dirt off her face and body. Her nimble, lean body that had been so accustomed to surviving in the wild. It was a thought to imagine what she might look like if she'd eaten more meals like the ones she'd been served in this castle. She was a good enough cook, but game was scarce in the woods. And fresh eggs were quite a rare treat.

And strangest of all was that she'd survived like this for so long, never having to show herself to another person that wasn't a target at the end of her arrow or a slimy merchant in Havenswood. Yet now, in an instant, her life had changed once again, and she'd spoken to more people in one week than she had in the past five years, trapped within this castle by a prince who blurred all the lines she thought she knew.

She could tolerate the feeling of grime and filth against her skin no longer, and her eyes fell on the bathtub in the corner of the room. She strode over, looking for the handle Azell spoke of.

It was polished wood, marked by some symbols or runes. One she recognized from the witch's books back in her cottage as the sign for water—the clear work of Spellbound magic. It took a moment or two, but the wall behind the handle rumbled with the sound of water rushing up just before it spewed out steaming clear liquid into the porcelain tub. She leaned over, feeling the heat rising to her face as every fiber of her being yearned to crawl into the hot water right then and there.

She worked to peel away the layers of her clothes. She pulled off her breeches that were nearly rubbed through from so much time in the saddle and spattered with so much dried mud it had hardened in the seams. A breath of relief slipped from her lips as she removed the leather belt around her chestnut-brown tunic that was so long it fit more like a dress. She was careful to twist her arm to conceal her marks as she slid her arms out of the sleeves, paranoid that someone may be watching or burst through the door any minute. And once she was out of the soiled clothing, she couldn't get in the tub fast enough.

She dipped a toe in, then sunk down into the warm water and let it wrap itself around her like a cocoon as the heat soothed her aching muscles. She simply soaked for a minute or two before scrubbing her skin with the soap sitting on the tub's edge. It smelled like lavender and was a treat to her nostrils. Scented soap was a luxury she tried her best to stock up on from Havenswood but often found herself running short. Her hair had long come undone from its braid, and she combed her fingers through the tangled locks before lathering some soap through it as well. When she dunked her head beneath the water to rinse it, she felt reborn.

She wrung out as much water from her thick locks as possible, and then coiled her hair up into a loose bundle on her head, securing the bone shard dagger deep in the tresses just in case she needed it.

And just as she thought of her, Azell's tiny voice chimed through the wooden door. "Lady Caramyn, the prince has requested to see you in an hour. Shall I help—oh!" She had opened the door just a crack, and Caramyn instinctively drew herself down into the water to make sure her arm marking was submerged. "I see you figured out the tub." She walked over to a drawer and pulled out a candle, lighting it and placing it on the vanity. Then she stooped over and picked up Caramyn's soiled clothing.

"You don't have to—" Caramyn began, but Azell held up a hand.

"Nonsense. I can't leave those filthy rags on the floor. There is plenty of clothing in the wardrobe for when you're done."

Caramyn leaned back in the tub, still relishing its warmth as she closed her eyes. "Thank you," she said.

"I can see you're making good use of that thing. I don't blame you after all you've been through. I'll leave you to it," Azell said with a half-smile, wiping her hands and gesturing toward the vanity. "But mind that candle. Asterious will be coming within the hour. You'll need to be out and ready before it's burned down to the third notch." She moved to light a single candlestick on a barrel beside the bathtub.

Caramyn nodded, and Azell excused herself from the room. Despite the disdain at the thought of having to see the prince again, she had never been so comfortable in her life. In the Woods she only bathed in creeks and streams, though sometimes she heated a kettle of warm water to soak her cold feet in winter. But now she indulged in that warmth across her whole body. And after a few moments, she drifted off in the comfort of the tub.

The sound of squawking and pecks on the window stirred her, giving her just enough time to see Nocthar outside fluttering the way he did to warn her. She shot up, grabbing the sides of the tub. But it was too late. Violent knocks on the door rattled her. She glanced at the candlestick, which was now burning long past the third mark. Asterious' voice boomed outside her room, growing closer with each word.

"If she's not answering then she might have escaped. We can't wait around out here to find out. I'm going in." The door burst open, the hinges nearly snapping from the force, and Asterious rushed in. "Caramyn?"

At first, she was shocked, completely frozen as the prince stood in the doorway staring her down as she sunk down into the tub. But then she noticed the way he withered, too, like a frightened dog that had barked at the wrong beast. And suddenly she didn't feel so small anymore. In fact, she felt as though she could turn his own game against him by doing something he'd never expect. It'd be the perfect chance to toy with him. To see how much she could bend him. "Yes, Your Highness?" She hummed, relaxing back in the tub, drawing his eyes to her.

"Shattered gods, this is highly inappropriate." The prince flushed red and his hand flew to his eyes as he turned away. But he still lingered in the room.

"Then leave." Caramyn leaned forward, propping an elbow over the rim of the bathtub. "Oh, but wait. You wanted to ask me something?"

"Yes...but please get dressed first." Asterious stumbled.

"Why?" She stood up in the tub, water droplets racing off her bare skin and trickling back down into the water. She was careful to keep the Shadowblood veins on her arm concealed by keeping it turned inward and pressed against her side, just in case he turned around. "Will whether I'm dressed or not make a difference in what you ask?"

"Caramyn please, just put on something." He sighed, his back still to her.

She reached for a towel, but beside it she found a thin silk covering with long, wide sleeves trimmed with lace and an open front meant to be wrapped shut. She slipped it on with a silent smirk, deriving far too much enjoyment out of humiliating the prince.

"All right. I've done as you've asked. Does this suit Your Highness?" She teased, the loose silken robe falling open to expose all but her arms as the hem dusted the floor behind her.

Asterious glanced over his shoulder, and when he visibly blushed again, Caramyn sneered. "What's the matter, Prince? Can't face your captive?" He was silent for a moment, and then the air turned heavy. Something darkened in his stance, and suddenly nothing was funny as Caramyn watched his fists clench at his sides. He whipped around and stomped toward her.

"You have no idea what you provoke with these insolent acts…what horrors you threaten to unleash." He seethed.

As his hulking figure closed the distance between them, Caramyn took a step back, nearly tripping on the train of the robe. The rabid look in his eye reminded her of the Inquisitor who'd lunged at her mother in much the same way, right before he shattered their world.

She flinched as he stopped before her, inches from her bare body. She readied herself to rip out the bone shard knife hidden in the pinned coils of her hair as he loomed over her, her head at the height of his chest—an ideal position for stabbing.

He growled through a tense exhale, his eyes firmly on hers. "Is this all just a game to you? This is absolutely blithe. Downright reckless."

"Fear tends to make the best of us reckless…" She stood firm as she threw his own words back at him, but a tremble in her voice betrayed her.

Something overshadowed him, perhaps the realization of the mere threat of his stature. He stared at her with haunted eyes, and she stared back for far too long. Her heart pounded like a mouse's until his broad shoulders relaxed, and he breathed out with a small step backwards. She should've just killed him. But she had far too many questions. Though if he ever approached her that way again, she couldn't promise her curiosity would be enough to stop her.

She closed the robe around herself and scowled. "You wanted to interrogate me?" She hissed, determined more than ever to get the truth out of Asterious before he could get it from her. "Well, then what are you waiting for?"

11

THE FORGOTTEN HEIR

Asterious

The prince flexed his hands, his chest tight as he stared at this ethereal woman who challenged the deepest parts of him in the strangest ways. She was insolent and wild and foolhardy, and had no idea the danger she was putting herself in. He could sense each of her breaths. The way she shifted and her heartbeat sped up when he came too near. Like a deer trying to stand her ground against a lion.

He would never be able to get it out of his head—the image of her standing there, facing him with bare dripping breasts and stomach, the sweep of her hips and perfect thighs peeking out with each step from the silky folds of that open gown. Her eyes shining like twilight stars above full, soft lips sparkling with water droplets like spring dew. A vision that would be unforgettable and equally maddening.

And when he moved toward her, she'd recoiled. It seemed to shake her far more than he'd meant to. He'd frightened her. Sometimes he forgot how easy it was to move too quickly, too harshly. Sometimes that inhuman part of himself slipped out in moments it shouldn't. But he couldn't let himself care. He didn't care. She was just a pawn...for now.

He held his gaze on her face as she stared up at him and breathed a sigh of relief when she wrapped the robe shut around herself. Fully clothed or not, he was going to continue with this interrogation.

"My question is the same, Caramyn." He tried to soften his voice, aware that the way he towered over her was likely intimidating enough. "Where...where did you find the ring?"

The girl shifted uncomfortably as she stood, glancing at the window nervously. There was a raven perched outside on the sill. "My answer is also still the same."

"Then this room will be your prison until it changes." When she bit her cheek and looked away, he pressed her, producing the ring from his pocket. "Let's try something else. A simple 'yes' or 'no.' Did you steal it?"

She looked back and narrowed her eyes at him, then at the ring. "No," she finally said, focusing again on the bird in the window. "Now I technically answered a question. So now will you answer one of mine?"

Asterious crossed his arms and leaned against the wall by the window, trying once again to distract himself from the way the delicate fabric clung to her curves. "Fair enough." He groaned. Perhaps it wouldn't hurt to tell her one small thing. "One question."

But her question wasn't as straight-forward as he'd hoped. He could smell her fear, her uncertainty, her mistrust. But he couldn't hope to guess what she would say next. He braced himself as she moved to take a seat in the windowsill and tossed out the words. "Why is the ring so important to you?"

"Because it was my mother's." He turned the ring in his fingers, watching the way the sun glinted off the metal and highlighted the outline of the moons.

"That doesn't count. You already told me that."

Asterious raised an eyebrow. "All right. Perhaps this will satisfy you. My mother was Queen Elysia Vaerwynd, and I've been trying to find out what happened to her since I was a boy."

It did not escape the prince's notice how Caramyn's eyes widened, and she leaned forward. "Was she not killed in the Lightborn Massacre or the purge of the witchlands?"

Asterious clicked his tongue and waved a finger. "A question for a question. My turn...Did you find the ring?"

A quiet pause held the air as Caramyn twirled her fingers in her lap. "Y—yes. On the bodies of some bandits I came across while traveling."

"Hmm..." Asterious purred. "So you're telling me you looted dead bandits while traveling alone in the wilds, found a magic Lightborn relic, and headed for the Shadow Woods with it around your finger, is that correct?"

"That's not what I said..."

"But it's what you've implied."

"I...I ran away from home some time back. I found the ring, put it on, hoping to sell it in Havenswood for supplies. But instead, the ring tried to kill me, and it made me feverish and disoriented. I must've stumbled into the Shadow Woods in my delirious state."

Asterious huffed. "So, you're from Havenswood? Because there's no other mark of civilization out there in the Bleak Wilderness apart from the bandit clans themselves. So unless you were part of those—"

"I'm not a bandit. And I'm not a thief. I trade herbs and remedies made from things that most don't dare to seek out in the wilderness."

"You still didn't answer if you're from Havenswood or not."

"And you didn't let me ask the question I'm owed for answering the previous one."

Asterious clenched his jaw. "Fine. What?"

"How is it that you are both of Blackwynd and Vaerwynd blood?" She didn't stall on a single syllable.

A long sigh slipped from Asterious' lips as he dropped his shoulders, bracing for the weight of the explanation. "Before my father openly turned on magic and decreed it a crime, he threw a grand ball in the human court, inviting all the Vaerwynd royals, and many magickind as well, even a High Shadowblood as an attempt at an allyship. The ball was meant to be a celebration to honor the Lightborn for their help in giving him a child—my half-sister, Sinevia."

"The Vaerwynd Massacre," Caramyn muttered. "The night the Shadowblood killed the Lightborn king?"

"That's what history says, yes. But the truth of it is...not quite so. The Shadowblood's presence was a scape goat. A place to shift the blame for when my father killed the Vaerwynd King." The prince turned his head, seeing that Caramyn was just as confused as he expected her to be. "The ball was nothing more than a trap. A plot for revenge for his wife's death in childbirth—the hidden cost of a life for a child. When all the Lightborn royals were gathered in the ballroom, my father subdued them with great iron bells he'd secretly installed throughout the castle, shattering their connection to their magic. He killed them all, but not before he made the Vaerwynd King watch as he took Queen Elysia—the king's mate—for himself. A queen for a queen. He promised to keep her alive as his prize for the rest of her days, knowing how greatly this would make the Lightborn king suffer before he died. But he didn't count on the cursed conception that would come of it." Asterious drew a heavy breath as he focused on a small crack in the floor, letting it out with one single word. "Me."

He looked up to see Caramyn's reaction, to see if it matched the way he sensed her pulse was slowing. Calmer. She was leaning so far forward listening he thought she might fall from the windowsill. He should've stopped there. Should've let that be the extent of his explanation. But for some reason, her gaze tugged at something inside him and he went on.

"The abomination of the Vaerwynd legacy. And the shame of the Blackwynd King. But still very loved by my mother regardless. And one day when my father grew tired of her pleading with him to recognize me as his heir, he locked her away in a location he kept secret from me. And I've been trying to find her ever since I—" Asterious bit his tongue, deciding he had said enough. "I've been trying to find her for a long time."

Something in Caramyn's gaze had softened. The way she looked at him now felt less like of a threat and more like...like something tender...almost compassion, maybe.

"I don't want your pity." Asterious grumbled, pushing off the wall to straighten himself. "I just want you to tell me the truth. Tell me something to give me some semblance of hope that I might not have wasted that journey to only end up no closer to finding her than where I started."

Caramyn stood up from the window and turned to stare out the glass, still clutching her gown shut. The sun rays broke through the stained-glass outline, casting a mosaic of heavenly light across her face and setting fire to those shimmering amethysts beneath her lashes. "I'm...not from Havenswood." She blinked and turned to face him. "I have told you everything I can remember."

Asterious leaned into her, careful not to upset her by moving too quickly as he did before. "You know, you're a terrible liar. High Lightborn cannot lie. Upon ascending the throne, spells are sealed into their oaths—binding them irrevocably to the truth. I watched my mother survive by working around that vulnerability time and time again. So, I know all about twisting or omitting details to work around the truth. I recognize it when I see it." Her gaze rained fire upon him. "And I see it. I sense the way your heart races when you try to explain yourself. And all it does is make me more suspicious of you. Makes me wonder what you're really hiding...or if you even know yourself." He raised an eyebrow as he propped himself up with one hand against the wall, amused at the way her flustered face twisted into a look of disgust.

"So you admit you're a master of deception. You do all this and tell me a sad story to get me talking, and then you'll kill me, right? Once I tell you what you want to know. This room, the food, everything. This is all just a trap, isn't it?" Her voice rose the longer she spoke.

"It's merely an interrogation. Not a trap."

"So, does an interrogation always come before the execution part, or am I just lucky? Does the next question come with a dagger to my throat?"

Something in Asterious sparked. If only she understood how he would absolutely relish what it would feel like to hold a dagger at her throat when she threw out her callous accusations. If only she knew how much it was in her best interest that he couldn't. But she knew nothing. She'd been sold the lie like everyone else, yet her judgements still stung. And the inexplicable way that it bothered him was salt in the wound.

"I'm hardly the monster you think I am. I took no pleasure in killing for my father. I wasn't given a choice. But perhaps you can be the first of my own choosing." Asterious bared his teeth, settling to tip her chin toward him with a finger instead of the dagger he'd like to imagine.

"Don't touch me." Caramyn hissed, yanking her face away. "Why are you toying with me? If you're doing all this behind the King's back, it's only a matter of time before he comes looking for you. So even if it's not your plan to kill me, he certainly will."

Asterious stepped away with a sly smile and began to pace, folding his hands behind his back. She'd managed to pique his interest in her personal secrets, and perhaps trading secrets was the key. So he decided to throw out one he could spare. One that might even get her talking.

"I wouldn't be too worried about that." He glanced back to watch her reaction. "Because King Daemar is dead."

He could see the way her body tensed even from over his shoulder, just as he expected. "You killed your own father?"

"No, no. I assure you, I did not have the pleasure. No one is quite sure who did, actually. It was a successful assassination and the key to my freedom." He whipped around, fighting back a grin. "Was it you? Perhaps that's why you were out running in the wilderness and won't tell me anything. Now it's all coming together."

Caramyn shot him a withering look. "I didn't realize I impressed you that much. You really think I could kill the king and escape?"

Asterious stepped toward her, prodding further as his game grew more interesting. "Why not? Maybe you killed him with magic. What more reason to want the man dead who placed a bounty on your kind?"

"I'm not magic. I've never even used a simple rune spell." Caramyn began to fidget, but then put her hands at her sides, her robe slipping open an inch. "My mother was half-Lightborn, like you. And you know as well as I do that magic does not transfer to children of half-breeds..."

"And your father?"

She flinched at the question. "I don't know. My father...he left before I was born. But if he was of magic blood, my mother would've told me..." Something in the girl's face shifted. The mask she wore slipped for all but a second as she threw her gaze to the floor and then back up. He noticed the way she kept her hands at her sides, but twisted the edges of her silky garment nervously.

"I see." He breathed in, truly intrigued. "And may I ask what was your mother's gift? Could it have had any bearing on your unusual eye color?"

"She...she was a wind weaver. One white eye, one sky-blue. She always told me she believed the reason I was born with eyes like these was because I was sick in the womb. And she found someone who used magic to save me...to keep me from dying. And it did this. I don't have magic of my own. Believe me, I've tried."

"You know there's only one kind of magic said to be capable of bringing back the dead...and it does not come without consequence." He raised an eyebrow.

"It wasn't Shadow magic, if that's what you're getting at. I wasn't dead. Just dying. Either way, it wasn't my choice to make. Healing magic has its own price. Mine was this—a deformity. The mark of a mistake. Of someone who wasn't meant to survive."

"And yet you did." His words came out softer than he meant them to. He was merely stating a fact, but she perked up at his voice and stared at him as if expecting more. That hard exterior she wore like armor cracking just a bit further.

But just as suddenly it returned, and she withdrew herself, crossing her arms. "You're damn right. I did."

"It's quite entertaining the way those eyes of yours catch fire when you're irked." She scowled at his words, blushing as she looked away out the window again. He paced for a bit, letting her simmer a second longer before bringing the conversation back around. "You have no reason to worry. At least not about being tried for high treason. I have a strong suspicion of who the assassin might be, and it's certainly not you."

"Then shouldn't you be there at Blackwynd doing something about it?" Caramyn raised her chin. "Or are you running from your duties like you ran from the bandits?"

Asterious pressed his lips together. He wouldn't let her get under his skin with such a childish comment. "If that's what you want to call it, sure. But it wouldn't matter anyway. I'm the forgotten bastard heir, remember? The throne is out of my reach...for now." He raised his hand casually, studying the ridges of his knuckles. "So, for the time being Evylere is without a king, and the Blackwynd Court's facade is falling because the news is spreading. But you see, my father's death wasn't merely...convenient. It was calculated. Precise. Not the work of some vagrant spell-dodger in the woods." His eyes flicked to her. "No offense."

"I'm not offended," she said flatly. "Just waiting for you to get to the point."

"My point," he continued, "is that my father's murderer was someone who knew the palace, the guard rotations, the hidden passages. Someone with the authority to get close, and the skill to vanish afterward. Someone who stands to inherit everything and who was starting to hate him almost as much as I did." He walked to the window, touching a finger to a blood red section of the stained glass. "And someone who hated me, too."

Caramyn's eyes begged him to go on, but she didn't say anything as he let the words hang in the air.

"So, yes. I ran. I ran from Blackwynd. Because there festers a dark power that grows stronger each day, and it was only a matter of time before it turned its gaze on me. And I refused to become the next pawn in the game, to be hunted or used—least of all by the one person I believed would stand beside me—my dear own sister."

12
LITTLE MYSTERY

Caramyn

"You believe your own sister murdered the king so she could take the throne?" Caramyn asked, entranced by his story, but no less suspicious of why he was telling her.

"Whether that was her reason or not, Sinevia is the recognized heir, and her ascension as Queen has already begun. But she has unleashed something...somehow...and it's far more dangerous to Evylere than my father."

Caramyn scoffed. "Whatever it is, it could hardly be worse than Daemar. Sounds to me like she did the kingdom a favor."

"I did not come here to debate kingdom politics. In fact, I did not come here to tell you any of this. I shared this with you in hopes you would see that I have no intention of being like my father, and that I don't have time to play guessing games."

"Then what is it that she's unleashed that has you running so scared?"

The prince glared at her, the sunlight framing the hard outlines of his jaw and the bridge of his nose, highlighting every bit of his tension. "She has summoned Shadow magic...and it's turned her into something unrecognizable."

"But I thought Shadow magic—"

"Could only be wielded by Shadowbloods? So did I. But I suppose now that they're extinct their Shadows need vessels to wield them—and will settle for anyone willing to sell their soul for power. It's a wretched magic, and somehow, it has a claim on my sister. And I fear it's seeking new vessels."

Wretched.

His words cut like glass, reminding her that she must stay guarded. That she couldn't dare get too comfortable and let something slip that could get her killed. She swallowed, thinking of how to redirect the focus off the cursed magic that tainted her blood. "Does Sinevia know you're here?"

Asterious walked to the door, placing a hand on the frame as though inspecting it. "I think she suspects I would've come here, but she doesn't have time to track me down right now. She hides her power for now so that the people don't oppose her claim to the throne. But she's already declared treason on anyone who aids me, so I try to keep my presence undetected. I'm not sure many common folk would recognize me...I haven't exactly been in the public eye. But I'm sure she has spies. I can't take any chances or put anyone in danger on my behalf."

"So that's why you didn't want to ride through Havenswood," Caramyn muttered, almost to herself.

Asterious tilted his chin, in the faintest hint of a nod. "Indeed. Now back to you. I've told you a lot. You've told me very little. My expectations aren't high...for now. But I still have one last question." He stood at the door as though he intended to leave.

Caramyn chewed her lip, her hollow stare following him as she gestured for him to go on.

"My men were only in the Shadow Woods for a few seconds before those wraiths came for us. It's a miracle they stayed away long enough for me to cross back in to help you." The prince drew a breath. "Do you understand that while you were lying deathly ill in those same Woods, you should've been destroyed by the dark power that infests it?" There was a twinkle in his eye that made Caramyn uneasy.

"I—I do. I guess I was lucky."

"Hmm. Lucky indeed." He grumbled the words and turned to go, but Caramyn stopped him with the question that had been burning in her mind since the day she met him. "Asterious." He turned around at the sound of his name, and she stood tall before the words left her lips. "Why were *you* trying to cross into the Shadow Woods?"

The prince's expression grew solemn. His gaze dropped as he looked to his left and right, as if he'd just woken up and realized he was in a place he hadn't meant to be. "I think our conversation is finished for now."

Caramyn clenched a bundle of the robe's silk in her hands and turned her back to him, looking back out the window at Nocthar perched on the far end of the opposite tower. Everything she'd told him had been laced with just enough truth that it served to keep her alive for now. But even that was too much. She should've kept her mouth shut entirely.

"I believe you're right, Prince. So don't come back to ask me any more questions. In fact, since there's nothing more I can tell you about your mother, or any of your other family issues, I think it's time you let me go."

"Well, I can't do that now," Asterious began. "You know far too much about me now, and those loyal to me. And your stubbornness gives me reason to believe you're hiding something. Maybe nothing. Or maybe something that could put me and my entire court in danger. So, until I determine you're not a threat, you're all mine. Welcome to the Forbidden Court, my dear little mystery." Then he closed the door behind him.

When he was gone, she turned and stared at the door where he had been standing just seconds ago. If what he said was true, and King Daemar really was dead, then there was hardly still a reason to kill Asterious. Her chance to make the King suffer was as much gone as him. Unless she just hated Asterious enough to kill him anyway...but would it be worth the trouble?

Gift. He'd called her mother's power a gift. It was unheard of to hear someone speak like of magic that way, especially a Blackwynd raised to hate it. But a few breaths later...

Wretched.

She told him she was just lucky that she hadn't been destroyed by the Shadows, but the truth was a secret she would take to the grave. Because she would never tell him that her father was a Shadowblood—a Shadowblood who'd fled and left her mother pregnant and alone, claiming she'd been unfaithful. Because though Shadowbloods had nearly been immortal, they were also sterile. It was supposed to be impossible for her to exist. And yet somehow, she did. And she had the mark to banish all doubt. The devastating proof of the dark heritage her mother had never explicitly admitted to, but had also never denied.

And the weight of what Asterious had said haunted her, making her doubt what little she thought she already knew. And she couldn't decide if it was for the better or worse. No one had ever questioned whether the Shadowbloods were truly responsible for the Lightborn massacre, because no one would've expected anything less from those wretched Shadow magic wielders. But if it was all a lie, like Asterious claimed, what did that mean? What else did he know?

But then...why should any of this matter to her? Even if the past was a lie, what did it matter now? It was better that she just left all this behind and returned to the Woods. Forget all the things she'd heard. For all she knew, Asterious was the real liar. And even if Sinevia was worse than Daemar, it would make no difference. Evylere had always been hostile to Caramyn, and she'd survived. And she would keep surviving. What difference would one more tyrant on the throne make? It wasn't her battle, and it never had been.

She'd leave this place. She wouldn't allow Asterious another chance to pry into her life any further. Wouldn't allow him to drudge up any more painful memories she'd rather not face. As she stared out the window and watched her raven take to the sky with a beat of his wings, she decided it was best for her to do the same sooner rather than later. Tonight, she would escape.

13

THE WOLF BEAST

Caramyn

A moonless sky darkened the night. In the distance, low thunder promised cloud cover that would darken the stars too. Caramyn cursed under her breath. It would limit her vision, but at least it also meant that anyone else out there wouldn't easily be able to spot her.

She watched the clouds coming in from the far sea's westward horizon. The castle faced the foggy cliffs of Mistwake Bay, and the rest of its walls were encompassed by the flourishing forest they rode through to get here. If she could reach those dense woods, she'd be back in her element and as good as gone.

As more thunder rumbled, drawing nearer, she ripped the sheets from the bed, tore down the curtains, and emptied the wardrobe of all its fine dresses, knotting all the fabric together into one thick cord.

A crack of lightning flashed as she prepared to break the window. She knew if there were guards outside her door, they might hear, so she waited for the next burst of thunder to shatter it with the leg of a wooden footstool. The glass splintered into pieces that tumbled into the darkness below. Caramyn leaned out the window and glanced down, the wind whipping her hair in all directions. The tower was far higher than even the mightiest tree in the Shadow Woods.

Nocthar circled above as ferocious lightning streaked behind him. It was only a matter of minutes before a deluge dropped from the sky, so she quickly anchored her fabric rope to the bedpost and tossed it down from the window. Her heart sank as she watched the end of it dangle a little less than halfway down, where wild brambles and vines covered the stone. If she just knew the state of the stonework, she might be able to scale the rest of the way.

As if linked with her thoughts, Nocthar dove downward to the bottom half of the tower and returned to the window with an ivy leaf in his mouth. She took the leaf and grinned, recognizing the plant by the swirl pattern in the veins. It was no ordinary ivy that laced the bottom half of the tower. It was Iron Vine, a species of ivy said to be strong enough to hold a dragon's weight. She remembered it from the books on plant remedies in her cottage. If it were true, it could easily support her. She gripped the fabric rope and took a breath. Then she climbed out the window.

"This would be much easier in my breeches," she mumbled to herself as the wind tugged at her dress, molding the heavy fabric around her legs. With her feet braced against the tower wall, she shuffled downward, her hands clamped around the cloth like vices.

She hurried, using her vantage point to study the castle grounds with each burst of lightning that illuminated the court. But as the raindrops began to fall, she moved quicker, barely reaching the ivy before the downpour began.

She wasn't far from the ground now, maybe twenty feet or so, and she was much more careless for it. Rushing to slide down as the wind and rain stung every inch of her skin, she reminded herself that at least no one would see her in this downpour. Cold wet hair clung to her neck and face, but she did not lose focus.

A few times the wet stone caused a slip along the vines, but she always managed to catch herself. She was no stranger to climbing, and once she was close enough to the ground for her liking, she leaped, finally feeling the earth beneath her feet.

By the lightning's fleeting illumination, Caramyn studied the great courtyard in which she found herself. A long path of those gleaming opal stones stretched out between rows of unkempt hedges and shrubs. What looked to be a grand fountain or sculpture formed a silhouette in the distance, but she couldn't be sure in the darkness. It would make sense that the Vaerwynd Queen's room overlooked a rose garden. Asterious' mother. The lost queen whose bedding and clothes she had just strung together to make her escape.

But she would never have had to do it if he hadn't brought her here to begin with...

She paused to lean against a pillar beneath a decorative archway as the rain beat down, her thoughts swarming. "What has that arrogant ass done to me?"

She didn't understand why the thought of leaving this castle—of leaving *him*—made her hesitate. Perhaps it was the way he'd contradicted everything she thought she knew of the Lightborn King's death, insisting it hadn't been a Shadowblood who started it all. Or perhaps because he'd talked about Shadow magic as though he knew its secrets, even while calling it wretched...

He was the wretched one, and yet she couldn't ignore the pull of him, the uneasy hope he had kindled that he might hold answers to questions she'd been asking her entire life. Or she could be entirely wrong about everything. And the consequences of staying and being wrong were far greater than if she just left this all behind and accepted that she may never be meant to know the secrets of her impossible magic heritage...because the alternative was that he discovered her mark and killed her for it.

Her stomach twisted her stomach into knots. If she left, perhaps she could find a new refuge somewhere deep in those towering snowy mountains. Or she could stow away on a ship docked at Magoth. If the map she carried in her head was correct, the trading port should be just a day's journey to the north. Or she could answer the call that kept beckoning her and return to those Woods to live out her days in darkness and isolation, never knowing who she truly was. Always wondering if she was meant for more...

She looked down at the sopping ground pooling around her feet, the reality setting in. She could be free. Free from all the tangled emotions the prince made her feel. Free from the burdens of being the Witch of the Shadow Woods. Free to step out from the weight of two conflicting destinies that should never have been hers to bear. If she'd just forget it all and leave...

Leave.

She squinted through the rain, looking for the stables to try her luck at stealing a horse. She thought perhaps a new horse that didn't recognize her wouldn't be so stubbornly loyal to the prince and would be willing to carry her away from here. It was worth a shot. Ignoring the wet chill seeping through her skin, she thought back to their arrival at the castle. A boy had emerged and led the horses away at the entrance gate.

That meant the stables were somewhere to the right of the castle's entrance. Caramyn turned on her heels in the cover of night, darting around the side of the castle. The growling thunder and deafening rainfall left no room for her senses to listen for the sound of Nocthar following close behind, but she knew he'd manage to stay near, as always.

A small, subtle glow directed her attention to an opening in a structure she hadn't noticed upon arriving. The rain let up just enough as she made the glow out to be a lantern over a wheelbarrow and pitchfork tucked away beneath an overhang jutting out from the castle. It appeared that the stables were built into the side of the castle itself, not separately like she had expected. A twinge of discouragement stabbed at her heart.

The wall. Even if she could steal a horse, how would she get through it? The only exit was guarded and locked by those massive gates. The only way to get out of here undetected was up and over. And that meant she only had her own two feet.

So she disregarded any hope for a mount and stepped up to the ivy-covered wall that encompassed the palace. After one last glance back, she climbed, the wet stone gritty against her fingertips. When she reached the top, she perched herself there to catch her breath and looked out. Nothing but a landscape of night veiled by rain, sloping into a dark forest below.

You've survived this long. You've always survived. You will survive again.

But was surviving enough anymore? She asked herself as she began her descent down the other side. She brushed her uncertainty aside, and let herself drop to the ground below, landing on her feet with a splash that sent mud spattering. The storm had strengthened again. But she was on the other side of the wall now. Completely free.

Before she could take a step forward, a desperate raven's cry pierced through the howling wind and rain. It meant danger, or that she'd been detected. She didn't take the time to ask which. She sprinted forward, down the hill, headed for the cover of the forest below.

She only made it about ten strides before she felt the presence of...something. It loomed, somewhere in the shadows she couldn't see, but close enough that she could feel. It was trailing her. Stalking. The footfalls were heavy, menacing, and getting closer.

A crack of lightning split the dark, and in its glare, she saw it—a wolfish horror fit to prowl the underworld. It charged straight for her, jaws parted around saber-length fangs, solid eyes gleaming like cold moonlight. Even on all fours it stood taller than a horse, its massive paws armed with scythe-curved claws.

It ran with speed far swifter than any ordinary wolf, icy rain rolling down its stone-black fur as it came for her. She ran, nearly slipping in the mud, but the beast leapt in front of her with a vicious snarl that chilled Caramyn to the marrow. It swiped at her, and she twisted aside to dodge the blow, but the tip of its claws still caught the edge of her shoulder.

She winced at the burning sensation of torn flesh. Blood surfaced quickly in the pattern of four bright red streaks across her shoulder. Nocthar dove down, flying into the creature's face as it growled and snapped its jaws, buying Caramyn a moment to flee. She ran as fast as her legs could carry her, back toward the wall of the castle, though she expected this beast could easily scale the wall, too, and likely faster than she could.

Just as she reached the base, she heard the padded footfalls of the wolf-beast approaching, howling as it neared. The sound of her own thudding heart roared through her chest as she realized there were no vines to climb on this side of the wall, and she scrambled to find a foothold amongst the crumbling stone. She clawed her way up, her fingers bleeding as she dug her nails into the rock wall in desperation. Nocthar had held the creature off as long as possible, and now it was coming for her. There was no escape. This vicious creature was going to tear her to shreds right here, far from where her Shadow Woods could protect her.

It lunged for her, but she ducked and rolled away, sending the beast crashing into the wall, demolishing it like it was made of twigs. As the creature shook off the rubble, she used the chance to dart through the break in the wall. But she wasn't fast enough, especially as her soaked dress clung to her legs. The creature roared and took off again after her.

A yelp cut the beast's cries short. From somewhere Caramyn couldn't determine, an arrow fired into the beast's shoulder. It did little to injure it, but was enough to distract it before the distinct sound of hoofbeats broke through its angry snarls. A saddled horse galloped towards her, and she readied herself to leap onto it. The horse slowed to a trot in front of her, and she lunged forward, latching onto the saddle. Before she could hoist herself all the way up, the horse burst back into full speed and circled back around to the side of the castle, halting at the stables where a cloaked figure awaited her.

14

TERRIN

Caramyn

A hand reached out from underneath the cloak. A grip like cold steel seized her arm, pulling her off the horse and guiding her into the stable entrance. The horse followed, and the figure quickly pulled the large doors shut behind them.

The warmth of the stable surrounded Caramyn and fought off the chill in her bones. She breathed in the scent of hay, manure, and horse, taking in the sight around her. A long cobblestone hallway lay before her, with a dozen stalls on either side, each housing magnificent horses that watched her with curious perked ears. The rainstorm was now no more than a clatter of sound beating down outside, as a trickle of water snaked along the floor beneath the doorway.

Caramyn's gaze followed the cloaked figure as they unstrung the longbow she presumed was used to shoot the beast. Watching carefully, she made a note of where they placed it in the corner by the door, beside the stack of hay bales towering to the ceiling—just in case she saw the chance to steal it later. Then she turned her attention to the cloaked stranger. "Who are you?"

The mysterious figure pulled back the hood to reveal a head full of flaxen hair glimmering in the torchlight. A youthful boy, probably no older than fifteen, gaped back at Caramyn with curious green eyes. He seemed just as surprised as she was, as though he had been caught doing something he shouldn't have been doing.

"What the hell was that thing outside?" She breathed in, shuddering at the mere remembrance of its glowing eyes. "That was no normal wolf. Is it some kind of guard for the castle?"

The boy only shrugged weakly, as though he couldn't be bothered to explain. *Damn it.*

"What is your name?" she demanded.

The boy began making symbols with his fingers, then looked at Caramyn with a nervous grin.

"I'm sorry." Caramyn raised an eyebrow. "I'm afraid I don't understand."

The boy rolled his eyes and then knelt down onto the dusty stable floor. She followed his finger intently as he formed letters in the dirt coating the cobblestone.

T-E-R-R-I-N

"Terrin?" She read aloud. "Your name is Terrin?"

The boy stood up and smiled proudly, signaling her with a nod.

"Can't you speak?" she asked.

Terrin shook his head, then pointed to his ears and used a cutting-off motion with his hand. She determined Terrin wasn't going to be able to tell her all she wanted to know about the beast. But he had saved her life, and that was enough for now.

"Well—thank you." Caramyn offered a respectful nod of her head. "And who's this? I'd like to give her my thanks as well." She gestured toward the dappled grey mare that she had clung to for dear life mere moments ago.

Terrin motioned for her to come near. He reached for her hand and guided it to the horse's steel grey mane. As she stroked the animal's neck, he walked away only to return with a leather halter, and pointed to the name engraved on the brass plate across the cheekpiece.

Frasya

"Frasya," Caramyn whispered. The mare turned to her and nudged her with a soft touch of her muzzle. "Beautiful."

After a few moments of silence as Terrin lingered nearby, watching her vigilantly, she glanced over at him. "So, you are the stableboy?"

The boy tilted his hand side to side, to indicate that she was partially correct. He then opened his cloak to reveal the elegant horse-head crest of the Blackwynd name, carved into a badge buckled to his tunic.

Then, he looked at Frasya, and gestured some type of hand motion to the animal, along with a clicking sound. The mare pawed and reared, as if on command. Then his hand went flat, palm down, and the mare steadied herself squarely in response, standing like a soldier awaiting orders.

"You train them." Caramyn fought a rather large smile that threatened to make its way to her face. She didn't want to make her excitement obvious, but she was truly fascinated with these stunning animals. So far, the rumor of the Blackwynds' exceptional reputation with horses was proving true—unlike everything else she thought she knew that only left her with more questions than answers.

Caramyn walked along the stable aisle, admiring the animals as she went. Terrin seemed so young. Yet the prince entrusted him with his entire stable of horses. There was an innocence about him that made her feel safe enough to turn her back to him, though by instinct she still watched his reflection in the decorative breastplate hanging at the end of the hallway. She thought about what Asterious had said—that anyone here would be put to death if found. This stable boy must have known the danger it would put him in to follow the prince, yet he'd chosen that path. Perhaps it was blind loyalty. Perhaps Asterious was worth following. Or maybe Sinevia was just the greater evil.

As Terrin tended to Frasya, Caramyn noticed the black stallion Asterious had ridden on their journey in one of the first few stalls. "Hello, Alofreise," she stretched out her hand to pet his muzzle. The horse let out a soft blow of warm air in response.

She was buying time, trying to figure out what she would do next, shocked that Terrin hadn't thought to alert someone of her trying to escape. Perhaps he knew she stood no chance to leave the safety of these stables, not on this night with that demon wolf outside. And if that creature lurked just outside the castle, what else would she encounter while traveling alone through these ancient witchlands? She was bound to this court for now. But what would happen when Azell or Asterious or whoever came looking for her in the morning? If the prince knew how easily she'd gotten out of that room, he might lock her up somewhere far worse.

"Can you help me get back into the castle? It seems I'm...lost."

The boy nodded with great confidence, his yellow hair flipping up and down across his forehead. Taking her hand in his, he led her briskly back down the stall hallway and to a dark corridor behind it, grabbing a torch off the wall along the way. There was a room stocked with saddles and boots, shields and lances, some clean, and some old as though they had been left there since the glory days of the old Vaerwynd tournaments. Terrin opened the door, nearly falling off its hinges, tearing the cobwebs down from the corners of the dark passage within. He handed her the torch and pointed. How could she trust where this would lead?

"This looks like it hasn't been used in centuries." Caramyn wrinkled her nose. The passage echoed the sound of a steady dripping of water. Her skin tingled at the thought of the dampness, cobwebs, and rats within. Stepping forward, she took a deep breath, trying to resist the stench of stale air.

"Wait, I'm forgetting something." She stopped herself. Terrin gave her a quizzical look. "You aren't the only one who can command animals."

She strode back to the front door with Terrin in tow, where an incessant pecking sound emanated from the other side. She quickly cracked open the door enough for Nocthar to flutter in, water droplets rolling off his ink-black feathers as he hopped onto her shoulder. "Sorry, Nocthar."

Terrin looked amused. Still holding the torch, she made her way back to the dark passage entrance.

"Thank you, Terrin. Perhaps someday you can teach me how to communicate with these magnificent creatures the way you can...if I'm ever able to return here."

Terrin flashed a genuine smile. With that, she stepped forward into the shadows of the dripping tunnel, where a cold air enveloped her, chilling her skin all over again.

15
MEANT TO BE

Caramyn

Caramyn walked along the corridor for what felt like hours, looking ahead for any sign of an end to the tunnel. Before long, she found herself facing a dead end.

"Great, Nocthar, now what?" She uttered to the bird on her arm in frustration.

Surveying the walls, she noticed a small latch peeking out from between two stone bricks in the wall. Fearful that there may be guards on the other side, she held her breath as she carefully lifted the latch. The door swung toward her just barely, only an inch or two. Catching it with her hand, she stopped it and held the torch away, so as not to draw any attention to the firelight. She peeked through the opening. It was the castle kitchen, and it seemed empty.

She pushed the door open further and slipped through to the other side. Awaiting her was a wooden table that extended the length of the wall, with pots, cauldrons and pans hanging overhead. Herbs hung drying on a line in the corner. On a large table next to a cutting block, a loaf of bread lay half-wrapped in a piece of cheesecloth, flanked by a small dish of apples.

Caramyn imagined how sweet those autumn apples must taste. After all, she was quite hungry after her encounter with the monster outside, so she plucked up a ripe red apple from the bowl and took a ravenous bite, offering some to Nocthar as well.

Apple and torch in hand, she made her way out of the kitchen and readied herself for a maze through the castle. She kept a watchful eye out for guards, often sending her raven ahead to scope things out before her. There were a handful of moments where she had to tiptoe around, but so far, she found the castle an easy place to sneak through, due to the lack of sentries. It was understandable, since Asterious only had those few at his service who had chosen to follow him. They could only be spread so thin, Caramyn thought.

As she followed the winding corridors through the castle, trying to find her way back to her chambers, she stumbled upon a structure that halted her breath. Two arched towering doors inlaid with pearl and silver beckoned, stretching to the ceiling, intricate symbols of vines, roses, and celestial patterns etched into their surface. She couldn't quell the curiosity that begged to know what grandeur lay on the other side. She pulled the heavy silver handles of one of the doors, only to open to a darkened ballroom. The floor was white marble, with an inlay of a silver crescent moon, and twisting thorns and roses snaking around it, still vibrant through the dust that had settled over it, marking the passage of time. The ivy beginning to overtake the cracks in the walls only added some natural, earthen beauty. The ceiling peaked into an arched dome of glass, open to the night sky above. At the opposite end of the room, a grand staircase carpeted in midnight blue, splitting at the top platform into two balconies held up by opal pillars that wrapped around the great hall. Hovering just above lining the glass roof were glittering diamond chandeliers that might has well have been clusters of starlight.

"Beautiful," she whispered to herself. It was most certainly Lightborn design. No human could have crafted something so enchanted. Her heart beat fast as she drank in the details and thought of how unfitting it was for her to be standing amongst such grandeur. She was born poor, in a village of such insignificance it rarely even appeared on maps. A place full of people so focused on surviving they hardly had time to notice the crystal white and icy blue eyes of the pregnant half-Lightborn woman who fled there alone to raise her child. A place hidden in the mires along the river separating the Bleak Wilderness from the human lands. A safe place, until it wasn't—Dawnmire.

Yet now she stood in this ballroom like something pulled from a dream, where once Lightborn nobility and their guests had once filled the air with their laughter, music, and magic. For a fleeting moment, she allowed herself the simple indulgence of imagining what it might have been like to steal a glimpse of such a world.

The sound of rhythmic footsteps yanked her from her reverie. She snuffed out her torch and darted to the corner of the grand room, where she hid and waited for the steps to pass.

When the footsteps faded, she sent Nocthar out to ensure it was safe to continue. He was gone for a worrying amount of time, but he finally swooped by with a reassuring croak and tilt of his wing, then disappeared into the darkness of the castle, and where he'd gone, she did not know.

She tiptoed out, back into the main hallway, and slowly recognized the entrance of the castle. She remembered passing the same elaborate opal lined hallways when Asterious and Wryan had first led her to the tower. She knew she was getting close. But how would she get past the guard Asterious had surely placed at her door?

For the first time, she second guessed her immediate instinct to kill. She had felt threatened by each man who crossed into the Shadow Woods, but the thought of a posted guard just following orders didn't make her feel the same way. Plus, it wouldn't be a good look to leave a dead man at her door either. That certainly wouldn't go over well with the prince in the morning.

She crept up the stairs, peering around the rounded corners to catch a glimpse of the guard and make her plan. But to her surprise, there was no one there. Had Asterious lied about the guard to discourage her trying to escape? Or was he yet again just toying with her? Or perhaps Nocthar was keeping the guard busy, which would explain his absence.

Whatever the reason, she didn't care, only counted it a blessing for the moment. As long as she could pick the lock, she'd be fine. She'd done it a handful of times during her trips to Havenswood, when she was desperate enough for food or supplies—mostly in the early months of surviving in the Woods, before she'd learned to acquire coin by looting trespassers. She also worked open small locks on chests or boxes that thieves left behind on occasion, but it had been well over a year since she had to do that.

She took out the bone-shard blade she'd made earlier from where she'd secured it to her thigh beneath her dress. It was a crude tool, but sharp enough to puncture flesh, and thin enough to poke around a keyhole. She worked for a while, growing frustrated as she felt the minutes passed the hour mark. It was imperative to get back into the room before dawn.

Finally, when her fingers were cramping and her neck stiff from glancing over her shoulder every few seconds, the lock clicked, and she breathed a sigh of relief. Proud of herself, she opened the door and entered quietly, her bird suddenly reappearing to join her. Now to clean up all the evidence of her late-night outing and get some rest.

As she closed the door behind her and prayed the lock would reset, she couldn't help but wonder why every step she tried to take away only seemed to draw her back to this castle, to this prince's world, as if maybe even the Shadows wanted her to stay...as if maybe she was meant to be here.

16
MAKE HER WANT TO STAY

Asterious

Asterious woke with a thrashing headache that threatened to split him in two. But he swallowed down the pain with disregard, as he was so used to doing. There was work to be done today.

The previous night's rain had left a rolling mist that welcomed that rose to greet the morning as he gazed out his window. The fog climbed so high it swallowed the view, leaving only the faint orange glow of dawn to hint at a new day. He dressed in a charcoal gray undershirt, black jacket and pants, and set out to meet Wryan in the dining hall.

Wyran could be harsh and rigid, but for all his severity, he's still given Asterious something his father never had—direction. It was Wyran who'd convinced the king to let him train in swordsmanship during all those years he was imprisoned beneath his father's castle—to ensure he was lethal in every form. And through each scar Wyran had given him, he'd learned control—and that had been the ticket to his freedom. He was a good nineteen years his elder, and

Asterious valued his counsel, from the dark depths of his cell in the Blackwynd dungeons to the gilded halls of this Lightborn palace.

He carried on, making his way to the dining hall, where Crisyn, the cook, and her assistant scurried to and fro as they prepared breakfast for the castle. When Crisyn brought him a plate of powdered pancakes with apricot preserves before he'd taken ten steps into the room, he shook his head. "It's really not necessary for you to make all this for us. My men and I would do well to prepare our own plates."

"We wouldn't hear of it, Your Highness," Crisyn shook her head, wiping flour from her hand on her apron. "You and your men need your energy to focus your efforts on far greater things."

"Keeping our stomachs full is no small thing, Crisyn. You're likely the most important of us all." He took the plate from her with a soft smile, the sweet aroma of the breakfast making his crackling headache a bit more tolerable. The cook curtsied with a smile in exchange and walked back to the kitchen. He'd lost count of how many times he'd told her she didn't have to curtsy, but she was just as stubborn as he was.

Asterious carried his plate of food to the table where Tyrios, Wyran, Gariel, and Riven were seated, discussing for the millionth time Riven's most recent intel about the dark creatures Sinevia was summoning as spies to help her crush any resistance before it began—and to track down the prince.

In fact, it was Riven's recent sighting of one across the Arengol River that had prompted their journey to the Shadow Woods. It was a clear sign they had even less time than Asterious thought. And though he knew that he should be wholly consumed by this and the urgency of it all, his focus strayed elsewhere—on finding his mother before it was too late—and now, the infuriating girl in the tower.

"Good morning, Your Highness," Wryan greeted, biting into a crisp apple as the prince approached.

Asterious rubbed his temples. "Morning Wryan."

"Another one of those nights?" Wryan frowned.

Asterious only grimaced and shoved Wryan's shoulder. "Still not as bad as you after a night of drinking."

Wyran chuckled with a headshake. "Boy, you'll never let me live that down, will you?"

"How could I?" A laugh rumbled from Asterious. "You came down for a training session wielding a broomstick, for gods' sake. I should've let you use it for our spar."

"You should have. All the more fun it would have been to beat you with a broom." Wyran brushed his knuckles against the table with a hearty laugh, his rounded nose widening as he flashed a grin.

When their chuckles died down, Asterious leaned an elbow on the table's surface and lowered his voice. "Wryan, you have more knowledge of the magickind classification than anyone here. And though I know we have our disagreements, I want your opinion on something."

Wryan hunched over, his expression growing serious. "Is this about the girl? Because you know what I think of the whole situation. The eyes don't lie, and hers have a hell of a lot to say."

"Yes, I know, Wyran...but that is where you and I differ. Her life is not ours to take, simply because she is something we don't understand."

Wyran grunted with a sigh, shaking his head, this time with disappointment. "I'll admit your father was a bit extreme, Asterious. But you can't let your desire to be unlike him become your fatal flaw. There was some wisdom in Daemar's ways. The world *is* safer without magic, and we cannot let our guard down just because it's taken a new form."

Asterious held his composure. "So you still think I should just kill her after I make her talk?"

Wyran lifted his hands and leaned back in a gesture of surrender. "I never said that. I only said caution has kept you alive this long. Don't abandon it now. Not everyone is what they seem."

"Well, that's exactly what's keeping me up at night." Asterious folded his hands across the table. "I think the ring might be the wrong thing to be focusing on, at least for now. The more I talked with her, the more I got the sense that she knows something—that she's hiding something—about the Shadow Woods." Asterious' grey eyes flickered.

"You think she might know about the weapon?" Wyran raised both eyebrows and straightened his shoulders.

"Maybe. Or that she has some sort of power making her immune to whatever horrors are in that forest. Which could certainly aid us in getting it, if that's the case." Asterious pressed a hand to the back of his neck as though trying to soothe a troubling thought. "Perhaps she escaped from the Veil? Do you think that's possible?"

Wryan knitted his brows together, his mustache twitching as he spoke. "Asterious, you know that's absurdity. The Veil is death. It was created by a Shadowblood. No one's breaking through it, on either side. Your father made sure of that."

"I know." The prince hung his head. Shadow magic was impenetrable by any other magic. And he feared it might mean his sister was beyond saving if it'd taken root too deep in her heart. His thoughts began wandering. "If Sinevia truly did kill our father, it's no wonder after what he did to her...to us."

"Your Highness," Wryan's face grew stern. "I won't pretend your father didn't make mistakes, but I served at his side for many years, and he was a good king, and a just man, until he was blinded by the loss of his queen. It made him rash, and paranoid, and—

"Cruel." Asterious looked up across the table, his eyes meeting Wyran's.

"In some ways, yes." Wyran sighed. "And think of it—it all stemmed from heartbreak. A ruthlessness awoken by grief. So guard that heart of yours the way you guard your secrets. Because nothing will ruin you faster than loving too deeply."

"Whether or not love played a part in his downfall if no longer relevant. The fact is he is dead, and Sinevia is blind to her power and we're running out of time before she destroys the rest of what he left behind." Asterious drew in a long breath. "And that's where the girl comes in. I think she can help us."

Wyran raised an eyebrow, his doubtfulness clear. "That's if you can get her talking. She's taking advantage of your patience." He smirked. "If you'd like suggestions, I have many methods."

Asterious shook away the comment. Wyran valued the effectiveness of force for these types of situations, but the prince was all too familiar with what it felt like to be forced, helpless against another's will.

"I'm sure you do, Wyran, but I'd like to try my own tactics with her first. I'm hoping at the very least I can get her to slip up and say something. Because I doubt she'll tell me anything else willingly. She's stubborn. I'm sure the last thing she wants to do is help me," Asterious sighed. "And I can't blame her." He circled a knot in the wood of the table with the tip of his finger as Caramyn's accusations echoed in his mind. She had every reason to believe he was a monster. And dragging her here against her will certainly wasn't helping to convince her otherwise.

"Careful, Highness. Sounds like you might be feeling something for your captive." Wryan's voice lowered. "Remember, this is just another form of what I've taught you. A strong leader has no choice but to close off the heart's connection to the mind, to put emotions aside at all times. You know that more than anyone. And if you forget it, look at those scars to remind you." As the man leaned back in his chair at his final point, he huffed out a distorted chuckle. "Though I can't say I fault you for it. She could certainly turn a few heads."

Asterious turned his gaze away, but felt his face run hot as he clenched his fist beneath the table. He didn't know why Wryan's comments about her enraged him so. He didn't care. He shouldn't care.

Tyrios appeared and slid into the seat beside Wryan, chomping down on a bite of pancake. "Do tell, Wryan, who could turn a few heads? I missed the memo on this clearly important meeting."

Wryan slapped Asterious on the shoulder. "Our prince here can explain. Seems he's got an eye for the girl from the Woods."

"Shattered gods, Wryan that is absolute nonsense." Asterious rolled his eyes and touched his fingers to his forehead as Tyrios and Wryan chuckled. "I simply said I think she may have more potential to help us if I can just get her to tell me the truth about herself. But to do that, I'll have to win her trust. I want her cooperation, not her fear." He noticed how Wyran shot him a look of warning.

Tyrios eyed the prince up and down, his smirk fading. "Well, it may not be my place to say this, but perhaps keeping her locked in her room isn't sending the right message. Make her want to be here. Show her you trust her, and then maybe she'll trust you. Isn't that what you always say when you're training new horses?"

"She's not a horse. I do not seek to tame her." Asterious snapped. Then he slid back in his chair with a sigh. "If I grant her freedom, what if she leaves?"

"Make her want to stay." Tyrios repeated with a shrug. Wryan shook his head and looked like he wanted to object, but to the prince's surprise, he didn't.

Asterious rubbed a thumb across his chin as he mulled over the thought of allowing Caramyn to roam the castle grounds. If she left, he may lose any chance of ever crossing back into those Woods. He was desperate, and she could be his last hope to keep both his sister and his kingdom from falling into darkness, as absurd as it seemed.

"You're right." The prince rose to his feet. "I'll give her a reason to stay. And I'll start by inviting her to dinner tonight."

Just then, the guard who had the night shift of guarding Caramyn's room passed by the table. Asterious reached out a hand to get his attention. "How is the girl?"

"It was a strange night, Your Highness." He shifted his eyes across the room, as if looking for something. "Lots of odd things shifting in the night. You'll have to forgive me, but I followed something I thought was lurking in the stairwell until I realized it was just a blackbird. Had me fooled, though. For a moment there it almost seemed like...Shadows."

"A blackbird?" Asterious raised an eyebrow. He didn't have to think too hard about where he'd seen one recently before. "But the girl is safe?"

"She never left the room, Sir. When I came back her door was still shut and locked."

He stood up, faster than he meant to, and addressed the men at his table. "If you'll excuse me, I need to check on something."

17
DINNER INVITATION

Caramyn

It was difficult to sleep without a blanket or even a thin sheet. Every piece of cloth in the room had been used for the escape plan. And Caramyn's grumbling stomach only added to her discomfort. She planned to devour breakfast once Azell brought it up. As she lay there curled up on the bare mattress, she worried what the maid would say about the shattered window and her blankets that had been tied into a rope and were now a soiled bundle on the floor.

"Good morning, dear." Azell peeked in through a crack in the door.

"Good morning, Azell. Come in." A yawn carried Caramyn's words as she sat on the edge of her bed and the maid pushed the door open.

"Goodness, you are tattered! What happened to your clothes? And your bed?" Azell threw her hands up as she shrieked. She placed the breakfast tray she was carrying on the dresser and dashed across the room.

Caramyn sat in silence as the maid inspected the bed and empty wardrobe, the scent of fresh warm fruit preserves making her salivate. As Azell made her way to the broken window, she clicked her tongue.

"I can't blame you for trying to escape. He shouldn't have forced you to come here." She paused again, looking out the window into the sunlight. "The prince is desperate enough that sometimes I wonder if he's thinking clearly."

"Desperate to sit on the throne." Caramyn crossed her arms. Her words tasted like salt. "He just wants power like every other king and conqueror before him."

"Well," Azell shrugged. "Maybe. Maybe not. He fears the weight of the crown, but trust me when I say I believe he is the one most fit to wear it. In his veins he carries both great bloodlines that ruled this land in duality for centuries. Asterious cannot change the things that have already passed at his father's hand. But he can do something about the future."

Caramyn huffed, not convinced, and shuffled over the tray of food, stuffing her mouth with a berry tart oozing a decadent filling that almost shimmered. Then popped a plump piece of starfruit into her mouth and washed it down with the creamiest milk she'd ever tasted.

Azell's dark eyes twinkled as she turned back toward Caramyn. "I've known him since he was just a young boy. He has a good heart underneath all that sternness."

Caramyn was surprised to hear such admiration for the prince. All her life, he'd been spoken of as a demon—said to have refused the throne simply to remain the executioner. Yet when he'd interrogated her, he'd implied that killing had never been his choice. And timid Azell hardly seemed the sort to dote on a monster. None of it added up.

Caramyn fidgeted with her tangled hair, twisting it in both hands over her shoulder. Even if he wasn't the demon they said he was, he was still a man. Best not to give him the benefit of the doubt. But she wouldn't say that out loud to this tender woman.

Azell approached, her eyes fixated on Caramyn's tattered dress that was nearly reduced to rags from last night's endeavors. She walked over to the dirty bedding and clothes on the floor and sorted through the pieces before gathering them up into a bundle in her arms. "Goodness you even ruined the dresses, too."

"Thank you for taking care of everything Azell." Caramyn offered a slight bow of her head. "When you have the chance, could you please bring back my breeches?"

"Yes, once they are cleaned. For now, I'll probably only be able to acquire more dresses, but I'll try to dig up some pants in your size, too. Try to keep them in one piece." She paused, glancing at the traces of crumbs left on Caramyn's tray. "Now that you've finished breakfast, let's get you into the bath. I'll work on finding you something to wear."

Caramyn had to fight back a smile at the thought of another hot bath. She had no intention of objecting to that. Moments later, the tub was ready, with hot steam swirling above the water like a welcoming mist. As Caramyn stood to undress, Azell let out a gasp. "Your shoulder!"

Caramyn had nearly forgotten about the gashes in her skin from the beast attack. The blood was dried and caked over them now, but the wound obviously fresh, and had caught Azell's attention.

"It's nothing. Just an accident from breaking the window," Caramyn uttered.

Azell stared hard at the cuts on her arm, walking even closer. As if she suddenly saw something horrific, her eyes widened, and she quickly averted her gaze. Keeping her head low, she simply walked out of the room, locking the door behind her.

As strange as it was, she returned shortly as if it had never happened, with a pile of clean blankets and a few dresses draped across her arms.

"I'll leave these here for you." She nodded at Caramyn with a smile and retreated again.

Nocthar flew into the room once she was gone and pecked the crumbs from her breakfast as Caramyn sank down into the warm tub. This time, she made sure not to fall asleep, as she didn't want to wake up to any more surprise visitors.

Once she finished, she selected a deep teal dress to wear. She admired the delicate beadwork along the bodice, and the color reminded her of the great waters on the horizon beyond the cliffs. The fitted sleeves were long enough to cover her marking, but an extra layer of fabric cascaded from her elbows, making her feel playful. She'd never felt something so soft and lovely against her skin.

It was quite a boring day otherwise. She looked out the window, longing to be outside. Unlike the stormy skies that had overtaken the night, the day was bright and cheery, but she could only enjoy it from her view from the tower. She was glad she had broken the window, for now she could at least feel the autumn breeze. If she had been in the Shadow Woods, she would have used a day like today for waxing her bowstring or digging up roots for her remedies, and if she had time, she might have read one of her books beneath a tree...a book describing what she could not see beyond the forest. But here she was, behind new walls, looking out at world beyond her reach once more.

As she daydreamed out the window, trying to make out shapes in the clouds, there was a knock at her door. It was much firmer than Azell's gentle taps.

"Don't worry, I'm clothed this time!" She called, presuming it to be Asterious. In some peculiar part of her, she wanted it to be him. She was so bored that it would have relieved her to engage in some banter with him.

But instead, a vaguely familiar face appeared in the doorway. It was Tyrios, if she remembered correctly.

"Lady Caramyn." He cleared his throat, seeming a tad bit uncomfortable to be in her presence. "The prince has asked that you join him for dinner tonight."

Caramyn raised an eyebrow. She had not at all expected that. "Well, perhaps he should invite me himself instead of sending his men like servants to do it."

Tyrios wore an expression of bewilderment. He scratched his ear and looked around. "I'm sorry, Caramyn. He had every intention to do it himself...but he had something urgent come up." A long pause drew out the seconds in which Caramyn refused to answer. "So shall I tell him you will be ready at six?"

"No!" Caramyn scoffed. "Tell him I won't be joining him for dinner or anything else for that matter, unless he can make his own appearance here to ask me himself." She turned away. "You may leave now."

Without another word, Tyrios was gone. It was less than an hour later that there was no knock at the door, but rather an aggressive turn of the key in the door's lock. Caramyn thought to reach for the bone dagger she kept hidden, this time in the bodice of her dress, just in case. It was her instinct to always have a weapon prepared, no matter the circumstance. She stood facing the door as it swung open and her eyes locked with those of Prince Asterious'.

18

BE MY GUEST

Asterious

The prince stood in the doorway, drilling his gaze into Caramyn's, wondering why she looked ready to pounce on him—and almost wishing she would. He'd planned to ask her to dinner himself. He wanted to check on her far earlier right after the guard's strange report this morning, and he was heading straight for her room when Terrin came rushing in to tell him about some equally disturbing occurrences outside the stables, involving the return of a vile monster he thought he'd taken care of.

"Tyrios tells me you've declined my request for dinner." He cocked his head to the side, his eyes still locked with hers. "How rude of you."

She stood firm, unmoving. "Hardly ruder than kidnapping." Her fierce pose was quite the contrast against the delicate blue dress she wore. "And I only declined because you sent your men to do your dirty work, as I'm clearly starting to learn is a pattern with you."

Asterious bit his tongue to keep himself from responding too hastily. Her words stung, but he knew how things must look to her—the way he kept his distance, and the way she had seen his men put themselves in harm's way for him. But he couldn't expect her to understand. At least not yet.

"I'll ignore that remark." He chose his words carefully. "I'm trying to be welcoming. I want you to feel as though you are my guest, not a prisoner."

"Guest?" Caramyn tossed her hair over her shoulder with a fake laugh. "I must've missed the invite because from where I'm standing, I don't recall choosing to come here."

Asterious moved toward her, just one step. To his surprise, Caramyn mirrored his movement and approached with a step, too. Now, they stood inches apart, so close that he picked up her scent of lavender and saffron.

"It seems there are a lot of things you can't seem to recall." He breathed with a low grumble. "Listen, join me for dinner tonight, and I'll let you ask me anything." He leaned forward and whispered into her ear. She flinched but didn't pull away. When he stepped back at her silence, her silent gaze flicked back and forth across his face.

"Why not ask one of your men to entertain you? Or are they not welcome at your table, only to do your bidding when it suits you?" Her never-ending remarks flew off her tongue effortlessly like venom.

Asterious clenched his jaw to retain his composure and turned aside. "I hope to see you at my table." He didn't give her a chance to argue further, only straightened the collar of his black coat and calmly walked out the door.

19

THE SHADOWBLOOD'S BLADE

Caramyn

"I should've taken off his head," Caramyn muttered to the raven that fluttered into her room through the window. In his talons, he carried her hunting dagger. Her eyes widened at the sight of it. "You couldn't have brought this back sooner? I could've had him bleeding out on the floor by now."

Though she spoke such threats, she was no longer so sure seeing him dead was truly what she wanted anymore. She couldn't deny the flutter in her heart that she'd felt when the prince had leaned so close to her, or the way his velvet voice sent shivers down her neck. It was a thought she abhorred—to think that she might feel even the slightest bit of desire for the son of the king who had driven her into exile. But it was surely just a physical reaction to the proximity of a man who could be considered beautiful, with that chiseled jaw dusted with shadow and those dark brows above keen eyes that seemed to weigh the world before speaking. Beautiful indeed, if he wasn't such an ass.

Nocthar crowed, demanding her attention. She whipped around to see him drop the knife onto her bed, nudging it toward her with his beak.

"I'll go...but only because he said I could ask him anything." She tucked the dagger away at her thigh into the sheath she'd made from a leather belt, then smoothed out her dress to ensure it was invisible. After the way he'd approached her before, with that dangerous look in his eye, she wasn't going to take chances. "And I certainly have some questions."

As the hour neared, Caramyn wondered what to expect, and wrestled with the idea of killing the prince, if it came down to it. She didn't know why she hesitated at the thought of it, when she had killed men before. Killing never wore on her conscience the way it did now. She didn't delight in it but simply felt it had to be done for the survival of herself and her Woods. For fear that if she didn't, something far worse would occur. But now...now she questioned everything and wondered if the Shadows she'd lived amongst for so long had hardened her to the weight of her deeds. And strangely enough, it was no longer the safety of the Woods she missed the most, but the blind certainty they gave her of who she thought she was supposed to be and what she was supposed to do, spared from any doubt.

As the sunset bathed the room in a golden orange hue, a soft knock at the door startled her. It was Azell. "Are you coming to dinner?"

"I—I am." Caramyn looked up from her seat at the vanity. For a moment she almost wanted to change her mind, but committed to stand by her decision. She had attempted to arrange her hair, but had given up and allowed it to fall in loose waves across her shoulders and down her back. She'd never been adept at styling, and her loose hunting braid was about as intricate as it got.

Azell took her hand and led her out of the room. This woman was motherly to her, despite how cold she'd been in return at times. Her touch was always gentle, and there was never a moment she wasn't hastening around to clean or help in whatever way she could. It reminded her of how her own mother had often quietly worked for the good of the village, despite the strange looks they gave her and her lilac-eyed daughter. She'd help in small ways that didn't draw too much attention, keeping the villagers none the wiser that she was using magic to do so—or that it was even her doing. Like when she'd send strong breezes to help dry clothes on the lines, or when she'd scatter the seeds on the wind during planting season. In quiet ways she helped in the safest way she could, never expecting thanks for her unseen work.

It was a meager life, but they were always both fed and warm. She often imagined how much different it might've been if her father had never left. If he had been there in Dawnmire to defend them the day the King's Inquisitors of the Order discovered them and turned her life to ash. If only...

Azell escorted her down the stairs and through a short maze of hallways to the banquet hall. Caramyn noted the corridors' familiarity from her night sneaking through the castle. Only now, everything was lit with life, torchlight, and warmth instead of cold, midnight emptiness. Finally, Azelle guided her to large wooden door with carvings of flowers and harvest fruits along the edges. A simple decorative touch compared to the rest of the castle

The door was opened, and there sat Asterious at the end of a long banquet table lined with an overwhelming assortment of roasted bird and smoked fish, assorted cheeses and stuffed mushrooms alongside glazed in-season vegetables. Tart cakes and fluffed pastries lined one corner of the table, as well as fruits drizzled with syrups and chocolate. The table was set with two silver plates and two chalices of wine at each end of the table. And a great mirror on the far wall stretched the length of the table, casting an eerie reflection of the emptiness of the grand space meant for so many more than just two.

Without a word, Azell patted Caramyn's hand and abandoned her, leaving her in the room with the prince. Caramyn sat down nervously at the seat at the far end of the table. She had never seen such a fine spread of food, and the seasoned scents of herbed barley and fresh roasted quail teased her nostrils. "This is all for me?" She hesitantly plucked a grape from its vine, curious as to where so much food had come from.

"If you want it. The Lightborn ensured their food sources were generous. The harvests in these lands still flourish as if by...well...magic. And as a result, the game is quite plentiful, too." Asterious nodded with a smirk. It was as if he'd read her mind.

She thought of what a shame it was that King Daemar had left these lands to rot, declaring them and anything that came from them as tainted by magic. If he was smart, he would've fed his people with its resources. Perhaps he didn't realize it would all continue thriving even without Lightborn tending it. But then again, she was glad this lush corner of the kingdom had not yet been exploited through human politics. And perhaps it was best kept that way.

She glanced up at Asterious, realizing she hadn't acknowledged the last thing he said. And for the first time, he flashed her what almost seemed like a genuine smile. "I'm glad that you accepted my offer."

Caramyn pursed her lips. "What else was I supposed to do? You probably would have starved me if I didn't."

"You think I'm horrid, don't you?" Asterious leaned back in his chair. "I'm not the monster they made me out to be."

Caramyn thought of how many times she'd had to tell herself the same thing.

I'm not a monster. I'm not a monster. She'd repeat the thought over and over as a child when she first started to understand the meaning of the shadowy markings on her skin. Then again years later, through shock and desperation as she traversed the wilderness seeking refuge in the only place left to run. *I'm not a monster.* She wished it were true.

And yet somehow it had all led up to this moment. A moment in which she sipped rich wine from a jeweled chalice in the castle of a man who should be her greatest enemy. She wondered what the prince would think if he knew of her past. If he knew she was blood bound to the Shadows, guarding their secrets in exchange for their protection. But she didn't know why she cared what he might think.

"How old are you?" She blurted out. He had said she could ask him anything, and she wasn't wasting the chance. But she wasn't sure why that was the first question she chose.

"Twenty-five," the prince said coolly. "And you?"

"The agreement was *I* ask *you* questions. Not the other way around."

"Right, yes." Asterious looked down at his plate and then flashed a tightened smile. "Apologies."

"If you must know, I will be twenty-one on the first day of the eleventh month," she uttered with a small shrug. She didn't know why she told him, but what could it hurt. "Now, back to you. You said you didn't want to kill for your father. And you claim you weren't even given the chance at the throne. You're nothing like what I've heard. So why is that you were made out to be a nightmare? Where do the stories come from?"

The prince hesitated, placing his silverware down. "The king—my father—wanted the people to dislike me. He tried to keep my existence a secret, but when that failed, he had to make it so that no one would ever expect to see me claim the throne and or recognize me if I tried." Asterious chewed his lip. Caramyn sensed there was more.

"So, you really did kill for him? Is that part true?"

"Yes. But not because I wanted to...mostly." His eyes flickered in the candlelight as he gave a fleeting, hollow smile. "Though I can't say there weren't the odd few who deserved it."

"Couldn't you refuse if you believed someone was innocent?"

"Sometimes that's far easier said than done." He spoke through a tense exhale as he tapped the edge of his plate with a fork.

The heaviness in his sigh signaled to Caramyn that she should probably stop while she was ahead. If she pushed him too far, she feared he'd simply end the conversation and leave like last time. She decided to change the subject, at least until she could circle back to her deeper questions.

"Why did you ask me to dinner?"

"Because...I've been thinking." Asterious swirled his fingertip around the rim of his chalice. "And I wanted to tell you that confining you to your chambers was a lapse in my judgment. I'm granting you freedom of this court. But understand that leaving the grounds would be difficult, so I wouldn't advise trying."

"Difficult? Is that a threat?" Caramyn repeated, thinking of the demon wolf she encountered the night before. Was he referring to that? Was it some sort of castle guard he hadn't mentioned? If she asked him about it, he'd know she already tried to escape, so she kept her thoughts silent.

"Not a threat. A warning. You see, there are things that lurk through these witchlands. Creatures once summoned by the Lightborn to guard these lands from enemies. Let's just say it would be in your best interest not to encounter them."

Caramyn's chest tightened as she feigned an unbothered nod. "Noted. I appreciate the...advice." She paused to take a bite. "You know, this almost seems like a charming attempt at an apology."

"If that's what you want it to be." Asterious continued, tilting his head with a curious spark in that one metallic silver eye. "Just keep in mind as you roam this castle, that there is one area that you must stay away from...for your safety. You must not go near the West Wing Hall."

Caramyn raised an eyebrow as she dug her fork into the quail meat on her plate, picking through the tiny bones with her fingers. "What are you hiding there?"

"Nothing at all." Prince Asterious' voice was soft as silk. "But it's very dangerous. You've seen how that side of the castle is nearly destroyed. It could come crumbling down upon you in a matter of seconds with one wrong step."

She didn't entirely believe him, but she let him carry on and pretended to accept his explanation for now. She had to make him trust her so he wouldn't redact her newly given freedom. "So, I can go anywhere else. Does that include the library? And the stables?" she asked.

"Yes, and yes. But you can't run away on my horses." The prince sneered. "Remember?"

"I know." Caramyn met his mocking laugh with a glower. "I simply want to see the horses. If I must be stuck in this dreadful place with you, I at least want to do something of interest. I want to learn more about them. Perhaps...how to ride. With real skill, not just sitting up there."

Asterious leaned back in his chair with a half-smile, almost as if impressed. "If that would please you, it's fine with me. My horses are more loyal to me than everyone in this court combined. My stablemaster, Terrin, uses methods from the ancient traditions, and they result in magnificently steadfast animals. I'd certainly trust those horses to keep you in line."

"Then I look forward to meeting them," she said, pretending this was the first time she'd ever learned of Terrin's existence.

She glanced down. Her fingertips were a glistening mess with oils from the meat she'd picked through. Normally she wouldn't care. Safe in her cottage, she'd tear into her dinner without a second thought. But for some reason she wanted to appear more refined here. She wiped her fingers with her napkin, a hint of embarrassment creeping in. Why did she feel this way in front of him? She shouldn't care what he thought, but she did. "I suppose you want a thank you."

"If that's as close to a thank you as I can get, I'll accept it." Asterious curled the corner of his lips into a smile, as though entertained by her.

Damn that handsome, devilish smile.

"It still doesn't change the fact that you kidnapped me." Caramyn played with the napkin in her hands under the table, twisting it back and forth.

"I could say I'm sorry for that, if that's what you really want. Since you refuse to let it go." Asterious leaned forward, placing his hands on the table with a smirk. "But really, if I had left you out there in the Shadow Woods, you think you would've survived? You would've been dead within another hour."

Caramyn hesitated before answering, still turning the cloth napkin between her fingers. She almost found it comical how he underestimated her. "I suppose it is rather strange. We all know the Shadows don't tolerate anyone crossing the forest." By feigning innocence, she was turning the conversation back now. Throwing out bait to see if he would reveal his reason for being in the Woods in the first place. "Why do you think that is? Do you believe the stories? Of ghosts and witches and all that?" She casually took a sip of the wine.

The prince tilted his head. "I once did. When I was a child. But now I have a theory of what they are." Caramyn perked up, her spine straightening as his words gripped her. It terrified her to think he might know the secrets of her Woods better than she knew them herself. He went on as she stared at him, unable to look away or even blink. "I imagine the wraiths are the spirits of the Shadowbloods that were killed there at the making of the Veil."

Caramyn shuddered. She'd often thought of the blood spilled in the Woods when the human and Lightborn armies infiltrated it, wielding their elemental magic against the Shadowbloods in retaliation for the death of the Vaerwynd King.

She never thought to consider that perhaps those ghostly Shadows might've been those same spirits. She lifted her chin, remaining her composure to keep him talking. "And why do you believe they prowl the Woods? Surely beings as powerful as Shadowbloods would have a more dignified afterlife than playing ghosts in a haunted forest."

Asterious gaze dropped to his lap, his eyes somber. "Not if they're guarding something."

"You say that like it's a certainty more than just a hunch." Caramyn urged him to go on, her fingers scraping the underside of the table nervously. Desperately.

"Because...I am certain. Mostly. Unless Wyran is somehow mistaken."

Caramyn blinked away the overwhelming urge to roll her eyes at the mention of Wyran before she demanded further explanation. But she couldn't hide the way her body stiffened at the name.

"I know he can be old-fashioned and hardheaded. But there's a reason. He was there when the blood turned sour between magic and mortals. He was there before the Order and saw the destructiveness already wrought from the conflict between Light and Shadow. He saw firsthand the damage magic could do, and it left him bitter."

"And he never once questioned it? Never considered that maybe the evils of the human heart could be just as destructive as any born of magic?"

"If he had, he would have been dead. Like anyone else who defied my father. But that's the thing—he stayed close through it all, and because of that, he knows what truly happened at the battle in the Woods...and he told me everything."

"So what information could he have provided you with that's valuable enough for you to tolerate his indifference towards the fate of magickind?"

Asterious flared his nostrils and looked aside, a brief pause before he explained.

"That the Veil wasn't the only thing left behind in the Shadow Woods by the last Shadowblood. He also created a weapon—a Blade—forged from Shadow magic and sealed with Lightborn blood to hold the balance between Light and Shadow...and I would dare say strong enough to bind the power of either."

Caramyn tilted her head at the mention of the Shadowblood's traitorous act of obedience to Daemar, sealing away the last of the Lightborn army into a void of darkness, leaving common magic folk to their own defenses when the hunts and purges began. And if this were true, what did it mean that she'd been blindly protecting something alongside the Shadows that they'd never revealed to her? Unless...they were revealing it to her now. Like this. So that she would know the weight of what she was meant to protect, and who to protect it from...

"Why would the Shadowblood leave something like that behind if he was helping your father eradicate magic?"

"Because magic cannot be destroyed. Only contained. So, he bound it to those Woods somewhere, and only someone worthy—someone strong enough—to bear the weight of its power can find it and free it. My father of course tried to take it for himself...and failed, thank the Shattered gods."

Caramyn's blood ran cold. If this thing was real, then she couldn't let the prince near it again. And she might as well forget the idea of running away to freedom. She must return to the Shadow Woods. She could not let that kind of power fall into the hands of a Blackwynd, half-Lightborn or not. And as a sense of urgency rose within, she had to hide all outward expression, careful not to reveal the storm of revelation that was stirring inside her. "That's why you were in the Woods? You think the Blade is yours to claim?"

"I don't think anything...I hope. Because I have carried darkness far greater than anything in those Shadow Woods." Something in his words made Caramyn shift her posture as goosebumps rose along her arm.

That sword is the only hope I have of stopping Sinevia from being fully consumed by darkness. Because she—and what's left of this broken kingdom—won't survive it if I don't."

"How..." Caramyn swallowed. "How can your sister be as powerful as you claim?"

"Because Sinevia isn't just an ordinary human Spellbound—she is a Seer," Asterious said. "And that has only accelerated her rise. She turned to forbidden spells that draw on Shadow, and though it granted her power, it darkened her heart in exchange. She was so desperate after a life spent concealing her abilities out of fear of our father I fear she doesn't even realize what it's done to her..."

Caramyn absorbed his words in silence, considering the weight of them. Seers were rare and impartial to magic or race. And Spellbounds were not defined by either Light or Shadow, because they weren't born from the god-Shattering. They were forged, shaped by those who mastered the ancient languages and wove them into incantations and runes that drew from Light. Anything derived from Shadow was strictly forbidden—and was supposed to have been destroyed with the Shadowbloods.

"So how do you plan to stop her with this Shadowblood's Blade?" she finally asked bluntly.

"I could kill her." The prince said without hesitation. "But I don't want to. There's been enough bloodshed in my family already."

Caramyn wiped her mouth with a napkin and cocked her head. "She clearly had no qualms with trying to kill you."

"Because she is blinded by the corruption of Shadows. But my hope is that if I can free the Blade...I can use its power to return balance to her heart—to reach whatever part of her has hardened." He paused, drumming his fingers on the table. "I refuse to believe I have lost the sister I once knew. The sister who promised me when we were younger, that one day she would learn to control her visions and help me find my mother."

Something brushed against Caramyn's spirit, the way his voice wavered. This was all still connected to her. His mother. The fate of the kingdom might as well have been intertwined with that of the lost Lightborn Queen. But she couldn't exactly blame him. If there was even the slightest chance she could've saved her mother's life, she'd do whatever she had to, at whatever cost.

"You don't hate your sister. Despite what she's done. You see her even through her darkness." It wasn't a question. It was an observation.

"No...I don't hate her. How could I, when I knew her long before she became this twisted version of herself? She was once just a curious young girl that snuck through the castle to visit me in my solitude, confused by strange visions, taught to suppress them, and ultimately broken by watching her closest friend put to death and being powerless to stop it."

"Let me guess," Caramyn huffed, shaking her head. "Daemar executed his own daughter's best friend?"

Asterious clicked his tongue. "She was the court physician's daughter, caught using magic to heal patients. Sinevia pleaded with our father to spare her, but he refused to change his mind. That's when she turned to forbidden magic in hopes to stop the execution. When that failed, she pursued it even more desperately in hopes of resurrecting her friend, only to find life raised by magic is not life at all."

Caramyn listened, brow drawn tight, half in horror at what he was saying, and half disgust that Daemar could order the death of such an innocent using magic for good.

The prince must've read her expression as he went to speak again. "Believe me, I'm the last person you need to convince that Daemar was horrid. Which is why I strive to be nothing like him." Something in his voice cracked, breaking through the illusion of his hardened exterior.

And then another realization struck. A horrible, terrible, gut-wrenching realization that made her blood turn to ice beneath her skin. There was a silence so thick it was suffocating, until Caramyn looked away, focusing on the patterns in the wall tapestry as she said, "You had to execute her, didn't you? Her friend. That's why Sinevia hates you."

She saw the way he swallowed and clenched his jaw, and she swore she saw a bleary glimmer in those grey and silver eyes that refused to meet hers. "Yes."

Caramyn's breath caught in her chest as the prince's eyes locked on her, and she could sense the way the air shifted in the room. She feared what he might say next, though she had been expecting it for a while now.

"You asked me why I invited you to dinner tonight. Granting your freedom was only part of the reason."

"What else do you want from me?" Caramyn glowered. "I've told you all I can about the ring."

"This isn't about the ring." The prince sat upright, his broad shoulders hunching over as he leaned forward, as if he was trying to whisper to her from across the table. "I want your help crossing the Shadow Woods."

Uneasiness crept through Caramyn. She had known it was coming—suspected that he was going to ask her this in some form or another. Still, she looked at him, sickened by the feeling of being backed into a corner. "Well, I'm afraid you're going to be disappointed, because I can't do that." Caramyn uttered softly, placing her elbows on the table before her. "There is no reason to believe I can enter the Woods safely, much less take someone else through them."

Asterious, stood up, stalking toward her as he talked. She didn't expect him to come so close, and her heart leapt at the sound of her name on his lips. "Caramyn. You're either lying or blind to what's right in front of you. Think about it. You survived for hours—maybe even an entire day—alone at the edge of the Woods. Lying there, right in the threshold of where the Shadows lurk. You should've been easy prey for them. You should've been dead long before I found you." His eyes swept across her face as he lingered at the corner of the table. "I believe you could be capable of something you don't realize. Magic has marked you like no other. Maybe it's because you're meant for something good. Something of Light, meant to combat the darkness. Something even the Shadows are afraid of."

Caramyn felt a shudder race down the back of her neck. Of all the things she'd expected, she didn't expect that. That he would suggest she could be a vessel of Light, when in actuality she was a conduit for the darkness that dwelled in her blood. That she was a conquering force who could tread over Shadows like the enemies they were. He'd destroy her if he knew she'd walked among Shadows because she was one of them, not because they feared her.

She wanted to hide, to cover her face, to bury her eyes from even her own reflection that watched her in the great mirror on the wall. But instead, she swallowed and managed to croak out. "You're mistaken."

"Am I? Think about it, Caramyn. The Shadows did not harm you. We could return to the Woods, and you could lead me through. You and I...we could find the Shadowblood's Blade." Asterious stood beside her now, his hand on the back of her chair.

And then it became clear to her. He did not hate Sinevia because of the darkness that held a grip on her. He did not want to kill her...because they were not a part of her, so there was a hope that she could be free of them. But for herself, that was not the case. Darkness was in her blood, and a part of herself she could not remove any more than she could scrub away the inky stains on her skin. And he would despise her for it if he knew. He would not be able to see past the cursed power she was bound to.

It was a trap. It had to be. If this weapon really existed, she would be the last person to help him get it. She would not freely trust a man's hidden heart, prince or not. Something within her crumbled, and she shot up to her feet, staring up into his dimly lit face as he towered over her. "So that's what all this is really about, isn't it? You just want to use me as your shield?" She gestured to the table. "This—all this—is just a way for you to manipulate me to do your bidding, the same way you send your men to do your dirty work. So that you can gain some god-like power you assume you are worthy enough to wield." She touched the corner of her eye while blinking back tears from both. She couldn't believe she had almost fallen for his charm and false generosity.

The prince's eyes hardened, and by his body language, her accusations had struck a nerve. "Don't you understand what's at stake? If Sinevia—"

"How can I believe anything you say? For all I know, Sinevia might not even be the real threat. Maybe she's saving the kingdom from you. You could be twisting everything and making her out to be the enemy. How would I possibly know the truth? How do I know you aren't just seeking power for yourself?"

The prince's gaze turned to steel, and his voice followed. "Even the rumors make it clear that I never wanted the crown. That much was true. I just wanted freedom, not to rule. But I don't have a choice anymore. I can't watch Evylere go to ruin at the hands of my own sister."

"Evylere went to ruin the day your father took the throne. And now you only show me mercy because you want to use me for your own gain. I have no way of knowing your true intentions. I don't even know that I am truly capable of leading someone through the Woods." She stepped away, turning toward the exit.

Asterious' footsteps echoed through the room as he rushed after her. "You have to try. You could be the answer to all of this!"

Caramyn whirled around. "To what? *Your* problems? How can you expect me to trust you—to risk my life for you? You wanted freedom? From what exactly? Living in a castle being waited on, hand and foot while the rest of us had to fight to survive? That's why you think I should be grateful that you dragged me out of my—out of those Woods—and brought me to your sparkling palace. You are just another spoiled, arrogant ass born into royalty, trying to manipulate your way into more power at someone else's expense. You are no different from the countless men before you." Caramyn looked away, swallowing a lump in her throat. "I heard the things Wyran said about me in the Woods. You listen to him. How do I know you don't really feel the same way? How do I know you wouldn't kill me once you got what you want?"

The prince's bewildered silence haunted her.

"Exactly. Those are the questions you can't—or won't—answer." She turned again and marched toward the door, ignoring his footsteps behind her.

As she reached for the door handle, a hand clasped around hers and yanked her back. She whipped around, seething, and with her unrestrained hand, smacked the prince across the face.

Asterious released her and glared at her, his eyes ignited against the torchlight. Something in his eyes shifted. A feral, devilish glimmer. He seized both her wrists and pinned her back against the door, his muscular arms like stone walls on either side of her. His chest heaved with each breath, his face inches from hers.

"Let go of me, you bastard! Or is this the part where you finally kill me?" Caramyn spat through her teeth as she struggled against his grip. "Go on. Get it over with! Show me what it is that makes you so ruthless!"

Her eyes met his for a moment, and he blinked, dropping his gaze to her shoulder. It was then she noticed that the top of her sleeve had been pulled down when he grabbed her, exposing the top of her collarbone and bare skin below it.

He blinked again. "What are those scars from?" The prince's voice darkened like a shadow, growling out the question as his eyes narrowed in on the faded claw marks that Caramyn had never meant for him to see. Four deep red lines that had begun to scab over against bruised flesh that betrayed evidence of her attempted escape.

Caramyn bristled as she felt the prince's grip tighten. "Whatever that thing you have guarding the castle is...it attacked me. It's quite a damn good way to keep me from leaving. But you could've at least warned me about it!"

The prince went pale, his widening eyes never leaving the scars. "That monster is supposed to be dead. It's not supposed to be out there. It could have killed you." His entire demeanor had changed, and the rage in his voice was now riddled with shakiness.

"And how terrible if it had, because you would've lost the chance to do it yourself, right? Or worse, lost the only person who can lead you through those Woods to get what you want?" Caramyn shouted the question louder than she meant to, shoving him off her the second his hold eased. She yanked her sleeve back up, moments away from grabbing the dagger at her thigh and plunging it into his neck, but his stunned, glassy-eyed expression was enough to make her hesitate.

"No...no!" The cries came through desperate breaths. Asterious' voice had never sounded so frantic, but his eyes hardened like stone as he stepped forward. "You *cannot* leave this castle if that thing is out there. Promise me you won't try to leave again. Promise me!" He reached forward with both hands as if to grasp her face between them, and then dropped them down to her shoulders, but stopped, trembling, his open palms hovering a hair's breadth over her skin.

She made a move for the dagger, but stopped when he didn't touch her. "It seems I don't have a choice. I don't understand what—"

"You don't have to understand, you just have to promise!" His voice trembled, and he took a step back, as if he suddenly realized how threateningly close he was to her. "I'm...I'm sorry..."

"I was right. You *are* like all the rest. You take what you want. You think you can force me to your will, whether it's dragging me to this court, demanding that I lead you through the Shadows, or stopping me from walking out this door." Hot tears stung Caramyn's cheeks. "And here I was actually starting to think you saw me for something more than just a pawn in your game."

"No, Caramyn!" Asterious pushed a clenched fist against the doorframe, hanging his head as if trying to collect his thoughts. "You don't realize what's at stake. This...this is not what I wanted..."

Caramyn stood with her back to the door, watching him stumble through his words. The room, his voice—everything about this moment felt like iron bars closing around her. All she wanted to do was run.

She wiped away a tear on her sleeve, ashamed to have been seen like this. She couldn't remember the last time she'd cried, yet now it felt as though every tear she had swallowed over the years was fighting to burst through now. He had stirred fears and doubts she thought she'd learned to shut out long ago, muddling the conflicts already raging in her heart. She couldn't decide what to think—not here, not now. She only knew she had to get away from him.

"It's not what I wanted either." She managed to choke out the words, and then slipped out the door.

20
MORE THAN THAT

Asterious

Asterious watched the door close behind Caramyn as she disappeared into the darkness of the castle, taking his last hope with her. Slamming his fist against the door, he released a howling groan. He trembled as he succumbed to the storm raging within. He'd held it back as long as he could. Long enough to keep from hurting her. But he almost had...

Marching back towards the dining room, his eyes blurred as he braced himself over the table. Trembling, he looked up and saw himself for what he was in the grand mirror on the wall. Pathetic. Broken. A vessel of destruction. He picked up a chalice and hurled it at the mirror, the glass shattering his reflection. That horrid reflection. He wanted to pick up the pieces and bleed himself out doing it, but as he dropped to his knees, a nagging voice warned him of the dangers if he crossed this line, if he lost himself to his fury and shame. Blinking, he eased himself.

He didn't know what pained him more—the fact that he'd failed to convince Caramyn to help him or the fear that he had pushed her away. And he didn't understand why the latter was part of the question. Why did he ache to be near her? Why did something in those eyes call to him like a siren he couldn't silence? Why couldn't he stop thinking of her, standing in the sunlight in that thin, flowing nightdress, staring at him like he was a murderer? Though he very much deserved for her to look at him that way. Because he was. Whether he liked it or not, he was.

And now he'd touched her. Grabbed her and nearly couldn't let her go. She had every right to be disgusted with him. Just as disgusted than he was with himself...with the way he held onto the fleeting memory of feeling her skin against his hands. He'd touched her...but not the way he should have. Not with the hands of a killer...of a monster.

Fearing for her safety was not an obstacle he'd anticipated. He brought her here to keep her safe, but he was beginning to realize he might have dragged her to a much worse fate than whatever she was already running from. He was a fool. And damn well the monster she accused him of being. He caught his shaking breath, desperately fighting the churning in his heart as he remembered the claw marks. If that beast was roaming outside in the night, it meant far worse was to come...especially if Caramyn stayed.

And how he needed her to stay...

It was late, but the prince knew Riven would likely be in the training room, as he often stayed up in the night hours sharpening his swordsmanship skills. It'd be the perfect distraction from himself, from the tangled emotions erupting within him.

Pain is a tool...a necessary teacher.

He repeated Wyran's instructions to himself, silently scolding himself for letting himself feel this much. Flinching was to be punished. Crying, never permitted. Anger should be beaten down until it learned to stay quiet. Discipline, Wyran called it. The only way to stay in control.

Train the body not to react, and neither will the mind.

He trudged down the castle halls, towards the training room, pushing through the simple wooden door bearing the Vaerwynd coat of arms—the silver moon phases—on a shield emblem. Sure enough, there was Riven, swinging his sword at an invisible opponent in careful formation as he perfected a striking technique.

Asterious' boot on the marble floor made the slightest tap, and Riven stopped to look over at the prince in the doorway.

"Care for a spar?" Asterious asked.

"Always, Your Highness." Riven dipped his head forward and walked over to the weaponry table to put away the sword.

"Don't address me with titles right now, friend. Just let me be your worthy opponent."

As the two men wrapped their knuckles, Riven raised an eyebrow. "Dinner didn't go too well, I'm assuming?"

Asterious shook his head. "It went to hell. She doesn't trust me. And I don't know what else I expected." He ran a hand through his hair. "I pinned her to the door, Riven. I almost didn't let her leave. I almost..." He trailed off, staring at the far wall. "And she had claw marks. *Beastly* claw marks."

"You think it's coming back?" Riven was trying to look composed, but Asterious could tell by the slight waver in his voice that he was just as concerned as he was.

"I don't know. But it's been like this since we brought her here. I've been fighting it more than usual." A long silence hung in the air before Riven eased the tension.

"Did you at least find out if she can lead us through the Shadow Woods?"

Asterious rubbed his wrist as he stared at his open palm before starting the next wrap. "I think she can. I think she knows she can, too. But something is clouding her head. Something troubles her beyond just not trusting me. But it doesn't help that she thinks I'm only using her as a pawn to get to the Blade."

"And is she wrong? Is she more than that?"

Asterious turned his head without offering a response at first. He didn't know the answer. He let the echoes of their footsteps in the cold chamber drown out his thoughts about questions he didn't want to ask himself. *Was she more than that?*

"Why the hell would she be?" He brushed it off and ripped off the wraps. He didn't need any protection. He should feel every bit of pain he could. That was the point. His magic would dull him to any pain while in combat, but he would feel it twice as severely later.

He stood squarely in position ready to throw the first punch, his Lightborn magic coursing through his veins. Riven positioned himself opposite him, facing him in a blocking position. Then the controlled hits went flying. With his precision and speed, Asterious would have battered his opponent to a pulp had he been making full contact. He pulled his blows, aware of the lethal force that would obliterate anything in his path if he didn't, thanks to the way his magic reinforced his bones and skin like armor during combat. He dodged every block with inhuman speed, moving before thought could form, pushing Riven back with each step forward into his swings. Riven ducked and made for a swift defense move, but Asterious was quick to counter faster than lightning could have struck. His silver eye sparked like steel, and he overpowered every possible movement Riven could make, his own body its own kind of weapon.

In a moment of pause, unable to stop replaying the way Caramyn had looked at him in that dining room, through her tears, he felt his heart twisting in knots. She looked at him with such fear and disdain, as if seeing what he was, as if knowing he deserved none of her. And since that moment, he'd been lost in a storm of rage, hurt, desire, and shame. And he had to stop it. He had to make it hurt. He had to attack whatever he was feeling. "Get your sword, Riven."

"Are you sure, Asterious?"

"Yes. Do it. And don't you dare hold back." Asterious panted, his raven hair sticking to the sweat on his forehead.

Riven returned with the sword and gave no warning before coming down swinging. Asterious dodged with a leap to the side and then grabbed the sword by the blade, twisting around in attempt to dislodge it from Riven's grasp. But his own grip faltered, slick from the blood seeping from his hand. With another jab of his elbow, he knocked the sword from Riven's hand and reached to catch it as it fell.

When his hand touched the hilt, searing pain surged through his arm and up through his heart like hellfire. Even with all the determination and pent-up fury in the world, he couldn't have willed himself to grasp the sword through the agony. Dark sparks flew from his hand and the weapon's handle, a force pushing them apart like magnetics, and the sword dropped to the ground beside the prince on his knees.

21
VIOLETS

Sinevia

The coronation had come and gone. Most of it was a blur to Sinevia, but the people didn't question it, and that was enough. Where a priestess of the old religion would have officiated decades ago, this was the first ceremony conducted by a clergyman of the Order. A remnant of her father's crusade sure to go once she plunged this kingdom into the darkness it deserved—a kingdom that must prove itself worthy of protection from the magic it fears, through sacrifices, tithes, and unfettered devotion to its queen and its queen alone.

But for now, she had recited the oaths, pledged herself to the crown and the people, and satisfied the illusion they clung to. A fitting starting point to set greater things in motion. A line lingered in her mind from the coronation vows:

"By the blood that binds me to this throne, and by the Blackwynd legacy, I pledge to honor what must be preserved—security and order—and to sever what must be destroyed—those things which are deceitful and feared. To uphold the Order. To keep the kingdom pure of magic and the lawlessness it sows."

Deceitful and feared.

Sinevia turned these two words in particular over in her head as she gripped the cold metal of the prison keys. To some, they were threatening ideas to shun, but to her, they were the path to power and strength. And some fools, like her brother Asterious, couldn't seem to fathom that path.

He was so powerful, yet he chose to fight it. To waste it.

She'd never forget that moonless night when she heard Daphne's screams from the depths of the dungeons. When he'd killed her. After she'd tried everything in her power to break those locks and get her out. Every spell, every rune, every key she could find. But it had been useless. As useless as begging her heartless father not to kill her best friend. And the weight of those keys in her hand reminded her exactly why she could never again be reduced to begging for someone else's mercy, only to be crushed when they chose not to give it. And why she would make Asterious pay for Daphne's death in blood.

His turn would come, but for now it was the bastard's who'd turned Daphne in after she used magic to heal his fatal battle wound. And here he was, standing attentive at the foot of her throne as though waiting for some noble orders, unaware of the surprise awaiting him. "You requested me, Your Majesty?"

She blinked. "General Arik. Thank you for responding to my summons so quickly."

"Of course, My Queen." He tucked in his arm and bowed at the waist. "It is my duty to meet your demands as swiftly as possible." Sinevia loathed the sound of his sniveling voice. He only cared about impressing his superiors so he could move up the ranks. He would kiss the ass of whoever was on the throne, so long as it suited him.

"How admirable of you, General." Sinevia stood and walked down to him, the keys jingling in her hand. "I requested you so that I could inquire your opinion of the state of our prisons." She noted the uneasiness with which his eyes shifted, but of course he didn't object.

"Come." She linked her arm with his, earning a startled look from him. "Let's take a walk down to the prisons for our inspection, shall we?"

She instructed her guards not to follow them down the long walk to the torchlit dungeons deep below the castle, where dripping sounds echoed in between the groans of prisoners and scampering rat feet.

"Tell me, General. Do you find these cells to be suitable punishment for say—a spineless traitor?" She ensured her arm was still linked with his. Her spells weren't yet strong enough to work without touching the subject. But that wouldn't be the case for much longer...

Arik fumbled with his answer, looking around, unsettled. "I—I would suppose so. At least until they are put to death, as the law demands of traitors."

"Good." Sinevia smiled. "Then you're in the perfect place to fulfill your sentence." Before the shock could even show on his face, Arik's body stiffened, his eyes wide with horror as Sinevia combined her Seer's visions with the power of a Shadow spell to force images of his greatest fears into his mind. And she ensured he would feel every moment of it as though it were real. And by the blinded whites of his eyes, she could tell it was working.

He was lying miles from the battlefield, badly wounded. The acrid metal taste of blood filled his mouth, and gasping for each breath felt like reaching for the moon. Blood pooled around him as his innards lay beside him, ripped from his body, and great birds circled above. He was dying a warrior's death, and yet no one would ever find him to know. Vultures would pick his bones dry long before anyone ever came across his flayed corpse. He would die this way, for nothing. Forgotten, food for the wilderness, and without a semblance of honor.

Sinevia watched the quivering lump in Arik's throat as he tried with all his might to scream, but he was paralyzed by her spell, forced to watch and feel the worst death he could imagine. Until finally, Sinevia decided he'd suffered enough, and plunged a knife through his stomach. He dropped to the floor, his muscles jolting from the pain and shock of the vision. And then he became another soul to steal. The perfect chance to strengthen her power. She carved a rune into his still quaking body, and he withered him from the inside out, into a hollow shell of a carcass, and another blackened scar seared itself into Sinevia's hands—the mark left behind from each soul taken in exchange for power.

This was the cost. This had to be done. All because of Daphne. If Daphne had just told her she was using magic to heal, maybe Sinevia could've talked her out of it, told her not to risk wasting it on those ungrateful patients. But she was too compassionate. Too weak to let them die. And she'd trusted that damn Arik more than she'd trusted her own best friend.

Sinevia blinked, haunted by the memory she viewed as all but a betrayal. Father was a fool, but he was right to fear magic. It had cost Daphne her life. It had made her weak and naive. Magic was dangerous unchecked. It couldn't be eradicated, no matter how hard father tried. It would always exist. So it only made sense that it should be wielded by one. One with the strength and judgement required to suppress any power that could ever rise up against it. To cut away weakness wherever it festered.

As she turned to go from the prisons, one cell caught her eye—the dark bloodstained dungeons that once held her brother. His chains still strewn across the floor in the same spot they'd fallen since the day he broke free. The dungeon she would visit so often to teach him songs and think of games to play through those iron bars. Those iron bars she had promised to find a way to unlock one day...

She'd deal with Asterious and his court of fools soon enough. But she was glad he ran. She'd planned on killing him at first, but his absence and the passage of time had birthed a far better idea for his punishment. She'd make him her slave, like father had done, except this time he'd no longer be shielded by prison walls. No. She'd put him on display for all to see, as a constant reminder of the power she held.

And until then, he wouldn't be able to take the high road forever. She just had to bring out his bloodthirst again. She was certain her curse would accomplish that with time—when the strength of his bare hands were no longer enough, and he couldn't stand to outrun the need to kill any longer. And by then she'd be strong enough to put that bloodthirst under her command...and trap him in it forever like he always feared.

She turned to leave, making the trek back to the throne room, where the Captain of the Guard opened the door for her and informed her of a visitor. She rolled her eyes and walked to the throne, permitting the doors to open once she was seated.

An interruption to her plotting burst forth in the form of the Captain entering the dimly lit throne room, his footsteps echoing on stone. As he walked the long, dark walkway towards the throne, Sinevia raised a perfectly shaped eyebrow at the dirty, hooded figure that limped beside him.

"Remind me of what this is about." She commanded gently, her voice like a nightingale.

"Your Majesty." The Captain bowed. "This gentleman requested an audience in your presence this morning. You told him to come back at midday."

"Ah, yes." Sinevia let a sigh escape her ruby lips as she smoothed the heavy velvet skirt across her lap. "And what is it you have come to ask?" Her dark gaze shifted to the man beside the Captain, who had now removed his hood to reveal his weathered face and balding hairline.

"Your Majesty." The man bowed so low he nearly kissed the floor. "I have come to ask once more that you send aid to our city. There have been so many raids from the mountain tribes that things are beginning to feel—well—out of control. They are taking our food and flocks."

"And which village is yours, again? Do remind me." Sinevia's tone was cold and her gaze unmoving.

"Misthelm, Your Majesty..." The man quaked, looking down at the floor.

"I see." Sinevia rubbed her fingers together, taking her eyes off the peasant before her. "If I remember correctly, there are those in Misthelm who..." she breathed a pause, playing with her words, "...oppose me. They've made it known that they refuse to close their temples as I have demanded. And now they dare to ask me to send them protection? Let them pray for protection to the gods they so fiercely defend."

"Well, yes, Your Majesty, but it's only a few—"

The queen cut him off. "A few who have chosen their fate. To oppose me is to lose." She stood, the long dark locks beneath her crown falling around her shoulders. "I am no fool to this game. You expect me to be merciful? To overlook outright rebellion? Your temple priestesses pray for my downfall, do they not?" She laughed gently with a chilling hum in her throat. "I have learned that mercy is a fool's game. And your deplorable citizens must learn that I do not play games."

"There's nothing you can do?" Tears welled up in the man's eyes as he pleaded up at the dark queen before him. "My children. It's dangerous for them. I worry each night that there will be another raid."

"Perhaps you should find a new place to live. Or convince those who oppose me to submit."

"But, Your Majesty, with all due respect, even King Daemar offered protection regardless—"

"Do not speak that name in my presence again," Sinevia hissed. "In case you have forgotten, Daemar is long dead. And I am your Queen now. Do not return to my court unless you can tell me every soul in your village has pledged their allegiance to me and me alone. And you can prove it."

"How...how would I possibly prove that, Your Majesty?" The man stuttered.

Sinevia smiled. "Bring me the head of your high priestess. Then maybe I will believe you." As the man's eyes widened in horror, the queen addressed the Captain. "Now get this man out of my sight."

The Captain took the dejected man by the arm, and led him away, back through the great entrance of the throne room. When the doors were closed, Sinevia sent a guard to request that the Captain return alone.

As she waited, visions of the girl from weeks past flashed through her head—the strange girl who'd appeared in a dream one night, only for a moment, before she vanished like smoke. Sinevia didn't know who she was, but something about her gaze unsettled her and drew her in all at once. She couldn't forget those eyes, no matter how fleeting the vision was. Some visions she could call on and control—but this one was sporadic and unclear.

She pushed the thought aside, having given up on it by now, replacing it again with thoughts of Asterious, and how she would make him suffer. He had always been the noble one, despite the darkness that plagued him. But that untamed temper of his left its ruin on him like the bloodstains of his cell. But perhaps it could be the most useful tool to her of all. She couldn't fight him with magic or weapons to bring out his dark power. He'd learned to control it too well by now. It would have to be a battle of the heart. She'd have to take something from him he couldn't live without, so that he no longer cared to lose himself.

She pocketed the thought for later, brushing away any inklings of doubt as she returned to her seat on the throne. She reassured herself that she would, in due time, break Prince Asterious.

The broad-shouldered captain returned, solemn and silent, ready to accept his next assignment. "Captain." Sinevia's midnight voice lilted through the great room. "Send troops to burn half the crops of Misthelm. And destroy the temples. I want the message to be clear enough."

"Yes, Your Majesty." The Captain bowed.

As he turned away, Sinevia considered how long she had been seated there, churning over her burdens as queen and her bastard brother, and decided some fresh air might help her clear her head. Perhaps a ride to visit Daphne's grave before supper would ease her mind. Though many of the palace horses had disappeared in the night with Asterious and the traitors who followed him, her stable remained well-stocked.

"Oh, and one more thing, Captain." Sinevia's perfect lips curved faintly. "Ready my horse."

Across the hillsides she rode at a slow and steady pace to match the thoughts lingering in her head. As she reached the field where the last few wild violets bloomed, she dismounted and picked a handful to carry to her dear friend's grave. Memories danced like ghosts of summers spent as children weaving flower crowns in sunlit grass. The lilacs had died out weeks ago, and the violets would soon follow. Winter would claim everything.

And so would she. She would become unstoppable. If she couldn't inspire loyalty, then she'd demand it through fear. And the world feared darkness. The Shadowbloods were long extinct, and now nothing stood between her and the concentration of their power—nothing but the Woods where wild Shadows roamed. But once she could figure out a way to get through those Woods, she could raise an army even Shadows couldn't kill.

As she walked alongside her horse, she looked at the violets in her hand and realized she hated them. They were fragile, weak, and mocked her pain and betrayal. With a summon, a whisper of Shadow withered the life from them, and she crushed them into dust between her fingers.

22

PICTURE OF DARKNESS

Caramyn

Caramyn tore off her dress down to the thin-strapped delicate chemise underneath remained and threw herself onto the bed, tucking herself under the covers to fight off the chill of the night creeping in through the window. Her meeting with Asterious had left her feeling sick, so much that she thought she might see the return of the meal she had just eaten.

She should've known better than to think he truly might've cared about her in the slightest. There was nothing genuine about his apology. She was just a pawn in his game, and she had fallen for it. Comforting her with this room, giving her these fineries, allowing her "freedom" in the court, the quick glances and flatteries—it was all just his attempt to convince her to do his bidding.

He'd probably lied about not having a choice to kill for his father. He'd probably lied about everything. He truly was as wicked as the rumors claimed he was. And for all she knew, he would kill her, or at the very least leave her behind once he got what he wanted and leave her abandoned once more in the shadows. Just like her father had done. Just like everyone did eventually.

128

The fleeting hope for some connection that he had kindled in her was snuffed out tonight. And it embarrassed her to think that she'd shown such weakness to the prince. How could she have broken down in front of him so easily? She hated that he made her feel so confused. That she could crave the sound of her name on his lips one moment and wish for his final breath the next. That she could long for the feeling of warmth that surged through her at his nearness, while also imagining plunging a knife through his heart. And some stupid part of her wished she could believe him, even as every instinct screamed at her to flee.

She closed her eyes as her raven settled on his perch at the top of the bedpost. Though her bruised heart still ached from disappointment, she planned to take advantage of her newly granted freedom. She hoped a visit to the stables in the morning would help her forget everything for a while.

As she lay there drifting to sleep on the pillow damp with her tears, an unearthly, bone-chilling howl in the distance made the hairs on the back of her neck stand up.

She didn't see the prince for days after that. Nor did she hear him or his men when she wandered the castle. And she didn't care. She didn't want to see him. And she didn't know what she would say if she did. So, she settled into a new routine of waking, having breakfast in the garden below her room, and then spending hours in the library, dusting off old books of Lightborn records, history, and legend.

She searched the texts for answers. Answers about her eyes, about the strange branching sigil etched into her chest, but found nothing. There was no mention of magic marking an unborn near death—aside from the Shattering, when the gods' essences first scattered into mortal wombs and created the Lightborn. She found no record of the Veil. No trace of the Shadow Woods that might confirm even a fragment of what Asterious had told her.

Perhaps that would make sense. The Lightborn had fallen, and the fallen did not write their own histories. What remained had been shaped by those who survived and gained power. Written by human victors who had likely manipulated their way there. And it was chilling to think that the only accounts of what truly happened lived on, filtered through their hands, their fear, their prejudice, and their need to justify the ruin they had wrought.

And that must have been why the more she uncovered about the past, the more it stirred something unsettled within her...

Then she found the spellbooks, tomes and grimoires. Some of Spellbound origin—which utilized spoken words and runes—and others for the enhancement or strengthening of the Lightborn's innate power through hand motions, breath control, body positioning, and gestures.

She thought to try, just to see if there was some hint of magic within her. Perhaps these magic books were superior to the old tomes from her witch's cabin. She considered attempting to control the flame on the candle flickering beside her but then decided that if she were a natural fire mage, she'd know by now. Fire had already given her too much trouble. And her purple-hued eyes were far from the burning ember flames found in a fire mage Lightborn.

Instead, she stared at a quill pen across the table, and touched it to join herself to it, just as the books instructed. Then she drew back, willing it to move with her inner strength, with controlled breaths and a flick of her hand, even reciting the incantation recommended to beginners to help summon the power within for those not used to doing so. She compelled the pen to move so fiercely that her hands began to sweat, both from nervousness and frustration. But her efforts amounted to nothing. And confirmed to her what she already knew, without any more answers than when she started.

She left the great library, a strange sense of both disappointment and relief weighted in her chest. As she rounded a corner, she heard the echoes of urgency in Riven's voice.

"Sinevia sent soldiers to Misthelm. A siege on the city. It was still burning when Gariel left." Caramyn stayed locked in place, listening from the other side of the corner.

"Did they leave anyone alive?" It was Asterious, his voice strained.

"I don't know. We couldn't get close enough to check for survivors. But the town is gone."

There was a sobering silence before Asterious' words carried through the hall. "We must help them if we can. I want to ride out there and see what my sister has done."

It was Gariel who spoke next. "We don't have time, Asterious. And even if we did. It's too dangerous for obvious reasons. What if it's a trap?"

"We can't just leave those people in ruins when we are merely a two days' ride away. If I am to rule these people one day, they must know that I am on their side. Gather Tyrios and Wryan and as many sentinels as we can spare. We leave immediately."

Caramyn peeked around the corner to see the two spies and the prince walking as they talked. The alarmed edge in their voices had sounded dire, and there was no way that they could've known she was there to fake it. If the siege they spoke of was real, then maybe there could've been some truth to Asterious' warnings. Even if he was a royal, arrogant, manipulative ass.

She didn't think before she stepped out from around the corner, blocking their path. "I want to come with you."

They halted, and she noticed the corners of Gariel and Riven's mouths curve into smirks. Asterious narrowed his eyes at her and tilted his chin curiously. "This is far from how I expected to meet again. But with you, I've learned to expect surprises. At least you're not naked this time." His comment earned a confused look from the men beside him. He must not have told them about that encounter.

"That wasn't a no." Caramyn squeezed her fingernails into her palm, wondering what the hell she was doing.

She could've sworn the prince was staring at her lips, before his gaze slid to her eyes, and he offered a single word in return. "Why?"

"Because..." She searched for the words to explain an answer she wasn't even sure of herself. "I want to see for myself just how terrible Sinevia is. Otherwise, all I have to go off is your word—and that's not enough for me. If she really is as bad as you say, let me come with you."

"This is already a great enough risk as it is. She'll only be a liability." Gariel's words cut like a knife.

Asterious glanced at him. "Maybe." He looked back at Caramyn. "But who am I to stop her? I won't deny her the chance to understand what's going on. Especially when I've already made the mistake of denying her the choice to be dragged into it." He paused, the look in his eyes softening. "And for that, I'm sorry."

It sounded real. Not an excuse, not a deflection. But the confession of a man who understood the weight of his actions and knew, too late, that he'd been wrong. But there was still an edge to the way he watched her, as if waiting for her to back down from her request to join them.

"At least you finally admit it." She flicked her gaze to the two soldiers, wondering if they knew she'd slapped their prince a week ago. Then she stared at him, brows drawn and posture stern.

Asterious bowed his head in acknowledgement. "The horses should be ready in half an hour. We won't wait for you."

"You won't have to." Caramyn turned away with one last nod at the men, then hurried to go change into something more suitable for riding and to pack a few things for the trip. Within twenty minutes she was back down in front of the castle, watching Terrin lead the horses out into the cobblestone courtyard. The prince's eyes met hers beneath the hood of his cloak as he appeared with his entourage in tow. With a silent nod in her direction, he mounted Alofreise, and they were off.

They traveled east, through the same lush, golden forest they had passed on the way in, but instead of continuing straight on, they took a northern pass, through a small mountain that looked more like a hill in comparison to the grand snow-capped giants farther behind it. The journey was quick, and thankfully the weather was fair, if not unusually warmer than it had been, with an overcast sky and light misty rain that marked the turning of the season. Caramyn rode Frasya behind Asterious' stallion, and she was grateful Terrin had taken the time to ensure the mare who'd saved her life could be her mount for this journey. She heard Nocthar's caw above them, but he stayed out of sight for most of the trip, her unseen guardian.

She refused to speak to Asterious aside from what was necessary, which wasn't much. As long as she kept pace with the group, there was little reason to interact. And it gave her plenty of time to think about what she'd gotten herself into. She feared if Riven's report was true, she would find herself facing horrors all too familiar. The whole town was gone...burned to nothing, he said. Just like her home. Some part of her hoped he was wrong. That he'd overestimated the damage. She didn't want it to be true, but it was the only way to even begin to confirm anything Asterious had told her.

Arriving at the charred remains of the city turned Caramyn's stomach. The rancid smell of death and burning smoke hit her nose like a ton of bricks. Mounds of ash and glowing embers scattered the ground where houses once stood, some blackened frames still intact. Smoldering black plains were all that was left of the crop fields on the town outskirts.

They dismounted to lead their horses through the rubble, and Asterious commanded his men to spread out to look for survivors. Caramyn stayed by him and Tyrios, her eyes drinking in the horror. Streets that were clearly once lined with shops and buildings were now crumbling rivers of cinders and ash. Elaborate pillars of structures that once must've been beautiful were demolished, strewn in pieces near the edges of the city. Wisps of smoke still rose from the charred remains of houses. She had to choke back tears when she saw an overturned baby's crib amongst the destruction, scorched to blackness.

"Why...why would she do this?" She couldn't stop the question from escaping, even through the quivering lump in her throat.

"Because we fought back." A voice emerged from the midst of the destruction. A man, his expression hardly readable through the grime and ash on his face, limped amongst the brokenness. The group turned to face him. "She sent them to burn our fields and destroy the temples, but we fought back. So instead, they destroyed everything. They killed everyone. My family. My children..."

It was then that Caramyn noticed what he held in his hand. A doll. A child's doll, covered in soot and mud...or was it blood? A wave of nausea overwhelmed her, and she thought she might vomit right there.

"Are there any survivors?" Asterious asked, desperation breaking through a tremor she swore he was fighting to hide.

"The only ones who survived were the ones who fled fast enough...so few of them. And me, so that I could suffer. So that I could see what I'd brought upon us because I dared to ask her for protection for our city...and instead she sent destruction."

"Who did? Who is she you speak of?" Caramyn asked through the tightness in her chest, sure that she was speaking out of turn, judging by the glance it earned from Asterious. But she didn't care.

The man looked at her through bleary eyes, his lip trembling as he stammered. "The new queen. Queen Sinevia."

"You're wounded." The prince gestured, drawing Caramyn's gaze to a bloodied ripped spot on the man's shirt.

"Yes, and the infection will take me soon enough," the man murmured, his voice cracking though his eyes were void of emotion, staring off far away somewhere.

"No, let us help you." Asterious stepped toward the man. "We have medics who can treat you. You can come back with us and stay in my court."

"No, no, that won't be necessary." The man's voice fell into a sudden calm, and the shift sent an eerie chill through Caramyn that left her cold with dread.

"You'll die without treatment." Asterious pleaded.

"That's the idea." The man turned to walk away.

The prince strode after him. "I know you feel hopeless. You've had everything taken from you. But please don't let yourself succumb to this. Don't let her win."

Caramyn and Tyrios followed close behind as the man reached out, grasping Asterious' sleeve with a gentle tug as if to lead him on. "Come," he said, and brought them to the edge of a hill that dipped down into a shallow valley. He pointed. "You see down there. I stayed behind to make sure there was someone to give them some dignity. Every last one."

Caramyn breathed in to keep herself from buckling to her knees at the sight below. Dozens upon dozens of bodies, lined in rows and positioned carefully to look as at peace as possible. The man continued as Caramyn closed her eyes. Even though she had watched Shadows destroy grown men and tear their souls from their bodies, nothing had ever disturbed her like this. The man continued, the unsettling calm still in his voice. "I buried my son and daughters this morning."

"I'm...I'm so sorry. Nothing can replace your family. But I promise you I'll do everything I can to stop this from happening again." Asterious' spoke tenderly, and Tyrios stayed back to allow him the space to persuade the man. "Just please, come with us."

"I don't even know who you are." The man said. "So why would I go with you? When the only place I want to go is with them..." He looked down at the graves of his children and then reached for the sword sheathed at the prince's waist. Asterious went to stop him, but when his hand touched the sword, he was jolted backwards by a burst of dark sparks, and he shrieked in pain. Tyrios had already lunged forward but couldn't pull the sword from the man's grasp before he turned it on himself and plunged it into his stomach.

"No!" Asterious cried out as the man dropped to his knees, blood filling his mouth as the life left his eyes and he fell forward off the hill and onto the graves below. Caramyn looked away, her stomach sinking.

The three stood silent at the top of the hill, the air too heavy for words. Asterious cursed and then mounted his horse. "Keep searching." It was a desperate command, but any hint of hope was gone from his voice.

As Caramyn settled back into the saddle of her mare, she shook her head, still in disbelief at what she'd just witnessed and the unfairness of it all. Tyrios rode alongside her as Asterious kept his distance ahead.

"What was that?" she asked, her voice low. "Why couldn't he take the sword from the man to stop him?"

Tyrios looked at her uneasily and then at the prince in the distance. "It's a lot to explain. And not really my place to tell you if he hasn't already." Tyrios sighed. "Just know it wasn't anything the man did. It's...the sword."

She blinked, perplexed and distraught, but no less intrigued. "Why does he carry it then, if he can't use it? Is it to deter someone from attacking?"

"Partly," Tyrios nodded, his golden hair catching the sunlight, highlighting the brown threaded through the curls. "But mostly, because he refuses to stop trying, even when it might kill him."

Caramyn watched the prince, a picture of darkness and despair—the shadow beneath his raven-black hair obscuring half his face, the dark scruff along his jaw, the black cloak cascading down to the flanks of the midnight stallion that carried him through an ashen sea of hopelessness.

They set out to return that evening, making camp when night fell on a starless sky. No one spoke of the day's events. In fact, no one spoke at all. Caramyn rested her head on the blanket she'd brought and pulled her mantle over her despite the warm evening. She couldn't stop thinking about the brokenness she'd seen in the prince, and she once again questioned everything she thought she knew.

She could no longer doubt his warnings about Sinevia. But that didn't mean she would blindly trust him either. It was clearer than ever that he still carried secrets. And even if she wanted to help him, she didn't know if she could accomplish what he was asking her to do. She hardly knew how to trust herself anymore. She'd killed men who could very well have been that broken Misthelm man. She'd told herself she was just doing what was necessary to survive, and to guard the unknown power at the Veil...and maybe she was...

But if she agreed to help Asterious, and to stay in his world for the time being, she could never let him know.

***

The next day's ride was uneventful, and the cooler crisp air of late autumn had returned. With only a few hours left until they reached the Forbidden Court, Caramyn decided to break the silence between her and the prince. She nudged her horse forward to match the pace of his. "Why Misthelm?"

She was surprised when he didn't hesitate to answer and replied without skipping a beat. "Misthelm was a bustling, popular city. A rare place where humans and Lightborn coexisted—mostly peacefully—and even thrived. Probably because of its proximity to Vaerwynd. The humans even built temples to the old gods that created the Lightborn in the Shattering. It probably started as a way to gain favor, but it grew to have quite the following. So you can imagine the resistance when my father decreed the Order."

"I'm sure..." was all Caramyn could manage.

"It was. As hard as my father tried, he couldn't quite eradicate the deep-rooted belief systems there. So, they were always a thorn in his side, a city of humans that revered magic long after it was outlawed. There were so few of them left after the Order purged the cities, and the magic wall around the city that once protected it was gone, so the city lost the strength to adequately protect itself from the constant thieves and loyalists that exploited its wealth of resources."

Caramyn shuddered at the mention of the purges that came after the Veil. Her mother told her of the horrors of how Blackwynd soldiers and Inquisitors would scour every city, destroying any inkling of magic they could find. Dawnmire had been safe from most of it...until it wasn't.

"Are you sure you never really wanted to rule this kingdom?" Caramyn asked, switching her focus back to Asterious. "Because you certainly seem to care for its people."

"I do. But they deserve better than me."

Caramyn wanted to say something, but she didn't know what words she could possibly offer after what they endured at the ruins of Misthelm. All she could think to attempt was, "It wasn't your fault what happened back there."

"Fault doesn't change the outcome," he grumbled. "Either way, it wouldn't be the first blood on my hands. And it likely won't be the last. I could've stopped him if..." His voice trailed off, as if he realized he'd said too much.

"If what?" Caramyn encouraged gently. She could no longer resist the urge to ask the question burning in her veins like the smolders of the city behind them. "I saw what happened with the sword back there. Why did it hurt you?"

"You saw that." The prince shifted his shoulders, breathing in a resigned sigh. "I suppose I'd have to tell you sooner or later...but, I hadn't hoped it would be today."

Another secret. Caramyn wanted to say, but it would be incredibly hypocritical of her. She was holding back everything from him, while he at least seemed to be giving her bits and pieces. Even if they didn't make sense.

He kept his eyes ahead on the road as he went on, the hesitation in his voice clear as he spoke through a deep exhale. "I'm sure it's obvious enough that I'm a steel singer. But, thanks to my dear sister, I've recently been burdened with an unfortunate curse that deflects my own magic back to me. So, when I touch a sword, axe, dagger—whatever—the very Lightborn magic that grants me speed, strength, and accuracy with my blades, is...warped...into pain that makes me unable to wield them."

Caramyn didn't know what explanation she expected, but it certainly wasn't that. She twisted the reins in her fingers as she started thinking of all the things this could mean. "And Sinevia did this to you?"

She noticed Asterious, too, fidgeting with his reins, and it was the first time she'd seen him look so uncomfortable talking about something. Was it shame, or fear of the vulnerability in telling her this?

"Yes," he snipped. "After our father's death, she gifted me a dagger. And the moment I touched it, I knew something was wrong. It was...excruciating. And I saw something in her eyes I'd never seen before, like she was reveling in my pain, though she tried to pretend otherwise. And that's when I knew I had to leave."

"She wanted to make it so that you can't fight back." She was thinking out loud, and all too late realized perhaps that was the wrong thing to say.

He was quiet, as though deciding what to say next. "Or she wants to unleash something far more dangerous than any sword in my hand."

Something about the way his words darkened the air sent a chill skittering through her body. What the hell did he mean by that, exactly? Clearly, he didn't want her to know.

So she asked the obvious, less threatening question. "And you believe the Shadowblood's Blade will be different? That it can overcome the curse? What if it hurts you too?"

He exhaled slowly. "The Blade holds the balance of Light and Shadow. It stands to reason that it can undo what they create. And if I'm wrong..." he huffed, humorless. "Then I'll hold on until it kills me."

Asterious clicked his tongue and nudged his horse into a trot without leaving room for a response, just as the grand towers of the castle came into view. Caramyn kept her slow pace, letting him go on ahead, and welcomed the scent of the flowering bright gold forest that was beginning to tarnish into shades of bronze and amber. She imagined what it might look like in a few more weeks, when the full fiery colors of autumn would contrast against the glimmering teal sea in the distance. She breathed in the fresh air, letting it cleanse her lungs of the smoke and death they'd left behind, trying to push away the vision in her head of the rest of this beautiful realm being turned to ash.

23

MIRRORS

Caramyn

When morning came the next day, she saw new hope in the rays of dawn that glistened through the open window and remainders of broken glass that still lingered. Instead of her usual studies in the library, she wanted to do something that would lighten her spirits after the bleak visit to Misthelm, and perhaps give her some clarity on what she should do now that she knew Asterious was telling the truth—at least part of it. She didn't wait for Azell to bring her breakfast before slipping on her shoes and heading out the door. It surprised her to see Tyrios posted at the bottom of the stairway standing guard, but she still greeted him with a nod and he returned the favor.

Her steps quickened as she swept her hair back over her shoulders, tying it up in a loose braid that she was sure wouldn't last the day. Though she was grateful Azell had finally found her a few more pairs of pants, she was starting to find the flowing skirts and elegant dresses to be rather flattering and lovely. She'd chosen a fascinating dress the deep shade of orchids, that cinched lightly at her middle, then fell away in a fluid cascade that brushed her ankles. The off-shoulder neckline that gave way to sleeves of intricate lace with winding patterns perfect for blending in with the Shadow markings across her arms, hiding them in plain sight beneath the sheer fabric.

She heard noises in the castle as she neared the kitchen. Through an open doorway in the distance, she saw a group of men eating and joking. She recognized Rivne, Gariel, and Wryan, but didn't see the prince. She was grateful that none of them looked her way. There was a lively warmth about the castle in the morning that wasn't present in the night hours.

She scurried to the grand doors of the castle, eager to get outside into the fresh air. The cool morning breeze that swept across her face greeted her like an old friend, and made her huddle further into her cloak. Making her way to the stables, her heart swelled at the thought of seeing Frasya, and the idea of learning to communicate with her as a friend instead of merely a beast of burden. She silently hoped Terrin would be there to show her where to start.

To her delight, he was. She found him mucking out the stall of a sturdy bay gelding. He greeted her with a wave and a confused look.

"Don't worry. I'm not here to run away." She reassured him. "Asterious lightened my sentence. I'm allowed here."

The young stablemaster simply smirked and returned to raking the muck and straw on the stall floor. Caramyn walked to Frasya's stall only to find it empty.

"Where is she?"

Terrin stopped and looked up. He pointed towards the door of the stables.

"Outside?"

Terrin placed his pitchfork against the stall wall and approached Caramyn. Taking her hand, he led her back out. He took her outside the wall to the north facing side of the castle and gestured outward. She peered out at the landscape to see the hillside dotted with a handful of horses grazing contently, her familiar dappled grey mare standing out amongst the others.

"May I visit her?"

The young stable master held out an open hand, as if to say "of course." Caramyn smiled, but then a twinge of something sinister ran down her spine, as she remembered that the last time she'd ventured that far from the castle, she was nearly torn to pieces by the monster wolf. But perhaps it would be different in the daytime. She hoped it would, at least.

Before she could walk away, a shrill whistle called her attention back to Terrin. He pointed at the horses in the distance, then back at his chest, tapping his heart with his fingers, then lastly pointed at Caramyn. There were a million things he could've meant by that, but Caramyn decided to smile and nod without thinking too hard about it.

As she crossed the fields, she ran her fingers along the tall autumn grasses that were clinging to their last tinge of green before winter absorbed their life. Nearing the horses, the mare lifted her graceful head from the ground where she nibbled and perked her ears toward Caramyn.

"Hello, friend," she uttered softly, holding out a hand.

The mare took a step forward, pushing her velvet muzzle against her open palm. Caramyn's lips widened into a grin. She was so amazed by the animal that she hadn't heard the footsteps behind her.

"I think that's the first time I've ever seen you smile."

Caramyn's grin quickly faded and morphed into a puckered scowl as she twisted around to face the prince. Refusing to meet his gaze, she turned back toward the horse, who'd resumed grazing.

"Am I still so terrible that I only deserve your silence?" The prince's voice was soft and light. She almost pitied him, but she quickly hardened her heart and reminded herself to keep it barricaded.

"Well, if you're not going to talk to me," he began, "they will." He clicked his tongue. Within seconds the four horses in the field came trotting over. "Morning, ladies." He addressed the horses, Caramyn realizing they were all mares.

She stood her ground, watching the animals prance in a circle around the prince as if he was a ringleader. One bay mare with a white blaze stopped and put her nose against the prince's cheek. He laughed and playfully pushed her away as she nibbled at his jaw scruff. "The Vaerwynd believed a horse and rider's hearts are linked." Asterious said, looking at Caramyn through shining eyes. "They reveal things about us we don't even realize about ourselves. They're like mirrors."

So that's what Terrin had meant.

"Why would you follow me here?" Caramyn finally asked, though she ensured the question came out sounding stone cold.

Asterious rubbed Frasya's forelock. "Because I saw you. I've been waiting for you to wander out here. I know the horses fascinate you."

"So?" Caramyn huffed. "Are you going to bribe me with one of them in exchange for completing your mission?"

"No," Asterious said simply. "But despite traveling for days together, I realized I never had the nerve to apologize for what happened at dinner. So here I am." His gaze held hers, and silence fell, except for a snort from a horse in the distance. Caramyn wanted to believe him, but she would not be so stupid as to fall victim to his charming manipulation tactics again. He ruffled his hair with his hand before speaking again, and she felt a rush of warmth that she didn't want to acknowledge. "I know you mentioned wanting to learn to ride and train. Terrin tells me you favor Frasya. She can be your personal mount." He paused to pet the mare's neck as she grazed beside them. "It...it can be my way of making it up to you."

Caramyn shook her head, sucking down the flutter in her heart. "I'd rather Terrin teach me. Not you."

"Well, he can, if that's what you want." Asterious looked back towards the stables, then back at her. "But either way, if you'd consider it, I'd like for you to join me for a ride soon. Just for fun. No talk of the Shadow Woods or magic or Sinevia or any of that. I truly just want to get to know you, Mystery Girl."

Caramyn scoffed. "I have a hard time believing you have any time for fun." She would resist him. She kept reminding herself that even if he meant it, it was all just an attempt to get her to let her guard down for his benefit. She'd learned not to misplace her trust again simply because he riled up something fiery within her that she wished she could ignore.

Just then, Frasya returned to Caramyn's side and touched her muzzle to her chest before lowering her head so that her large brown eye was level with Caramyn's. The horse stared deeply through her, as if she was seeing through to her into her very soul. Then she nudged her with her velvety nose, knocking her off balance enough that she brushed into Asterious.

Caramyn flushed as she stumbled into the prince's solid chest. Heat rushed through her at the contact, his steady hands catching her before she could falter, but not before she could keep her gaze from snagging onto those star-rimmed silver eyes. She glanced away just in time to see the horse behind her tossing its head with an energetic whinny, looking far too pleased with its own mischief.

If horses truly could read hearts, then Frasya certainly saw right through to hers. No matter how fiercely Caramyn fought the feeling stirring inside her, she could not vanquish it. She knew that she had every reason to hate Asterious, and her conscious had no difficulty reminding her of that. But her heart betrayed her, blurring the line between hatred and desire until she could no longer tell where one ended and the other began.

24

THE PERFECT PAIRING

Asterious

Asterious let out a quiet laugh, shaking his head. "I truly didn't expect Frasya to take to you," he admitted. "She's... selective."

Caramyn arched a brow.

"She's always had a mind of her own," he went on, clearly amused. "Doesn't suffer fools. Won't tolerate mediocrity. She certainly makes you *earn* her trust." He glanced at the mare fondly. "She once nearly took my head off with a back hoof just to make a point."

"A perfectly acceptable statement," Caramyn snipped. "I'm sure you deserved it."

"I probably did," Asterious shrugged. "Which is why the more I think about it, the more perfect of a pairing it seems. A fiery mare who speaks her mind and refuses to settle for less...of course she'd choose you."

He pretended not to see the tender smirk that slid across Caramyn's face as she turned to stroke the horse's forehead.

She looked so lovely here in the golden haze of morning, her loose braid coming undone so that her hair tumbled over her shoulders—where those faded scars from the claw marks that made his blood simmer if he focused on them too long. So instead, he focused on her. He'd not been able to get the vision of her unclothed out of his head since that day, and it was enough to drive him to madness now seeing her in this dress that was almost ethereal against her smooth, flushed skin. Her radiance would've drawn any living creature to her right then. For a moment he wondered what it might feel like to have her lips against his, to tangle his fingers in those beautiful brown tresses—but he knew better. This wasn't supposed to be part of the plan. Just get her not to hate him.

He'd hoped Misthelm might have cracked open the part of her she kept so fiercely guarded, or at least forced her to see what was truly at stake. Instead, she only deepened the mystery, giving him no sense of whether it had changed her, or simply taught her to hide herself better.

"Let's make a deal," Asterious began, still letting his gaze softly travel over her as he fought back more unholy thoughts about her. "Let's get you some breakfast, and then we shall start your first riding lesson today. If you still can't stand me afterwards, then I promise to never speak to you again. You can have Terrin teach you all you want, and I'll never interrupt your time here again."

"Today?" Caramyn tried to maintain her indifference, but Asterious could plainly hear the excitement in her voice.

"Why wait?" Asterious shrugged. "You want to learn horsemanship? There's no one better to learn from than a Blackwynd prince."

Caramyn only responded with an eye roll, but he also saw the faint smirk she was trying to keep him from seeing. She crossed her arms, pretending to consider, until she finally offered an outstretched hand. "Deal."

He placed his hand in hers for a firm shake, and he could've sworn she almost laughed. "I'll get the horse's ready. That should give you plenty of time to change into something more suited for riding."

"Perhaps there is hope for you yet, Prince." She pulled her hand from his and stared at him with a gaze that could pierce a man's heart through those amethyst eyes like veiled depths, guarding secrets she would not name. She turned to go, a flicker of that half-smile still teasing him with its elusive ambiguity. And as he watched her leave, that lovely dress flowing behind her as she crossed the meadow, he flexed his fingers, fighting the trace of warmth her touch had left behind.

25

TRUST

Caramyn

Caramyn observed with careful eyes as Asterious showed her how to harness the horses using their head collars. She watched him lead his stallion through the stable, finding herself staring longer than she should have at the slip of bare skin and muscle peeking through the open collar of his shirt and the taut strength of his scarred forearms rippling beneath his rolled-up sleeves. She'd never seen him look so casual as he did then, wearing a simple pair of charcoal pants, a light grey shirt, and his black riding boots. She couldn't help noticing the fit, powerful lines of his body, so often concealed beneath those dark coats, and heat curled low in her stomach before she could stop it. She cursed herself for the traitorous thought that she wouldn't mind seeing more—far more.

She hung onto every word the prince said as he explained how to properly groom and saddle the animals. He handed her a brush and gestured to Frasya, who stood calmly in the stable aisle. At first, she was reluctant and concerned about moving too quickly and agitating the mare, but Asterious' voice reassured her.

"It's all right," he urged. "They love the attention. And if they don't, they'll let you know. Especially this one."

As if on cue, the mare pinned her ears but pricked them forward again once Caramyn placed the brush back along her neck. She stroked the fur gently, just like he had shown her. The mare's eyes softened as she stretched out her neck and wiggled her muzzle, earning a soft giggle from Caramyn.

"You must've scratched an itch she couldn't reach," Asterious said, chuckling with her.

Something about the sound of his laugh reached a deep part of her heart that wasn't meant to be accessed. She had never heard such weightlessness in his voice, and after the way she'd seen him burdened in Misthelm, it was a welcome relief. For a heartbeat, he had shed the mantle of the arrogant, somber, temperamental prince to reveal a carefree soul, unshackled from the weight of burning cities and bloodied crowns.

"All right, next comes tacking up." The prince walked to the room of the stables where all the saddles and bridles lined the wooden walls. He selected the equipment needed and showed Caramyn how to position the saddle on the horse's back and attach all the buckles and bits of leather to secure it.

Caramyn drank in every word, her mind stretching to catch each thought. For most of her life, her only teachers had been books and the harsh lessons of survival. She had taught herself everything she knew, forever grateful to her mother for teaching her to read.

Whenever she tried to join the children in the village for anything from elders sharing stories around the fire or helping with the harvests and mending fishing nets, she was met with cold, sideways glances. And then after her first bleeding, when Shadows began appearing in places she'd been, parents began dragging their children back inside. Soon enough she wasn't allowed outside during the day—only at night, alone, after the village had gone to bed. So, she spent her days poring over the knowledge that others gained from mentors, always out of necessity, rarely out of choice.

But now, here in the Vaerwynd stable, sunlight spilling across the wooden beams, the sweet scent of hay in the air, she was learning something new simply because she *wanted* to. Not because survival demanded it, not because fear dictated it. And someone—someone who could have been anywhere else—was willingly taking the time to teach her, in the light of day, as if she mattered. The realization made her chest tighten and her heart lift all at once, and it was almost enough to make her forget that he was the cold-hearted Blackwynd Prince and his every kindness could be a trap.

The prince allowed her to finish tacking up the horse, only assisting if she asked or if small adjustments were needed for security. Then, together they led their horses to a place behind the castle that Caramyn had not yet discovered, facing the sprawling cliffs that overlooked the Shattered Sea, was an arena. Where a once flawless layer of sand had covered the ground, it was now mottled with clumps of spiny grass peeking through.

As they stepped up to the gate, Asterious slowed with some strange hesitation, and then stopped entirely. His hand hovered over the latch, fingers curled as if he'd forgotten how to move them. For a few too many breaths, he stood there, unmoving, eyes glassed and distant, like something had pulled him somewhere far away to another place and time. His jaw tightened. He opened his mouth as if to say something, then closed it again, swallowing hard, the silence stretching uncomfortably thing.

"Is...is this where the Vaerwynd held their tournaments?" Caramyn asked, the question half a probe, half an attempt to snap him out of whatever trance he was in. She stroked her mare's forehead, disturbed by how still the air suddenly felt.

Asterious didn't look at her. His gaze slid instead to the covered platform beyond the gates, where two-throne like seats loomed beneath weathered flags with the kingdom's crest. "Yes," he said at last. His voice was unsettlingly steady, void of emotion. "No doubt many victories were celebrated here. As well as failures." A pause. "I'm sure they were...memorable."

Only then did his hand finally close around the latch, but not before his knuckles whitened, as if bracing for something he didn't dare name. Once they passed through the gate, the worst of whatever had seized him seemed to loosen its hold, but it didn't vanish entirely. His shoulders eased, and he spoke freely again, but his movements remained guarded and tense, as though something still weighed on him.

Caramyn's gaze drifted past him to the tiered benches that lined the outside of the arena, and she could almost imagine the ghosts of an audience cheering as knights of old raced on their steeds, magic flames or wind patterns swirling above them for entertainment, and whatever other competition the Lightborn indulged in. She wondered how many a lance had splintered in the same spot where she stood, or how many mages and witches had performed or dueled here. The cheers of the crowd echoed in a memory of history she didn't possess but could envision clearly thanks to the stories she'd read as a child to pass the painful hours in hiding.

"Didn't you see tournaments in Felhold?" she asked. "Surely your father hosted them, too."

"He did once upon a time." Asterious cocked his head. "But by the time I was born, he was too busy alienating our allies to risk tournaments. He no longer welcomed neighboring kingdoms. He thought it showed weakness to allow them into our lands. That they would corrupt our ways and culture and make it 'impure' with foreign magic influence. Too many opportunities for intel, he believed."

"So many have suffered for his paranoia and prejudice." Caramyn shook her head.

Asterious looked down as he put a hand on his horse's muscled neck. "I'm sorry for the pain my father's laws have caused. It couldn't have been easy for you growing up. To have to hide and live in fear that one day you might be found and—"

He stopped, as if choking on the thought he couldn't finish. So, she finished it for him. "And brought to you for execution." He had no knowledge of what he apologized for, and some part of her wished she could tell him that she *did* live in fear, and that she *was* found, and that the only way to escape it had been to run to the darkest part of herself and to make sure no one could ever find her again.

But he'd found her. And he was so foolish to think she was Light, that she might be something greater than darkness. She told herself that was the only reason he hadn't killed her yet. She watched him mount his horse, and the image of him astride his black stallion conjured up the memory of the way he'd looked at Misthelm—

"Caramyn." The sound of her name ripped her from her spiraling thoughts. "Everything all right? That's the third time I said your name."

"Yes, I'm fine," she stuttered. "Just admiring the...view." Her face flushed with embarrassment as she realized what she'd said, while she'd been staring straight at the prince, and Asterious raised a teasing eyebrow before gesturing for her to mount up. She blinked away the voices in her head and hoisted herself into her saddle with ease, a natural feeling from the nimbleness she'd acquired from years of climbing up branches and prowling through treetops. The prince nodded with an approving look. "That was graceful," he said. "This will be quite different than when you rode with us to Misthelm. Or when you rode with me when we met."

"Oh, good. I hope so." Caramyn wrinkled her nose, "That was unpleasant. I could smell you the whole time." She hoped he didn't notice the way she blushed at the memory of sitting against his warmth when they'd shared the saddle on their journey from the Shadow Woods nearly a month ago.

"What? You didn't enjoy being snuggled up to me?" The prince sneered, and she made a face at him. "Now, take up the reins." Asterious grasped the leather straps between his ring and pinky fingers, making gentle fists, and showed her how to do the same. "A skilled rider will use these sometimes for subtle things, but not as much as you'll use your legs and shifts of your weight. The reins don't control the horse. In fact, nothing we do controls them. We only communicate with them. And if they trust us, they listen."

Caramyn blinked as he explained how to shift in the saddle, tense and relax certain muscles, and use leg signals to ask the horse to move, turn, and maneuver. "Let's try a lap around the field. Don't use the reins. Use only your body."

As the pair steered their mounts around the border of the arena, Caramyn concentrated on controlling her body enough to move the horse where she wanted, but sometimes Frasya seemed to have her own ideas of where she should be and how fast they should go.

"Don't focus so hard on just yourself." Asterious advised. "Remember there is a living creature beneath you, and she feels everything you feel. She has to trust you, but you also must trust her. Trust is everything."

Trust is everything.

Caramyn soon realized this was far different from climbing trees and pulling the weight of longbow drawstrings. Those things required her to rely on nothing but her own strength and ability. But riding this powerful animal, asking it to respond to cues as refined as her breath and posture, as though their bodies were connected, required a sense of partnership she wasn't used to. All her life, she was strongest when she was unyielding and guarded. Yet now, only by becoming vulnerable and surrendered could strength become hers for a little while. It was an exchange of power and freedom that she could never achieve on her own.

Glancing over at the prince riding beside her, she wondered, if she could just allow herself the luxury of trusting, what else might her thorn-wrapped heart be capable of feeling? Was trust a matter of learning, like any other skill...or was it a choice, a willful surrender? She hadn't stayed alive this long by giving out her trust, and she wasn't about to start with this damn prince, no matter how some unspeakable force seemed to draw her to him. She belonged to the Woods—alone, untethered. Perhaps it didn't promise happiness, she'd admit, but happiness was another thing altogether, and hardly necessary to survive.

Once they unsaddled the horses after the lesson, Caramyn joined Asterious as he brushed down Alofreise once more.

"Well, you didn't slap me and run away this time, so did I do something right?" The prince placed an elbow on the horse's back, propping his chin against his hand as he stared playfully at Caramyn on the other side of the stallion.

"What if I say no? Will you really honor our deal? That you'll never speak to me again? Even if I walk out of this court with no intention to return?" Caramyn spoke without looking up from the section of the horse's shoulder she was brushing.

"I would. If that's what you want. If that's what you need to believe that I'm sorry...for everything." The playfulness in the prince's voice was gone. Only warmth and promise.

Caramyn felt his eyes on her and fought the urge to look up. "But that would mean you'd be giving up your chances of getting through the Woods, wouldn't it? You seemed so sure you can't get through it without me."

"It would mean that I realized I never should've asked that of you. It would mean that I expected you to trust me without ever giving you a reason to. It would mean that I was wrong. I can't control you. I don't want to. So, maybe you won't be the one to lead me through the Woods. But that doesn't mean I won't keep trying to find a way. With or without you."

He refuses to stop trying. Tyrios' words from Misthelm echoed in her mind. He was letting her go. He was giving her a choice. A real choice. And she could take it and run, if she wanted. She could go, and forget her past, forget her duty to the Shadow Woods even, and find a city like Misthelm that perhaps wouldn't treat her like a mistake...and then watch it burn at the hands of an evil queen.

And Asterious would stay here, hiding out in this forgotten castle that he'd dragged back from ruin, chasing an answer for his sister, and his curse, and this quickly crumbling kingdom. And one day he'd return to the Woods in desperation and be killed by the Shadows the moment he crossed their threshold. She knew it with terrible certainty. And some part of her would always know that she was a coward. Because staying here, with Asterious, meant returning to face a past she had spent her life hiding from. His burdens were not hers to carry, she reminded herself. And yet, no matter how hard she tried to outrun them, his unraveling truths only continued to draw hers into the light.

"Well, what if we extend the deal? Today might've just been a fluke. One more session tomorrow, and then I promise I'll decide." Caramyn said through tightened lips.

"I think you're taking advantage of me." The prince joked, a smile riddled with mischief across his face. "But alright. I think I can survive one more morning with you." He took the horse from the crossties and led it back into a stall.

"Very well. Until tomorrow, Asterious." Caramyn found her cheeks warm as his name left her lips, and she dared not to look back at the prince as she made her way out of the stables and back to the castle.

Riding had made her hungry. To silence her growling stomach, she grabbed a warm piece of pastry bread on her way through the kitchen castle and walked down a corridor she hadn't explored before. She feared being alone in her room with her thoughts and didn't feel like facing the turmoil of her confusion quite yet.

In this hallway, adjacent to the one that led to the great library, she found glass cases lining the wall, each displaying armor, shields, or royal garb of Lightborn nobility throughout the ages. She paused, studying them and their intricate craftsmanship, functional as they were beautiful. One in particular caught her eye, and she stood before it, imagining what kind of fierce female might've worn it. It was clearly designed for a woman's form, mostly leather, except for the pauldrons on the shoulders layered with silver and gold, and a breathtaking metal breastplate that rested just over the leather corset at the waist. It was molded to look like wings, spread apart from the sternum and reaching across each breast, a shield for the heart.

Caramyn wondered how it would feel to wear such armor, or to fight in a battle that required it. Would killing on the battlefield stain her heart the way killing in the Woods had? Or would it make her noble and good and proud?

The sound of boots tapped through the hallway, and she looked to see Gariel approaching, swinging his sword as though he'd just been using it. She noted the sweat beaded above his brow and crooked nose, and the dampness of his dark, close-cropped hair. He was the tallest of Asterious' posse, and it was obvious when he took up a spot next to Caramyn, who was already a whole head shorter than the prince.

"Combat training?" Caramyn asked.

"Aye," he said. "We've been training every night. In case Sinevia were to send troops here. But deep down I fear it'd not be enough to stand against Shadow magic." He nodded towards the armor. "Just ask the Lightborn how they fared against it."

Caramyn touched a finger to the glass separated them from the armor, haunted by the thought of the Lightborn who might've worn it last. "Did this belong to Queen Elysia?"

"No, but it was her ancestor's. The original Lightborn created from the rift in the Shadows—the great Shattering that killed the gods. Long ago, before these kingdoms existed, the Lightborn and Shadowbloods were perpetually at war with one another. Both incredibly powerful, but Lightborn had sheer numbers on their side and eventually won the war simply because the Shadowbloods were sterile and dying out. The outcast god who created them made them immortal unless killed, but in doing so it cost them the ability to reproduce, their Shadow power too strong of a burden to be passed on without killing any offspring."

"And the ones not killed in the war were the ones banished to the Bleak Wilderness?"

"Yes, to keep their dark power at bay. And for a time there was peace. At least the illusion of it. They were no longer hunted again until..."

"Until Daemar," Caramyn murmured.

"Exactly. And he didn't need magic on his side to defeat them. He just needed to resurrect the old fears between the Shadowbloods and the Lightborn and watch them destroy each other. And at their weakest, he tricked a Shadowblood into creating the Veil...and killed him anyway." Gariel crossed his arms, still focused on the case of armor in front of them.

The demise of the last Shadowbloods. She often wondered if her father had been among them. She pictured it now, the strongest Lightborn witches and mages driving the Shadowbloods deep into the Woods, scorching them with fire, splitting the earth beneath them, commanding thorny, twisted branches to subdue the Shadowbloods. All as King Daemar watched them slaughter each other, his perfect plan in motion.

"That's the only thing I don't understand. How Daemar managed to convince a Shadowblood to help him. Why would he create the Veil for him if his people had already lost the battle?"

"A Shadowblood hardly needed a reason to be wretched. It was simply the nature of their dark magic." He must've noticed the way Caramyn shifted uncomfortably, despite her every effort to refrain from showing any emotion, because he seemed to scramble to add more. "Though I suppose it might've just been his last stand against the Lightborn. Either that or Daemar had some kind of leverage over him. Knowing Daemar, it was probably the latter." Gariel was silent for a moment before speaking again. "The uncle who raised me was a fire mage. Daemar executed him and made me swear loyalty to him in exchange for sparing my aunt. And years later, I found out he didn't keep his word. So, I was glad when Asterious broke free of him."

Caramyn turned her head to look up at the soldier, whose eyes now looked heavy and tired. "He's lucky to have you all."

He smiled weakly in acknowledgement as if to say, "thank you," and then departed down the hallway.

Though the conversation had been pleasant, that damning word stayed with Caramyn.

Wretched.

She stood admiring the armor for just a few seconds longer, and then continued down the hall wandering more uncharted sections of the castle, until she noticed a dark corridor leading to the western edge of the castle.

Do not go near the West Wing. It's dangerous.

Maybe he had been telling the truth. It was nearly pitch black, and cobwebs and crumbled stone peppered what she could see of the corridor. But her curiosity called to her. She stood staring down the dark hallway, but thought of the prince, and their morning together, and decided it was best not to disrupt whatever small trust they'd started to build between them.

Then, as if on cue, she heard her raven calling to her. She turned on her heels and left the West Wing far behind.

26
URGENT NEWS

Caramyn

The next day's session was spent on the ground, where Asterious showed her how to cue the horses for things like rearing and trotting in circles and patterns around them with no more direction than a movement of her fingers. At the end of the session, he tapped the ground and his magnificent stallion lay down like a playful puppy by his side.

"Want to ride Alofreise?" he asked, patting the horse's rump.

"With no saddle or reins?" Caramyn raised an eyebrow with a chuff.

"The best way. Remember, if you know what you're doing, you don't need any of that. We'll just keep it at a walk." Asterious reassured.

Caramyn hesitated. She feared Alofreise might not listen to her the same way Frasya did, but she wanted to try, if for no greater reason than to test herself. She walked to the horse lying down, and with an encouraging nod from Asterious, swung a leg over his back. Asterious gave a cue, and the horse tucked his hooves beneath him to stand. The motion of the horse rising from beneath her felt like getting caught in a wave. She grabbed a handful of thick mane to steady herself on the way up.

Asterious pointed and gave a voice command that sent the horse plodding along slowly in a circle around him.

"I can't believe you haven't ridden much in your life. You've taken to it quite well," Asterious said, his eyes fixated on Caramyn.

"Well," Caramyn took a deep breath, carefully weighing her words before speaking. "There's a lot I haven't done in my life. Growing up, my village was small. And I didn't leave the house much. I've...been on my own a lot since."

Asterious looked down at his boots. The horse's steady walk became even slower as he continued the circle, and Caramyn watched on to see what the prince would do next. "It seems we have something in common. My father kept me locked away, too. In a place where the only company I had were the damned souls he sent me to kill."

Alofreise lazily halted in front of him and stomped a hoof. The prince glanced up at Caramyn, squinting from the sun that made even his duller grey eye look starlit silver.

She felt her heart quicken. She knew all too well what it felt like to be alone and forced to kill. "But you broke free of your father. How did you do it?"

"Someone let me out." Asterious brushed back a few stray locks of black hair that had fallen across his eyes. Then he looked back at the ground, shifting his weight from one foot to the other.

"Someone?" Caramyn repeated softly. "Do you know who it was?"

"Wyran." Asterious shook his head ever so slightly, almost with an edge of disbelief. "I know he can be an asshole, but in some ways, I owe him my life. I am only free—only here—because of him."

She couldn't fault him for thinking that way, for feeling some loyalty was owed to someone who helped save him. She couldn't deny that she felt indebted to the Shadows in much the same way. Perhaps there was more to Wyran beneath that cobblestone exterior, she thought, though she still wasn't convinced. So, she simply said, "No wonder you tolerate him and that grating voice of his."

"Someone has to." Asterious said, almost joking, but with a dullness in his voice.

"Where did you go once you escaped?" Caramyn said, trying to move on.

"I didn't want to go far, because I still needed to stay close in hopes to find my mother. So I posed as a soldier at the training camps outside Felhold at the base of the Silver Spine mountains. They're cold, harsh, and isolated, and the perfect place for me to go unnoticed. It was originally Wyran's idea—to keep me disciplined and focused. I think it did me good. I'd been treated like a monster so long it helped me unlearn how to be one...mostly. If there were any who recognized me, they likely feared me far more than they feared my father. And as I trained with them, some became close friends."

"Gariel, Riven, and Tyrios." She smiled, almost wishing she could indulge him in her past the way he opened his to her. "So that's how you were able to convince some of them to follow you when you fled?"

"Yes. When I heard the king was assassinated, I returned to Blackwynd Court to confirm it and to make sure Sinevia was safe. That's when I noticed she was...different...and then she gifted me that thoughtful 'welcome home' cursed dagger. Thankfully I didn't have time to tell her where I'd been hiding the past year. So, I returned to the camps to garner support. Most of those in Daemar's army were there long before he betrayed the rest of the realm, and not all of them agreed with what had become of the kingdom. Some of them were forced into his army during the purge, either to protect loved ones or themselves. So, I suppose that was reason enough for some of them to see me as the better option."

"That's all very truly impressive." Caramyn nodded with a teasing sneer. "Now you just have to convince me that you're the better option."

"For whatever reason, I can't seem to stop trying." Asterious purred, and for a moment, everything seemed...terrifyingly, suspiciously...safe.

Almost safe enough to indulge him in the full truth of what she knew about his mother's ring. It was clear he still tortured himself with his search for her. She could put his searching to an end if she simply told him she'd overheard the bandits say they stole it from a royal grave—no doubt his mother's grave. Or she could spare him the pain by guarding that secret as fiercely as her own. After all, it was a weighty claim to make without being absolutely sure his mother was dead. And it would only raise more questions about her...questions she wasn't ready to answer in case they cost her life.

A cool wind blew. The horse shook its mane. Light grey clouds shifted and blocked the sun's warmth. Caramyn shuddered against the sudden chill, and Asterious reached a hand upward. "I can help you down if you'd like, and we can go inside."

Just as Caramyn reached for his hand and leaned over to slide off the horse, another gust of wind burst through the air, carrying a torrent of crisp yellow leaves that whipped up near the stallion's head. He snorted with a startle and side-stepped, sending Caramyn toppling down onto Asterious.

They tumbled to the ground together, the prince catching her on the way down and taking the brunt of the fall. She looked up, realizing she was nestled between his arms, her body on his, pressed against muscular chest, where she could feel the beating of his heart.

She failed to stifle an awkward laugh, trying not to acknowledge the way some part of her wanted to stay there forever, lying against him. But she noticed when he didn't laugh back, and suddenly found herself caught in his gaze. He studied her, and she returned the favor, lingering on the subtle tiredness in those steel eyes and the alluring curve of his lips. She only then realized that she was clutching his shirt with one hand, the other pressed against his tan skin peeking through the unbuttoned collar.

She blinked in surprise when he reached up to sweep her hair back from her face and tucked it behind her ear. "It's a pity you had to hide those eyes away all this time. They're actually rather...beautiful. Like blazing amethysts, hiding the mystery you are."

Beautiful.

She used to think they were beautiful, too, when she was a child. Before she learned to hate them. The prince breathed against her, and she felt herself melting into the feeling of her body against his as he stared at her with some kind of look in his eye she hadn't seen before. For a moment, she almost felt free enough to tell him everything. To tell him she was a shadow-marked magicless witch bound to the Woods and a life among the Shadows. And she almost started to...but then a screeching call from Nocthar above reminded her to keep her head. So instead, she simply smiled as though it was all just a joke.

The sound of the arena gate opening startled her, and she scrambled to her feet at the thought of someone seeing her lying on the ground with the prince. She dusted herself off and Asterious did the same, a sly smirk briefly flickering across his face.

It was Wyran. He walked with purpose in his steps, tossing a glance at Caramyn that made her uneasy, and then refocused Asterious. Something was wrong.

"Your Highness, the scouts you sent to Felhold have returned. With urgent news."

A moment of tension lingered in the air before Asterious responded, as if he feared saying too much. "Where are they?"

"In the meeting hall. They've brought something."

Asterious exchanged a quick glance with Caramyn, before addressing Wryan. "I'll have Terrin take care of Alofreise. Tell them we'll be there as soon as we can."

"We?" Wryan's eyes shifted to Caramyn, thick copper brows raised over his hazel-green eyes.

"Yes, if she wants to come." He turned to Caramyn. "You don't have to. It's up to you. But you are welcome if you decide to."

Caramyn fiddled with her fingers at her side. Did she want to enter a meeting room full of former Blackwynd soldiers and spies? It was enough for her to be here with the prince, alone, but to face his inner court at his side...what would they think?

"All right." A disgruntled Wryan shifted his shoulders and turned away. "I'll tell them you're on your way."

As they watched him leave, Asterious turned to face Caramyn. "The choice is yours. That was our second lesson. If you want, you'll never have to see my face again. But just as much, if you choose to accompany me, I'll take it to mean the opposite."

Caramyn drew in a shallow breath and bit her lip before looking up at the castle. She started walking.

"What does that mean? Are you leaving?" The prince called after her.

"You heard Wryan...it's urgent!" She smiled just a tease over her shoulder and caught a glimpse of him shaking his head with a grin before striding off to catch up to her.

"Then I suppose this means I can officially welcome you to the Forbidden Court, little mystery."

Caramyn cocked her head to the side at the sound of the nickname, doing her best to hide her blushing smirk. "Yes, but I'm only staying for the horses."

"Can't say I blame you. Though I hear the prince is rather charming, too." Asterious chuckled. Their laughter subsided as they neared the great doors at the castle's entrance. Caramyn followed him through and up of one of the many staircases in the castle, until finally they stood before a large room lit by simple chandeliers and a vast table where Asterious' four head soldiers sat, along with who Caramyn presumed were the scouts. And in the middle of the table, a covered, unmoving figure—the shape of a body.

There were three scouts, one female, to Caramyn's surprise. Women weren't permitted to be warriors in Daemar's army. But this fierce, blonde woman in her thirties, perhaps, seemed to be the leader of this unit, for she spoke more than the two men with a commanding voice that could cut through bone. "We got as close as we could to Blackwynd, but Felhold is a hostile place to outsiders right now. Anyone and everything is met with suspicion. And no one can leave without permission. It's madness."

Asterious sighed, nodding towards the body. "I'd expect nothing less. And what's the story with that?"

"This is what we are most concerned about. She deployed a warband to the southern towns to demand allegiance from their leaders. But the soldiers...they're...they're not all human."

The woman lifted the cover to reveal a creature, it's body like that of a human, but it's skin ashen and pale grey, the color of death, scarred and marked by deep cut markings that resembled patterns and illegible writing. Instead of hands and feet it had unnervingly long claws of bone protruding from rotting sinew. Where eyes should've been, there were only two deep empty hollows, and its mouth was forced shut with a few jagged stitches. Caramyn nearly gasped but managed to conceal her horror for the time being.

"What the hell is this, Leejia?" Asterious stared down at the dead creature in disgust or concern, or perhaps a mix of both.

"An experimental Shadow soldier," Leejia replied. "Sinevia's practicing forbidden spells on the bodies of dead soldiers and men to create an undead army fully under her control and impossible to kill. But she's still not powerful enough to bring back the dead. The most she seems to be able to do is temporarily reanimate their bodies with the rune carvings, but not much more. In this, she seems as limited as any other Spellbound blood witch. Her magic can't seem to sustain them longer than a few hours, and they're easy to kill...for now."

"How many did you see?" Asterious asked.

"More than you'd expect. Maybe a hundred."

Asterious drew his brows together. "Where is she acquiring so many bodies? Evylere is not at war."

Leejia's eyes darkened and a heavy silence filled the room with something grave and brooding. There was no explanation Caramyn could think of that didn't send a shudder down her spine.

The prince gave a somber nod of understanding as he looked around the room, and then back at the lead scout. "Is Sinevia still in Blackwynd Court?"

"Yes. Would she have reason to leave?" One of the other scouts asked, brows raised.

"She'll be looking for a way to strengthen her spells, and once she finds it, she will. Shadow magic is the only magic capable of bringing dead back to life. But it must have a constant source to draw from to keep the host alive. Like a heartbeat. One spell won't simply sustain forbidden life. Sinevia knows this from trying to bring back Daphne, and that means she'll be seeking a greater source...and I fear it won't be long before she finds it." He clenched his jaw and swallowed. Caramyn noticed the way he flexed his hands at his side and chewed on his lip before continuing. "And the moment she does, that's when our time truly starts running out."

"A greater source?" Wyran asked. "What are you talking about exactly?"

"The source Sinevia needs to resurrect her army is in the same place as the thing we need to stop her—in the Shadow Woods." His gaze slid to Caramyn. "The Veil. It's a living wall of raw Shadow power. It's the only plausible explanation. And if I've thought of it, no doubt Sinevia already has."

There was a long silence in the room, and each second carried the weight of the question everyone must have been thinking until Tyrios finally asked it. "So then, what's next?"

Caramyn's eyes flicked to Asterious, noting the tension in his jaw, and the unsettled curling of his fingers back and forth into a fist. He drew in a deep breath before speaking, never taking his eyes off the table where the horrid Shadow soldier lay, its soulless sockets like empty voids of oblivion. "We make it there before she does."

An uneasy feeling crept its way into Caramyn. How was it that Asterious knew so much about Shadow magic? The things he so confidently explained were supposed to be secret laws and forbidden knowledge—things that even she didn't know after living amongst Shadows for five years. He surely couldn't have learned it here in this Lightborn haven, or in his father's court...unless he'd been looking for it. Unless he was hiding something still. Unless there was something about him that made him more deadly than just being a skilled steel singer.

Or perhaps she was just overreacting. It was her instinct to assume the worst—to immediately mistrust any and all intentions. Perhaps he was just thinking one step ahead of the enemy, and he was very good at it. And she could help him. She could lead him through the Woods. Either way, she would have to go back. All eyes were on her Woods, and she would not abandon them.

As she stared at the rotting creature on the table, at the puncture wounds in its chest and neck, from either blade or arrow, where clotted black blood had dried, it reminded her of how many times she'd inflicted the same wounds on those she'd killed defending the same darkness Sinevia was trying to reach. The same darkness she was bound to by birth. If she didn't stop this, it'd make her more of a monster than she already was. She'd fail everyone—Asterious, her mother, herself, and even her Woods—and that thought scared her far more than Sinevia ever could.

Something drew her attention to the patterns carved into the monstrous thing's flesh. They were runes and spells and symbols she vaguely recognized through glimpses. But then her eyes snagged on the symbol etched deeply by jagged cuts along the right arm of the deathly soldier—a thick middle line with two smaller swooping lines outward, forking down like broken wings—the same mysterious symbol that had become visible in her Shadowblood veins the day she ran to the Shadow Woods. The day one curse became another. A curse she hardly understood, but a curse nonetheless. Whatever she was, whatever she was born to be...she was anything but Light.

Wretched.

As she stood, the blood draining from her face at the realization, Wyran pulled Asterious aside to discuss preparations for leaving within the week. As they spoke, all the other gazes in the room fell on her, and the air became heavy. A tightness coiled around her chest like thorny brambles choking out her breath. She couldn't focus here. Not with that thing on the table and everyone silently questioning her presence. She'd talk to Asterious later. She'd tell him she would help. But not now. Not here in front of everyone.

"I...I must go." she uttered to no one in particular before exiting the room. And the moment the door closed behind her, she could breathe again.

27

FOR ALL OUR SAKES

Asterious

"We'll leave within three days at the latest. That will give us enough time to prepare rations and avoid any potential run-ins with travelers for the harvest celebrations." Asterious gave the order loud enough for everyone to hear, though Wyran had pulled him aside to ask.

"I'll get started on preparations this evening." Wryan nodded, hands on his waist.

The door clicked shut, drawing both of their attention to the fact that Caramyn had left without much warning. A sly grin took over Wyran's face as he lowered his voice and tapped his forehead. "Now I see why you brought her in here. That was good thinking, letting the scouts get a good look at her."

Asterious pressed his brows together. "What do you mean by that?"

"Aren't you going to ask if they recognize the girl? If they ever came across the likes of her during their mission?" Wryan asked, his voice near a whisper.

"I imagine they would've told me by now. Besides, Caramyn has never even been close to Felhold." Asterious spoke just as softly, aware of the curiosity looming in the rest of the room.

Wryan clicked his tongue. "Because that's what she told you? What if she's lying?"

"I believe her."

"You've let your guard down with her, Asterious. She still hasn't told you anything. What if she's working for Sinevia? You saw the way she ran out of here. She could be sending her word of everything we say. Ever since we found her, things have worsened in the kingdom far faster than anyone would have imagined. And you've been unravelling in ways I thought we'd finally beaten out of you."

Asterious bristled at his words. He wasn't wrong. Something about Caramyn had triggered the return of the most beastly part of himself, and he didn't know why. The part Wyran had worked so hard to teach him to subdue through blood and tears, quite literally. But that was because of his own weakness. Not hers.

"That is not her fault," he said plainly.

Wyran frowned. "She doesn't even want to help you. In fact, she's putting us all in more danger. You know the consequences of falling for that pretty face. You know what will happen if you lose a grip on that heart of yours. *Do. Not. Feel.*"

"Wyran, you of all people know I'm aware of what can happen. Don't worry. I'll fight it. I'll discipline myself more to keep anything from happening. I'll get it under control again. Long enough to just get her to take us through the Woods. And then I'll be free...of everything."

"You mean she's going to help you?" Wyran's face snapped into a doubtful expression quickly.

"She hasn't said that exactly. But she's going to stay, and that's a start."

Wyran groaned with a sigh and looked away. "Hopefully a good start. For all our sakes."

"Your dismissed, Wyran." Asterious shook his head. Wyran especially knew better than to provoke him, so he didn't understand why he seemed so intent on doing it.

But Wyran was right about one thing. Asterious certainly did notice the strange way Caramyn left the room in a hurry, as though she'd seen a ghost. And it troubled him deeply to think that it was one more layer added to her—to his mystery that he was growing ever more desperate to unravel.

28

THE LETTER

Caramyn

Two hours had passed since the meeting. Caramyn had wandered outside, waiting in the garden as she mustered the strength to tell Asterious of her decision, and to ask something of him return. She stared into the petals of a withering rose, unable to get the image of the undead soldier and the sigil on his arm out of her head. She had no idea what it truly meant, or if it was just a disturbing coincidence.

And to think moments before, in the arena, she had been so close to revealing herself to Asterious. She had almost told him who she was, because he'd made her feel like she could. But now thinking back to that vile corpse on the table and the nightmarish possibility that she might bear any connection to it...she was certain that if anyone in that room—if Asterious—knew, it would change everything. It might even cost her her life.

When the sun was hanging low in the sky and she'd walked the garden's perimeter a countless number of times, Nocthar appeared, briefly landing on a sculpture nearby before flying down to rest on her shoulder. She stroked the bird's glossy feathers with a sigh. "Nocthar, how do I know if am I making the right choice?"

The truth was, it hardly felt like a choice anymore. If she didn't help Asterious find the Shadowblood's Blade, his sister was coming to steal her Shadows' power. Either way, a Blackwynd wanted something from her Woods, and it seemed she needed one to stop the other.

And she would stop it, even if it meant partnering with this prince that twisted her heart in knots. The prince who would likely cast her aside once he realized she belonged to the very darkness he thought he saved her from. This prince that had let her taste a life beyond the Woods she thought she'd never find—a life never meant for a Shadowblood—and it made some part of her balk at the thought of hiding herself away once again.

Nocthar cawed and flew away into the castle where Caramyn followed. She hadn't made it far into the arched torchlit corridors before Asterious' looming figure appeared at the other end, concern written across his face even from a distance. He approached, broad and tall, the ends of his black coat flowing behind him as he walked. "I was coming to check on you," he said. "Are you alright? You seemed troubled earlier in the meeting. I'm sorry you had to see that thing—"

"No, it wasn't that. I just...I was actually coming to find you, too." There was a pause as they closed the distance between them. She looked up at him, and Asterious nodded for her to go on. "I wanted to tell you...to tell you that I'll do it. I'll lead you through the Shadow Woods to find your weapon. I can't promise you it won't be difficult. To be honest, I don't know what will happen. I will try...But seeing as you like bargaining, I'd like to ask something in return."

"Ask anything. I'll see to it that it's done." The prince said, the warmth of his voice chasing away the chill from outside.

"Show me the West Wing."

There was a flicker of hesitation...a shadow of reluctance he must have thought she couldn't see. He blinked a few times, and his shoulders lifted with a sundered breath before he merely said, "I told you it's not safe."

"Neither is crossing the Shadow Woods. But it's what you're asking me to do. This is what I'm asking of you."

"You believe I'm keeping something from you." It wasn't a question. Just a cold, emotionless statement.

"Are you trying to convince me that you're not?"

The prince's eyes narrowed. "No." He drew in a breath and glanced up briefly, as if catching a fleeting thought. Then he reached out his hand. "Come on then. I'll take you there now."

She was surprised it came that easily. But she wasn't about to ask questions. She placed a cautious hand in his, and he swept her away with a gentle tug, taking a torch from the wall as they passed into the dark heart of the castle.

She was silent for a long time, observing the way he drew inward, his eyes cold and haunted as though he was about to expose her to something from her darkest nightmares. They passed the armor hall and the garb displays, and turned down the hallway leading to the West side of the castle until they found themselves face to face with that dark hallway lined with cobwebs from before. That eerie, chilling portal that led to whatever secrets Asterious had tucked away.

As they stepped into the darkness, with only the single torch's light to guide them, she spoke to ease the tension, and perhaps to reassure herself out loud. "For what it's worth, whatever it is can be no worse than what I've faced before. You said it yourself. Even Shadows must fear me. I've been on the other side of the Woods and lived to tell the tale."

"Indeed, you did." Asterious hummed as he stopped her in front of a great red door at the end of the corridor, only smaller than the great doors to the ballroom entrance. He pulled out a key, unlocking the door, and Caramyn watched carefully, thinking about what she might do if this was all a grave mistake.

"Go ahead." He pushed the great door open, leading her in by the hand into a room truly ravaged by time and brutality. Frigid air made her stiffen as she looked around the dark chamber, where stone walls crumbled and left gaping cracks where night air slipped through, and thorn-covered vines claimed every inch of the walls and furniture...A shattered dresser mirror lie on the floor, the shards coated in a layer of dust. Everything was blackened by dust—everything but a black torn velvet curtain against the wall, and the bed, draped in heavy crimson sheets that stood out like a drop of bright blood against this cold, gloomy room.

"I hope this is what you wanted to see. Perhaps it doesn't live up to the horrors you witnessed in the Woods that you still refuse to share, as well as anything else about you, but this is it." There was an edge like steel in his words. For whatever reason, bringing her here had seemed to upset him. He stood behind her, and she could feel him watching her back.

She swallowed. "Is this...your room?"

"It's where I sleep sometimes, yes."

"Why? Why would you choose to sleep in this cold, horrid place?"

"Because it's uncomfortable. Necessary to keep myself...under control. It's what I must do to stay numb to whatever feelings could cause me to become...well...reckless."

Something shifted. Something ominous and forbidden. The coldness in his voice felt like icy serpents slithering beneath her skin. He stepped toward her, his footsteps hollow echoes on the cracked stone floor.

"What kind of steel singer can be so deathly powerful? Who are you really, Asterious?"

She could feel him so close behind her, standing just a hair's width away at her back as he whispered in her ear, his voice gentler, but still just as unsettling. "I've shown you exactly who I am. And I'm still waiting for you to return the favor, little mystery."

She ached to tell him. She truly did. But at the same time, she feared the consequences more than ever. And she didn't know why. He'd shown and told her everything she'd asked him to, but she still couldn't so easily forget the image of him looming over her against the banquet hall door with that bloodthirsty look in his eye. Something—some dark part of him—had peeked through then, and she was wary of when it might slip out again. Her heart wanted to trust him, but her mind refused to let her.

A tear trickled out, and she squeezed her eyes shut to keep another from falling. She opened them at the feeling of the prince's knuckle across her skin, wiping the single tear. His other hand clasped her waist, and he slowly spun her around to face him. "Who are *you*, Caramyn of the Shadow Wood?"

Who was she? She was the abomination offspring of a Shadowblood and Lightborn who carried the shame of it away from the world that wanted to destroy her. She was the magicless witch claimed by the Shadow Woods and the bearer of its mark. She was a frightened backwoods girl from a pathetic village, and she was a swift, silent killer in the treetops. But here, she was simply a young, lofty woman who dreamed of dancing in glittering ballrooms and racing on horseback, who loved steaming hot baths and sweet gooey pastries from the kitchen, and who—secretly, stupidly, regretfully—pined for the touch of the handsome prince standing before her. A woman so starved of any semblance of enjoyment from life and love that she'd convinced herself she didn't need either of them. Didn't deserve them.

"I...I'm not sure I know anymore." Her breath hitched as she took a step back. The prince watched her, as though his eyes were searching for answers in her face.

"I look forward to the day you remember," he said. "But until then, promise me something for tonight."

Caramyn blinked back the threat of another tear, and forced a half-hearted smile with a tilt of her head. "What more do you want from me?"

Asterious matched her weak smile, cupping her head in his hands. "Promise me that you'll get some rest."

"I promise." She whispered, noticing the exhaustion in the prince's eyes. He must never have known a true night's rest in this prison-like place. "But only if you promise to do the same."

"Don't worry about me," he smiled with a devilish lilt in his voice. "This room is a luxury compared to the war camps and my father's prisons." He slid his hands from her face as she turned to go. She touched her cheek to feel the place where his hand had been. And for a moment, she was almost convinced that everything was fine, and that the strange feeling she'd had when she stepped into the room was nothing more than her instinct of being overly cautious. But as she turned to go, a wind blew through the cracks in the stone, ruffling the velvet curtain against the back wall, and she glanced back just in time to see what looked like heavy chains with shackles peeking out from underneath. And all at once that bristling, frigid terror came back, gripping her like a winter's noose.

She didn't keep her promise. Her thoughts taunted her all night, hardly allowing for any restful sleep. Before the first light of dawn could illuminate the castle, she threw a coat over her nightgown, descending the tower to make her way to the library with one lone candelabra lighting the way. She searched by dim candlelight through the shelves, desperately seeking a particular book on runes she'd vaguely recalled seeing before.

And as she searched, something called to her from a corner of the library. Something whispering in the darkness like the familiar sound of Shadow wraiths creeping through the forest—something guiding her. It felt like Nocthar, only it wasn't. It was more like her own intuition, drawing her to some obscure section of the room so strongly that she couldn't ignore it. And as she found herself shuffling through the dust-covered books where her impulse had led, she felt her vision heightened —as though she was seeing with impossible eyes—seeing light and shadow in places where they wouldn't normally be visible. It almost seemed like...magic.

But it couldn't be magic. She was simply feeling what she'd always felt when she was deep within her Woods—a draw to the shadows, like a dance partner that guided her through each step and linked with each movement through her soul. She just didn't understand why she felt it here, far from her shadowy refuge. As she brushed her hand across a selection of old, cracked books, she felt the strong urge to pluck the books off their shelves, and she did. One by one, she pulled out the books, letting each drop to the floor. Until one fell open perfectly at her feet to reveal a crumpled, folded piece of paper nestled in its pages.

She picked the worn paper up, unfolded it, and let her eyes scan the words.

To the Esteemed High King and Queen of the Lightborn Court,

I write to you from a place I cannot reveal, and with a name you may have long forgotten. Yet silence now would make me complicit in what is to come.

King Daemar speaks of a celebration to honor your kingdoms' unity and to show his gratitude for your magic's intervention that granted him a child. But the truth is, the event is a trap. Even my fellow ambassador has been deceived, and plans to attend in good, but misplaced faith, despite my warning. Perhaps you will heed it.

The King blames your court and your magic for his misfortunes, and he no longer sees magic as an ally, but as the greatest enemy to our realm. This grand celebration is a snare carefully set to exterminate your court and mark an age of persecuting your people. And he will call it justice, security, and order.

I do not send this out of loyalty to your Court, nor out of sentiment. I send it because I know how this ends if I do not—and it ends in blood. Our kind have warred for far too long to allow the horrors of war to flourish again in the name of eradicating the magic that marks our blood.

The man who once believed humans and Lightborn can rule alongside each other peacefully no longer exists. In his place stands a king who has decided that the Lightborn must suffer the same fate as my people, if not worse.

I know that you will have suspicions because I am a Shadowblood, and you believe me to be your natural enemy. Act as you will. Delay, prepare, expose him—or dismiss this as shadowmongering. I will not write again.

—Morveth

Something chilled her to the marrow. This Morveth, a Shadowblood of all people, had sent a warning to the Lightborn about the ball where they would be ambushed and massacred. He was trying to save them, strange as it was. And they had clearly not heeded his warning...

Or perhaps they never received it. Why else would it be tucked away here, hidden in a decaying section of the library? Unless someone had hidden it here to keep the warning from ever reaching the Lightborn king.

But why had it called to her? What did it matter now?

She placed all the books on the floor back on the shelves as best she could remember their order, keeping the note folded in her free hand. Then she returned to find her rune book. When she found it, bound in dark red leather, she tucked the letter away between its pages and carried it back up to her room.

Swathed in a heavy blanket to fight off the autumn chill, she shifted through the pages, quickly scanning the meanings of various runes and their meanings, hoping to find a match for the mark the Woods had given her when it'd drawn out the patterns of her Shadowblood veins into tree-like lines and reaching roots. All Shadowbloods were said to have had black veins somewhere on their bodies to mark their tainted blood. But she'd never heard of the veins taking the form of a symbol.

Near the middle of the book, a section on binding and confining magic caught her attention. She slowed her reading, examining each category of symbols, searching for something that mirrored what marked her skin. But each one seemed so rigid, so crude in its form and simplicity.

The mark on her arm was nothing like them. It might as well have been alive, with its subtle violet sheen and its intricate design. It spread like a living thing, black lines branching outward like the roots of a tree driven deep beneath the skin, each line tapering and twisting as if it had grown rather than been carved. The sharpest angles lay in the way the two end tree roots spread outward from the center one, almost like bird wings, before swooping down to coil in fluid, delicate lines across her skin. As though the Shadows had chosen their own shape, and left a hidden meaning buried beneath it.

She lowered her arm, unsettled. Whatever she was, whatever secrets marked her, she was no closer to understanding it than before.

As her eyes began to grow heavy from lack of sleep, she yawned, the words beginning to blur on the page before her. She stopped to stretch and rest her eyes, shuddering from the morning cold. The window had been somewhat repaired, but the draft still snuck in on windy days. She looked down again, determined to push through her tiredness and continue. As she turned another page, the echoes of footsteps in the stairwell drew her attention to the door she'd left open. Within seconds, Asterious stood in the doorway, drawing a breath as he leaned on the doorpost. "Sleep well?"

"Well enough." Caramyn said, not even looking up as she continued flipping through pages.

He took two steps into the room. "I grant you freedom of the entire castle, yet you choose to stay up here." He purred.

She pulled her blanket close around her, shifting to hide the book pages from his sight. "It's just that it's freezing in this castle, and I'm too cold to move."

The prince eyed the blanket wrapped around her, then glanced back at the fireplace behind her. "Have you used the fireplace? I'm sure it would help."

"What a novel idea." Caramyn shrugged with a playful glance. "It's out of firewood if you haven't noticed."

Asterious walked over to inspect the stony hearth. "Indeed," he cooed.

Turning around, to face Caramyn, he sat down beside her on the floor, his long black coat trailing on the floor. "What are you reading?"

"Nothing important for now. I was just finishing up actually." She closed the book, mindful of his glance down at the pages.

"Then...would you like to join me to get more firewood?"

Caramyn eyed the prince at her shoulder. "You? Firewood? Who's going to carry the axe?"

Asterious rolled his eyes, leaning in towards her. "Guess we'll find out if it counts or not. I haven't tried an axe yet." He chuckled. "And if not, it'll be a nice change of pace to go for a ride anyway. I think we could both use a little fun before we set out tomorrow and head towards imminent death and darkness."

"Alright, fine." Caramyn shoved the book away. "I suppose the fresh air could do us both some good."

"It will. We can ride to the cliffs by the sea. It's quite the view by horseback." Asterious practically leaped to his feet, and Caramyn couldn't help but feel a warm prick of endearment at his excited reaction. "I'll have the horses readied. Meet me in the courtyard in twenty minutes."

When he had retreated back down the tower stairs, she unraveled herself from the blanket and readied herself for a ride. Perhaps it would do her good to give her mind a break from forbidden runes and secret letters.

29

SELF-SUFFICIENT

Caramyn

The fall air was crisp and bitter on her skin, but the beauty of the leaves in their fiery arrays of gold and red made the cold's bite easier to ignore. A velvet midnight blue cloak draped around her, lined with thick fur that warded off the chill. She reached down to pat Frasya's neck, sliding her hand underneath the horse's thick mane to warm her hand.

For the first time since she'd arrived, she would get to explore the side of the castle facing the great waters, and it secretly thrilled her. Their horses carried them at a brisk walk, crunching leaves beneath hooves as they weaved through the shallow forest that separated the cliff's edge from the rest of the landscape. As they neared the end of the trees, a small herd of deer stopped their grazing and frolicking to look at them, on high alert. With a twitch of its tail, one deer took off, bounding away into the thick of the woods, and the rest followed. Caramyn had never witnessed so many in one place before. In the Shadow Woods, they were a rare prize to come across when hunting, and it was always a lone deer. She couldn't have imagined such an abundance of prey in that dark place, and now seeing this vibrant forest bursting with life, she understood why. Where the Shadow Woods had always been smothered by a veil of haze and looming evergreens like a weight on the soul, this forest was a parade of colors amongst widely spaced branches that left large openings to the sky, like open portals to freedom.

Nocthar trailed along, fluttering from branch to branch and cawing periodically.

"I have to ask." Asterious shifted a bit in the saddle, turning to Caramyn. "Ever since I met you, that damned bird has lingered around. Is it your pet or something?"

"Pet? No. Friend, yes." Caramyn's eyes flashed. "And he doesn't just linger around. He's far more intelligent than you realize. Probably even more intelligent than you." She wrinkled her nose at him.

"Shattered gods, I should have known better than to offend your crow."

"Raven." Caramyn corrected. "And his name is Nocthar."

"Ah." Asterious lifted his chin, looking ahead. "And did you acquire him yourself?"

Caramyn thought of what she could say that wouldn't reveal too much. "No, not really. He found me at a time when I needed him most...and for some reason he's just always looked after me."

"I've certainly heard of falconry, but you'd be the first raven tamer I've ever known."

Caramyn laughed. "I'd hardly call him tame. He only does what he wants to do. And he's usually right."

Caramyn recalled how much she had been through with Nocthar. Flying down to her from a branch above, he'd shown up for whatever reason after she'd killed Number Three, and never left her side since. He'd led her to fresh water and warned her of coming danger more times than she could count.

"He has always been loyal to me, and I've never had a reason not to trust him. I can't say the same for people." She fiddled with the reins in her hand, squinting to see the dot of blue in the distance through the other side of the trees.

"I can't say I blame you. People do terrible things to each other through hatred and fear. Which makes love and trust that much more precious..." He tapered off. "So tell me, is there still anything about me you don't trust? Or have I won you over completely yet?" Asterious shot a sly glance her way, riding past her into a swift trot and breaking ahead of her.

Caramyn urged her horse forward with a nudge of her legs. Frasya surged onward into a canter, breezing past the prince's horse. "If you have to ask, what do you think?" She made a lewd gesture as her horse whipped past him and she called out with laugh. "Good thing you taught me I don't need my hands to ride!" Nocthar soared above, his wingspan casting a shadow above as the horse picked up speed.

"Fair enough! But if I catch you, you have to tell me something about yourself!" The prince called out, pushing Alofreise into a gallop.

Caramyn did not know these woods, but she let the horse carry her as fast and far as she dared, dodging low-hanging branches and jumping small logs in her path. The thought of Asterious racing to catch her made her heart flutter as fast as the wind against her face. Like children, they chased each other, a game of cat and mouse. Not that much earlier, she had been so shackled by her mind, but now here galloping through this radiant forest and laughing into the sea wind, she felt her frustrations dwindling as she let them stay far behind thundering hooves and fallen leaves.

She finally slowed her horse up when she came to the edge of the forest, where she was faced with the vast expanse of sea stretching out beyond the cliff on which she stood. She drew a breath of balmy air, dazzled by the sight of the waves crashing against the rocky bluffs that encapsuled this great body of water.

As she stared in awe at the sight of where the forest's edge kissed the sea, she heard the hoofbeats of Asterious' horse nearing as he joined her on the ledge. As the prince caught his breath, Caramyn looked over at him, and couldn't help but find his disheveled appearance comical—his normally neatly-placed hair, now disarrayed from the ride, a few bits of leaf sprinkled throughout, and his cheeks so pink from the cold wind nipping at his face. Where he once always looked so regal and somber, now he looked quite the opposite. "Did you hit a branch or something?" Caramyn asked through a chuckle.

"Or something." The prince ruffled his hand through his hair and pulled a twig out from the fastener of his cloak. To her surprise, Caramyn felt a genuine cackle rising within her, and she couldn't contain it. She allowed a small bit of it to escape, but soon she had lost control and it grew into a roar of laughter.

"I'm glad you're so easily amused." Asterious' tone started off firm, but he too began to laugh mid-sentence.

"What fun that was!" Caramyn beamed, reining her horse around to face Asterious. "It almost made me forget how terrible you are!"

"The feeling is mutual. Remind me not to question the bird." The prince nodded with a dwindling chuckle to the raven now fluttering down to perch on Caramyn's shoulder. Then the only sound that remained was the crashing of the waves against the rocks below. They both watched, soaking in the last bit of silence and stillness as the air became heavy once more. For in just another day's time, they'd leave all this behind and march back towards the darkness. Back towards her home.

"You didn't catch me, for the record, but I'll grant your request anyway." Caramyn reached forward to stroke Frasya's mane. "I grew up in Dawnmire. A village so small I'd be surprised if you know it."

"I'm afraid I'm not familiar with it. Where is it?"

"In the northeast. Far from Felhold, somewhere between the hills and the sea. Known by few outsiders, and *very* self-sufficient."

"Self-sufficient." Asterious huffed. "I suppose that explains you." He gathered the reins between his fingers and rested a hand on the pommel of the saddle, looking out at the misty abyss beneath their ledge.

"Perhaps it does." She said, watching the waves roll on the horizon. "Or perhaps it is the harshness I have been shown from the world. Either way, I have no need of anything it has to offer."

"There it is."

"There's what."

"The immediate push back. The refusal to accept that there could be anyone out there who cares for you. You've convinced yourself aloud that you are utterly alone."

Caramyn snorted, offended, shocked, and bewildered. She turned her head toward him then, brows knitting. For a moment she was ready to snap back, but the words stalled somewhere along the way. Frasya shifted beneath her touch with a shake of her mane, as if sensing the change in her mood.

"I learned early not to rely on others. They only see what they want to see when you're different from them. They assume because they don't understand you that you're something to be wary of...something...not good," she said at last. "In a place like Dawnmire, one thing out of the ordinary and everyone knows before the next day. And rumors start. People start talking and making assumptions." Her fingers curled into her horse's mane. "When I left, I was fleeing from Inquisitors who finally found me. And though I'd grown up there—though those people had known me from a child—not one of them cared to help. Not one of them tried to stop..." She clamped her mouth shut. She'd said far too much. "All I'm saying is it's easier to believe no one is on your side than to believe they are—and be proven wrong."

Asterious never stopped looking at her, the wind blowing his hair over his forehead as he watched her from his stallion, waiting for her to go on. When she didn't, he said. "Rumors and assumptions are wicked things. And speaking from experience, I've found it's often people who've known you all your life that can be the most merciless of all."

Her jaw tightened. "But what about when the rumors aren't all wrong? What about when there's some truth mixed in, and you start to have trouble differentiating truth from the lies about yourself?"

"Then treat their misunderstandings like questions and answer them. Show them who you really are, so it leaves no room for doubt in their mind—or yours. Then let them decide if they still want to be cruel or indifferent. And if they are, then, let them choke on the truth they chose to ignore." She glanced at him, surprised at how deeply she'd felt his words.

"You seem to have an easy time doing that. You seem to have numbed yourself to everything," she sighed.

"Not everything," the prince exhaled, swinging a leg over his horse to dismount. "I still haven't quite figured out a way to keep you from getting under my skin." He laughed, walking over to her and giving friendly tap on her boot as he looked up her. "Come on. There's a spot with a view best traversed on foot."

Then he stretched his hand up. She didn't need to take it. She could dismount just fine on her own. She hesitated, the perfect picture of the war in her mind right before her. This prince reaching for her, and her pulling away, failing to believe there was a kind of reach that wasn't meant to hurt her.

He blinked and his mouth twitched, a small dimple forming where he sucked in the corner of his cheek. "I know you don't need my help. I know you don't need me or any of this, or anyone here. I don't offer my help in small ways in effort to diminish your capabilities. I do it to show you, that despite what you believe, you are not alone."

The admission lingered between them, fragile as glass. She wanted to say something, but instead she stared at his outstretched hand, convincing herself that if she showed him her true self—if she gave him even the faintest glimpse into her past—he would yank that hand away.

"What are you so afraid of?" he asked, his voice a gentle, steady haven in the chaos of the wind and waves crashing below.

The truth. Of herself. She almost said it out loud. But instead, she took his hand, and swung a leg over so that her boots touched the ground. And she cocked her head with a smirk. "That you're leading me to my death. How do I know you aren't going to push me over this ledge?"

"Because if you truly believed I might do that, you wouldn't be here with me now." His tone wasn't playful. It was warm. Certain. Safe.

Leaving the horses behind, they walked to the cusp of the ledge, where the cliffs spilled down to churning turquoise waters below. The sea was so vastly different from the forest, and yet in some ways, it was very much the same. It could feel infinite, and it could claimed who it wanted, and no one could stop it. It did not rage without reason, nor was it merciful just because it was beautiful.

But like the woods, where sometimes there was a patch of glade where everything felt peaceful and soft, there were no doubt places on this shore where the wind did not batter the tide against the rocks so harshly, where the water stilled and bubbled in secret tidepools, gently, peacefully. There were always hidden places beneath the raging dangers that offered sanctuary. One simply had to find them.

Something lush and crimson caught her eye beneath the wild shrubs sprouting from the ledge. She knelt down to examine the batch of thorny blooms and their tiny bulb-like petals. "Blood Briar," she muttered under her breath.

"What's wrong?" The concern in Asterious' voice almost made her giggle.

"Nothing's wrong," she said, carefully plucking a flower and standing up to show him. "It's just a type of plant I've read about in apothecary books. They're very rare. And tend to grow in rather harsh conditions. I've just...never seen one before." She offered it to him.

Asterious took the bloom, studying it, careful of its tiny sharp thorns. "Rare things are often the most remarkable," he said, voice low. "What are they used for?"

"They're good for ailments of the blood, as the name suggests. They can slow down bleeding and temporarily suppress the effects of poisons and blood curses. Highly sought by medics."

A smile flickered across Asterious' face as he handed the red flower back to her. She tucked it away into her dress pocket, where the Shadowblood's letter nearly slipped out, but as Asterious went on, he didn't seem to notice. "You study plants. You tame ravens. You're a natural rider. You notice the world around you. And you might just be the most fascinating woman I've ever met."

His eyes lingered on her, and she blushed at the terrifying sensation that she might want to feel his touch, desperate to redirect the conversation to something that felt less...personal. "Speaking of fascinating things, you asked me what I was reading when you came to find me this morning," she said. "I...found a letter...in the library. From a Shadowblood named Morveth. Did you know of him?"

At Asterious' intrigued expression, she reached into the pocket of her cloak and pulled out the folded letter, handing it to him. She watched patiently as he read it quietly, and then read it again.

"Morveth..." the prince repeated, looking out to the sea. "I can't recall the name. But his letter implied he had a fellow ambassador representing his people to the Lightborn and human courts when necessary. That would've made him a High Shadowblood." His eyes slide back to the paper in his hand. "Why would a letter from him be in the library?"

"Your guess is as good as mine. I think someone tried to hide it."

"Well," he muttered, bringing a hand to his chin. "If someone hid this away, clearly the Lightborn had a traitor of their own in their midst. I suppose none of it matters now. But just think how it might've changed things if they'd listened."

"There likely would've still been a war eventually, I suppose," Caramyn said. "But it sounds like the Shadowbloods might've stood with the Lightborn. The humans wouldn't have stood a chance."

"It's certainly surprising—*fascinating* even—that a Shadowblood would warn them."

"Perhaps not all Shadowbloods were so...wretched."

"Perhaps. Legend says their dark powers were a result of the darkness in their hearts during the Shattering...but maybe there was one better than the rest...or maybe this *Morveth* had something to gain." His voice lowered. "The sad thing is there's really no way to ever know the truth."

"And that's the worst thing about it," Caramyn shook her head, still staring at the horizon. "Sometimes the truth...about the past, about who we are even...gets written for us and twisted before we even have a chance to find it for ourselves."

Asterious flashed the faintest smile, specks of sea spray dusting his face. He folded the letter and handed it back to her. "Then we rewrite it. Refuse to be something you hate."

Was it a choice that easily made? Was choice stronger than blood?

What if you don't hate what you are...but the world does?

She wanted to say, but the words stayed stuck in Caramyn's throat. He must've known she was holding back. But he didn't push her farther.

She noticed him watching her. She wanted to look away, but the steadiness in his silver eyes felt like a calm harbor in the midst of a stormy sea. Maybe he would understand. Maybe he truly cared. After all, she'd already told him she would lead him through the Shadow Woods. She'd already agreed to what he wanted. If treating her kindly and spending time with her was a manipulation tactic, he no longer needed to do it. So why was he here with her when he should be doing a hundred other things? When his kingdom was splintering at the few seams left, and his sister was out to kill him, yet he was focused on showing her the cliffs of the Western Sea.

The wind on the cliffs rose without warning, a sharp gust knocking Caramyn off balance. She stumbled forward, boots scraping stone, just before a steady hand closed around her arm.

Asterious pulled her back from the edge in one firm motion, her shoulder colliding with his chest as the space between them vanished. His other hand came to her waist, steady and unyielding, anchoring her as the wind tore at their cloaks.

Heat flooded through her at the contact, settling low as he held her there a moment longer than necessary.

"Careful, little mystery." His voice dipped close to her ear, warm despite the cold air. "The view is beautiful. But look too closely and you might fall into something... dangerous." A sly curve touched his mouth.

Caramyn looked up at him, at the way his midnight hair whipped around his face, at the sharp attention in his gaze as it traced from her eyes to her lips. His arm remained at her back, firm and possessive. Not quite an embrace, not quite a release.

She leaned into him without meaning to, drawn by the scent of pine and leather, faintly spiced. His breath brushed her temple as he spoke again, close enough that she became acutely aware of how little stood between them—and how easily he could pull her closer still.

And then a twig snapped behind them, shattering the calm. Ripping the stolen moment right from Caramyn's grasp, as the sound of something stalking through the forest overshadowed the rhythm of the waves below.

30
THE CAVREN

Caramyn

Asterious tore himself from their embrace as the rustling sounds of the forest neared. Two shapes emerged from the tree line, hulking and malformed, their bodies massive and uneven as they prowled forward on all fours. Their cracked skin looked carved from the earth, like stony hide stretched too tightly over sinew and muscle, cracked in places as though it might split under the strain of movement. Their legs were too long, their gait lurching and predatory. Thick, curled horns like a ram's jutted from skulls encased in rock-like armor that tapered down their spines and along a jagged tail.

And where faces should have been, there were none. No eyes. No nose that was visible. Only a vast, monstrous mouth lined with rows of jagged teeth. The grating growls that rolled from them ceased all at once as their heads tilted. Even without eyes, it was easy to see they were locked on to them.

Caramyn's breath caught. The air itself felt as though it had tightened around her chest. "What... what are those?" she whispered, horror crawling up her spine.

"Cavren," Asterious said, already moving in front of her. His arm came out instinctively, shielding her. "Relics of the Lightborn army summoned from the depths of the earth. They guarded the land from Shadowbloods." His jaw tightened as he watched the creatures prowling before them. "They don't come above ground to wander," he continued. "They're after something."

The Cavren's mouths opened wider, their bodies lowering, claws scraping against the soil mixed with silty stone.

Then one lunged. Past Asterious and straight for Caramyn.

She barely had time to scream before the creature slammed into her, its weight driving her backward toward the cliff's edge. Stone bit into her spine as she fell hard, the Cavren's jaws snapping inches from her face, hot breath reeking of rot and magic washing over her. She clawed at its armored hide, useless, just before some force pulled it back.

Asterious. He seized the Cavren by its horns and ripped it off her as though it was no more than a yapping dog. The ground shook as he slammed it down once, twice, then wrapped his arms around its body and crushed the air from its lungs. Its form crumpled beneath his bulging arm muscle. The sound was sickening. Bone cracked like rocks. Flesh gave way.

The creature went still.

Caramyn lay frozen, gasping, staring up at him as he stood over the ruined body, chest heaving, hands slick with rust-colored blood. For a heartbeat, he did not look human, and those silver eyes gleamed an unearthly white.

The second Cavren was gone. Asterious' gaze snapped around, sharp and searching. "It didn't flee," he called, the sound of restraint in his voice buried in a guttural growl. "It's circling."

Caramyn pushed herself upright, trembling. In the prince she'd seen something she could not name as he'd cracked that vicious creature in half like he was squeezing a lemon. No Lightborn could possess strength like that. Not even the strongest steel singer in the world.

Asterious followed the motion of the second Cavren as it returned, prowling, closing in. Once again, it's sights seemed focused on Caramyn.

Asterious' eyes widened. "The letter you're carrying from the Shadowblood. They're designed to hunt Shadow magic. It must be the letter they sense. You need to get rid of it. Now."

The word landed between them like a blade. Caramyn knew the truth. She knew why they were really here if they were truly Shadow trackers. But she had to at least hope by some miracle disposing of the letter might be enough.

Her heart lurched. She tore into her cloak with shaking hands, pulled the letter free, and hurled it over the cliff. The wind caught it, spinning parchment into nothing before it vanished into the foaming waters below.

A distant, furious roar echoed from the forest. Asterious gestured toward the horses. "Run. Get to your mare and go. I'll handle the other one."

"No—"

"Caramyn." He started to grab her shoulders, but then hesitated. "It will come back for the letter, and I can fight it...but you *cannot* be here."

"I'm not just going to—"

"Go!" He howled, a burning white flashing in his eyes. Enough to horrify her.

Enough to recognize them from the moonless night she'd tried to escape the castle.

"Go!" His voice boomed again.

She didn't argue. She ran.

Her mare whinnied as Caramyn vaulted into the saddle, heels driving her forward just as the second Cavren burst from the trees, not slowing or hesitating, but locking on to chase her.

Branches tore at her cloak as she drove the horse into the woods, heart pounding so violently she thought it might shatter her ribs. The forest closed in fast. Too fast. Hooves thundered. Stone claws struck earth behind her.

Then the Cavren leapt.

Instinct took over. Not thought. Just a hand in front of her face, shielding herself.

And then Shadow surged outward in a violent burst, swallowing the space around her in cold, living darkness. The force slammed into the creature midair, earth-colored blood spattering over Caramyn like hot rain. The Shadow hurled it back with a bone-rattling impact that split bark and sent it crashing through undergrowth. And then it withered, like the soul had been yanked right out of it.

The woods fell silent. The shadows receded, dissolving in thin air.

Caramyn slowed her horse, and stared at the dead beast's gargoyle-esque form. Then felt a presence long before she even looked. But when she finally did, she saw him. Asterious stood at the forest's edge, staring.

Not at the Cavren, but at *her*.

The distance between them felt wider than the cliff, wider than the sea. He took a step back, as if she'd struck him. Betrayal warred with grief in his eyes, raw and unguarded.

And Caramyn knew before he spoke another word that whatever they had almost been to each other moments before had just been torn apart, as surely as that creature had been crushed between Asterious' hands.

31
HYPOCRITE

Caramyn

The forest did not feel the same once the Shadows had answered a call she did not realize she'd made.

Caramyn sat rigid on her mare, her pulse still skidding unevenly through her veins. The Cavren lay broken somewhere behind them, and the thick, watchful silence that weighed down the air between them was haunting. As if the trees themselves waited to see what would happen next.

"Show me," he finally said, those glowing eyes now dimmed back to steely silver. The simple two words struck harder than any accusation.

Caramyn swallowed. "Show you...what?"

"You know what." He finally looked at her then, in a way that made her chest ache. "The markings."

Her breath caught. For a moment she considered lying again, feigning ignorance or stupidity. But that ruse was old now. And the taste of deception had long gone sour in her mouth. If he wouldn't accept her, that was one thing. If he wanted to kill her—well, at least she was already poised to flee on her horse.

Show them who you really are... Then let them decide...

She slid down from the saddle. Each step toward him felt like walking toward fire. Her hands trembled as she reached for her sleeve, gently tugging it upward to peel away the fabric covering her inner elbow, the smoky black veins peeked out more with each roll of her sleeve, branching black lines that curled and twisted like roots seeking water. They pulsed with a faint violet shimmer now, as though stirred awake by whatever magic she had unleashed.

Asterious inhaled sharply. He didn't try to touch her. He did not step closer. Instead, he took a step back. And Caramyn felt it like a blow.

"Now you know," she said hoarsely, forcing herself to hold his gaze. "What I was so afraid of. Why I wouldn't tell you anything about me. And why I was in the Shadow Woods."

Silence stretched between them.

"It's impossible," he said at last.

"I know. And I don't understand it any more than you do," she croaked out, disgusted by the patterns on her arm they both couldn't seem to stop staring at. "I—I don't even understand what happened just now. The Shadows have never protected me outside the Woods before."

"Outside the Woods?" Asterious repeated, a spark of troubling realization settling in his eyes. "You're...you're the Witch."

She looked up at him, lost for words, her silence a damning confirmation. And she decided there was nothing worth holding back any longer.

"You want the whole truth? The whole damn truth you've been trying to pry out of me all these weeks?" She drew in a breath, steadying herself against the memories clawing their way up.

"Your father's Inquisitors found me when I was fifteen," she said. "Dawnmire had been spared from their reach for so long. Until one day they came, searching the village for any signs of magic. My mother hid me well, but our house sat on the outskirts of the village. Far away where it was harder to hear the screams of an outcast, abandoned wind witch..."

Asterious remained silent, lips pressed together in a thin line. Unreadable.

"They took their time with her. I left my hiding spot when I couldn't take the sound of her screams anymore...disillusioned and stupid enough to think I could try to stop them. They killed her in front of me and burned down everything, but not before she begged me to run." She went on. "They hunted me through three villages, across the river, and finally through the Bleak Wilderness. I ran until my lungs tore and my feet bled. And when I couldn't run anymore, I fled into the Shadow Woods." Her voice dropped. "I knew they wouldn't follow me there. I knew no one would."

The forest seemed to press closer, branches creaking faintly overhead. She laughed softly, without humor. "And you took me from them—from the only place I've ever truly been safe—and expected me to just let you in."

"You lied to me." Asterious said it quietly, but his words cut deeper than if he had shouted.

"I didn't tell you. There's a difference." She corrected, bitterness creeping into her voice. "You would've killed me. Don't pretend like you wouldn't have."

"I don't kill without reason. I've tried to make you see that. To make you see that I was more than what my father made of me. But instead, I only let you make a fool of me."

"Then I suppose we're even. Because you are hiding something, too. You've created this illusion that you've told me everything there is to know about you. But there's still something you're holding back, and you think I'm too stupid to notice. You're a hypocrite—no, don't deny it! It's clear to see by what you did to those creatures..." Her throat burned. "What you did to *me*." She tore at her collar, pulling it down to reveal her scarred shoulder, forever marred by the wolf beast's claws.

His lips twitched and his eyes narrowed, jaw clenching as though restraining some underlying emotion he dared not show. As if caught in a trap he didn't want to face.

"And that's exactly why you need to leave." Something dark flashed across his expression. Too quick to name.

Her heart stuttered. "You...you want me to leave? After all that work to get me to agree to help you."

"That's just it," he growled. "I don't think you can help me anymore. Not like I thought."

The words stung, but worse the callousness beneath it. The distance. As if he were so easily willing to throw away whatever bond was starting to form between them. As if all of it—every moment between them, with the horses in the meadows, the shared dinners over campfires, the stolen glances and lingering touches—meant nothing. As if all she'd ever been to him was a tool. A tool he no longer knew how to use.

"So you discard me when I no longer serve your purpose?"

"Rather when you are no longer safe with me." Asterious exhaled, staring at the ground. "I wanted your help when I thought it could fix things. But now I see that it would only destroy us both."

It felt like a kick in the gut. She swallowed down the sting. "What does that even mean? That I'm so *wretched* you'd rather let the kingdom fall apart than let me have a hand in saving it?"

"That's enough," Asterious said sharply.

She stopped, her vision bleary as tears burned behind her eyes. She wouldn't let him see her cry again. But if he'd just explain himself instead of speaking in circles...

For a long moment, he said nothing at all. Then he turned away from her, dragging a hand through his hair as though trying to ground himself.

"You cannot stay," he said.

Her stomach sank.

"You need to leave," he repeated. "Immediately."

She stared at him. "What about the Shadowblood's Blade? Your sister? Your *mother*?" Surely the mention of that would make him realize how unreasonable he was being.

"This changes everything," he went on. "Being near you...it's dangerous."

"Because I'm a Shadowblood," she said bitterly. "Because despite what you say, you can't believe that I could ever *choose* to be better than the darkness that marks me. Because you don't *trust* me."

"Because I don't trust myself," His jaw tightened again, his whole body as tensed and rigid as his voice. "And if you remain here, I fear I *will* kill you."

Caramyn blinked. "You don't mean that."

"I do." His eyes finally met hers again—and there was something feral beneath the restraint, something tightly leashed. "You don't understand what you provoke. What you *awaken*."

Fear crept cold along her spine. "What are you talking about?"

"I can't make it any clearer. We will be the doom of each other if you stay. You've unleashed something...powerful...without realizing it by coming here. And the closer you are to me, the greater the consequences. The darkness you see in me...I thought I'd laid it to rest. But it seems in finding you, it has resurrected. And I've come too far to let it defeat me now."

"So, in true Lightborn and Blackwynd fashion, you cast me out to spare yourself."

His jaw flexed. "I'm trying to spare you."

"It doesn't feel like it."

He whistled a precise string of notes that summoned Alofreise. He mounted his horse in one smooth, abrupt motion, as if afraid that if he lingered, he would falter.

"You can stay at the castle for one more night. *One night.* Then you can ride out with us when my men and I leave in the morning to ensure you're a far enough distance away from here, where no more Cavren or other Shadow hunters can sense you."

There it was. That damn confusion he stirred without end. He wasn't banishing her here on these cliffs like she expected. He wasn't leaving her to fend for herself. He didn't want her dead.

And that was the matter of it—the way he could seem so cold and heartless one moment, and then the next a glimpse of concern or compassion would slip through. Like he couldn't quite keep the mask from falling off fast enough.

He focused on her for a moment, and then the heartlessness returned. "Then when we're far enough...we part ways. For good."

"And you and your men will ride on to the Shadow Woods. And you'll die trying to cross into them," she said firmly, like cold, hard truth.

"Perhaps," he said, his voice hollow. "And why would you care?"

It was an excellent question. Why would she care? Why would she care that Daemar's son, who'd torn her from her Woods, locked her in a tower, interrogated her, and pinned her against the wall might die? A few weeks ago, she'd have been leaping at the thought. But now...now she knew the Asterious beneath the monstrous mask. The Asterious who'd begged her forgiveness, who tenderly wiped tears from her eyes, and who laughed alongside her during thrilling chases through the woods. At least, she thought she knew him...

"I *don't* care. But just know you're only giving me a headstart there. And when you get to the Woods, I'll be waiting."

The prince arched an eyebrow. "To do what exactly?"

"I haven't decided yet." Her chest twisted with a hollow ache as she uttered the vague threat, but she was so furious with him, she couldn't help herself.

"We leave at first light," he said. His gaze sharpened, something dangerous flickering there. "Let's get back before we run out of daylight."

With that, he turned his horse away, and Caramyn gave a weak nudge for Frasya to follow, a sick feeling weighing on her as her heart and stomach twisted in knots. Mist had shrouded the forest like a veil now, and the grey mare and black stallion moved through it like phantoms, their riders merely ghosts in the silence.

Caramyn shivered more from her shame and anger more than the cold air against her Cavren blood-soaked clothes. Asterious would never trust her again, and she'd never see the court again after tomorrow. She had expected all of this eventually, but secretly she'd been foolish enough to hope for something different.

32

RIGHT BACK WHERE WE STARTED

Asterious

Everything made sense. So why couldn't his mind stop racing? It was clear that the woman covered in Cavren blood riding behind him was the reason he'd begun losing his grip on the beast. She was the reason it had all come back, and more vicious and bloodthirsty than ever. The reason it'd almost taken over when he fought the Cavren off her.

It was already difficult enough to keep his forbidden burning desire for her from unleashing the curse within. But her Shadow-touched blood explained why it was becoming impossible. With every accidental touch, every momentary brush of her skin against his, he felt that dark magic pulsing beneath his veins, threatening to take over. And now he knew why.

He despised Shadow magic not because he feared it. But because he was at its mercy. Because it was the very thing keeping him breathing, at its cruel discretion. The reason he couldn't face his sister again until he had a way to shield himself from its influence. He didn't want to kill her. And he didn't want to kill Caramyn.

Guilt nibbled at his conscience. He knew he'd hurt her. But what choice did she leave him? It was too great a risk. To this court. To this kingdom. And to her. He was running out of lives to take…and above all, if he took hers…there would be no coming back from it. He would never forgive himself. So why did knowing that he'd broken her heart bother him so much?

You're a hypocrite.

Yes, he was. He couldn't tell her what he was. What he thought she might've been able to save him from. She'd blame herself. And she'd try to stay out of defiance or guilt. And that was far too dangerous. For both of them.

He forced thoughts of her from his mind, redirecting his focus to preparations for tomorrow. And for tonight. He'd make sure there were guards outside Caramyn's room to keep her safe. He'd ensure he slept chained tonight, though there were times even that hadn't been enough.

He breathed out his relief at the sight of the castle as the grounds came back into view. As they passed through the stone walls, Terrin awaited them to take the horses back to the stables. He was grateful he wouldn't have to deal with the horses for now. He just needed to get away from the Shadowblood girl.

Caramyn slid from her horse with a lifeless slump. Her expression could only be described as some sort of hopelessness Asterious had not seen on her before. Was she truly so shattered by this? Was it all another act? Trying to unravel her only created more questions than answers.

"I'll escort you back to your chambers," He spoke low, exhaustion wrung out in each word. He knew he should just walk away. But he wanted to make sure she was secured as far as possible from him for the night. And…perhaps some part of him also wanted one last moment alone with her, though he knew it was absurd for him to even consider it. It was more than absurd. It was absolutely reckless.

"Nice to know I'm your prisoner again for the remainder of my stay." Caramyn's violet eyes flashed like lightning as she spoke, but her voice was weak, almost timid.

"You are not my prisoner. But yes, there will be guards. Not to keep you from leaving. But to keep you safe."

"From what exactly?" she mumbled in a hoarse whisper.

"From me."

Caramyn's icy silence cut through him, bringing more uncertainty creeping into his mind. But he had to see this through, no matter how much it hurt her. It was the only way. The only way to protect her. Just like when the bandits attacked and he ran with her. She didn't understand it then. And she wouldn't understand now. It was just the way it had to be.

The trek to the top of the tower felt like an eternity. His boots echoed with each step up the stairwell. Caramyn hardly looked at him as she stepped into the room, and he was almost certain he caught a glimpse of fear in those eyes. Or hatred.

"Pack your things. Whatever you want to keep, it's yours. I'll have supplies and coin brought up as well. And in the meantime, you'll be safe here for the night." He squeezed the doorknob. He should've left it at that. "Your guards will escort you to the stables tomorrow at sunrise. And then I never want to see you again."

"The feeling is mutual, Prince. Looks like we're right back where we started." Caramyn muttered, turning away.

At loss for a reply, he gently closed the door, as she kept her back to him the entire time. With trembling fingers, he slid the key into the lock and turned it until it clicked, knowing she would've heard it, loud and clear. And she would always think he was the monster he'd tried so hard to convince her he wasn't.

She'd lied to him. But now it was he who was the liar.

As he made his way down to the Great Hall, tapping Caramyn's room key against his palm, Wryan greeted him with a grin spread across his bearded face, but it faded as he neared. "Why so downcast, Your Highness?"

"Caramyn..." Asterious groaned, tossing the key to Wyran. "She's..."

She's a Shadowblood. He almost said it. But then he thought better of it. Wyran would want her dead and he would hound him for letting her go...for letting her live. And he didn't want to hear any of it right now.

"She's...not who I thought she was. She fooled me. She fooled me well. Can you find some guards to post at her room tonight?"

"Of course. In fact, I'll stand guard myself. That way you won't have to worry." Asterious didn't like the idea, but he didn't know why. Wyran had always been loyal, despite his combativeness and stubborn mind.

Wryan tucked the key into his pocket and straightened his shoulders, shifting from one foot to the other, a coy smile forming on his face. "And, if I may say, I've had my suspicions about the bitch since day one."

Something ignited inside of Asterious. "What did you call her?" He drew out the question, his voice like low thunder.

"A bitch?" Wryan stepped back with a nervous laugh. "All right, maybe 'whore' would be better? I mean look at what she's done to you. If I didn't know better, Your Highness, I'd wonder if she's put you under one of her witch spells."

Asterious felt a simmer beneath his skin, hot rage flooding his every vein and muscle. And for once he no longer cared if Wyran saw it. He took a single step forward, the air around him tightening as something feral strained beneath his control. "You insult her, you insult me," he said coldly. "You may have helped me, Wyran, but I am still your prince. Do not speak of her again. She's dangerous. Powerful. And if you ever call her those things again, I'll have you repeat them to her face so she can show you what she's capable of." He flexed his hand, the strength within him screaming to be released. "And then I'll remind you of what I am."

Wyran threw his hands up in a half-mocking gesture of surrender. "Apologies, Prince Asterious. I can see you're feeling a bit...unwell. Be careful. You may need to inflict some...discipline...on yourself before it's too late."

"You're right. I am indeed unwell." Asterious stormed away, not meaning to have lost himself so easily on Wyran. But his emotions were taking over, and when they were in control, nothing good ever came of it. He could no longer distinguish between his anger and his heartbreak. All he knew was that he was feeling both. And he shouldn't feel anything. With nowhere left to go, he stalked off to the far end of the castle, retreating to his chambers in the West Wing.

33

NOTHING LEFT TO LOSE

Caramyn

Caramyn stood in the same spot for what felt like hours, staring into the lifeless fireplace that was supposed to be kindling with the firewood they had set out to find. Instead, they had only found disaster. Just when her heart had finally begun to open, her past reared its head and closed it, stitching it shut tighter than before. But there was still a wound left that she couldn't seem to repair so easily.

She had experienced her fair share of betrayal and rejection, but this time it was different. She'd never felt rejection from someone she had begun to trust. Never from someone she was starting to...

No. I feel nothing for him.

She knew she must tame these thoughts that churned like the waters beneath those cliffs. It was the only way she would be able to win the war within herself. She couldn't let herself continue to care about Asterious. Caring about him had cost her everything.

But her desire to find out the truth was fully alive and well, fueled by the pain left from their interaction. She would not be able to leave this place, these people, and just forget it all like Asterious expected her to. Whether he liked it or not, he had entangled her in his mess, and now she wouldn't be discarded so easily. If he didn't trust her, fine. But how dare he pretend he had the moral high ground when he was so clearly concealing something too sinister to even imagine. How dare he try to threaten her with killing her after toying with her emotions all this time.

It was all a trick. It had to be. There was something he didn't want her to know, and it had shaken him that she'd gotten so close to figuring it out. He wasn't sending her away to protect her, or to keep from killing her. That was horseshit. He was sending her away because guarding whatever secret he kept was far more dire than even getting his precious Shadowblood sword. More sacred, apparently, than saving his own sister and mother.

And now that he had unmasked her secrets, she intended to do the same to him. She'd not forgotten those disturbing chains in the West Wing. And surely that's where she'd find the truth. She had one night left here in this castle and nothing left to lose.

And as though he'd heard her very thoughts, Nocthar swept in and landed on the windowsill, the gleam of his eye catching the last bit of daylight as it faded beyond the horizon. And in his beak—the key to her room.

She didn't even care to know how he'd managed it. All that mattered was that he did. And she could either run...or unmask Asterious. The bird dropped the key into her open palm. "Well done, my friend." She stroked him, running her fingertips along his sleek, black feathers as a plan took form in her mind. "Nocthar, make sure your wings are well-rested. Tonight, we're going to take a little visit to the West Wing."

34
THE WEST WING

Caramyn

Caramyn crept to the door. The castle would be sleeping now, she hoped. Putting her ear to the door, she listened for a sound, sure there would be guards on the other side.

To her dismay, the creaking of the floor and a muffled man's cough in the distance warned her there was someone out there. But then silence. She waited, but no more sounds ever came. She crouched down to check the space between the door and the floorboards, finding no sign of shadows or boots. Did she dare risk it? Surely the prince wouldn't have ordered them to kill her if she tried to leave.

He wouldn't. She repeated it in her head more than once, trying to convince herself.

She tiptoed back for her dagger she'd been keeping under her pillow. Gripping it in one hand and the key in the other, she unlocked the door to open it just an inch. She looked through the small gap, holding her breath. And to her surprise there was not a soul to be found.

So what—or who—had she heard? It hardly made sense, but she refused to stuff herself back in that room and waste her last chance to find out who Asterious truly was.

She sent the raven ahead to scope out the rest of the tower. He returned with an encouraging coo, reassuring her she was truly alone. The bird perched on her arm as she made her way down the steps in silence. The sound of his wings wasn't worth risking. She tucked the key away safely into her corset, and gripped the dagger, ready to strike should the need arise.

But it wasn't enough. She wouldn't be caught in another devastating situation unarmed like she'd been at the edge of the Woods or the Western Sea cliffs. Taking a torch from the wall, she carried it to light her way to the first destination. Using the secret passageway from before, she made her way to stables. The bow and quiver of arrows still rested against the wall where Terrin had placed them the night he saved her. It was exactly what she had come searching for.

Caramyn took the weapon and slung the quiver over her shoulder. The familiar feel of the leather strap across her body and the weight of arrows on her back was like a hug from an old friend. Satisfied, she crept back up the passageway to search the rest of the castle.

It was an unsettling trek. As she wandered the cold stone halls, she couldn't rid herself of the feeling that someone was following her. Nocthar would circle every now and then, checking the surroundings, but he could find no indication that her feelings were true. She shook it off. She was simply being paranoid.

Caramyn remained on guard as she crept through the shadows. Sneaking around was her specialty. With a bow, the cover of darkness, and a clear view of her surroundings, she was more than capable. It was exactly in these conditions that she thrived—when she was outside among the living, breathing forests she knew. But here, within unfamiliar stone hallways, her confidence waned.

Finally, after passing through the hall of armor she'd visited before, she approached the forbidden wing of the castle. Just like last time, as she stood peering down the corridor, something called to her, holding her spellbound despite her unease. She felt it in the way the air shifted, and in the groans the walls sang out as the night wind battered them. Something was different on this side of the castle. It wasn't just the crumbling walls or the cracked, ivy and moss-covered floor. It was something otherworldly.

She decided to nock an arrow, just in case, and kept it ready. She had lived years carrying the weight of the Shadows, yet she had never felt more pelted by darkness than she did stepping foot into the hall. There was some strange magic here. Something sinister. Something Asterious didn't want her to see.

For a moment, she thought she heard the heavy rattle of chains in the distance, and a small gasp took her breath. As she settled her pounding heart with an exhale, the sound subsided.

Something within her pushed her to keep going. Perhaps it was curiosity. Perhaps it was the desperate hope of uncovering whatever Asterious wanted hidden, to prove she wasn't the only one guilty. Perhaps it was a mixture of both. Whatever it was that spurred her on, she listened.

Each silent footstep brought her closer to the dark red door at the end of a corridor. The same one from before, but now that she was alone and could examine it better, she noticed how the door might've once been bright and rosy, but now it was the deep color of blood. As she neared, she could just make out some intricate carvings that were slowly succumbing to their age as the wood chipped away. Thorny vines that had long ago burst through from the floor encompassed the threshold in a protective manner, some with small rose blooms that were beginning to wilt.

With eyes wide and hands trembling, she crept towards the beautifully grim door. She stretched out a hand to turn the tarnished door handle, but before she could touch it, Nocthar swept across her line of sight and let out a dire screech in urgent warning.

But it was too late a warning.

"Scheming whore!" A voice from behind struck her like lightning.

She whipped around, an arrow ready to fire, but before she could release the twine between her fingers, something hard and unforgiving met the back of her head.

Her arrow fired into nothingness, and everything blurred. Her vision was fading, and she was stumbling. Down. Down.

Collapsing.

"He warned you not to come here." The gruff voice was familiar, but she couldn't quite identify it as she perceived it through distorted, far away senses.

She touched the back of her head and felt warm, wet hair that stained her fingers scarlet with her blood. She could hear Nocthar making a fuss at the attacker, but there was little he could do.

"Who are you? What...what did you do?" The weak words spilled out of her mouth as the world around her faded away, dull spots like ink blots overtaking her vision.

"I just stopped you from ruining everything." The voice was marred by her disorientation.

She fought to stand, but the ground slipped out from under her as her senses faded. She felt the hands of her attacker and used her bow to fend him off with what little strength she had left. She struck him with the end of the bow, but he pulled it from her weakening grip and tossed it aside.

Then a sharp prick in her neck. A final sting to accelerate her descent into darkness by what could've only been a poisoned dart.

"That should keep you quiet for now."

"I wasn't going to kill him...I wouldn't kill him..." She managed to breathe out the words as everything faded once and for all. By the flickering of the fallen torch, there was just enough light to make out the face above her with the last bit of consciousness she had left. She recognized him now. It was Wryan.

35
QUIET AS DEATH

Asterious

Asterious opened his eyes to his cheek pressed against the cold stone floor and chains shackled around his ankles. At least they'd held this time. His clothes were tattered, and his head throbbed maddeningly. The fear that he was losing himself once again pierced him like an icy dagger to the chest. All the discipline and pain he'd endured to control his emotions now seemed it had been for nothing. Because now, because of Caramyn, they were returning with a vengeance. Each night since she'd come to the Forbidden Court, they'd grown stronger. And he'd grown weaker. He could lose himself. He could lose the kingdom. He could be its very downfall if he did not regain control.

He reached for the key to the shackles, ashamed he'd had to resort to this. He would *have* to stop caring about her. He couldn't be angry with her, or hurt, or even concerned. He must simply make himself feel *nothing*, whatever it took.

When all else fails, make it hurt worse. Until the pain makes you forget the feeling.

But now, that was much harder to do. Now he couldn't just pick up a blade to dig into his own flesh like Wyran had taught him to do. In the war camps he could easily gash himself open whenever he felt the feelings growing too powerful. But his current condition prevented him from so much as touching even a butter knife. And he needed the pain, needed the distraction—the catalyst for numbness—more than ever.

Unlocking himself and rising to wash the night from his body, he splashed water across his face in the stone basin in the corner. The cracked mirror above it stared back at him, a reminder of the man behind the monster—behind the silvery black veins ominously claiming his body—the shattered pieces on the floor like the missing pieces of himself. He ran a hand through his black hair, brushing it back from his eyes, and then dressed in pants, a well-fit tunic, and his typical dark overcoat, ensuring he buttoned it all the way up to his neck. He couldn't risk those newly formed creeping veins peeking through. As he reached for the handle of the great blood red door before him, he drew in a breath, leaving his demons behind with his shackles. Now it was time once more to play the part of the noble prince.

The walk through the maze of hallways in the castle still wasn't long enough to reset his thoughts. "Morning." He nodded to the men in the breakfast hall as he entered.

Taking a seat next to his usual four friends, he guzzled down a fresh pint of ale. "A bit early for drink, eh, Your Highness?" Tyrios nudged him, flashing his teeth. He noted Wryan's uncharacteristic silence and watchful eye from the corner of the table, and knew he was probably still sulking over their interaction yesterday evening.

"Perhaps." He braced his brow at the pungent taste as the drink stung his insides. "But it was...a rough night."

"That's a bit worrisome, given we have such a big day ahead of us." Tyrios took a bite of bread spread with some sort of orange jam. "You're certain you're still...controlled...enough to make this journey?"

"I'm certain I have no other choice but to try. Time is running out." Asterious nodded, forcing himself to eat a bite of food. "Are all preparations made? Weapons? Rations?"

"Everything should be ready. It's just a matter of you giving the order." Wryan spoke up, leaning back in his chair.

"Which, respectfully, should be sooner rather than later." Gariel chimed in with a nod. "There have been more reports of Sinevia burning crops to punish resistant cities. She'll send the whole land into famine soon. The whole kingdom will be too weak to rebuild before long if we don't—"

Asterious held up a hand to spare himself the lecture. "I'm well aware of the urgency of the matter." He glanced between the four men. "But our best hope of reaching the Shadowblood's sword lies locked in the tower with the girl. And, unfortunately, she's no longer part of the plan." When met with questioning eyes, he realized Wryan must not have shared the news amongst them.

"But if she's a Shadowblood...why are her eyes violet instead of solid black? Why don't her markings cover her entire body?" Riven shook his head in disbelief.

"She says her mother was a Lightborn." Asterious sighed.

"Her mother? How? Shadowbloods aren't *born*. They were...well—*made*...at the Shattering." Tyrios stuttered. "How can that be?"

"I...I don't know. And she claimed she didn't understand it either." The prince glanced between them. "But it doesn't matter now. You know as well as I do that Shadow amplifies my curse. I cannot let her come with us. I can't risk this thing taking over out in the open again. I can't risk killing you all and being trapped as a monster forever." Asterious hung his head.

"We don't know for sure that she's the only way to the weapon." Gariel interjected. "We were close before."

"Yes, we were. And then we found *her*." Asterious nodded, taking another swig of his drink. "I don't know what fate we will meet by venturing in there without her. Which is why I will be the only one going in to find the Blade without any of you. My curse might serve useful for once if it at least gives me a chance of surviving long enough to find it. But I won't risk any of you."

"That's admirable, Asterious, but you know we will gladly give our lives for your cause if need be." Tyrios clasped his hands together and leaned forward on the table.

"I do know that. And that's why you are not dispensable to me. I will not risk your lives for mine." Asterious looked down at his nearly empty cup before speaking again. "I'll figure out how to get through the Shadow Woods, even if I have to do it alone." He said, trying to convince himself as much as them. "Speaking of the girl, I haven't had a chance to inform Azell of the change in arrangements. I need to give her the key so she can bring her breakfast. Wyran, do you still have it?"

He held out a hand to Wyran as he stood, scanning the large hall for any sign of Azell. Wryan stood as well and placed a hand on his shoulder. "I can bring a meal up to her, Your Highness," he offered. "To spare you the trouble."

"Hmm, all right." Asterious raised an eyebrow, putting his hand back by his side. "I assume last night was uneventful?"

"Quiet as death, inside and out." Wryan selected a plate of fruit, poached eggs, and oatmeal and exited the great hall.

Asterious watched him until he was out of sight and then sat back down with his head in his hands. Something felt wrong. But he concluded his mind was too burdened to differentiate the sense of foreboding from stress. There was truly so much to be done, with no idea if any of it was truly the right answer. Time was running out for his sister, the kingdom—and for him. And he was beginning to doubt himself.

A few moments later, hurried footsteps burst through the dining hall, demanding everyone's attention. The prince whirled around to see Wryan, his face looking like he'd just dropped something fragile and valuable and watched it shatter on the floor.

"Prince Asterious!" He spat out the words as if he was going to choke on them if he didn't speak fast enough. "The girl is gone! She must've escaped this morning!"

"What? How? She wouldn't..." He should just let her leave. He shouldn't care if she was gone. But he did.

"There's no sign of her. The door was unlocked."

"And you're certain you have the key?"

Wyran pulled the key from his pocket and held it up, something smug about his movements.

Asterious shook his head. "I want round-the-clock guards posted everywhere we can spare. Be vigilant. I've angered her. She could be hiding out in the castle somewhere waiting to take her revenge." That wasn't true. That wasn't true at all. But it was the only thing he could think of to justify why he would order his men to waste their time looking for her when there were far greater things at stake.

"We'll search for her all we can while you're gone, Your Highness," a guardsman reassured from the hall.

"I won't be gone today." Asterious said, earning himself shocked expressions from Riven, Tyrios, and Gariel. "Not until she's found. We'll push off the journey— at least for one more day."

"Your Highness, we can't afford much more time." Riven said.

"Just one more day." He swallowed, looking straight ahead.

"Isn't this what you wanted, Asterious?" Wyran asked, stepping close. "She's gone. You were going to send her away later today anyway."

"Y—yes. It is what I wanted." The prince stuttered, not sure why he couldn't explain the sinking feeling in his heart. And not sure why it was even there, as he watched the dining hall clear out as his men went to search the castle. "Just...not like this."

No further words were spoken amongst the five, and they disbanded. Asterious saddled his horse to search the grounds, the forests, and the cliffs by the sea, and he stayed out searching until the moon called him back.

He wished he could have at least said goodbye, and that he could've at least watched her ride away on Frasya and known she was safe. And he wished he knew why he cared. He'd disciplined himself not to lose control to grief, pain, anger, or even joy—and he had the scars to prove it. But he'd never prepared himself for this kind of feeling that seemed to have complete power over him. A feeling he could not name and therefore did not know how to defeat.

As he rode beneath the stars in the crisp night air, he questioned everything he thought he knew and forced himself to accept that if Caramyn was truly gone, he'd give anything to change the last thing he said to her, because it stung like salt in a wound, replaying in his head.

I never want to see you again.

36
SOMEWHERE TERRIBLE

Caramyn

The scent of fish and brine filled Caramyn's nostrils. It was still dark, but the light was starting to come through, bit by bit. She felt as though she was rocking back and forth, floating, but she couldn't move her hands to steady herself as they were bound by thick rope. Someone pressed a cold rag to the back of her head and was mumbling something to her in a gritty whisper. "You're waking up. It's all right."

She wanted to open her eyes, but she was afraid to reveal herself if they were an enemy of magic. She fought the tempting urge to look at her surroundings, and she strained her ears to listen for any small sound that might be familiar. So she held her eyes shut, still pretending to be unconscious. But it was too late to fool the person at her side.

"It's all right. I know you're awake," he said, a kindness in his voice. "I'm sorry that someone did this to you. And I'm sorry you ended up here."

She still didn't open her eyes. She wanted to hear the reassuring call of her raven. But as her senses returned, even with her eyes closed, she realized she wasn't imagining the floating sensation. The sounds of water and creaking wood were clear as the frigid, moist air on her skin. She had never seen a ship before, but she was certain she was on one.

She listened quietly as the sounds around her all melded into one chaotic orchestra—the crew above rowing in unison to steady chants. Gulls screeching faintly. Waves lapping the sides of the boat and the captain calling out orders. And a low, haunting sound of women weeping that pierced her to the core.

"What are you doing, healer? Get back up here and stop wasting time!" The booming voice from above bellowed nearby suddenly.

The male voice at Caramyn's side responded. "This one is not well. If I don't tend to her injury, she'll be in no shape to make port. She certainly won't be fit to make it up the mountains."

"So what? It's not our problem if she doesn't survive once she's their property."

"But Captain..." the voice was pleading. "This one is exceptionally lovely. They'll be willing to pay a high price for her, but not if she's half-dead. Think of the profit you could make from her if she's at her peak."

"Aye, very well. Fix her, then, Brenn. But be quick about it."

"Yes sir."

The sound of heavy boots grew faint, leaving the sounds of only the man tending to her. He pressed a palm to her head. Then pulled away briefly only to return and lay something across her forehead—a small chain or string of jewelry. With a few whispered words from the voice, she felt the bruise on the back of her head fade away. The swelling subsided, and the ache was gone.

She realized from her readings that this was a complicated healing spell. The chain over her forehead must've been enchanted to channel the magic. And that made this man a skilled Spellbound. So she decided it was safe to open an eye. The piercing sun shining through slats in the deck above nearly blinded her, but once she blinked and turned away, her vision adjusted to see a man, perhaps a bit younger than Asterious, peering down at her.

She lay on a blanket beneath the ship's deck, both her arms and legs bound with rope, and this Brenn fellow was positioned kneeling at her side in a simple brown tunic with a hood. She had managed to catch a quick glimpse of the golden glimmer in his pupils as the magic faded out, right before they faded back to a normal brown—a side effect of Spellbounds with diluted Light in their bloodlines. And after surveying the small group of other terrified females tethered to the ship's walls, Caramyn was only sure of three things. This man had just used magic. She was on a ship. And they were headed for somewhere terrible.

PART II

37

ONE AND THE SAME

Caramyn

"Don't move so much," Brenn's raspy voice carried the sea within it, along with the slight windburn on his cheeks that gave away his profession. "You'll hurt yourself again."

"Who are you?" The question leapt from her lips. The man had met her gaze briefly when she'd opened her eyes, and she knew he recognized what they meant by the way he locked onto them and nodded. But he didn't say a word about them.

"You used magic to heal me." She tilted her head to the side, hoping to get him talking. Brenn turned away, concealing his profile beneath the hood of his tunic. "You could be killed for that," she added.

It surprised her when he spoke. "The king's law can do nothing to me here. His rule does not extend to the seas."

"The queen's law, now, technically."

Brenn shot a puzzled expression her way, looking back at her. "Does it matter? King or queen, either way, we must hide and scrape by in whatever ways we can."

Caramyn kept her gaze on him, unbreaking, noting his ash brown tousled hair and the facial hair that lined his stout jaw. "Tell me where this ship is headed and how I got here."

Brenn cast his dark eyes to the wooden floor between them.

"Please. I'm not a fool." Caramyn gestured by lifting her bound hands. "I can clearly see this isn't meant to be a pleasure cruise. Obviously the destination is not a desirable one, wherever it may be. So why not just tell me of my fate?"

Brenn nodded, his forehead wrinkling in a worried manner. "Because if I tell you, you'll hate me for being a part of it."

"Well, if you're so ashamed of it, perhaps you shouldn't be a part of it. Have you considered that?"

Brenn lowered his voice and his eyes pleaded with her to do the same. "Have you considered that serving as a healer on the black-market trade boats is the only way I can use my gift and not die for it?"

"You're a Spellbound healer. But you have Lightborn ancestors, yes? That's why your eyes lit up gold for a second?"

"My great grandfather was a druid elder and a vine caller. He was good at making things grow and flourish. So, I guess I must've gotten lucky with an affinity for learning healing magic." Brenn's voice was unwavering. "Or unlucky."

Caramyn was silent, thinking of what to say next. Brenn certainly hadn't retained any regal Lightborn features besides the magic. He was handsome in a hardened, rugged sort of way, with a slight crook in the bridge of his nose and a stern jaw covered by brown unkempt stubble.

She was still itching for a direct answer about her whereabouts, and disgruntled that he hadn't given it. She took in the sight around her once more, focusing on the women bound in here with her. They were mostly near her age, a few a bit older, and two that looked far too young to face whatever horrors awaited them. One girl met Caramyn's gaze—a girl with big brown eyes and hair like night. An icy feeling snaked its way across Caramyn's chest as a chilling realization found its way to her.

"Black market," she repeated. "And what is the cargo?"

Brenn was silent. For a moment, Caramyn thought he looked like a young boy ashamed for having told a lie, but too afraid to admit it. But he finally spoke. "The Silvereans pay a high price for brides. There is a shortage of women on the mountain."

"Brides?" A pit formed in Caramyn's stomach. "Who brought me here? Tell me!"

"I—I don't know. I make my living on the docks. I board whatever vessel hires me. I'm just here to do a job."

Caramyn pierced him with a gaze of iron.

"I swear it when I say I didn't see who brought you here. The ship was already loaded when Captain Tharvold paid me for hire. I'm supposed to be here mostly for the crew, not you. But when I saw the shape you were in, I knew I couldn't let them bring you into the Spires like that."

"The Silverean Spires? As in...at the edge of the Silver Spine?" Caramyn practically choked on the name as her blood ran cold. The Silver Spine Mountains were a massive mountain range that made up the backbone of the realm, cutting across from east to west. Most of them were passable with preparation and common sense. But the Spires were a frozen shelf of mountains that jutted out far past the fjords and kissed the sea. Unreachable and inaccessible by outsiders and those not conditioned to traverse them. The Silverean mountain clans rejected the rule of courts and kings, and there was little any king could do about it. Caramyn remembered this from the many maps she had studied, but she never thought she'd have need to be familiar with this forsaken part of Evylere. "I wasn't brought here of my will."

"I know you weren't. Very few are. I'm sorry." Brenn hung his head.

"I don't believe you're sorry at all." Caramyn turned up her nose at him. "You're just as bad as the rest of the disgusting bastards above rowing us there."

Only then did she notice how cracked her lips were from the blistering cold, and it felt like swallowing sand to talk. She closed her eyes, thinking back to the most recent memory she could manage to summon. She remembered approaching the door of the West Wing. The sound of chains. She remembered saying Wryan's name. He was there. Had he done this to her? Had he *sold* her?

"Healer," Caramyn snapped, her voice hoarse. "Where and when did this ship leave port?"

"Please call me Brenn. And Magoth. We left from Magoth. In the dead middle of the night. We've been sailing all day."

Caramyn steadied herself. Though she had expected the answer, the impact still hit like a rogue wave. Magoth was a small port on the river, and the nearest to Asterious' Forbidden Court, likely only a few hours' ride. Wryan had certainly brought her here.

If they'd been on the water for the whole morning, that meant there was at least another day or two still ahead of them. By now, they had almost certainly sailed past the river's mouth, the last thin vein that could have carried her back to Evylere. They'd be past the fjords now, at the edge of the sea, making escape impossible. Whatever waited for her lay only forward.

"Why are you still talking to the cargo, healer?" The captain's steel voice cut through the air and made Caramyn jump. "You've fixed her, so now go find somewhere else to be until you're needed. You want to talk to her? You can put in your bid against the Silvereans like every other man."

Brenn scrambled to his feet and retreated back up to the deck, keeping his eyes on Caramyn until he could no longer manage. She wouldn't easily forget that strange, broken look in his eye.

As the ship swayed beneath her, she thought of Asterious and wondered if he knew what happened...or worse—if he'd planned it. Perhaps that was why it was so easy Nocthar to get the key. She wrapped herself in the blanket and shuddered from both the cold and the way the dire realization settled within her.

The prince would've surely been glad she was no longer an issue. Now he could go back to fretting about his sister and taking back his throne without her in the way to complicate things or uncover his secrets. He was probably praising Wryan right now for a job well done at getting rid of her.

But where did that leave her? To face the icy throws of the Spires. Alone. If surviving in a frozen mountain fortress wasn't enough, she'd have to survive the people—cold-blooded, iron-strong clan warriors as harsh and unforgiving as the snowbound peaks they called home. No one could breach those mountains on foot. Not even the king's soldiers. But perhaps an undead army could...

Seawater leaked down through cracks in the ship's deck, leaving behind its cold, salty mist to sting Caramyn's frost-chapped skin. She licked her dehydrated lips, soothing the cracked skin for only a moment before the frigid air sapped them again. She wished she had asked Brenn for a drink of water.

She curled up on the floor as night came, thinking of Asterious and thinking of lofty, impossible ways to escape. But she had never been at sea before. There was no way out. She didn't even know what had become of Nocthar. If he had tried to follow her, he might not have survived for long in these conditions on the water. She yearned for her raven, for now she was truly, hopelessly alone. Alone and betrayed in a new way that stung more than ever before. At least those who'd hurt her before had always made their intentions clear from the beginning. There was no luring and pretending to care about her, only to turn on her like this.

Let him hate me. Let him assume the worst. And let him choke on it...Let it torture him more than if I had driven my knife into his heart...

Because he might as well have driven one into hers, the way it ached in a way she'd never felt before. And the pain was like a poison that lingered in a way she'd do anything to be rid of. A way that disgusted her.

Silence fell during the night. Even the women's weeping had died down. A couple of them had been willing to speak to her. Most of them were sold by families who owed a debt...and one was sold by a soldier who'd kidnapped her after raiding her village. Caramyn wondered how many more there would be next time.

The moon above shone through the open hatch in the deck, casting rays through white clouds and icy haze. The crew did not row much during the night, and they seemed to be moving far more slowly. Caramyn refused to close her eyes, for she was too keenly aware of the way the hungry eyes of the crewmates ogled the captives down here. She wouldn't sleep while such dogs occupied the same space as her.

Suddenly footsteps called her attention. They were quiet, but she heard them from behind. She braced herself, waiting to be touched, groped, or harassed in some way, and quickly intended to meet their face with the back of her elbow. But instead, a hand lowered down beside her shoulder with a canteen of dripping water.

"Drink." It was Brenn's voice. "I managed to get this for you since you weren't awake earlier when the rations were given out. I know you must be parched."

Caramyn said nothing, but took the canteen as best she could manage with her restraints around her wrists. Guzzling down the water, she had never tasted anything more refreshing in such a moment of physical desperation, even despite the leather aftertaste from the canteen skin.

"Won't the captain have your head for this?" She whispered, looking up at Brenn's looming figure.

"What he doesn't know won't hurt me."

"You shouldn't help me. Let me die of thirst here in the bottom of this stinking boat. I won't allow myself to be sold as some man's blushing bride—as someone's property."

"I know," Brenn uttered. "But if you'll trust me, I'll do my best to help you."

"Why?"

"Because you're magic. We are one and the same. I know why you're wary. I know what it's like to live your whole life hiding who you are."

Caramyn studied his face, which in itself was a nod to his druid blood. Everything about him was rough like the earth, like the unkemptness of nature, but his eyes somehow maintained a softness that made him seem gentle. He reminded her of soft, velvet moss on a splintered, solid log.

He was the first person she'd ever known who could have claimed to know what it was like to face her struggles and really meant it. To be forced to do something he didn't want to do in order to survive. And if he, too, had spent his whole life running and hiding, then maybe he could be more useful to her than she wanted to admit.

"The ice has slowed us down. We'll arrive at the Silverean docks late tomorrow." Brenn knelt down to take the canteen from her slowly, muttering his words discreetly. "I'll not talk to you anymore till then, to keep up appearances and keep suspicions down. But I'll try to think of something to help you survive when we get there."

As he turned to go, she shifted, and noticed the crushed Blood Briar petals that laid scattered beneath her, remnants of the flower she'd put in her pocket.

An idea sparked.

"Brenn, wait!" She called hoarsely and he shuffled back over on tiptoes. "You're a druid...do you have any elixir vials? And, and can you possibly bring me some water from the sea?"

Salt could sometimes strongly enhance the effects of some shrubs. If she could amplify the Blood Briar with seawater, it could possibly coagulate the blood of someone who drank it to a dangerous degree...to either put them in a deep sleep or clog their heart. It was a desperate idea, but it just might be her only hope of a defense where they were headed.

Brenn shot her a confused look. "I might have some. Why?"

She shifted back to reveal the red petals at her side. As a healer, he of all people should've understood. The corner of his mouth lifted every so slightly into a smile as he whispered. "Yes, I think I can find what you need."

And then she didn't see him again until she heard the captain above calling out land.

38

BLOOD BRIAR

Asterious

The prince paced the moonlit cobblestone of the courtyard, his eyes tired and his nerves shattered. They had been searching for two days with no sign of her, and he had delayed their journey to the Shadow Woods yet again. Riven and Wryan had given him hell for it, but he didn't care. He couldn't leave until he knew what happened to her.

The thought that she might have decided to betray him—to destroy him—plagued his mind. That she might run straight to Felhold and tell his sister everything. The thought of it tore him to pieces, and he wasn't sure which outcome was more painful to think about—if she was on her way to betray him or if she was in danger. He scratched at the prickle in his chest where the scars were. The flesh scars, obscured beneath the cursed magic ones. A scar for each time he'd been betrayed by those who were meant to care about him. What was one more if she betrayed him too?

"Your Highness."

He hadn't even noticed when Azell's frail frame appeared in the archway. She carried a small plate with a meager amount of meat and bread.

"I don't mean to overstep, Prince Asterious, but I fear you'll grow weak from hunger if you don't eat something soon."

The prince straightened himself, conscious of his fatigued appearance. "Thank you, Azell." His voice was weary, and he was ashamed for how he'd let the mere thought of this girl burden him so much. "You've always known best, Azell, and as such, your concern is always welcome."

He took the plate from her and forced down a few bites which his stomach did not welcome. Leaning against a cracking stone column, he stared across to the other side of the courtyard garden, lost in thought. Azell reached to take the plate from him, and he handed it back to her without hesitation.

"I don't understand it." He crossed his arms, his steel eyes shifting to a rosebush wrought with thorns growing wildly beside him. He leaned over to pluck the single remaining rosebud from its brambles. "I should be focused on everything but this. Sinevia, finding Mother. The kingdom and its people. But it seems I've been cursed yet again...and this time I don't know how to break it."

"Oh?" The maid's reply was barely audible.

"It's so stupid of me, Azell. It's madness to say it out loud, but...thoughts of her consume me day and night. I crave her with every dawn and yearn for her under each moon. Like a fool I find myself whispering her name in the silence, as though somehow it could call her back to me."

"You speak of the Lady Caramyn?"

"Unfortunately." The words drifted from Asterious' in one breath like smoke in the dark as he clutched the withering rose in his hand. "I don't understand what she's done to me."

Azell stepped closer. "Your mother once confided in me about a similar feeling," she said. "About the consuming passion she'd felt for King Vaerwynd before Daemar killed him, and how it ached like a hole in her chest every day that she had to live without him."

"Yes, but of course she would feel that way. He was her mate," Asterious muttered, shaking off the thought before it could take root. Mates were rare. A fated Lightborn bond created only when two souls carried fragments of the same god's heart from the divine Shattering. And there was no possible way a Shadowblood could be his mate, if he even had one.

He sighed and hung his head. "What I feel for Caramyn has no explanation."

As he concealed the rose in a closed fist, he thought of his last words to her, and still felt their bitter sting on his tongue.

I never want to see you again.

When he'd said those words, he didn't know that despite what he thought he wanted, he *needed* her to stay. He hadn't known how he would break for her when she was really gone. Had he known the anguish her absence would bring, well...

He didn't know what he would do—because no matter how badly he wanted her, he couldn't let himself destroy her.

All he hoped for now was the reassurance that she was safe.

"There's...there's something..." Azell's voice quivered but strengthened as she spoke. "There's something I need to—"

The rapid beating of wings above interrupted. Asterious looked up to see a raven—Caramyn's raven—sweeping down to them with its talons curled around something sharp and metallic.

"That damned bird." He clenched his fist, and his voice lifted, suddenly filled with hope that she was near. "That's *her* bird."

The raven swept down near to the ground, as though it had used every last bit of strength to perform the maneuver. Azell gasped as the creature ruffled its feathers and stared upright at the prince, dropping the object at his feet. A dagger.

Asterious reached down to pick it up, but then remembered the jolt of pain he would feel if he so much as grazed it with a fingertip. So he crouched down instead to get a better look. It was a hunting knife with the unmistakable craftsmanship of rural mountain folk. Marks of frequent use stained the well-worn black handle, but the blade was just as sharp as new.

"What is this supposed to mean? Whose is this?"

The bird fluttered to his shoulder and immediately began to preen its feathers. Asterious cursed under his breath and shook his head. Whatever puzzle this strange, confusing creature had delivered, it was quite unclear...and he didn't have time for more puzzles.

"Did someone hurt Caramyn? Did this belong to her?"

The raven poked up its head to let out a caw and then went back to preening nervously.

"Someone hurt her? Is the dagger hers? Is that a yes or no, damn it?"

"It is hers." Azell added suddenly.

Asterious turned to her, his face wrought with surprise.

"I noticed it strapped to her leg one evening when I was preparing her bath, and she began to undress behind me. I never let her know that I saw her in the reflection of my silver pitcher."

"You knew she had a dagger? All this time? She could've tried to kill me with it."

"But she didn't. And we both know she would've had quite the difficult time trying to kill you. I wasn't worried." Azell's voice held firm with a hint of a laugh as she met the prince's gaze. "Don't you see, Asterious? You and her aren't so different. You both hide beneath these hardened exteriors, both terrified of someone looking closer and seeing your true heart."

"The only thing true about my heart is that it would destroy both of us. It's for the best that she's gone."

"Is it?" Azell raised an eyebrow.

Asterious stood, catching a brief glimpse of his hated reflection in the blade. "If she wanted to betray me, she could have done it long ago. She had every reason to hate me from the beginning." He gently poked the bird to get its attention, hardly believing he was desperate enough to be asking it questions. "If this is her dagger, then why isn't it with her now?"

The bird lifted into the air and clamped its beak around Asterious' coat lapel, tugging insistently. "I think he wants you to follow him," Azell said, a twinkle in her eye.

"I'd say so." The prince remarked, stepping forward as the bird flew off, soaring into the palace halls.

He and Azell rushed back through the castle corridors, following the flight of the raven. It led them to the West Wing, where it dove to the ground and pecked urgently at floor of the hallway leading to Asterious' chambers. The prince knelt to examine the area, his eyes scanning the deep red of the rug lining the hall. He strained to see, unsure of what he was looking for, until he spotted stains of blood, well-camouflaged against the ruby carpet.

"What's this?" Asterious' voice darkened.

"Your Highness." Azell interrupted. "Earlier in the courtyard I came to tell you about something I saw that seemed...unusual. I was hesitant, but now I'm convinced I have good reason to be suspicious."

"Well, what is it?"

"Well, I didn't want to accuse anyone without cause, but I can't deny the blood here. The morning Caramyn disappeared, I awoke earlier than usual. There was a noise outside keeping me awake—now I think I realize it was the bird." She narrowed her eyes at the raven and took a deep, nervous breath. "Anyway, since I couldn't sleep, I decided to get an early start on the day's tasks. And as I was preparing things for the day, I passed by a window and saw Sir Wryan returning from a ride with a riderless horse, which I found odd at such an hour. But I thought maybe he had just been returning from hunting for the journey." Asterious listened with intensity, leaning into her words.

"Wryan?" he repeated. "I certainly didn't send anyone on a hunt that night. In fact, he'd offered to guard her room. That's where he was supposed to be. You're sure it was him?"

"There's more." She lifted her chin and unfolded a shirt that was tucked in her apron pocket. "He came to me later that day and asked if I could mend his shirt when I had time. I thought nothing of it until I sat down to fix the tear this morning and noticed small specks of blood." She handed the shirt to the prince.

He stared at the faint red dots as a sick feeling rose within him. "Are you saying you believe Wryan had something to do with Caramyn's disappearance? You think this blood is hers?"

The raven cawed and beat its wings, only calming down when Azell spoke again and lifted her hands in a surrendering motion. "Your Highness, I'm not saying I believe anything. I am only telling you what I saw."

Asterious meditated on her words. It was no secret that Wyran wasn't fond of Caramyn, but surely, he wouldn't have done something to her, especially behind his back. He thought back to how calm he'd seemed the morning she'd gone missing. He'd even pretended to be the first to notice—and perhaps that's exactly why he'd offered to bring her breakfast. Something simmered inside the prince. "I'll talk to him. It must be a misunderstanding."

But then, just as he turned to go, his eyes snagged on something bright red in the darkest corner of the corridor, just at the base of the doors to his room—crushed, broken petals from a flower he'd only seen once before. Blood Briar.

Without another word or second wasted, clutching the blood-specked shirt, he stormed back into the castle towards Wryan's chambers, leaving the raven and the maid behind.

He slammed a fist on the door, second guessing why he wasn't tearing it down instead. And if Wryan didn't answer it within the next minute, that was exactly what he was going to do.

Wryan opened the door just a crack and poked his head through. "Everything alright, Your Highness? What brings you—"

Asterious pushed past him and forced his way into the room. "Do you know anything about Caramyn's disappearance?"

Wryan stood still, frozen in place, his eyes wide as though he was offended by the question. "Of course not, Asterious," he finally said. "You were there when I went up to her tower and she was gone. I was just as shocked as you."

"Is that so?" Asterious took out the shirt and tossed it at Wryan, who was backing up into a corner. "Is that why you look so astonished that I would ask? Is that why there's blood on this shirt? Tell me, whose blood is it?"

Wryan clenched the shirt in his hands, glancing between it and the prince as his lips stammered. "I—I know it might be difficult to accept, Your Highness, but the girl left of her own accord. She had every reason to leave once you discovered who she was. Her plans to kill you were probably ruined."

"If she wanted to harm me, don't you think she would've tried it much sooner?" A smoldering burn rose in Asterious' chest as he spat the words through a tensed jaw. "Now answer the question. Whose. Blood. Is. It?"

Wryan laughed nervously, crumpling the shirt into a bundle and tossing it on the floor. "My own, of course. We're soldiers, for gods' sake. Is it so unbelievable that we bloody up a few tunics?"

"Enough of your shit, Wryan. You hated her. You made that clear." Asterious prowled toward Wryan, closing in around him like a lion on its prey. "What did you do to her?"

Wryan's sly eyes narrowed like a viper. "I did what you couldn't do, Asterious. She would've been your ruin. Like your father." Wryan cocked his head. "You refused to see it. So someone had to see it for you. Someone had to protect you from yourself. You should be thanking me."

A rush of rage flooded Asterious. Fury flashed before his eyes like steel lightning and in an instant, he had pinned Wryan to the wall, rattling the torches on their hooks.

"What did you do to her?" He growled, pressing his thumbs around Wyran's throat.

"Easy now...Your Highness..." Wyran choked. Asterious eased up his grip to let the man talk. "Watch that temper. You're risking a lot right now. I found her snooping in the West Wing. She had nothing good planned, I assure you."

"Did she see me? Did she see what I am?"

"That's what you're worried about? Asterious, I trained you. I thought you were stronger than this. She's poisoned your mind."

Asterious closed his grip on Wryan again, fighting every urge within him to squeeze the last breath from his lungs. "You think I can't think for myself? You knew my plans to make sure she was safe. You defied me!" he seethed through his teeth. "You had no damn right to go behind my back! Now tell me what you've done with her!" He slammed Wyran against the wall once more, the blaze in him searing like wildfire, the beast one wrong word away from taking over.

"My sincere apologies, Prince..." Wryan coughed, his fingers prying at the prince's grasp in desperation.

"Where is she now? I won't ask again!" The prince roared.

"She's...." Wryan rasped. "She's probably on the other side of the ocean by now. I took her...I took her to Magoth."

"Magoth?" Asterious released Wyran at the word, because if he knew if he didn't let go, he was going to kill him. "It's taking every bit of strength I possess to keep from tearing you apart right now."

Wryan huddled on the floor, grasping at his neck as he wheezed out the words. "Now remember, Asterious, that's not you talking."

"Oh, but it is. This time, it is very much me. Push me one inch further, Wryan, and I'll end you here." Asterious leaned down to grab Wryan by the shirt collar and pulled his face to his. "When did her ship leave? And to where?"

Wyran croaked out the words between coughs, his fearful gaze cutting into Asterious. "I...I don't know. I didn't ask. The ship was preparing to leave as I got there. They were just some smugglers. Said something about taking women for the Spires? I don't know for sure, I just took the money and left."

"The money? You *sold* her, you fucking bastard?" His breath was shaking. He yearned for the weight of a sword in his hand so that he could run it through Wryan right there. It'd be much cleaner that way. But his bare hands would still do the job just fine. "My curse is your mercy. Because without it, I would kill you right now."

He could scarcely believe the words coming out of his own mouth. But he would have to deal with Wryan later. Because he couldn't afford to lose control now. Because now, only one thing was worth pursuing, no matter what it may cost him. He couldn't let a moment more pass without knowing she was safe.

He flung Wyran down, ripped the door from its hinges, and departed into the shadows without looking back. "To hell with you, and to hell with this kingdom! I'll stop at nothing until I find her."

39

A HIGH PRICE

Caramyn

As the ship docked, Caramyn's bones shuddered as the ship groaned through the icy shallow water. With dread gripping her heart, she watched the prisoners as the crew forced them to their feet.

Her head whipped around, looking for Brenn, but she caught no sight of him. She clutched the withering Blood Briar petals ferociously, praying they still retained their potency.

Her heart pounded and twisted as a calloused crewman appeared at her side, undoing her shackles to offboard her with the rest of the captives. When she resisted, the back of his hand met her face. She managed to keep her footing against the blow, and pressed a hand against her bruised cheek as she looked up at the man through reddened, vengeful eyes. Her breath shortened, and she pulled her hand from her face, ashamed of herself for showing him even an instance of weakness. And then she spat on him.

The man reached for her and raised his hand to strike her a second time, but a voice approaching made him pause.

"Wait! Stop!"

It was Brenn. He was panting as though he'd just finished dealing with something urgent. Rushing to the man's side, he uttered his words between heaving breaths.

"She's barely recovered! If you damage her, you'll cost the captain," he hissed. "Since I am her medic, I was instructed to see her to the bidding grounds. You are relieved of your duty here." Brenn held an unwavering gaze on the man, who reluctantly turned away after an intense stare down.

As Brenn tended to Caramyn and pretended to chain her wrists together, he leaned forward so that she could hear the words he whispered under his breath. "I got what you asked for." And then he slipped a tiny vial of seawater into her hands. She quickly added the petals and then snapped the plug back on.

He made it appear as though she was still bound, but really, he'd left her shackles unlocked as he led her up to the deck of the longboat.

The searing sunlight on the white snow-capped mountains almost blinded her after two days in the dark belly of the ship. But the sun's warmth on her dry, frigid skin was a welcome sensation.

At the docks, where the black water froze into jagged panes along the shore, a small settlement awaited. Towering above it, the mountains rose sheer and merciless, their snowy peaks vanishing into a sky perpetually choked with ash-colored cloud. No road led in, and none led out. The only access point was the narrow throat of the fjord itself, hemmed by cliffs so steep and slick with ice that it would be impossible to escape from here even if she could run.

A scattering of tents huddled against the wind, their hides stiffened by frost and smoke. Between them, a crude market sprawled across the frozen ground. Splintered tables, bone-carved trinkets, slabs of salted meat traded in silence by figures wrapped head to toe in furs. Caramyn found her body trembling uncontrollably, desperate for warmth, and could only imagine if it was already this brutally cold down here, what chance would she stand against the elements further up into the Spires?

At the center of it all lay the bidding ground—a ring of trampled snow and dirt, and a few charred fire stains. Voices rose from around the ring, mostly of men naming their prices for the women who stood in the midst of it all. Women stood rigid in the cold, eyes forward, as brooding, towering men examined them like livestock.

The crew began lining up the women they'd brought from the ship at the entrance of this bidding ring. And she was part of the inventory.

"Run as soon as you have a chance." Brenn whispered, hardly moving his lips as they stepped off the pier. Caramyn gave a subtle nod, but deep down, she didn't have the faintest idea where she could even go. She would die in this place without shelter and warmth. But better to freeze to death than be caged as some man's pet bird.

Then she saw her—a young girl, barely a teenager—standing amongst the group. She was different, her skin the deep tan of the arid desert lands far across the sea and her hair like smooth raven's feathers. She might've been from Gahmea, a prominent kingdom of sand and sun. Her terrified brown eyes met Caramyn's for a moment, and like the girl's on the ship, they haunted her. She looked away, sickened at the thought of these young girls forced to this desolate, cruel place, and desperate to distract herself from this unfolding nightmare she could not stop.

"Have you ever been here before?" Caramyn asked Brenn, eyeing the meager tents and rune jewelry.

"Just once. Briefly." Brenn didn't turn around but slowed his pace as he lagged behind the rest of the group. Then he gave her a nudge. "Whenever you're ready, run. Maybe if you can hide out long enough you can catch another ship that comes in and stowaway."

Not a bad plan, Caramyn thought. She ripped her hands from the chains and ducked away, running for her life in the opposite direction towards another unknown fate, but hopefully better than this one.

She hadn't gotten far, when icy mist appeared around her ankles like lassos. A rope of ice and snow coiled around her like a serpent, knocking her to the ground before dragging her back through the unbothered crowd to a hulking one-eyed man who stood back at the dock covered in thick furs and hides.

"I'd be careful if I were you. The sale isn't kind to those who try to run." He spoke through the thick scarf across his mouth, looking down at her lying in the cold mud. The look in his bright blue eye and the calm of his voice told Caramyn he must've done this a million times before. And he was clearly a Silverean water witch—quite skilled with manipulating ice and snow. "Best behave or you could end up with a buyer who is rather...cruel."

The way he drew out the last word made Caramyn shiver. For the first time since Asterious had found her in the Shadow Woods, she felt completely helpless. Of course magic would be prominent here. There was no authority to stop them. Strange and ancient magic had likely flourished here in these untouchable peaks while it suffered its grueling death in the rest of the kingdoms.

"All that power and you choose to use it for this," she spat through desperate pants.

"Let's just say I make the most of my talents." The man grinned and flexed his arm in a mocking way that made her want to claw out his remaining eye.

Brenn ran to her side, but the man shoved him back. "You couldn't keep her contained. I don't think your captain would approve of you taking her the rest of the way."

"I'm sorry," Brenn said, producing the shackles he'd removed from Caramyn. "It was an accident. It won't happen again...I promise."

The Silverean man watched Brenn with suspicion, then snatched the shackles from him and placed them on Caramyn's wrists himself, securing them so that there was no chance of her getting out of them again.

"Try again." He growled, pointing to the bidding grounds. "If you so much as step in the wrong direction, I'll kill you both."

Caramyn hoped the focused look on Brenn's face meant he had a plan, because she was out of ideas now. But as they walked, she sensed Brenn's nervousness as he guided her, noting the sweat starting to form on his forehead even in this frigid air. She wondered if he could tell she was just as worried.

She could see up ahead. Smoke from nearby fires shrouded various men of status, draped in their fine furs and laden with axes and leather, laughing and drinking. A breath caught in her throat when she realized they were discussing the price on a helpless young woman who stood displayed among others in the center of the ring.

"I can't imagine why there's a shortage of women in this charming place." Caramyn shook her head. "Who wouldn't want to stay here?"

"They tend to sire mostly sons. Daughters are rare, so I've heard, and more susceptible to the harsh climate. Then there's the matter of death in child-birth...No doubt women are kept like broodmares in hopes of increasing the female population." Brenn murmured, his voice low. "Though I suppose they finally realized it was more effective to smuggle wives in."

She swallowed, nausea tearing at her stomach. "I've fought off vile men before. A little ice won't stop me from doing it again." She said it under her breath, more for herself to hear than for Brenn. But within her insides were twisting in knots.

"Just be careful." Brenn touched the top of her knuckles of the hand containing the vial, and his eyes flashed gold for a heartbeat.

"What did you do?" Caramyn asked, taking another reluctant step toward the bidding ring.

"I made the vial invisible. But it's only a small enchantment and it will only last for a few hours. Keep it close. It's all I know to do."

Before Caramyn could ask him more, a solid, unforgiving grip yanked her away from Brenn. "Time to go!" It was captain Tharvold. "I'll not risk you escaping again."

"No!" She cried, twisting and tugging without success to escape his grasp.

Brenn chased after her two men from the crew were quick to restrain him. Caramyn heard the captain reprimand him and order the men to take him back to the ship. She watched the distance between them grow as Brenn, shouting and grunting in objection, was restrained and dragged away until she could no longer hear his voice. She hadn't even gotten to tell him thank you.

The captain yanked her along until he brought her to a man sitting alone on his own private platform. By this alone, it was easy to note his wealth.

His head was shaved to the skin, marked with pale scars and dark paint that traced his temples and brow, highlighting the grease and grime along his scalp. A circlet of bone and beaten metal rested against his skull, more talisman than crown, a faint tang of blood and rot clinging to it. He watched her with hard amber eyes sharp as ice under a winter sun. Eyes that flickered with a simmering hint of cruelty. Though at least middle-aged, his body was thick with muscle beneath layers of fur and hide, and when he stood, he towered over Caramyn as just as she imagined a Silverean clansmen would. Broad, immovable, and forged by the cold, and radiating a predatory stench of a man who took things by force and did not care who he crushed along the way.

Tharvold spoke to the man in an unfamiliar tongue, likely the ancient Silverean language that she thought only the mountains knew. He gestured to her as though she was an object he was presenting, no more alive than the shackles on her wrists. After an exchange of gold coins, he left Caramyn in the presence of the man, still bound.

"That's quite an unusual eye color. What kind of wielder are you?" The man surprised Caramyn as he spoke in the common tongue, his accent thick. She did not respond as the man eyed her up and down in a way that made her crave a long bath.

"It doesn't matter to me if you answer me or not. My house is warded to suppress your power, whatever it is. I bought you for the only thing you're good for. And that's not speaking." He reached up and touched her swollen face. She flinched and pulled back as much as her chains would allow. He clicked his tongue. "Oh no, they didn't tell me about that. I couldn't see the bruise from there. I paid a high price for you because of your rare beauty. Too stunning to be ruined by senseless injuries like that." He paused, running his fingers down the curve of her neck. "But you can prove you're still worth the price tonight. I don't think I'll have the patience for to wait for the binding ceremony."

Caramyn felt her head spin and thought she might vomit there on the spot, despite the fact that her stomach was empty. Memories stirred up of the Inquisitors who had looked at her mother with the same filthy, vultures' eyes. He placed a thick fur pelt around her, and though she winced at his touch, she welcomed the much-needed protection against the cold.

She clenched the vial in her sweating palm. Her last hope. Unless those Shadows had followed her across these frigid water as they had followed her to Asterious' court. Unless they would come to her aid now again as they did with the Cavren. But she couldn't take the chance in assuming they would show up. And if she had somehow summoned them in her own power, she was clueless as to how to do it again. She would survive with or without the Shadows' help. Whatever awaited her, she could only pray that when night came, and this horrid man tried to touch her, she would have quite the surprise for him instead.

But first she'd have to survive the trek up the mountain.

40

THE SPIRES

Caramyn

The climb up the Spires was a punishment measured in hours.

Caramyn rode a stocky, slate-coated mountain horse bred for the cold—short-legged, wide-chested, and covered in thick, wooly fur, its snorts steamed in violent bursts as it hauled her up switchbacks carved straight into the mountain's stone. Her new captor led the horse, trudging up the snowy pathways with impressive ease and familiarity. The wind scoured the path, flinging specks of sleet that stung her face and crept through seams of her borrowed furs. When the trail narrowed to a ledge barely wider than a cart, she fixed her eyes on the brutish animal's wiry mane and counted breaths, afraid that one slip or misstep would send them both tumbling into the dark waters below.

By the time the ascent ended, her limbs burned and her lips were cracked raw by cold.

Clutching the invisible vial in her palm, Caramyn counted the minutes, keeping track of when it was due to become visible again. She was afraid to relax her hold even just a little bit, for fear that she might lose it, since the faint pressure against her skin was her only reassurance that it was still there.

There were other travelers too, hauling their newly purchased women and goods up the same icy path. Through intent listening, she had learned that the man who'd bought her was called Hrothvor, and bore the title of Frostlord. The language barrier left some things unclear, but the man's obvious position of rank needed no translation.

Still, she watched everything. Every bootprint stamped into frosty gravel. Every runed post and iron-ringed door of homes carved into the mountain. Every turn of the road as the group led her to a place where they finally found some mark of civilization. She had to know the way back to those ice-claimed docks if she would ever hope to find her way home.

Home.

The word taunted her. Was it the dark, mist-laden Woods at the edge of Evylere that called her home? Or was it the towers of Vaerwynd Castle she found herself aching for?

As she tightened her grip on the vial, she wondered if Asterious had even noticed her absence. Would he remember her? And why should she care if he did or didn't?

She shook the thoughts away. Whatever haunting imprint the prince had left on her heart could not matter now. He wouldn't—couldn't—be her reason for surviving. She had never needed faith beyond herself, and she refused to let fleeting emotion change that.

Hrothvor's stronghold rose from the rock like a clenched fist. It was little more than a reinforced lodge set apart from the tents around it. It was a low, broad structure built of stacked stone and timber, with a roof layered with sod and hide to brace against wind and snow. Smoke puffed from a tiny chimney, the scent of pine pitch and burning peat clinging to the air. It wasn't larger than the others by much, but perhaps housed an extra room or two.

Hrothvor muttered something to another man with him as he dismounted, perhaps a servant of some sort. The man ran to a tent outside and returned with a figure robed in furs, slimmer but nearly the same height. It was a woman, and her piercing ice blue eyes met Caramyn's as she approached and held out her hand.

"Ragna the Binder." Hrothvor's voice ground out. He gestured to Caramyn. "She'll prepare you. Go with her for now."

Prepare.

With no other choice, she followed the woman back to a large half-cabin/half-tent, where a fire burned in the center and Caramyn nearly collapsed before it to soak in the warmth.

She glimpsed a small back room, where it appeared other young women waited, some mending wool, some polishing bits of metal, some simply staring into nothing. A few murmured to one another, and others sat apart in corners like abandoned tools, the absence in their eyes unmistakable.

She was shoved forward before she could stare too long. Ragna stood behind her, statue-esque and imposing, she carried herself like a crane. She might have been old enough to be Caramyn's mother, her features sharpened, not softened, by time. Her long hair, streaked bronze and ash, was braided tightly in a long thick strand down her back. Deep set blue eyes—human blue—pinned Caramyn in place. A heavy fur mantle draped from her shoulders, and steel jewelry gleamed at her throat and throughout her woven braid.

"Not fond of the cold?" She spoke crisply and slowly.

Caramyn stared, unmoving, still caught by the woman's presence, before finally shaking her head.

"Hrothvor isn't a patient man." Her brow arched as though unimpressed, but her words conveyed quite the opposite. "You'll be the envy of the other maidens with those eyes. You might just become his favorite, if you're smart. And that could make you more powerful than the rest of us."

She reached out, and Caramyn jerked her wrist away, frozen restraints biting into her skin.

"I will not live as anyone's favorite caged bird."

"*Ijia*, you will accept it as those before you have. And those after." The woman's stark, thin lips curved faintly. "They cry. They bargain. Then one day they understand their purpose. Where else do runaways and refugees end up? Dead, destitute, or unprotected. But to be the maiden of a Frostlord offers...security."

"So do prisons," Caramyn snarled.

Ragna turned to the wall, lifting a coiled leather scourge weighted with metal.

"What was that word you called me?" Caramyn asked.

"Ijia. 'Canary.' My term of endearment for new maidens." The way she said it made Caramyn's skin crawl, but she swallowed down whatever intimidation it made her feel.

"And your word for raven?" Caramyn asked.

"Raven?" Ragna circled her, eyes keen. "Raven is *Kuhrissi*." With a flick of her arm, the scourge cracked. Fire ripped across Caramyn's back, stealing her breath. Her legs folded, and she met the cold hard ground like stone.

"You belong to the Spires now, little bird. Hrothvor bought you. I will perform your binding ceremony tomorrow, and he will own you. You are Hrothvor's maiden, and soon you will be his wife."

Face pressed to the ground, Caramyn forced back tears and whispered the word. "Kuhrissi."

"Up," Ragna said coolly. "Hrothvor expects you ready by nightfall. Impress him—for your sake."

Caramyn wanted to scream. To fight. To do anything. Instead, the weight in her chest settled into something hard and patient. There would be a chance. She would wait for it, or die making one.

Other women were summoned to prepare her. They washed her with icy water, scrubbing away grime with stiff brushes that burned the welt on her back. It was nothing like the baths of Vaerwynd. Nothing gentle at all.

She feared what they would do when they removed her clothing and saw her creeping Shadowblood marks framing the root-like sigil within them. They did stop and look at them, and muttered something in Silverean, but they didn't seem concerned with any of it. And she didn't know if that was a good or bad thing.

All the while, she kept the vial clenched tight. When Brenn's invisibility spell faded, she never opened her hand. Just before they painted her nails, she feigned a sneeze and slipped the vial into her mouth, praying it wouldn't spill. They braided her hair into intricate knots, weighted with metal beads, and painted her lips a deep wine shade. As Ragna lined her eyes with soot black kohl, she spoke again.

"No wonder he paid so dearly. We don't have eyes or markings like yours here. You're quite a rare gem."

Caramyn bit her lip, focused on hiding the vial. Perhaps the Silvereans didn't recognize Shadowbloods because they were too far removed from any of their impact on the realm. They wouldn't know much of Shadowblood history, or even how to recognize them, when they existed so far from where they'd once dwelled, isolated in this fortress of frost, stone, and iron.

When Caramyn's preparations were complete, the women retreated, but not before one leaned close and whispered, "I'm so sorry." Caramyn flinched, unable to see which of them had spoken—but she would never forget the sound.

Night crept in as torches were lit. Food was brought—a tasteless sludge of fish stew and bread. Even though she was starving, she only pretended to eat, wary of anything that might dull her senses. She couldn't keep from shivering beneath the sheer woolen wrap they'd given her to wear over the fitted crimson gown that clung to the shape of her body, and that was certainly not meant to keep the body warm.

Ragna watched from the door, tapping the whip in her hand. When the last of daylight faded, she stepped forward, dabbing Caramyn's neck and arms with fragrant oil.

"It's time."

If a night to remember was what Hrothvor wanted, it was what he would get.

41

RED DRESS

Caramyn

"Don't look so dismal, Ijia" Ragna muttered. "You'll realize your place is here, among the maidens. They all accept it sooner or later."

Caramyn finally broke her hours-long silence. "Have they accepted it? Or do they simply have no choice because this place has broken their spirits as well as their bodies?" Caramyn shook her head, biting her tongue before she lost her temper and ruined her chances of escaping.

Ragna walked her to the great lodge of Hrothvor, where a heavy door with an iron ring awaited them. Caramyn scrutinized the layout of Hrothvor's outpost. Beneath the snow-coated slopes of the back roof, there was an opening. An icy glass window that overlooked the settlement of tents and snowcave homes. A promising exit point, if needed.

She missed having Nocthar's eyes. He would have found the best route.

But he wasn't there. And without him, she'd have to trust her own instincts on the ground.

She was taken into the clan leader's home, and her thoughts raced. How was she to administer the vial of poison tucked away in the bosom of her dress? How would she administer it? She couldn't assume there would be a drink in his room, or that she would even have a chance to slip the potion into it if there was. What if he kept guards *inside* of his room? He probably wouldn't be the type to mind an audience... But as she dared to entertain all the things she was sure he would try to do to her, she thought of something that just might work, if it didn't kill her first.

The vial was so small that it hardly contained a sip's worth of liquid. She couldn't waste a drop. As she walked, she popped the lid off, hiding her movements underneath her woolen shawl.

Ragna knocked on the door. Hrothvor's voice on the other side granted them permission to enter, and her skin turned to ice. She felt sick but forced herself to maintain her focus. The crane-woman shoved her forward into the fire-lit crackling room and closed the door. The space was dim, just as she'd hoped. Scanning her surroundings as quickly and discreetly as she could, she was relieved to see that there was no one else in the room besides the hungry-eyed Frostlord. Her window of freedom lay just across the room, an open gateway into the night sky.

She waited for a brief moment when he looked away as he adjusted himself, and with one swift motion, brought the vial to her lips and took in the liquid, careful not to swallow the small amount. It burned, and tasted like sour blood and sea, but she ignored the bitter taste and feigned normalcy, her face nonre-active and unreadable.

"Come here." Hrothvor demanded from his spot on his elaborate, fur covered bed. He sat up, braced against the timber headboard underneath a wolf pelt, naked and baring out all his jagged scars. Caramyn fought the burning urge to resist his command, and slowly strode over, drawing near to the bedside with a feigned smile.

"I see Ragna has taught you some manners." He laughed in a way that made Caramyn's stomach turn. "Already doing as you're told without a word. And so damn beautiful. I don't think I can share you among the clan like the others. You might just have to be my special little pet."

His odor was that of sweat, horseshit, mead, and something with a bitter copper twang. He reached up to stroke her arm, trailing up to her chest, and bile rose in her gut. But she couldn't show any of it. As he groaned, Caramyn fought her desire to grab the nearest object and slam it into his face. Instead, she feigned willingness, quiet and docile, just as he'd want.

Still holding the poison in her mouth, she knew she must work fast, before he got her into a position she couldn't get out from under. Though it repulsed her, she climbed onto the bed and over Hrothvor's hulking body, pressing her open mouth to his, ignoring the grating feel of his cracked, wind-worn lips. As he expressed his pleasant surprise with a nauseating moan, she pushed out the poison from between her lips, ensuring that his mouth was open and praying that at least some of the liquid would wash down enough to take effect.

The man choked a bit as she pulled away, but he didn't react as she had expected him to. "You taste like the sea," he grumbled, wiping his mouth. "A bit defiant. But I like you. Do it again."

She hesitated for a second, watching with bated breath for the elixir to take effect, and hoping it would be enough.

"I said, do it again." The Frostlord's voice deepened as he reached for the back of her head and pulled her down to him, forcing her mouth to meet his again, the warm stench of his breath making her ill. She pressed her mouth shut tightly, but he fought his way in between her lips, his anger clear in his violent movements and the force of his slimy tongue against her teeth. Her heart raced with fear, and all at once she felt glad for every man's life she'd let the Shadows' take. She wished more than anything to give this vile clan chief the kiss of an arrow in his chest, but for now, poison would have to do.

Suddenly, Hrothvor's lips fell loose. The iron grip he held went limp. He muttered something weakly as she quickly pulled away, and his eyes fluttered until they shut completely. It had worked.

She watched Hrothvor's chest rise and fall. He wasn't dead, but merely in a sleep, his blood likely thickening and slowing within his veins.

She glanced around for something she could use to finish the job. She found a mirror near the bedside and took it as far from the door as possible, placed a blanket over it, and stomped it with the heel of her shoe to break the glass. She carefully bent over and selected the sharpest shard of the broken mirror, eyeing her own broken reflection as she held the makeshift glass weapon in her hand.

As she stared back at herself, something within her made her take pause. To reconsider, just for a breath, whether she was meant to bring judgment upon this man. Perhaps killing him in cold-blood was not the answer, no matter how easy or justified it felt. Unlike when she was in the Woods, her certainty wavered over whether she had the right to choose whether this man lived or died.

She didn't know what had shifted within her these past few weeks. She hardly recognized herself in this moment. If a man like Hrothvor had so much as stepped a toe in the Shadow Woods, she wouldn't have thought twice about killing him. Yet now, here, despite how horrible he was, she couldn't fully convince herself that it was her place to stop his heart. Even if he truly was a monster, perhaps she didn't have to let that make her into a monster, too.

She laid the glass shard down and rushed towards the door to make her escape. And found it locked.

She turned and fled upstairs to find the window she'd seen earlier. And no sooner was she striding towards it than when she heard a cry from outside. She crouched and crawled to the window to keep hidden, watching as below, outside, a young girl, fourteen at most, was being forced to move along by another elder woman, similar to Ragna but softer, and with the looming presence of a man walking with her. Decorated and wearing a similarly seductive dress as Caramyn's, she resisted the entire time they dragged her along toward Hrothvor's door.

It was the Gahmean girl from the docks—the one with the terrified eyes. As Caramyn took in the scene, the girl's intended fate became horrifyingly clear. Rage flared hot in her veins as she watched them force the girl inside. Caramyn held her position, waiting for them to enter the house.

But the door was locked, and if they couldn't get it open—if Hrothvor couldn't answer them, it'd alert them that something was wrong. She scurried back to the main room, searching in the dim, space by only the hearth's light. She found a key on the small wooden stool by the bed, by Hrothvor's sleeping body, and she rushed to take it to the door where someone was now knocking.

As she thought of the Gahmean girl on the other side, any inkling of hesitation was gone. Hrothvor was exactly the type of monster that needed to be put down.

In that young girl, Caramyn saw herself, scared and trembling, fighting to run away. No one had been there to save her when she needed it. And her soul had become distorted and merciless for it. But she would not let this girl suffer a similar fate. She would not let her become prey to this traumatic horror and lose herself in darkness as she had. Maybe it was too late for her. But it wasn't for this girl. And because of that, she wouldn't leave this let this abhorrent man in the room draw another breath.

She crawled back over the balcony and retrieved the broken mirror glass, a revived need for vengeance coursing through her veins.

Another knock at the door. Caramyn held her mirror shard behind her back and opened it to see the servants and the girl as she expected.

"The Frostlord is in the middle of a massage. He told me to answer the door and said not to disturb him further." She said with a gentle smile, as calmly as possible, not sure if they even understood her. They nodded and sent the girl forward into the room with her. She closed the door and locked it, tossing the key into the heart. It wouldn't matter. They wouldn't need it. And she didn't need to be carrying evidence on her later.

Caramyn peered at the girl, whose face was stained with the tracks of tears. She bent down towards her with a finger to her lips, warning her to remain quiet. The girl nodded fearfully. Caramyn placed a hand on her shoulder to calm her, then gestured for her to turn around to face the hearth and to keep staring into the fire. The crying girl complied, and Caramyn guided the girl's hands over her ears as she whispered her only instructions. "Don't listen."

When the girl was standing with her back turned and ears covered, she slowly crept away and snuck to Hrothvor's bedside. She preferred killing from a distance, but she knew how to do this, too. She'd make it as quick and clean as possible. She looked down at his sleeping figure, then at the young girl's silhouette in the corner. It was all she needed to reassure her that her choice was the correct one. It had to be. She lifted the razor-sharp spire above her head, and then in one swift motion, swiped the glass across the man's throat.

She was glad her dress was red.

42

A FAIR EXCHANGE

Caramyn

I am not a monster. I am not a monster.

Caramyn clung to the words like the shadows clung to her as she ran through the streets under the cover of night. They'd stolen some fur cloaks, broken the window and made their escape out the back. The village was as dead as Hrothvor, everyone tucked safely away from the frigid night in their homes. And she could see why. The cold was even more numbingly bitter without the sun to fend off its bite. And she couldn't imagine lasting long out in it.

She led the girl through unfamiliar frozen paths beyond, and crags slippery with ice, taking turns she only recognized because of the trek to the outpost earlier that day. But she had no idea how to get back down the mountain alive. They'd be frostbitten within hours. They couldn't hope to navigate the mountain's terrain on foot. And how soon would it be before Hrothgar's death was discovered and her absence noticed? And what was she supposed to do with this young, terrified girl for which she was now responsible?

With the questions racing through her mind, the only things she was certain of were that she couldn't allow herself to end up back in that cage again, and that she had to find a way back to Evylere.

She found something that looked like a stable, with open stalls facing away from the heavy north winds. Fingers nearly frozen, she fumbled with the metal latches and freed two sturdy mounts, horses that looked more like buffalos with their stocky bodies covered in thick shaggy layers of fur. She helped the girl up on one—a white and black spotted gelding—and then mounted her own, a slate-gray mountain pony.

At least with the animals' warmth beneath them and their surefootedness in these mountains, they might stand the slightest chance of making it through the night. Caramyn glanced at the moon, nearly shrouded behind snowy mist and mountain clouds. No one was yet aware of the murdered Frostlord she'd left behind, but she was certain that come morning, they'd all know what happened and who did it. And they'd be looking for her.

She chided herself. If she had just left Hrothvor unconscious, she might have escaped without such drastic consequences. But instead, she had put a target on her back. She wanted to indulge in regret, but one look at the timid girl huddled on her furry pony, and she was reminded that the price was worth paying.

The girl, thin and delicate, was obviously shaken, but still held herself with an air of confidence. She reminded Caramyn so much of her younger self. She was nearly the same age as when Caramyn's own horrors began. And she didn't want her to have to face the same cruelty she did. She couldn't let her tenderness, her innocence, be butchered at the hands of such evil. No. She would not allow this gentle girl to become molded by darkness, fear, and vengeance as she had been.

As they wandered the village, Caramyn took notice of a small open stable where a few horses were stalled. She strode toward it, careful not to make a sound, the girl trailing like a shadow.

"Can you ride?" Caramyn whispered, gesturing towards the horses.

The girl hesitated, as if to make sure she understood, then nodded boldly.

She had no idea where she was going, but she knew she had to get far from the city whose name she still hadn't learned.

Their horses slogged through the snow with slow, heavy strides, but they covered far more ground than they could've managed without them. They'd escaped the outpost village only to find themselves wandering a barren wasteland of snow that went on for what looked like miles beneath the black starry sky. The wind was intense, and Caramyn thought her teeth would shatter from chattering, even buried beneath the stolen furs. Unrelenting gusts carried a constant shower of snowdust over them, further limiting visibility that was barely there to begin with. There was ice in her eyelashes, ice in her hair, and what felt like even ice in her veins. She tried to instead focus on the stars overhead of this vast white expanse of nothing, and the dancing aurora that she was only accustomed to seeing during Frostlight, yet here seemed to fill the sky with endless, constant color.

The sound of her mount's hooves pounding the powdery fluff below reminded her of the day she'd raced through the forest with Asterious. She failed to stop a small smile that sneaked its way to her lips at the memory. But it quickly faded when she remembered that it was also the day everything had changed. And she wondered if that simple fleeting kind of happiness would ever be within her reach again.

After an hour of wandering, half-frozen and tempted to turn back and risk capture just for the mere hope of warmth, Caramyn noticed a line of shadows stark against the white blanket surrounding them. A soulful sound of hollow chimes reached her ears, carried on the wind, as if drawing her to them. Squinting in the moonlight, her eyes tired by the monotony of endless white tundra, she noticed the dots seemed to be moving. Prompted by a mixture of desperation and curiosity, she rode towards them, the girl riding at a distance behind her, both cautious not to come up too quickly.

Once Caramyn was close enough, the rattle of the chimes grew clearer, and she could make out that the dark silhouettes were those of wagons from a small caravan of travelers. Their wooly goat-like beasts and thick-furred horses shouldered large burdens, and their handlers carried nearly just as much across their bundled backs as they trudged through the snow in thick leather fur-trimmed boots.

Caramyn hoped there might be someone in the caravan who spoke the common tongue. After all, they appeared to be nomads. Perhaps one of them had encountered a Evylerean from below the Silver Spines before.

She waved to them, riding up slowly with her hands visible to show she meant no harm. The girl followed on her pony, silent as usual.

"I mean you no harm." She spoke boldly in her warmest tone, despite the fact that her lips were numb and her jaw felt frozen in place "Do any of you speak the common tongue?"

The travelers halted in their tracks, staring at her with quizzical looks. Even here under the moonlight, it was plain to see the confusion in the tired eyes with which they watched her. Finally, one of them spoke, from the caravan sled laden with chimes carved from what appeared to be bones.

"I do." An elder woman's voice rose from near the back of the caravan. It would've been impossible to tell otherwise, as every bit of her except her eyes was swaddled beneath furs and wool wraps. She stepped forward with spritely energy for her age in her voice. "Who are you?"

Caramyn hesitated, unsure of giving away her name. Even if no one here had known it since she arrived, perhaps it was best to keep it that way considering the circumstances. "Call me Kuhrissi." She said, for some reason clinging to the Silverean word. "I don't know the girl's name. She is Gahmean, I think. Or at least from somewhere in the far West lands. I was hoping someone here might be able to help."

The old woman stared, unmoving and unblinking. "Hmmm." Caramyn wondered if she was studying her, trying to recognize who she might be. What if news had already spread? What if there was some sort of bounty on her already? Would these people try to take them back if they realized they were runaways?

She tensed her leg muscles, ready to send her pudgy horse off into a gallop if need be.

But the woman simply held up a mittened hand and turned her head toward the sky. "We were just about to stop and make camp. We travel at night because the snowstorms can be fierce during the day. But the sun will be up soon, and we are tired." When she looked back down at them, her eyes glinted in the dim light of dawn, revealing the thick white film covering them. She was blind. "You are both welcome to rest in my tent and I can translate...if you can prove you're worthy of it." With a grin, she held out her hand. Caramyn opened her cloak and looked down at the assortment of metal jewelry that adorned her from her preparations back in Ragna's hut. She was no stranger to bargaining stolen gold for survival. The jewels meant nothing to her, and she would give just about anything for even just a flicker of heat from a candle.

She glanced over at her young companion, who was trying to control her feisty pony as it tossed its head impatiently, puffs of white breath blowing as it snorted. Then she dismounted, her bones rigid as icicles, and took a stiff step towards the elder. "Of course," she said, sliding a golden bracelet off her wrist and placing it in the woman's outstretched hand. "A fair exchange."

43

ZERA'S BOW

Caramyn

Caramyn and the girl sat quietly as they watched the nomads set up their tents with the kind of effortless skill only acquired through repetition.

The elder woman, who'd said to call her Zera, offered them each a bowl of some unfamiliar hot liquid. Caramyn accepted, despite her wariness, and only took a few sips of it before desperately wanting more. Whether it was the faint taste of juniper berry that lingered in the spiced sweetness of honey mead or her thirst finally setting in, she didn't know. But it was doing a wonderous job of thawing out her insides.

Once Zera's tent was ready, she ushered them inside.

Zera seemed younger than her voice and clouded eyes would indicate. She moved with swift grace and fluidity, completely unhindered by her blindness. She knelt on the floor, across from Caramyn and the girl, and then gestured for them to do the same. Then she took off her fur hood and pulled down the wool covering over her mouth and nose to reveal more of her deep bronze skin, a flood of warmth in this cold, grey place. "So, you want me to translate, yes?"

"You're...not Silverean?" Caramyn asked.

"Not at all. Most of us in this caravan aren't. We come from all over the place, for various reasons, mostly necessity or desperation. And as your luck would have it, I hail from Gahmea—though what a long time ago that was..."

"Well," Caramyn nodded, still feeling the blood returning to her face. "If you can talk to her..." She glanced at her young companion, who sat with a faraway look in her eyes. "I—I found the girl. She seems lost, and I want to make sure she's safe. But I know nothing about her."

"Hmmm." The woman pursed her weathered lips. "Well, you might start by telling me the whole truth if you expect me to do the same."

Caramyn blinked. "The whole truth? What more do you want?"

"I mean that if you expect me to believe you just found this girl wandering around—-and you both like *that* beneath those cloaks—you're fooling no one but yourself. I know that you were brought here by pirates. Purchased for the House of Hrothvor, the Frostlord of Ironfell, the strongest clan village of the Spires. Yet now you're here. The only thing I don't know is why."

With her mouth agape at all that the woman knew, Caramyn managed to croak out the question. "Why" It seemed absurd to ask. "Why? Because we don't want to freeze to death. Because I refused to be some vile Frostlord's property and object of pleasure..." she took a breath, slowing her words to calm herself before continuing. "And I refused to leave her for him either." She stopped, feeling the eyes of both Zera and the girl on her. Then she looked up. "Will you ask the girl her name for me, please?"

"Well, there it is. That wasn't so hard, was it? Now that I know your heart, I have no use for this in these gods forsaken peaks." Zera tossed the bracelet back to her and lifted her chin. "Now..." she said, "I will translate."

She turned and spoke perfect Gahmean to the girl, who answered back timidly. "Her name is Narahbi."

"Narahbi," Caramyn repeated. "That's quite lovely."

"She also asked me to thank you. I told her to call you *Kuhrissi*, though make no mistake, I know that isn't your real name. You hail from Evylere. And you're running from something."

"How do you know all this about me?" Caramyn snapped, feeling vulnerable.

"My dear, Gahmea is not renown for the same kind of magic Evylere once boasted. Our people were blessed by the Shattering in other ways. Some can shift the sands with their mere voices, some can shape glass, bone, and sunstone with their touch, and others see far beyond horizons into past, present, and future." Zera paused. "I am one of those. I believe your people call us Seers."

"Well..." Caramyn stammered, still trying to choose her words carefully, though she should've known by now it was a fool's plan to try to hide anything from this woman. "You're right about Evylere. But I'm not running from anything. In fact, I want to get back."

"Ah yes. You do." Zera grinned slyly, "But there is still something you're running from. You've almost convinced yourself otherwise. And that's exactly what it is. You're running from yourself, child."

Caramyn swallowed, a tickle in her chest welling up as she clenched her fingers in her palm. "That's not what I asked you to do. Just...just tell me about the girl. How did she get here? Ask her that."

Zera addressed Narahbi once more. They exchanged a few words, and Caramyn noted the desperate expression on Narahbi's face as she spoke, her deep brown eyes glossy. Finally Zera turned back to Caramyn.

"She says her parents sold her to settle a debt. Gahmea's High Council has forbidden slaves of any kind, so they could only hope to sell her across borders. She's very grateful for what you did. But she can't go back home to her family. They'd send her right back or sell her again elsewhere." Zera paused, looking the girl over. She reached over and brushed a loose hair back from her face and began speaking again to the girl in the Gahmean tongue.

"I offered her an apprenticeship with me. She can stay with our caravan and assist us, until she's old enough to decide if she'd prefer a life below the mountains. We always need more hands. And if she begins to show Seer or sand singer abilities as she grows in age, then I'll mentor her. She's right at the age when most Seers would begin to realize their abilities, but it must be nurtured or it will never develop past unclear visions and blurry dreams...and if it is suppressed, it often leads to a catastrophic unraveling of their power."

Perhaps that was what happened to Sinevia. Shadows or not, it was no wonder she succumbed to the overwhelm of having to hide herself within her own father's walls. No wonder it had led to a fracturing of her soul...

And no wonder running from her own cursed blood had led to hers...

Caramyn looked at Narahbi. At least this would spare her from such fates. "Is that what you want?" She asked her. wanting to assure she was doing right by the girl. "Do you agree to this?" Zera translated the offer and the question.

Narahbi nodded with confidence.

"Then welcome home, Narahbi." Caramyn agreed, studying the contents of the tent around them. Beside Zera's bed, there were jars and chests of all sorts, and a crate containing some scrolls, carving knives, and weaving sticks. From a small hook hung some talismans and bone chimes. But it was a well-crafted ivory bow leaning against the tent's support that caught her eye.

"How much for that bow and a quiver of arrows?" Caramyn asked suddenly.

"Oh," Zera turned around to look. "That's not for sale, dear one. That's my hunting bow."

"How can you hunt blind?" Caramyn asked.

"There are ways of seeing that have nothing to do with eyes." Zera smirked.

Caramyn ran her fingers along the curve of the bow. "It's a fine weapon. I'll give you anything on me." She reached up and tore a golden circlet from her head. It was inlaid with the finest gems and rubies and had been woven into her hair until this moment. "This?" She held it out to the woman. "Surely this is enough."

Zera took the jewelry and felt around its ridges and stones carefully before speaking again.

"I have a better idea," she snickered. "You keep the tiara, and you prove to me that you're worthy of the bow."

"And how exactly do you want me to do that?" Caramyn leaned forward.

"Stay with us for four nights. Go hunt for us. All of us. Prove you can use it, and I'll let you keep it."

Caramyn pondered the idea for a moment and agreed. She was confident in her abilities with a bow. She almost never missed a target during her time in the Shadow Woods, using only a bow she'd handcrafted from the trees around her until she was able to purchase a better one.

This bow of Zera's was of the highest quality, carved from yew wood and decorated with ivory and intricate carvings all along its length. She longed to hold the weapon, her hand on the shaped grip, the string taut against her fingers. There was no doubt in her mind that she couldn't easily take down prey with such a bow in her possession. As long as she could find something to take down in this frozen wasteland...

"I'll do it," she said, standing to reach for the bow. "But I'm gone after the fourth night. No exceptions."

"That's the deal." Zera smiled. "We're glad to have you along."

So Caramyn remained with the caravan to fulfill her obligation, eager to relish the feeling of a bow in her hand once again. The first night, she crept out into the tundra and returned with two handfuls of snow hares. She'd anticipated difficulty in finding the prey, especially without Nocthar. But it was as if standing under the aurora-kissed night sky, alone in the barren snowy wastelands, without twisted trees and branches she was so accustomed to using for cover and stealth had forced her to awaken some part of her senses she hadn't known existed—some otherworldly part of herself that made her almost feel...magic.

It made sense. These shrouded peaks were ancient, and would've been the first to have been touched by the divine fragments in the Shattering that made the realms and the magic in them. Maybe that explained the constant color dancing above that only appeared on Frostlight everywhere else. And maybe it explained why the Shadowbloods were created far, far from here, deep in the wilderness by an outcast god who saw the darkness already in their hearts and wanted to mark them with it forever. Perhaps the closer she stood to the sky, the closer she'd get to the Light. She didn't seek the favor of any long dead gods, but perhaps for a fleeting moment, she could almost believe she wasn't a mistake.

On the second night she stood and listened to the gentle whistle of the frosty breeze, almost feeling the touch of her mother's wind magic on her skin. And she felt the snow beneath her boots, ignoring the wintry bite of the cold seeping through them, and something—something in her blood—guided her to wherever the prey was, just as it'd guided her to the letter in the library.

A snow lynx.

She would return, feeling something refreshed in her spirit, and Zera would help prepare the meals and talk with her and Narahbi.

On the third night she relied once again on that magic sense of blood and air to show her where to go, and it took two men from the caravan to carry back the great winter ice-stag she'd found.

That night, the caravan celebrated their feast, building a large fire around their camp and playing instruments that made Caramyn's heart sing. She sat swaying to the hum of the flutes and strings as the men carved into the roasted venison, and Zera blessed it as a favor from the gods, both Gahmean and Silverean.

Narahbi danced around the fire with a boy her age, smiling with stars in her eyes, and Caramyn thought of Asterious as she watched them. By now she'd accepted that he really must have hated her. It was the only way she could move on. Wryan was his right-hand man, and if he did this to her, Asterious had to have known. And he didn't care.

As he shouldn't. And neither should she.

He hid behind lies, and so did she, but at least she hadn't denied it. In the end, they both refused to fully remove the masks, and this was the outcome. And they deserved nothing less than to despise the other for exposing the darkness they already saw within themselves.

She wasn't meant for Asterious' world. Shattered gods, she was starting to think she wasn't meant for any world at all. And if her heart was too dark for Asterious—her broken magic too heavy to bear—he wasn't worthy of it anyway.

Zera brought a plate of deer meat and ale over to Caramyn as the great fire flickered, casting shadows on the golden sand. "You aren't going to eat, Kuhrissi? The first cut is reserved for the huntress. You'll offend the gods to waste it."

Caramyn took the plate and gnawed on a bit of meat. It was tender, and much more flavorful than any deer she'd ever hunted in the Shadow Woods. "These people celebrate well. I never had the chance to attend the feasts where I grew up. I always watched from afar."

"They judged you harshly. Because of that marking on your arm, yes?" Zera sat beside her, sucking the meat off a bone like it would be her last.

Caramyn startled at the mention, and Zera clearly noticed enough to explain. "I sense it. Shadow magic and something...something else. Something even I can't see clearly."

"They had a reason to." Caramyn watched the fire. "The King convinced everyone all magic was evil. He made them believe it was the reason for all their problems. So, when your story is already written for you—twisted before you can even tell it, let alone understand it yourself—it's hard for people to see you as anything other than a threat."

Zera sighed heavily as she tapped Caramyn's arm. "The mark of a Shadowblood isn't a curse unless you choose to let it be one. Shadowbloods were feared, yes, simply because they were powerful. And much harder to read because they are far more complex than most." She smiled a smile that warmed Caramyn more than the drink in her hand.

The hair on Caramyn's neck stood straight. Zera couldn't physically see the veins forming a tree and the deliberate pattern of the roots beneath it, but that had yet to limit her. Caramyn rolled up her sleeve, desperate for something—anything—this woman might be able to tell her. "The only other time I've seen anything like this mark was on a soldier whose body had been brought back from the dead."

Zera leaned in close, lifting a hand. "There is no magic that can truly resurrect the dead...and the distorted life it gives is not without great consequence." She touched her fingers to Caramyn's arm. "Let me feel the marking. Perhaps I can identify it."

Caramyn shifted and turned her inner forearm towards the woman, holding still as Zera removed her gloves and slid her fingers along the vein cluster of crackling lines like twisted brambles that that joined in the center like a twisting tree trunk in the hollow of her elbow. She traced the path where the trunk spread into roots, and the lines sharpened into that three-lined forked sigil that trickled like lightning toward her wrist.

"This...this is very much like a forbidden binding rune of the old religion, used to tether a life to something else, mostly used to take control of a living being. To put them under the dominion of their anchor." Zera's voice quivered ever so slightly. "I suppose in some rare cases it could be used in effort to resurrect the dead, perhaps by binding a dead soul to a power source strong enough to revive it...perhaps if someone powerful truly knew what they were doing..."

The vision of the Shadow soldier's lifeless gray skin flashed before her eyes, the haunting picture of the body lying there with symbols of magic carved across the rotting corpse. A vessel reanimated solely to be Sinevia's puppet.

"I am under no one's dominion. I am no one's puppet." Caramyn sat upright defensively, as a feeling of violation crept in. "I was born like this. It can't be the same thing." She refused to believe it could be.

"I wish I could tell you more," Zera sighed. "But so much of you is shrouded, as if behind a veil. You are so much more than what I can perceive."

Caramyn couldn't find the words to respond, and instead shook her head and dropped her shoulders, for once again, she was left with more questions than answers. She closed her eyes, letting the steady drums and flutes of the feast music lift her spirit.

She thought of Asterious and loathed herself for it. It was a wound she couldn't seem to stop reopening—to imagine what it might've felt like to dance to music like this with him, to twirl carefree in that glorious ballroom in Vaerwynd Castle without the darkness breathing down her neck. She pinched her eyes shut, but the memory only sharpened. The way he'd made her feel almost human, almost safe, and the quiet pull he had set in her heart. It was all reduced to ash now. And better for it, because it was never real anyway.

A touch from Zera made her jump. She opened her eyes, realizing how desperately strange she must have looked. But Zera only nodded, as if she knew exactly what she'd been thinking about.

"Back in Gahmea we believe the wind is sacred—the messenger of the old gods." Zera's change in tone made Caramyn open her eyes. "Tell it your message and send it to him on the wind."

To him.

She knew.

Caramyn felt her face getting hot at how foolish she must seem. She didn't like the thought of putting her trust in gods, or magic, or whatever else was out there, when she'd made it this far by the faith she had in herself. But something in her craved rest in something stronger, just for a moment, even if it was just pretend. So, when she next heard the caravan chimes, she laid her burden into the wind. And as the breeze swept over her skin as though it had heard her thoughts, she told it just what to say.

On the final night, Zera insisted there was still enough leftover meat from the stag that she didn't have to hunt. But something back out on the silent, ancient ice plains called to Caramyn, and she wanted to go anyway.

She packed for her journey back home, surprised at the heaviness she felt in her heart at the thought of leaving in the morning. She'd grown close to Zera, and enjoyed their meals and chats. Zera often shared with her stories of the caravan's travels and traditional remedies from the desert plants of her homeland. She even taught her some Gahmean and Silverean words that would be helpful as she navigated this land alone.

She'd proven herself worthy of the bow, but Zera had left her with a much greater gift, whether she'd meant to or not.

Hope.

She would return home, to her Shadows, the only truths that had never betrayed her, and together they would never let anyone in again. Certainly not Asterious. Because he was a lying Blackwynd prince, and she was the witch of the woods.

But first she had one last hunt to complete.

She was dressed for the tundra, bow strung and in hand, as she glanced at the bundle of belongings and food for her departure in the morning, when something from outside—from above—called her attention. It was a sound so familiar she almost convinced herself it was her imagination. But when it called again, she couldn't deny it amidst the sound of beating wings. Her heart swelled at the sound. She knew those wings. She knew that call.

She ran out of the tent, looking desperately for any glimpse of a raven in the snow. But instead, she only found empty, frozen nothingness.

44
TO THE WOLVES

Caramyn

She set out for the plains, venturing further than she had before. Far enough that she could make out a low glimmer of orange lights in the distance from a tiny clan village where the plains ended and sloped back down into jagged mountain edges. It wasn't Ironfell, but it was similar enough.

She lurked, creeping along as deep snow crunched beneath her boots, listening for the echoes of the heartbeat of any creature that might be nearby. Her breath, silent and steady, warmed her nose as she breathed into her woolen face covering.

And then, a crisp cold whistle whirred past her just before snow plopped from the edge of a snowbank behind her.

An iron-tipped arrow.

She twisted to see it just before a second one flew and lodged itself next to the other. And when she glanced back, she was surrounded, flanked by clansmen from all sides.

Her luck had run out. She was wanted. And they had found her. And if that was the case, they likely didn't want her dead. She was worth much more alive.

And who knew what punishment would await her after they collected their bounty.

There were eight of them. One moved toward her—the leader of the group, his cold eyes more crystalline than the snow flurries dusting the air. "You come quietly, and you might still recognize yourself when we're done with you," he said. "You resist, and we will return you broken and so ruined, even the wolves won't want what's left."

They closed around her, axes and spears raised, eyes raking over her like hot coals. She swallowed down a gulp of frigid air, the sting in her lungs only worsening the way her chest tightened. There was nowhere to go. They backed her against the snowbank, like ravenous animals playing with their food. She raised her bow, arms trembling from fear more than cold. She knew it wouldn't save her, but she would not go willingly. She fired an arrow before they could blink, and struck a man straight through the eye.

The leader lunged at her, gripping her shoulder so hard she thought it might shatter, and threw her to the ground. She reached for her hunting knife, fumbling as he crouched down and wrapped his hand around her jaw, bringing her face to his.

"The wolves it is," he sneered. His grip tightened and the other men closed in.

A flash of black feathers streaked across the sky behind him. A monstrous growl and a familiar chilling howl pierced the night.

No, it can't be.

And then a force like a stone wall slammed into the man, ripping her from his grasp and leaving his torch dropped beside her so that she could clearly see his fate at the mercy of his attacker.

At the mercy of the wolf beast.

It dragged him away between massive jaws, bones crunching as the great wolf hurled the man to the ground before tearing him open with those vicious blades of teeth. A spray of crimson rained down and stained the snow red. Snarls mingled with the sound of flesh and tendons tearing filled the air.

Nauseated and horrified, Caramyn's heart raced so wildly she thought it might burst through her ribs. She fought to keep her breathing steady as her blood ran cold watching the wolf mangle this man just steps away from her.

The hard snow cracked beneath the beast with each movement, as though the earth might collapse under its strength. Shouts arose from the other men as they sent a barrage of spears and arrows flying at the beast. Even with their mighty Silverean stature and strength, they looked like frail adolescents compared to the colossal monster. Their weapons struck the wolf, but the creature hardly seemed weakened.

It charged at them, blood dripping from its mouth and eyes glowing ghostly white. With ease, it grasped the nearest man in its jaws and flung away a handful of others with one swipe of its claws. The remaining three tried to flee, but the wolf was already upon them, a hellish blur of black and white. It slammed the first man into the ground, jaws closing with a wet snap and tearing away in a spray of blood. The second couldn't even choke out a scream before claws tore him open from shoulder to hip and tossed him aside like a skinned deer. The last managed to run a few steps before the wolf dragged him down, fangs raking deep as it shook him until the snow beneath was steaming scarlet.

The creature released a guttural roar and Caramyn scrambled across the snow to hide in a dip at the snowbank's edge. But the wolf took notice. It stopped to smell the air in a moment that felt like time had stopped. It turned its blood-soaked nose in her direction, as if some familiar scent had pulled it there, and those grim moonbeam eyes caught her in their hold. Eyes that she was certain hid a prince behind them. Eyes that she had to aim for if there was any hope of making it out of there alive.

The wolf catapulted towards her. Her hands shook as she readied an arrow, drawing her bow back as tightly as her shoulders could manage. But her trembling fingers faltered, and she released the arrow too early. It struck the wolf's shoulder and did no more damage than the many arrows and spears already jutting from his body.

She drew another arrow as she leapt to her feet, sprinting across the snow, glancing back as the wolf shortened the distance between them with ease. It pounced, and she ducked so that it leapt over her. The earth rattled when it landed in front of her, and she skidded to a stop so quickly she nearly tumbled over. Now she faced the beast, its hungry eyes locked on her like a target.

In an instant, black feathers broke the trance. Nocthar soared between them, his wings cutting through the air like knives. And the wolf stilled, as if captivated or exhausted, or perhaps both.

She inched towards the beast with caution, ready to turn and run if it so much as flinched, and fearful of even taking a breath too quickly. Even in the cold night air, she was dewy with sweat from fear.

While she studied the wolf beast's face, a strange comfort washed over her, as though she'd just settled into some place familiar in her mind. A place that felt like home.

Then the beast blinked, slowly, strangely, and when it opened its eyes, they were no longer that unnerving glowing empty white, but instead a calm, steely, starlit grey. Nocthar screeched from above and landed gently on the beast's heaving back. A sign that she was safe.

She trusted Nocthar, no matter how absurd it seemed, and some part of her recklessly, stupidly, yearned to find the man buried within this beast. Knees threatening to buckle, she stepped forward and knelt beside the wolf, laying her bow on the ground. If she was going to die here anyway, it might as well be on her own terms. Better this way than being chased like a frightened rabbit across this never-ending stretch of snow.

"Asterious?" She whispered.

A low growl made her shudder as his eyes focused on her once again.

He exhaled, and black mist appeared, creeping over his body. The fur and armor-like hide faded, as if dissolving into the mist, leaving behind human skin and muscle. She touched his arm through the black fog, as the mist transformed the furry, sinewy limb into smooth flesh. Claws became fingers. The bloody snout became a face—the familiar, beautiful, and weary face of the Lightborn Prince of Blackwynd.

He lay before her, unclothed. He blinked with tears in his eyes, but he couldn't seem to speak. Caramyn, still reeling from what she'd just seen, glanced at the spears and arrows in his back, and her own arrow embedded in his left shoulder, where crackling veins of black scars covered that half of his body, as if crawling up and around his waist and ribcage. As if reaching toward his heart. And between them were dozens, if not hundreds, of flesh scars, from deep wounds that had long healed.

"Cara...Cara..." He tried to stammer out something but couldn't get any farther. He had so much to explain, and some part of her still hated him, but she pushed that aside. His wounds were already taking their toll in his human form, and if the blood loss didn't kill him, the cold would. Questions could wait. For now, she had to keep him alive.

Putting aside her shock, she tried desperately to move Asterious, but she lacked the strength. He groaned like a man drunk on wine, and she stayed with him, removing her fur coat and cloak to give to him. As she moved to cover his naked body, she couldn't stop herself from staring. Her wandering gaze took in every tensed muscle, every well-formed ridge and bulging vein decorating his powerful build. She didn't mean to draw in a breath so loudly at the sight of him, but she did, and she was sure he'd heard it, much to her embarrassment.

Why was he here?

The questions burned through Caramyn as she struggled to drag him as far as she could, past the scattered, mangled bodies in the snow. But before long, she could pull him along no farther. She collapsed beside him, gasping from the effort and the frigid air burning her lungs.

"I can't believe you came for me." She couldn't manage to hold back. It burst forth from her lips like rushing water from a dam.

The prince gazed up at her, weak, battered, exhausted, but still managed to string together his hoarse reply. "I can't believe I let you go."

45
NO MORE SECRETS

Asterious

With sore muscles that flinched with each breath, the prince lay shivering beneath the cloak that Caramyn had laid over him. Normally his Lightborn magic kept him from feeling the wounds until much later, but his body was already worn down from his relentless trek across the Silver Spines. But though the injuries were significant, nothing had pierced his heart. He wouldn't die from any of it. He could ignore the pain of open flesh on his back, but he couldn't ignore the way he wanted to wither away into darkness, far from where Caramyn could see him like this. This was not the way he'd hoped to find her.

"Did...did I hurt you?" he asked desperately.

"No." She placed a gentle hand on his chest, calming his breathing at her touch. As she leaned over him, the stars framing her face in the night sky behind her, he longed to reach up and touch her. To hold the face of the woman who had not left his thoughts since she vanished and lose himself in those enchanting eyes of amethyst galaxies.

But those eyes had grown cold, and he turned away. How could she be gentle to him? After everything he'd done. After seeing him rip those men apart. After seeing him for the beast he was.

The arrow wound from Caramyn in his shoulder stung particularly, the bloodied tender flesh around it throbbing. The iron tipped spears in his back ached too, but the skin of his wolf form was thick enough to have kept them from penetrating too deep into the muscle.

"Will you take them out?" He uttered between labored gasps.

Caramyn's eyes widened. "You'll bleed out right here. We can't just—"

"No," he huffed. "I won't. I mean...yes, I will bleed—but I will not die. I cannot die."

Her face twisted in clear confusion. He knew she wouldn't understand. But he didn't have the strength to say everything now. "Believe me," he mustered a smile. "I've tried."

"What?" Caramyn did not seem amused by his efforts to reassure her.

"A curse. A terrible curse...that keeps me alive—not by blood..." he sputtered. "...but by a heart replaced with Shadow. Just please...remove the spears. Then I can try to walk."

He could see her hesitation and her horror all at once. None of this was supposed to happen. None of this was supposed to be explained this way.

But she did it. She carefully pulled out each spear—three of them, to be exact. He gritted his teeth as each one tore through his skin once more as she freed the sharp tips from his flesh. They didn't have hooks, at least, thankfully, and slid out with relative ease. But the arrow...it didn't seem as promising.

"I'm not taking that one out here," Caramyn grumbled. "I don't care what you say, it's embedded far too deep. I'll wait until we can get somewhere safe to treat your wounds." She paused and her gaze caught his. "And you can explain this all to me."

Asterious rose to his feet, pulling the cloak around himself as tightly as possible to fight off the bitter cold against his bare skin. Each step through the snow made his feet grow increasingly numb, as he left a trail of red blots behind him. Caramyn did her best to support him, but it wasn't enough. They couldn't continue this way, with him slowing her down like this. She'd freeze to death.

"I didn't come all this way so you could die on my behalf," Asterious muttered. "Put the cloak back on. You're freezing."

Just as she opened her mouth, presumably to argue, a horse snorted in the distance. Caramyn glanced up, grabbing her bow and nocking an arrow without skipping a beat. The raven fluttered around her in sweeping patterns, as if in a desperate attempt to guard the two of them. And then her protective stance softened, and she breathed out. "I didn't think it'd work," she said, almost laughing.

"What worked?" He asked faintly, squinting to make out the faint outline of a figure walking across the snow towards them beside a hefty mammoth of a horse. He thought perhaps he was hallucinating from the blood trickling down his back. But Caramyn assured him it was very real, even as his vision darkened the closer the figure came.

"I called someone...on the wind," Caramyn said, her voice sounding miles away. "A friend."

He didn't remember closing his eyes, but when he opened them, he was warm and staring up at dark smoke puffing up to the night sky through a hole in the roof of a large tent. His first thought was Caramyn. He shot up, the cloak falling off him and exposing his bare chest and abdomen. Her voice startled him.

"Welcome back." There was an icy edge in her voice colder than anything he'd faced in these mountains. She sat beside him, ringing out a bloody wet rag into a bucket of red water. "Lie back down so I can finish cleaning these." She touched her palm to his bare chest, pushing him back down to the cot on which he rested.

"Where am I?" he breathed.

"Zera's tent. She's helped me in many ways since I've been here." She turned and addressed a young girl who'd just entered the tent. "Narahbi, can you please bring more *arrjhu?*"

The girl left. Asterious raised an eyebrow. Caramyn noticed. "It means water," she said flatly, with no further explanation. Then she gave no warning before dousing his wounds with liquid from a flask. The overpowering smell of licorice permeated the air as Asterious grimaced in pain, gritting his teeth to keep from yelping at the burning sensation. When he focused again, Caramyn was holding a blade to the flame of a burning candle, her face stoic. "I'm going to remove the arrow now. It's going to hurt."

She dug the blade into flesh, carefully working the arrow tip loose to keep the hooks from ripping him open further when she pulled it out. Asterious fixated on a talisman hanging from the tent wall, his mind going to places that were now second nature.

Train the body not to react and neither will the mind...or the heart.

"I never thought someone could be so emotionless while having an arrow removed. But then again, I've only ever removed them from dead men." Caramyn grumbled.

"I have plenty of experience with pain."

She tossed the arrow aside. "Is that another one of your cryptic clues or can I expect an explanation this time?"

"I will tell you everything...I promise..." Asterious hardly knew where to begin.

She said nothing as she wiped away the last of the blood and then stood to rummage through a basket, pulling out a hook needle and line, each movement swift, purposeful, and defensive.

Asterious shifted in his cot. "But first tell me, please. Have...have you been safe?" he asked, his jaw tightening at the thought. "Has anyone here touched you? Tell me, and I'll scatter their pieces throughout these mountains. And don't try to lie to me."

"I am unharmed and untouched. And I survived. Self-sufficient, remember?" She sat down beside him again, voice unwavering. She didn't even look at him. It burned like salt in a wound, but she had every right to be withdrawn. She had every right to hate him, and she should have left him on the snow, bleeding and naked.

"I know you're more than capable of taking care of yourself—"

"Then why did you come here? After everything you said. After telling me you never wanted to see me again?"

"Because..." he turned his body at her urging, where she began stitching the first wound on his back. "I had to make sure you were safe. And fearing that you weren't was a torture I had yet to experience."

She continued working quietly, with no reaction. No response.

"Caramyn," he breathed. "Are you afraid of me? Of what I am?"

She hesitated before answering, pausing her stitch. "How could I not be? Especially when I don't even understand what it is that you are."

"I wasn't always like this." Asterious touched the scars at his chest, his voice weary. "When I was a boy, and Daemar finally grew tired of Elysia's pleas to recognize me as his heir, he offered her a deal. If I could pass his trials, he would accept me as his son and place me in his court." Asterious swallowed. "I was barely old enough to even grasp the weight of it, but I still managed to complete whatever ludicrous tasks Daemar thought up for me, whether by luck or skill. They started out simple enough. Like finding a rogue arrow fired into the forest or harnessing the stable's most unruly stallion. But with each success, the trials grew more sadistic. Things like choosing the cup of wine that wasn't poisoned, walking barefoot over hot embers, standing outside for days without food or water...you get the idea. I'd pass the trial, and then there'd always be 'just one more' before I'd be worthy of a father's acceptance...worthy to be an heir to his kingdom. Until I finally failed. I was put in an arena with nothing but a sword, my hand nearly too small to grasp the hilt. There was a door...and my task was to kill whatever was behind it..."

He closed his eyes, remembering his mother's words as she kissed his forehead before he entered the arena.

It's the only way to take what is rightfully yours. I know you can do this, my son. You are stronger than whatever waits beyond... Don't be afraid.

"And then?" Caramyn's voice pulled him back to the present as she finished the stitch. "What was behind it?"

Asterious sat up slowly and turned to face her, his eyes flicking to hers. "A wolf." Some horrific feeling hit Asterious like a wave. He'd delved too deep into this memory he'd tried so hard to forget. "A snarling, rabid wolf, with gleaming yellow eyes. I fought...and I might've killed it. But I realized too late the sword I was given was blunt."

He still heard his father's voice from the platform where he watched.

He's only a child. We wouldn't want him to harm himself on a sharp blade.

His mother screaming. Pleading.

I swear, Daemar, I swear on my son's life, you will pay! You stole my honor, my kingdom, and now my child. I will have my vengeance for all you have done to me and my people. I swear it!

He could still feel his mother's hot tears as she rocked his bloodied, lifeless body back and forth in her arms—

"That's why you acted so strange in the arena that day." Caramyn spoke so low it was almost a whisper. Asterious offered a subtle nod of confirmation, and her violet eyes brimmed with the light of something unnamed. She leaned in, her shadow dancing on the walls of the tent by the flickering of the fire.

Asterious licked his lips before he continued, distracting himself from the lump forming in his throat. "I was dying. My mother took me somewhere far away after that. I don't know what happened there, except that when I returned, I was no longer on the brink of death. I was completely healed—but at the cost of becoming...this. Left with no memory of how it came to be, except a single small vein of Shadow that would end up taking me over like a weed...claiming more of my body each time I succumbed to the beast within. It crept farther across my skin, branching out whenever I spilled blood—see, even now, there are seven more branching out here from the men I killed tonight."

He pointed to the thin tendrils covering most of his torso. Caramyn tilted her head, her brow furrowed as she scooted closer, examining the black raised veins working their way to the center of his chest. As she studied them, he went on.

"Because I technically survived the last trial, my father twisted the bargain and agreed to make me part of his court...as his killer." Asterious stared at the blood still caked beneath his fingernails. "I was not the son he wanted. But I could be the perfect executioner. That's when he imprisoned my mother somewhere I could not find her, and it became his leverage—the hope that one day I could save her. He quickly learned that fear or anger made the beast take over. And so, he used me...Turned me into nothing more than a weapon and a message to his enemies—disposing of them by locking them in a prison cell with me, letting terror do the rest. That cell became my home from the day I returned from death until the day I finally escaped. Until I learned how to gain control of the beast by numbing myself to fear, anger, and any emotion in between. Until I learned to feel...nothing, by punishing myself for the monster I am."

He gestured to the scars that marred his flesh from the length of his arms to the skin beneath the Shadow veins. The raised lines of white and pinkish pale ridges from uneven healing and jagged blades that had cut crooked and deep.

Caramyn shifted uneasily, still holding the needle and thread. "Then why did it come back? Why did you lose control of it at the Forbidden Court?"

"That's just it," Asterious whimpered. "I hadn't...until you came. And I didn't understand it. I didn't know why your presence was making me lose myself again. So when you turned out to be a Shadowblood, I thought it was because of your Shadow magic. But now I realize...it was because..." his voice gave like cracking ice.

Caramyn's eyes softened, warmth blooming there as she touched his hand, and he knew, without her saying a word, that it might destroy him if he couldn't muster the courage to finish the thought. "Because I was terrified of the possibility that I'd begun to care for you."

The tent fell silent. Even the crackling fire seemed to have quieted. Asterious stared at her, the pain of where the arrow had been suddenly throbbing through his chest. Or perhaps it was the feeling of his heart growing heavy, weighted with sorrow as he laid out his dark secrets for her to see. Most of his men knew. Azell knew. But he had never wanted Caramyn to know.

He squeezed her hand. "Please say something." He said finally, his words like shaky whispers.

Caramyn stared at him, drawing a breath as she straightened herself. "So, my heart is not too dark for you, then? You think you can look past the mark of a Shadowblood?"

The prince stared at her, a desperate look in his eyes. "I can look past anything as long as I'm looking at you," he said. "But I don't want to look past it. I want to see all of it—all of you. You've shown me how beautiful darkness can be. But you also hold so tightly to your darkness that you forget there is Light in you, too."

She smiled for a breath and then curled her fingers around his hand tightly. "Spoken like a true hypocrite."

"You call me a hypocrite, and you're right. So don't forgive me. Damn me. Damn me to hell for all I care. Just don't leave me again."

Caramyn pushed her forehead to his, closing her eyes. He breathed in her sweet scent and let the warmth of the gentle air from her nostrils trickle over him.

"Then let's stop trying to hide from each other." She breathed in deeply. "We have both been forced to become what we never wanted to be. I know what it's like to spend each day fighting the darkness inside you—fighting to prove to yourself that you're not the monster everyone believes you to be."

"So where does that leave us?" Asterious asked the question, his breath grazing her lips.

She leaned in, letting her words linger against his mouth. "Two monsters in the dark, helping each other find the Light. No more secrets."

"No more secrets." He repeated.

Her lips brushed his. Brief, barely there—and it was enough.

He felt it immediately. The bloodthirst, the coiled need to kill. Hatred and fear surged together, a sickening rush of sensation as control began to slip. It was the same feeling that always came just before the beast possessed him. His worst fear, realized in a single breath.

He couldn't touch her like this. Couldn't allow himself this closeness. Her presence overwhelmed his senses, her kiss dragging him toward depths he might never crawl back from. And if he ever let it happen again—if he ever forgot himself for even a moment—he knew with chilling certainty that he might kill her.

46

THE BLACKHEART

Caramyn

The tent flaps rustled, and they drew apart, the moment breaking like fragile glass. Caramyn was still reeling, her skin alight where he'd touched her, her pulse echoing the memory of it. Every instinct urged her to close the distance again, to sink back into Asterious, to reclaim the fleeting warmth of his mouth against hers, but she stayed where she was, pushing it all away as Narahbi returned, this time with Zera at her side. Nocthar flew in along with them and fluttered to perch on a basket handle.

Zera was carrying a bundle of clothes, and Narahbi held two steaming cups of tea that she offered to each of them.

"I see Kuhrissi has brought back a *kuhrissi.*" Zera noted as Nocthar fluttered to Caramyn's shoulder. Then her gaze flicked to Asterious. "And oh, good, he's awake." She crooned with a sly smile and a wink. "I can excuse you from your hunting duties tonight, because you still managed to return with quite a handsome prize."

Carmyn noted the way Asterious' face flushed at the woman's teasing and found it endearing.

"Thank you," Asterious said. "For everything. For this. For helping Caramyn."

Zera gave him an acknowledging nod, and then her eyes creased with that mischievous smile again, gesturing at the needle in Caramyn's hand. "Are you ever going to finish stitching him up? I understand if you've been distracted."

Caramyn rolled her eyes playfully, but she, too, felt her face warm at the taunt. "She's right. Hold still." She refocused on the arrow wound at Asterious' shoulder.

As she leaned forward to suture him, she fought to ignore the surge of heat and desire that coursed through her when she touched him again. She tried to keep her eyes on the wound as she threaded the line through, but she couldn't help stealing glances every now and the way his muscles flexed between each needle prick. A desperation wound tightly inside her, an ache in her core, taut and distracting. But she clenched her jaw shut and focused, drawing the stitch closed with a sharp, deliberate pull.

She noticed the prince watching her, his eyes following her every movement. She leaned in closer to tie off the string, her face inches from his once more. She tightened and cut the last bit of thread, fighting fiercely to ignore the desire humming in her veins.

"How did you do it?" Zera's voice broke the tension, her presence bold and unyielding as she tossed a wool shirt and pants in Asterious' lap. "How did you survive crossing these peaks alone, and in so little time?"

Asterious glanced at Caramyn and then back at Zera. "I didn't. The wolf did. I survived with the heightened senses and strength it lends me. It can endure what a man cannot. I scoured the Silver Spines from one end to the other until I picked up her scent. It was the longest I've ever remained at the beast's mercy. I was even afraid I might not be able to come back from it. But it was the only way I could hope to find her."

Caramyn watched his eyes as he spoke. The way one gleamed silver in the firelight when he turned his head, like a remnant of the untamed predator within him.

He'd come for her. Asterious had left his kingdom and come for her. He'd crossed these uncrossable mountains in a form he hated more than anything, yet was willing to endure...for her.

"You're a Seer. I know by the talismans. What else do you know about me? Can you tell me where my mother is?" Asterious asked, sitting with the clothes bundle bunched in his bare arms.

"You certainly don't waste opportunities," Zera muttered. "I can try...but as you can see, my eyes don't quite work as they once did. It's better if you have something of your mother's that I can touch...something I can feel to link my visions to her."

"The ring?" Caramyn gasped, looking around as if she expected to see it lying nearby.

A defeated look fell over Asterious' face, a flash of sorrow in an almost hopeful moment. "I don't have it. I couldn't carry anything with me here."

It was then that Caramyn thought to tell him what she'd overheard the grave robbers say back in the Woods. She knew that it would likely crush him, but he deserved to know. After all, hadn't they just agreed to no more secrets? She decided she'd tell him at the first chance. But not here. Not in front of Zera and Narahbi.

"Let me try." Zera came closer with a sigh. "If Kuhrissi thinks you were worth dragging back here, perhaps I can at least offer the effort."

The old Seer leaned down to touch Asterious, feeling the scars along his body as she'd touched Caramyn's marking, studying their design with her fingertips. She closed her eyes, as if calling on some ancient magic, summoning a power unseen. Her wrinkled mouth curved into a frown—almost a look of pain, before those cloudy white eyes opened again, staring straight ahead.

"I'm sorry," she murmured, her voice as feeble as her bony fingers. "There is no present or future I can read with your mother in it. But the past is clear enough. She loved you."

"Loved?" Asterious nodded gently, a faint, forced smile settling across his face, but then disappearing as he hung his head. "What does that mean?"

"I cannot say for sure. But perhaps our Kuhrissi can." With that, Zera waved her hand and said something to Narahbi in Gahmean as she gestured for her to follow. They both exited the tent, and left Asterious and Caramyn kneeling before one another.

"Go ahead. Tell me what I already suspect." Asterious swallowed, clutching the clothing in his hands tightly.

Caramyn fidgeted with a piece of twine, staring at it as she formed the words slowly. "I didn't steal your mother's ring off dead bandits—I mean...I *did*—but they weren't already dead when I found them. I...I killed them." It felt strange to say the words out loud, but Asterious seemed unshaken, as if she'd merely told him what she'd eaten for breakfast. "And before I killed them, I heard them talking. Saying that they'd stolen everything from a grave—a royal's grave."

She expected Asterious to be quiet. She expected him to struggle upon hearing it. But she didn't expect him to stare at her with no indication of what he was thinking, unmoving. The silence stretched thin between them as she picked at her nail, unsure of what to say. "I'm sorry I didn't tell you sooner," she added.

Asterious looked away, his mouth drawing tight as his jaw worked beneath the strain. She couldn't tell if it was anger or something closer to resignation. Until he finally spoke.

"I already knew," he said quietly. "I just didn't want to believe it."

He unfolded the clothes before pulling the shirt over his head. "I didn't want to give my father one last victory over me. But like everything else..." His voice hardened. "He took her from me too."

There was nothing Caramyn could say that would soften the blow. She stepped closer anyway, lifting her hand toward his stone-cold face, aching to bridge the distance between them. But he pulled away, and something fragile inside her quietly caved in. Confused, and more hurt than she cared to admit, she let her hand fall.

This wasn't the moment for questions. Whatever he was carrying, he needed to face it alone, and all she could do was give him the space he'd chosen, even as it carved out a hollow in her chest. He reached for the pants and rose to his feet, his lower half no longer obscured by the blankets that had covered him while on the cot.

Then Caramyn realized how long she'd been staring.

"Are you enjoying watching me dress?" He asked, a tinge of warmth returning to his voice, as if he had just taken the news of his mother's death and stuffed it down as fast as possible, adding more confusion to Caramyn's already muddled emotions.

"I was just leaving," she snapped as blood rushed to her cheeks, thinking back to him lying fully naked in the snow. "Besides it's not like I haven't seen all of you already anyway."

"I suppose we now both have that in common with each other." Asterious' words caught her like a sudden snowstorm as she blushed at the memory of standing in front of him, dripping shamelessly in the tub at Vaerwynd castle. Back then she had felt so bold, so careless for what he thought of her. But now, there was some invisible force between them that she couldn't distinguish from a barrier or a bond. And because of that, she stepped out of the tent to join Zera and Narahbi.

"You care for him?" Zera nodded, her dark plum lips parting into a pearly grin.

"Why ask? You already know the answer." Caramyn shook her head.

Zera tilted her head. "In nature, the raven and wolf are bound. The raven flies ahead and sees what the wolf cannot, warning of danger or prey. The wolf is her strength, hunting and fighting where the raven cannot. Alone, they endure. Together, they live."

Caramyn kept her gaze fixed on the approaching dawn, enchanted at the sight of the aurora of colors sweeping over the stark white snow with the promise of morning. The promise of warmth after a long, cold night.

"What did you see when you touched his scars? What are they?" Caramyn asked.

"A countdown." Zera said ominously.

"What do you mean? A countdown to what?"

"Until the beast takes him completely, and he's trapped in that form forever. It feeds on darkness—on fear, pain, grief, but most of all, death. Each life he takes strengthens it, growing the veins, bit by bit, until eventually they reach his heart, overtake it, and he can no longer fight the darkness within himself."

Something sinister gripped Caramyn's own heart, a hopeless, broken feeling of dread and foreboding. The veins were so close to his heart. Mere inches away from completing their dark purpose. She pressed her lips together, still hung on the weight of Zera's words. "How...how many more times can he kill before—"

"One. Maybe two."

Caramyn stared at her, her lips stammering, and her voice hoarse when it finally came. "Is there any way to stop it?"

"*It* is a Blackheart—it's what happens when Shadow magic is used in attempt to heal by someone who has no business using it. Someone powerful enough to do it, but foolish enough to try. Someone desperate enough to try pulling someone back from the edge of death. When a soul is already slipping beyond the reach of Light magic, the Blackheart binds to what remains, keeping the body alive while slowly devouring the soul. In time, it takes full control, until it permanently manifests as the deepest fears of the host." Zera lifted her chin, her calloused eyes bleary. "And there is no way to be rid of it that I know of—except to pass it on to another dying soul, which may very well cost the host the life it was sustaining."

"He was just a child..." Caramyn whispered, imagining the young Asterious, thrown to the mercy of a ravenous wolf, all for the mere hope of earning his father's acceptance. Forced to become the very same bloodthirsty beast that sent him to this fate.

"Yes...he was." The way Zera said the words made Caramyn glance twice at the woman.

"You speak as though you knew him." Caramyn narrowed her eyes, as if trying to see beyond what was in front of her.

"Because I did know him." Zera's voice quaked. "I'm the one who cursed him with the Blackheart. And I've regretted it every day...I recognized him the moment I touched his scars. I knew exactly what they were. And I knew I was the one who caused them."

Caramyn nearly choked on what she'd just heard. The air turned heavy. It took a few breaths too long for the meaning of Zera's words to land, and when they did, it was like a dagger to the heart.

She thought she might suffocate. She stared at Zera, stunned, horrified, her mind spinning like a broken compass. As she searched for the words to demand an explanation, Zera seemed to already understand that one was owed, and offered up the rest without any prodding.

"I was much younger. I was a skilled healer, but I'd never saved anyone so close to death before. His mother brought him to me, years before I had to seek refuge in these mountains. I'll never forget the pain in her eyes. He was a bloodied, battered mess, and there was barely a heartbeat left to save. I told her there was nothing I could do, but she begged me with all the fierceness of a mother. She cried, bargained, pleaded with me to try." Zera spoke through broken sobs now, each one stronger than the last. "I...I couldn't find it in me to turn her away. To let her watch her son die in her arms at my doorstep. I...I thought I understood the consequences...I thought maybe it would be worth it. I warned her. I knew Shadow magic came with a price. But neither she nor I could have imagined how high a price it would be."

"They left, and she thanked me, and the sound of her gratitude haunted me every day after, leaving me to wonder what would become of that poor boy...until now."

Zera's words echoed around in Caramyn's head, snaking their way through her thoughts like vile serpents. She wasn't angry with Zera. Her remorse seemed true, her inner turmoil genuine. But none of that helped Caramyn to see the path forward. None of that changed the fact that behind her, on the other side of the tent, was a man cursed by a darkness so deep it might destroy them both long before they found a way to outrun it. And she had been the one to reawaken it.

And then the question plagued her. Did he know? Did he know how close he was? How many kills he had left before he became the beast forever? Did he know that he could never be free of it, without damning someone else to the same fate? "You should tell him." She finally managed to utter to Zera.

And then the tent doors stirred behind them, and Asterious emerged, the image of a hardened hunter in the midst of the cruelest winter. He was clad in thick wools and leather boots, and a cloak lined with stone-colored fur drawn closed around his shoulders. His once regal air now partly eclipsed by the rugged edge of a weathered warrior. Unshaven dark scruff shadowed his jaw and chin, accentuating sturdy cheekbones beneath that steel-hard gaze. His hair was a touch longer than when Caramyn had first met him, stray midnight locks falling in sharp waves across his forehead and brows, framing his face.

"No need," he muttered as he ducked beneath the tent entrance. He pulled a covering over the lower half of his face as the icy wind blew, but it couldn't hide the brokenness in his eyes. "I heard everything."

47

NO MORE ROOM FOR RISK

Caramyn

The rest of the day was awkward, tense, and almost more unbearable than the bitter chill of the mountain. No one spoke. No one knew what to say.

By nightfall, Asterious insisted that they leave as soon as possible, despite his injuries. His reasoning being that they would heal quickly regardless, and that he couldn't give Sinevia any more time to steal the Veil's power and build her army. Though Caramyn didn't doubt that was part of it, she found it far more likely that he just wanted to get away from this place that had stirred up so many horrible memories and uncovered one too many dark truths.

She couldn't blame him. She was more than ready to return to the witchlands, and eventually, the Woods. She'd thought about it all night—about the Shadowblood's Blade. If it was as powerful as Asterious said, then perhaps it could save him from the Blackheart. Perhaps he'd already thought of that, too. Perhaps he hadn't. But either way, whether he admitted it or not, it was yet another reason to find it. Another reason to try.

As they sat around a fire that night, Nocthar fluffed his feather, perched on Caramyn's lap as she shielded him from the evening breeze. In what was the first attempt at breaking silence amongst the three of them all day, Zera spoke up, poking the fire.

"You won't be able to cross these mountains the way you came with your Kuhrissi. It's far too harsh. And the skies are showing signs of a blizzard soon. Get caught in that and there will be nothing you can do to keep her from freezing to death."

"I know," Asterious said, elbows on his knees as he stared into the flames.

"Then, how do we get back?" Caramyn asked, not directing the question at either of them.

Zera smacked her lips and pointed out into the horizon of white nothingness where the edge of the mountain awaited. "Take the mountain path back down to the docks. Best to travel at night, just to be sure no one from Ironfell is passing through for trade. I'm sure they're keeping an eye out for Hrothvor's lilac-eyed assassin." She gestured to Caramyn

"If women are sold to these clans, won't they find it suspicious that one is trying to leave?" Asterious asked flatly.

"They will. But you might find a fishing boat with a captain named Veylan there. Tell him Zera sent you, and he'll take you wherever you need."

"Then we'll leave tonight," Caramyn said without a hint of hesitation. "We can take the horse. Asterious, you can pretend that I'm your captive to at least throw off suspicion."

"It wouldn't be the first time, strangely enough." Asterious grumbled, and for a moment, the weakest smile flashed across his face.

"Very well." Zera slapped her hands on her lap and stood. "Narahbi and I will go and prepare some food and supplies for you. I'm very glad to have met you both." She disappeared into the tent with Narahbi in tow.

Asterious went to tend to the horse, and left Caramyn sitting in the company of only her raven. She watched the prince, his movements slow and stiff, likely from the soreness of his muscles and the stitches pulling at his skin. Caramyn stood as Nocthar fluttered off to the tent, and pulling her coat around herself, shuffled over to Asterious.

"Need a hand?" She asked, already determined that she was going to stick around regardless. "Just because it won't kill you, doesn't mean it doesn't hurt."

Asterious was silent as he picked ice crusted from the horse's hooves and picked up a brush. Caramyn walked around to him and touched his wrist before he could swipe the brush across the animal's coarse fur. He glanced away, but not before she could glimpse the shine in his bleary eyes.

"Don't do this to me," she said. "Don't come all this way for me and then act like you can't even look at me. Whatever it is, whatever is hurting you...you don't have to face it alone."

"If I don't face it alone, everyone suffers." He brushed the horse with quick, defensive strokes. "It is my burden. And mine alone to control. No matter how painful."

"Who told you that?" Caramyn's face hardened. She already knew. "Was it Wyran? Was he the one who trained you to stuff down every inkling of emotion? The one who told you to abuse yourself to learn to drown out your own feelings? Because how's that working out now? It appears to be destroying you far faster than the Blackheart ever could." She noticed the way he flinched. "You think the answer is numbing yourself to pain and fear. But in doing so, you numb yourself to the good feelings, too—to happiness, to joy, to..." The word snagged on her tongue, and she realized she'd been speaking faster than her mind could keep up. But Asterious was looking at her now, waiting every so intently for that last word, and she couldn't leave him empty. "to...caring deeply for someone," she said in place of the real thought she left lingering on her lips.

Asterious stopped brushing the horse and turned to face Caramyn. He gripped her shoulders, firmly, desperate and slow, with intention.

"You think I don't *care deeply* for you?" he breathed. "You are a thorn in my side. And yet you are also the rose. And you are the rain that falls on its petals, and the sun that warms its leaves and lifts the world from the night. *You* are the ruin of my existence. Where once I knew my purpose, and my duty, now I am hindered by you in every step because...because...to say I merely *care* for you is not nearly sufficient."

He flexed his jaw and flared his nostrils, as though trying to cage the next words as he held her gaze through those eyes holding back an ocean. Then his hands slid from her shoulders, and Caramyn could have sworn they were trembling.

"Caring deeply is exactly the reason I must stay away from you. The feel of your skin ignites me in ways I cannot explain. Your touch is a relentless pull toward tragedy. I cannot risk what could happen if I were to...to...lose myself." He glanced down at her lips with hunger in his eyes. "I must protect you—I *will* protect you. And that means even from myself. I've lost my mother. I've lost everyone I ever cared about. I will not lose you, too."

Asterious went back to brushing the horse, and Caramyn stood, something in her shattering like ice. "The Shadowblood's Blade can save you. I believe it has to. If it's enough to pull Sinevia from the darkness, it can surely save you."

"Maybe it can. Maybe it can't...but Zera was right. If I kill *one* more time, whether in this form or the other, the chance will be gone. For me, for Sinevia, and for Evylere. There is no more room for risk."

Caramyn searched the furthest reaches of her mind for something to say, for anything she could possibly grasp to counter what he said, but deep in her heart of hearts, beyond the shadows that shrouded her own soul, she knew he wasn't wrong. If they ever allowed themselves to give in to that pull between them—to that abyss they both ached to fall into—it could destroy them both, along with the very kingdoms they were trying to save. And she would be the reason for it.

It only made sense. She was a Shadowblood. And Shadowbloods always brought ruin.

"You're right." It was all she could manage to get out. "I'll go help pack. And don't worry," she said, her voice tired and heavy with so many unspoken thoughts. "I'll tie my own hands up this time."

And she turned away, leaving footprints in the snow as she trudged with slow, half-hearted steps back to the tent.

When they'd packed enough dried meats and bread for the journey, and a few extra coats and cloaks, Zera and Narahbi sent them off with gentle, heartfelt goodbyes.

Zera reached in for an embrace and wrapped her withering arms around Caramyn in a way that reminded her of the warmth and comfort of her mother. Then she handed her the unstrung bow.

And as they loaded Caramyn onto the horse, wrists loosely bound and her cloak hood pulled over as far as it would go, she addressed Asterious one last time. "I'm so sorry for what I've done to you. I hope you can forgive me."

Asterious, silent and somber, dipped his head towards her in a nod. "The Shadows have a way of tempting the best of us. You were only trying to save me. I forgive you for that."

Zera sniffed, dabbing a tear at the corner of her eye. And then, just before they turned away to take their first step out into the mountains of the Spires alone, she paused, drawing a steady breath as though this might be the last kindness she could offer. "My final words to you both—the darkness that marks you does not define you. What you do in spite of it, does."

Caramyn uttered the delicate syllables of the Silverean word of gratitude. "*Inejiah*. Thank you for everything, Zera. Truly."

And then they set off for the mountain pass, Nocthar flying above and leading the way.

48

CAPTAIN VEYLAN

Caramyn

The harbor was quiet as the dawn crawled in. The journey down the mountain had been uneventful as Asterious led the sure-footed gelding down the icy, crooked path for hours through the grueling slog that had taken the entire night to complete. Even the horse seemed to let out a sigh of relief when they reached the bottom.

"How do we find Veylan?" Caramyn whispered, slipping out of her bonds and sliding down from the horse, her frozen legs nearly shattering when her feet hit the ground.

They took the bags they could carry and released the animal. Then they hid, ducking behind some crates on the docks.

"The better question is how do we even know he's here?" Asterious grumbled as he peeked around the frost-covered crate. "There are two fishing boats moored, but if we pick the wrong one, we're in trouble. A hated Blackwynd royal traveling with the Frostlord's assassin will get some attention if whoever is on the boat recognizes us."

"So, what do we do?"

A sudden voice from the shadows gave them the answer they needed. "Ask someone who can help you." A brazen, but familiar voice startled Caramyn from behind. She whirled around to see a cloaked figure.

"Brenn?"

He lifted his hood to reveal those warm, caramel eyes. "I took the next hire on a boat passing through here—don't worry, not more smugglers. Just a spice merchant." He flashed a strange half-smile. "I hoped we'd cross paths again. I presume you escaped and you're safe with..." and then shot a cold glance at Asterious, a questioning look.

"Prince Asterious Blackwynd." Asterious unfolded from his crouched position behind the crates and stood to his feet. "And exactly who are you?"

"This is Brenn," Caramyn stated, standing up between them. "He was on the ship that brought me here. He's a healer, and he also helped me make the elixir that I gave the Frostlord."

The prince eyed the cloaked man up and down, as if he was trying to determine whether he was looking at a venomous snake or a harmless one, and he secretly hoped it was venomous so that he could have an excuse to crush it. "I'd not be so not quick to put much faith in a man found working on a ship with *people* as cargo." Asterious growled.

"Nor would I be so quick to trust a man whose kingdom allows it." Brenn's eyes narrowed.

"My father's sins aren't mine." The prince clenched his jaw and met Brenn's gaze. "And I ensure you I will put a stop to this disgusting practice when I am king."

"Oh, so you plan to take the throne after all?" Brenn scoffed. "I thought you were just the executioner."

"Stop it, Brenn. He is not what you've heard." Caramyn interjected, irritated with the both of them. "We are safe with him."

Asterious bit his cheek before speaking. "Well, *Brenn,* thank you for whatever part you played in her safety, but as you can see, I no longer think she's in need of your assistance."

Brenn chuckled dryly, looking out at the two small boats docked in the harbor.

"I'd say that since you don't know which ship to get on, you're very much in need of assistance."

"He's right," Caramyn said. "We need his help. And we can't waste any more time." She turned from Asterious and leaned in towards Brenn. "Do you know of a captain named Veylan? Is he here?"

"I've heard the name. He's a quiet one. I'll see if he's here. You can come, but lay low. Keep your faces covered until I give the clear."

There was no chance for response before Brenn strode off towards the harbor. Caramyn followed without question, urging the prince to do the same. They moved in silence, swift and low, trailing Brenn as he took them close to the sailboat on the left, a slightly smaller vessel than the other, with a narrow hull that looked like it could slice through even the roughest waters with ease.

"Wait here." He left them standing at the edge of the dock while he leapt aboard and knocked on the door of the captain's quarters.

Caramyn strained to listen over the evening tide lapping the pier.

"Captain Veylan, you in there?" Brenn's voice rang with another rap of his knuckles against the door.

A door creaked open, followed by coughing and a few grunts. "Who are you and what the hell are you doing here this time of night?"

"It's actually morning now, sir." There was a long pause before he spoke again. "Can you grant passage inland to Magoth?"

"You'd better be paying me enough to buy a new ship to go that far. I don't leave the fjords." Veylan grumbled.

Asterious stepped forward to Caramyn's surprise, joining Brenn on the ship. She followed in attempt to stop him, but was too late before he put himself between Brenn and the captain. "I'll pay you whatever you want upon arrival. I'm an Evylerean noble."

The man crossed his arms, revealing a rum bottle in one hand. "My answer is no."

The man turned away, slamming the door, but Asterious stopped it with the tip of his boot. "A woman named Zera said you could help us," he said, holding the man's gaze.

Veylan slowly looked up, inching the door open again just a bit further. "Zera? I figured she'd be long dead by now." He shook his head with a weary groan. "I should've known she wouldn't go to the grave without cashing in a favor."

"So you'll help us?" Caramyn spoke this time, feeling more confident at the mention of Zera's name.

"If it's for Zera, I'd damn better do it." Veylan brushed a hand over his weathered face, smoothing back his head of sloppy greying hair. "Get on board. We'll leave in an hour or two. Just let me go back to sleep till then, damn it."

He muttered and disappeared back into the darkness of his quarters, leaving the three of them standing on the foredeck. Caramyn and Asterious glanced at Brenn, then at each other.

"Well, that could have gone worse, I suppose." Asterious shrugged, turning to slap a hand on Brenn's shoulder. "Thank you for leading us to Veylan, but I think we can take it from here."

"Oh, I'm coming with you. My home is inland as well, as unfortunate as that may be." Brenn feigned a grin, yanking his shoulder out from Asterious' clasp. "Besides, Veylan will need another experienced seaman whether he admits it or not. A trip through the inlet and upriver is not ideal for a lone sailor. So if you want to avoid the possibility of getting swept out to sea with a drunk captain, I'm coming along."

Asterious rolled his eyes. Caramyn nodded and looked out at the sea beyond the mountain's edge, where the sun just peeked over the black glassy surface stretching into forever. She looked forward to the voyage, where she wouldn't be trapped beneath the damp deck, but instead free to feel the sea's breeze.

Then she felt the exhaustion hit all at once as she failed to stifle a yawn.

"We've been traveling all night. We should get some sleep." Asterious dropped the words like an anchor as he made his way across the deck to the hatch leading down belowdecks. "We're safest out of sight."

Caramyn followed, but Brenn stayed back. "Suit yourselves. I'm staying up here."

As Caramyn carefully climbed down the wooden ladder behind Asterious, she felt a strangeness in the wind just as the last bit of breeze tickled her skin before she dipped below the ship. Nocthar circled above and landed on an unfurled topsail.

"You're sure we can trust him?" The prince pushed past some old barrels and nets, working his way through the cramped confines of the ship. They passed a small galley, a storage space, and finally a small room for sailors' barracks. Or rather, a single sailor's barrack.

They both stood in the doorway, staring at the small cot in the corner that took up most of the space available. "I'll take the floor." Asterious made a move toward the room but then stopped and backed out. "The floor in the galley. We shouldn't be in this small of a space together."

The prince turned to leave without another word.

She wanted to call for Nocthar so she wouldn't be alone in the room. It reminded her too much of being tucked away in the depths of her home as a child, confined to the walls of that too small house and never allowed to interact with the world outside it. But she knew it was safer here, and for Nocthar to be up there. He could watch the entire harbor and warn them far faster than Brenn could.

She laid down her bow and emptied the contents of the bag she carried—a few bits of dried flatbread and berries, a new dagger she'd been gifted from one of the nomads in Zera's caravan since she'd lost hers to Wryan. And a flask of fresh water. She took a long, drawn-out sip, knowing she should conserve it but too parched to care.

Then she lowered herself down onto the cramped cot that was secured with rope tied to metal rings in the wall. She tried to sleep, but couldn't stop thinking of the scars on Asterious' body, and the mark on her own. She refused to believe it was some sort of binding rune—that she bore the stamp of anything other than herself, anything tying her life to something she could not see. She survived because she chose to, not because her destiny was anchored by something else.

Flee to where shadows hide the light...and when you find it, guard it with your life.

She had chosen the Shadow Woods, she told herself. It just so happened that they chose her back.

Her eyes grew heavy as her thoughts wandered, and she snuggled deep into the fur-lined cloak she was now using as a blanket, still wrapped in her coat. The gentle bobbing of the boat rocked her to sleep far more quickly than she expected. And she slept until the sound of sails unfurling and hefty boots treading the deck stirred her awake.

49

REASONS

Asterious

He didn't sleep at all. Partly because of the cold, but mostly because he didn't trust Brenn or Veylan, and he never took his eyes off the hatch in case they decided to sneak down to Caramyn's quarters. But he knew he'd have to rest eventually.

When an hour had passed, he emerged from the hatch and found Brenn tying down some rigging. He rubbed his hands together to warm them in the frozen morning air as he approached him.

"Ah, Your Highness, did you enjoy your nap?" Brenn spat out his mockery without even turning his back. "I do sincerely apologize that there's no one here to bring you hot breakfast on a silver platter."

Damn, this man was certainly going to be a pain.

Asterious ignored the comment, despite imagining slamming Brenn's head into the railing. "I came to ensure we're still departing as planned." He scanned the deck and the helm. "I don't see the captain."

"Keep your crown on. He's coming."

"He'd better be." Asterious grumbled, glancing at the captain's door before taking a step closer to the ropes Brenn was rearranging and tugging on. "Need a hand with that?"

Brenn stopped his work and straightened to face Asterious with a hand still on the rigging. "Do you know anything about sailing? Have you ever even left the comforts of your castle long enough to have the slightest idea of what it's like out on these waters? You'll be most helpful by just staying out of the way."

"Have I angered you in some way, Brenn?" Asterious practically spat out his name, stepping forward.

"Only a bit," Brenn snarled back. "It's not easy for me to accept that I'm helping the son of the man responsible for imprisoning my entire village—my family—behind the Veil."

"And I'm sorry for it. But that wasn't my doing." Asterious held his threatening gaze on Brenn, shifting his jaw as he leaned forward ever so slightly.

"Then will it be your undoing?" Brenn cocked his head, squinting from the rising sun's light that illuminated his wind-chapped face beneath his hood. "If you rule, are you going to break down that damn Veil and let the witches and the druids and the creatures your father despised return to these lands without persecution?"

Asterious was silent as he focused on the frost coating the ropes beside Brenn.

"That's exactly what I thought." Brenn shook his head and went back to working the tethers. Asterious watched him, startled when he caught him moving his hand over the ropes, and sending them to work tying and untying themselves, weaving through the rigging as needed as his eyes glowed gold. He'd never seen Spellbound druid magic before, but it was fascinating and unsettling all at once.

"You think I don't want to free those people? Of course I do. And I plan to, once I know how." Asterious said sternly, turning his back to the chilling wind. "But no one knows how to break the Veil. And even if I figure it out, there could be dire consequences. It's a giant living force of pure Shadow magic—breaking it could be catastrophic. So, I can't make promises of something I don't understand yet. These things take time."

"You can't make promises because you don't actually care." Brenn secured a knot with his hands, his eyes returned to their normal brown color, and then he brushed past the prince to the other side of the ship.

Asterious wasn't in the mood to argue. This fool was just that—a fool, and a bitter one to which he had nothing to prove. Nothing to gain from indulging in his petty spite. But he had everything to gain by making sure they arrived back to Magoth in one piece. He leaned against the hull, blowing out a huff to see the vapor crystallize in the air as he replayed the intriguing display of magic he just witnessed.

Just as his thoughts shifted to her, Caramyn emerged from the hatch, huddled in her coat and cloak. She smiled at him softly, then looked up and down at the masts. "Are we still leaving?"

"Your friend says we are. But if we're still at this dock in five minutes, I'm taking the damn wheel myself."

"Ha! Good luck with that." Brenn called from across the deck.

Just as Brenn finished the words, a heavy door swung wide open, and Veylan appeared, stumbling out of his room and teetering across the ship to the wheel, clad in his thick furs and leathers. "Let's get a move on. The sooner I get you fools off my boat, the better." He grasped the wheel, taking a swig of drink from a flask before pointing with it towards the horizon. "Around the mountains and up the river. Then you all get off my ship and never involve me in your business again."

"Quite a bargain." Asterious narrowed his eyes at the man, watching him carefully as he set them on their course from the docks. The ship cut through the icy waters with ease, navigating the coast where snow-banked rocky edges gave way to deep velvet waves rolling in from the sea itself.

He tore into a piece of dried deer meat he'd found in the galley, walking over to Caramyn, who stood near the bow of the ship, watching the blue water below as they sailed between the fjords.

"Are you hungry?" He handed her a piece of jerky, and she took it with a slight nod. "Sorry it's not Crisyn's pastries you like. But it's something."

A small laugh escaped Caramyn's lips. "I miss Azell. I miss everyone—well, except Wryan."

"Wyran." The name tasted bitter in Asterious' mouth. "A snake in the grass. I ordered the others not to let him leave. I don't know what else he would do in my absence. I don't understand what it is about you that's made him so hostile." He stared ahead. "It feels like another person I've lost, but in a different way. I trusted him so much, but now I fear I don't know who he truly is."

"He's shown you who he truly is for a long time Asterious. He gets in your head and uses it against you. But you try so hard to see the good in people, even when they don't deserve it.

"I still haven't decided if it's a weakness or a strength."

"Maybe both." Caramyn shrugged. "But there has to be a line."

"I guess I finally found it at the edge of the Shadow Woods."

He said it through clenched teeth, half-joking, but the truth was much harsher. The line hadn't been crossed when Wyran flogged him until he bled, or when he'd driven knives into his own flesh at Wyran's command, all in the name of "discipline." It hadn't been when Wyran spoke openly of his hatred for magic, or of what a pity it was that Asterious was a tainted half-Lightborn.

None of that had been the line, because Asterious hadn't been looking for one. He'd made excuses, told himself he owed Wyran his freedom, only to realize too late that it had been another kind of prison. Wyran hadn't chained his body. He'd caged his mind. And the line hadn't been drawn by anything done to him, because he could endure it.

But the moment Wyran hurt Caramyn, the line became unmistakably clear as day.

"What do you plan to tell him when we get back?" White fog puffed from her reddened lips with each word, and she buried her nose into her cloak.

Asterious tilted his head, never taking his eyes off her. "I'm going to tell him to fall at your feet and beg for your forgiveness...because he'll never gain mine." He caught a glimpse of the small smile she tried to hide just before it flickered from her face. She looked away, refocusing on the open water ahead.

For a while, there was only the sound of the churning water and creaking ship, and the sound of Brenn uttering things back and forth with the captain. Until Asterious could no longer stave off his curiosity. "Speaking of deception, how do you know this *Brenn* is trustworthy?" The question must have caught Caramyn off guard by the way she blinked and shot a quick glance over.

"How do you know he isn't?" Caramyn asked, dropping a curled fist on the hull. "If he hadn't healed me, I might not have even survived. And if it weren't for his help with the poison, I might still be getting passed amongst Frostlords as we speak."

Asterious grimaced at the thought of those vile men anywhere near Caramyn, and he had to draw in a slow breath and focus on his heartbeat to keep the wolf in him tame. The chill of the cold didn't feel so bitter anymore as something like fire rose within him.

"Then for that, I suppose I owe him a chance to prove himself. But if he truly thinks I hate his kind, he's certainly a bold fool to wield it in front of me so carelessly the way he does."

"A bold fool...or simply bold? Because he doesn't hide who he really is? It's what we're so used to doing, isn't it? You and me. We've spent so long hiding who we are, it seems dangerous to finally meet someone who doesn't." Her stare cut him like the cold. "Maybe it's time we consider that the parts we hide might just be our greatest strengths."

"I've considered it. But I don't want that strength if it costs me everything," he sighed.

She held his gaze, the wind sending wisps of her hair flying out from beneath her hood. Asterious reached up to sweep her hair back, and then hesitated, withdrawing his outstretched hand as soon as he had lifted it. He couldn't risk touching her here.

"And what of you, my lovely mystery?" he asked, closing his fist at his hip. "Are you so bold now to let the world see the Witch of the Shadow Woods?"

"I don't want to hide anymore," she said. "Not the mark, and not what I am. The Shadow Woods gave me a purpose, and I'm done believing I should be ashamed of it." As she spoke, her voice strengthened with each word, and something lit up within him as she went on. "If the world sees me as an enemy, then let it. I'll walk this path if there's a chance at saving what's left of this kingdom...and a chance at saving you."

Those final words caught him off guard, and his heart sank.

"Don't do this to try to save me, Caramyn." He stepped forward, placing his hand next to hers on the hull, but still ensuring space between them. "Do not make my burden yours. Don't you dare find your strength only for my sake. Do it for *yours*. I will not allow my wretched heart to be the cause of your undoing."

"You can't ruin me like you think you can. I'm stronger than that."

"I could very much ruin you, Caramyn of the Shadow Woods." Heat rose in his face at the thought of his body entwining with hers, in a dance of passion that he could hardly imagine without destroying him right then and there. A kind of heat that coiled around him and surged down to the stiffening feeling between his legs.

"Even if I say it isn't because of you, I'd be lying. And we promised not to do that anymore, didn't we?" she said, blinking at the wind. "Because of you, I was pulled from my solitude to witness the world falling into a darkness I thought could never touch me again. Because of you, I had to face the uncomfortable truth that there are those in this world who cannot outrun it—who have no means to fight back. And because of you, I have realized that darkness does not rise because it is stronger, but because no one chooses to stand against it." She reached for his hand, then stopped herself. "And I refuse to believe any of that means I must sacrifice the hope of saving you."

She seemed like a queen right then—the way she spoke, and the way the warmth of the rising sun's light brought color to her face in this colorless frozen sea. The heightened senses within Asterious caught her scent as the breeze carried her laughter. The sweet smell of pine and wildflowers mingled with the frosty saltwater mist, creating a fragrance that he longed to chase after.

"You've changed me too, Caramyn," he said. "I once had but one purpose—to save my kingdom and take my rightful throne...But now, I'd let it all burn if it meant protecting you. I won't let you risk yourself against the darkness I brought you into."

"I've lived amongst the Shadows for a long time. I'm not afraid of your darkness," she chuckled. "So, no more running. I'm ready to return to my Woods. This time, for all the right reasons."

The corner of Asterious' lips curved into a smile as he studied her features. Her beauty shone even brighter through her confidence. There was a fire in those violet eyes he'd never seen before, and they burned like beacons of hope in the darkest of nights. He took out a flask tucked away in his coat pocket and drank a swig before offering a drink to Caramyn. "To all the right reasons, my dear mystery."

"To all the right reasons." She smirked, sipping from the flask as her raven swept down to perch on her shoulder.

Asterious turned to leave, forcing himself away before the urge to seize her and claim her lips became unbearable. What once sparked fury in his veins now consumed him as pure obsession. He could hardly imagine a more dangerous place to be with her than aboard a small ship with no escape beyond the endless waters. He would have no choice but to keep his distance until they reached land, unless he wanted to risk tearing everyone aboard to shreds and damning himself forever.

He passed Brenn as he strode to the other side of the ship, who gave him a passing glare. Asterious noticed his direction, noticed he was heading for Caramyn, who still lingered at the bow with her bird. Without thinking, he grabbed Brenn's arm.

"She tells me I should trust you. So I will. But if you break that trust, or if you bring any form of harm to her, I will make you pay for it in ways that leave you begging for death."

"Oh, I see. Your suspicions about me are all because you don't trust me with her, not that you don't trust me with magic. That's why she gets a pass from the killer prince for her own magic, isn't it? Because you want to fuck her." Brenn glanced past the prince toward Caramyn's direction. "Or perhaps you already have."

Muscles tensed like steel in Asterious' arms, every nerve screaming as Brenn's words hit him. Caramyn's scent still clawed at his mind, sharp and maddening, driving him toward the edge of control. He knew he was losing reason. The beast was stirring beneath the surface, the shadowy veins scratching at his skin like razors as they threatened to claim control one last time as the sting of that insult from Brenn fanned the fire hotter. If he gave in now, there would be no restraint, and Caramyn would pay the cost. He had to bury the animal within, to find the strength to stay anchored to himself. Before he snapped.

He growled at Brenn in response, "Like I said, you'll beg." He forced his hand open freeing the man from his grasp and stormed away to the steps leading belowdecks.

50

A DAY LIKE ANY OTHER

Caramyn

Veylan said it would take an extra day to get back since they were sailing upriver. The old captain kept to himself and refused to speak to any of them, though Caramyn and Asterious took turns bringing him food whenever they'd found enough ingredients to put something together to give them a break from the dry jerky and berries.

Caramyn prodded him once when she was bored, when he was at the helm and couldn't leave it to escape her questions. She begged him to tell her how he knew Zera in exchange for her silence the rest of the way.

"If you must know. I suppose it don't matter. But every question after costs you a finger." He grumbled his threats as his tongue drew out the last word, but Caramyn noticed the inkling of a smile that broke through as he spoke of Zera. "She was once one a High Council member of Gahmea, revered for her visions—until me and my father were caught stealing from one of the consuls there. She defied the other council members and argued that the son of a pirate shouldn't pay for his father's deeds. Instead of letting them put me to death

320

alongside him, she freed me against their knowledge. They banished her for treachery. She fled to Evylere years before the King purged out all the magic. And here I am, an honest fisherman makin' it far longer than my father ever did. And there she is, wandering the Silverean mountains in exile. A damn shame really." There was a long pause before Veylan spoke again, gesturing with his hands for Caramyn to leave his post. "Now go clean all the bird shit off the deck before I feed that raven to the sharks."

If anyone else had threatened Nocthar like that, they wouldn't have lived to see the next day. But Caramyn had come to learn that Veylan was all bark and no bite, and almost found his bitter mutterings humorous—that, and the fact that he was their only way home. And they were almost there.

On the last night before making port, Caramyn woke, disturbed by something she couldn't name. Her immediate thought was of Asterious, and she went to check on him in the galley. She found him tossing, groaning in agony or fear, and tears streaking from his eyes that were shut tight. His blanket was tossed aside, and he was shivering, shirtless, curled up defensively, bracing for an invisible foe and sometimes trying to fight back.

She ran and dropped to his side, calling his name. He didn't rouse from his nightmare, so she said his name louder, grabbing him with all her strength and trying to still him. He fought harder, until he clasped his hand around her wrist and the other hand gripped her throat. His eyes flew open, still shining from the tears.

"Caramyn!" He ripped his hand from her neck as though she were on fire. His voice was broken, jagged, and hoarsely desperate. "I could've killed you!"

"But you didn't." Caramyn whispered, shocked, but not afraid. "What's happening? Are you...changing?"

"No." He panted, tears rolling down his face. "Just nightmares."

She put a hand on his shoulder, soothing him as his quick breaths slowed. He'd ripped some of his stitches open, and bits of blood streamed down his back. She reached for the blanket in the corner, pulling it over him. "I get them, too," she said.

"I imagine living in the Shadow Woods made them all the worse." Asterious put a hand to his head, damp with sweat despite the cold.

"Not exactly," she tilted her head, kneeling beside him and drawing him close. "Mine are never about Shadows. Only fire."

"The fire should fear you." The prince rested his head against her breast. "Mine are mostly Shadows and blood. I don't remember them when I wake up. I know they're memories. Memories I can't reach."

It was dangerous, she knew, to be here with him like this, to run her fingers in soothing patterns along his bare, scarred back in comfort. But she would not leave him alone to face this.

"Sometimes I wish I couldn't reach mine." Caramyn exhaled, feeling the warmth of the prince against her chest. She watched him rest, closing his eyes peacefully as the tears dried along with the bloodstains on his back.

"You're much more comfortable than the floor," he mumbled softly, earning a small laugh from Caramyn.

The knob on the galley door turned with a click and she bolted upright. Asterious sat up, facing the door.

"Brenn," she muttered at the sight of him in the door frame.

"I heard some commotion and thought I'd check to make sure everyone was all right." Brenn's gaze snapped from her to Asterious as he shifted a step backward, seemingly uncomfortable at the sight of them on the floor together, Asterious shirtless and damp with sweat. "I can see that you are."

Caramyn stood to her feet. "Thank you for your concern. We're fine."

His expression didn't soften. He walked away, leaving the door open, but not without calling back. "We'll be docking at Magoth in an hour or less. We hit a current that moved us along faster than expected. The queen has posted soldiers in all port cities to search boats and watch for rebels—especially magic ones. You'll need to be ready to sneak off quickly."

Caramyn gestured towards her room. "I should go get my things together." The prince nodded.

She rolled up her blankets, packed away her flask, and slung her bow and quiver around her shoulder so they would be ready to take up to the deck when it was time. And then she decided to watch the stars fade with the sunrise during her last morning on the water.

As she climbed up, she was grateful that she didn't need her thick fur hood around her face, as the air was already noticeably warmer than the frozen coastlines of the Spires. The chill of winter creeping in was still very much present, but it felt like a furnace compared to the frigidness of the mountain fjords.

She noticed Brenn watching the sky, seated at the stern with his arm propped up on his knee against a barrel. "You didn't have to leave him, you know. I meant what I said. I came to make sure he didn't kill you or something. I wasn't trying to...interrupt."

"It...that wasn't what you think." Caramyn breathed. "I understand why you're cautious with Asterious. I know his father is the reason our families are dead. But he is nothing like his father was. And he would never hurt me. You must try to understand."

"What must I understand? Your willingness to help this prince of nothing doom us all? You could run away once we make port. Think of it. You—we—could start a new life somewhere, in a place where we're not just pieces left behind of a dying breed. We could travel to Gahmea, where magic is not just tolerated, but revered." He spoke lowly, through bared teeth so as not to allow anyone but her to hear. "But if you help get that man on the throne, what makes you think he won't do exactly what his father did? He'll finish off those of us left."

Caramyn shifted uneasily. "I once considered that possibility, too," she uttered, taming the frustration in her voice with a low growl. "Because I, of all people, do *not* blindly trust. But I have seen what he has faced. What he has overcome. I have seen the way he cares for his people—even ones with magic." She turned to look back at the hatch entrance. "He is selfless, and he only wants to heal this land."

"Emotions can easily tangle with our judgments. But if that's what you wish...I suppose that when we dock, we'll go our separate ways." Brenn shook his head, his locks of cinnamon brown brushing his forehead. He glanced around, as though checking the deck of any previously unnoticed presence. "But if you ever decide to change your mind—or if you ever desperately need help—use this. I will come."

He must've noticed her puzzled expression as he pressed a talisman on a leather string into her hand. It bore the image of a falcon with open wings. "It's a summoner. Enchanted so that if you simply hold it completely and whisper my name into it, I'll hear."

"Why have you done so much to help me?" Caramyn was lost for words as she traced the intricate carvings in the small wooden totem with her fingers. "You hardly know me."

"Because, like I told you before. We are one and the same."

Caramyn had no further words, fearful of deepening the connection if she asked him anything more. Instead, she resigned herself to watching the sky as the dark expanse of stars overhead slowly transformed into a palette of gold, white and heavenly hues of pink and lavender. Leaning against the hull, she stared up into the place where the gods of old were said to reside, and for once she thought maybe they might've been real.

Veylan's gruff voice calling out to announce their arrival tore her gaze away and back to the misty cliffs of Evylere coming into view ahead. Brenn stood up, belongings slung across his back. "Goodbye, Caramyn. I'll be off this ship before you can notice I'm gone. I'd like to avoid another interaction with your dear prince. And if it's what you wish, you'll never have to see me again." He waved at her and then gestured at the talisman in her hand. "Unless you decide to use that."

As she studied him for what she knew might be the last time, she looked into his eyes and nodded in a way to thank him from the sincerest part of her. Looking down at the talisman, she stood with his words still swirling around in her mind. Asterious appeared on the deck, and she hurried to tuck the charm away in her pocket.

Veylan navigated the ship through the rocky waters, and the familiar scent of the forgotten Lightborn lands swept Caramyn into a dream. The smell of apple blossoms, cedars, and the edge of the sea, and the crisp wind of autumn's end that cloaked itself around her.

Brenn huddled beneath his cloak as Asterious neared, distancing himself by heading to the masts to lower the sails. Veylan docked the ship, working it between the tight-spaced piers of the Magoth docks. Once the vessel was moored, he stomped over to the edge of the boat and dropped the gangplank with a slam. "A favor repaid for a favor granted. Now get off my boat."

"You have our gratitude, Captain Veylan." The prince nodded and handed him some coins Zera had given them. "Stay here a few days so that I can send someone with further payment."

"No need," Veylan coughed. "I think the sailing did me more good than any gold. And I'd rather get back to the fjords than linger around this noisy place another minute."

Caramyn thought she saw the old seaman smile again.

Brenn whisked past them across the deck and down the gangplank into the commotion of the docks where sailors were preoccupied with loading and unloading their vessels. He spoke with a Felhold soldier, directing his attention to the water as Caramyn and Asterious snuck past with their cloaks shielding their eyes.

Nocthar flew far ahead of them, beating his wings as though he'd just been released from bondage. Once their feet were on dry land once more and they were far enough away from the patrols, Caramyn surveyed the busy port to tell Brenn goodbye, but he was gone.

Marching through the harbor, she and Asterious set their sights toward the south. Caramyn shed her outer coat, finding it too bulky and unnecessary for the temperate late autumn chill. Her cloak over her long-sleeved wool dress would suffice on its own.

"I'd thought you would've learned by now not to hold onto mysterious relics." Asterious said suddenly.

"What?" Caramyn stopped in her tracks.

"The talisman." Asterious said. "What if it's cursed? What if he's lying?"

"And what if he's not? Do you really think he would curse it after all he did to help us?" A trickle of doubt crept into Caramyn's mind. "You're the one who told me to trust more. Now maybe it's you who need to have a little trust," she said. "Not in him. But in me."

Asterious glowered. "I do trust you."

"Good. And just to make you feel better, I have no intention of wearing it. I'll just keep it here in my pocket—just in case."

"I'm not going to tell you what to do with it. But I have difficulty imagining a situation we could possibly get into that would require his help."

Caramyn shook her head, and for a moment she thought of tossing the charm out in the dirt. But even if it seemed absurd, the subtle fear of ending up in a situation like being sold to Frostlords in the Spires, or running from soldiers through the Bleak Wilderness with nothing but the clothes on her back—of facing danger alone again—made her hold onto it instead, nestled in her pocket...just in case.

Asterious' smirk faded as he looked ahead toward the miles of terrain before them, far beyond the fishing villages of Magoth. "Now we make our way back to the Court. It's at least another day's walk on foot." Asterious said with a tired but firm tone.

"Then let's get walking." The aroma of warm bread drifted to Caramyn's nose, overpowering the smell of fish and stale bilgewater. "But first let's grab something to eat. I can't stomach another bite of that dry jerky."

"Agreed," the prince said, pulling his cloak even further down over his face. "Just keep your guard up and your head down."

"A day like any other."

As they entered the village market of Magoth, wary of their surroundings but keeping a normal pace, Asterious nudged her gently. "Actually, it's not a day like any other at all. Today is a special day."

Caramyn raised an eyebrow, still focused on the selection of food at the vendor table they approached. "Oh? Why is that?"

"You said you were born on the first day of the eleventh month. That's today."

Caramyn realized it was, and she hadn't even noticed. She'd forgotten her own birthday, but he'd remembered. And it was certainly not what she'd expected him to bring up. But she replied inquisitively. "I...I suppose it is."

"Well after all I've done, after all you've been through because of me, I'd like to give you something. It can never make up for everything. But it's a start." He cleared his throat, purchasing two cinnamon pastries and two legs of roasted lamb from the busy market seller, who hardly gave them a passing glance. "So, what would you like? A garden for your plants? Another horse? Books?"

Caramyn thought for a moment as she stuffed the warm pastry into her mouth. She pictured the Vaerwynd castle, remembering the night she snuck back to her tower, passing the magnificent ballroom in all its haunting midnight beauty. She closed her eyes as she imagined how it might have felt to twirl gracefully across the golden marble floor when it was once in its glorious prime. She knew exactly what she wanted.

"A dance. In the castle ballroom." She smirked, swallowing the last bit of pastry. "But I hardly think this is time for birthday wishes." Caramyn wrinkled her nose and bit her cheek, looking ahead and the worn dirt road before them.

"Maybe not. But I swear to you, when the time is right—and it *will* be—you shall have your dance." His eyes shone with a twinkle that rivaled the stars.

"Don't make promises you can't keep, prince." Caramyn laughed. It was part-joke part-truth. How could he ever hope to dance with her when he couldn't even touch her?

"And why wouldn't I be able to keep that promise, apart from the obvious?" Asterious raised an eyebrow, passing a clever glance her way.

Because what if I'm wrong about everything, and we can't break your curse, and you can never find the strength to be near me?

"Because I imagine you're an awful dancer."

"Then that just shows how little you know of me." The prince's chuckle filled the air around them and warmed Caramyn's soul as they trudged through a cool, dense fog. "I'm quite a skilled dancer, you should know. I wasn't allowed to attend any of the feasts or banquets my father held, but they held private balls for just me alone in my cell." He was nearly grinning ear to ear at his own cruel sarcasm. "I was still required to learn all the most popular dances and courtesies of the ballroom as part of my training—just in case, they said."

"Just in case you ever met the Witch of the Shadow Woods who asked to dance for her birthday."

"In case I ever met the *Queen* of the Shadow Woods and needed to impress her." He feigned a bow, nearly tripping as they walked.

Caramyn beamed at him in a way she hadn't thought possible, and in a way she knew didn't make sense. Here they were joking about dancing, pretending the hideous truth wasn't keeping them apart—that he could kill her if he so much as thought about her too long. And it would trap him in his eternal consequence. And yet she would be willing to risk it a thousand times over just to hear that laugh, low and unguarded, meant only for her. For the way the sound of her name on his voice made her breath falter, for the warmth that spread through her at the smallest brush of him, and for the ache that followed when he pulled away.

Nocthar cawed overhead, gliding past them as if to urge them onward. Asterious' smile faded as he took a slow breath inward. "I hate to ruin the fun, but if we hope to reach the Court by tomorrow, we can't afford to stop for more than a quick piss and drink."

Caramyn readjusted the bow at her back and straightened her shoulders. "Then let's shut up and move."

Without any further exchange of words, they followed the raven, pushing themselves to walk faster and farther. Into the night they carried on in silence, too tired to speak even if they wanted to. When the great towering steeples of Vaerwynd finally came into view, and Caramyn spotted a torch burning in the distance, she started to smile, thinking it was Terrin waiting to greet them. But it was only as the flame approached, faster than faster, she realized it was Tyrios, panicked and rushing to meet them.

"Thank the Shattered gods you're back." He skidded to a stop, panting out the words.

"What's wrong, Tyrios?" Asterious' weary eyes suddenly opened wide with concern.

"The scouts have received word that Sinevia has left for the Woods. And she has an army of Shadow Soldiers waiting in Felhold, ready to be resurrected. And their first order—" Tyrios breathed. "To destroy Vaerwynd and burn the witchlands."

Asterious bit his cheek. "She believes she's finally powerful enough to steal the Veil's power for their life source. If we hope to beat her there, we have no choice but to leave before sunrise."

Caramyn sucked in a deep breath, trying to hide one of many countless yawns, her exhausted joints aching with each movement. Asterious glanced at her with bloodshot eyes before continuing. "We'll sleep a few hours tonight while we can, but tell Terrin to have the horses ready at midnight."

"So be it. I'm eager to meet your dear sister." She lifted her chin, finding buried strength at the thought of someone infiltrating the forbidden forest she'd spent so many years guarding. "And I'm very much beginning to miss my Woods."

51

PAST THE POINT OF NO RETURN

Sinevia

Sinevia watched as the snow drifted over Felhold, marking a new beginning, sealing old sins beneath white silence. A cleansing of sorts. And once she destroyed what was left of the Lightborn Court, Blackwynd Court would rise as the symbol of one central, final, and unchallenged power.

The queen turned her horse away from the looming stone castle, leaving her precious throne behind for this necessary journey. It would not be easy, but once the Veil was within her reach, her power would be unlimited. She'd studied the runes, she'd translated the spells and reworked every single word down to the last syllables to ensure her illusions would work in conjunction with the Shadow magic and the blood she'd prepared for the ritual. To ensure she could siphon that living source of power from anywhere, once she had claimed it. It stirred deep satisfaction in her to think that once her soldiers rose, she would lay siege to the last rebelling cities and crush the resistance before it could fully take root. Even the Silvereans would no longer be exempt from her dominion.

She blinked, the pride of her efforts and pain laid bare before her in the form of her guards marching through a blanket of white. "A beautiful sight, wouldn't you agree, Captain?" She patted her horse as the Captain kept in pace alongside her on his own mount.

"Glorious, Your Majesty," he nodded.

She took a cold, deliberate pleasure in every part of it. An entire realm would bend to her will, backed by a military that could not waver, doubt, or betray her. And above all, she would have her revenge for Daphne's death. Against the ancient belief systems that had nurtured weakness and misplaced compassion in the first place. They had crept into Daphne's mind like a slow rot, convincing her to waste her power on those least deserving, to mistake mercy for virtue, and to get herself killed by defying the law for a love that was a lie. Such defiance was no less dangerous than unchecked magic itself. And unlike her father, she would not tolerate either.

And what fun it would be to watch it take shape. Her brother could not slaughter an army that was already dead. He would tire long before her immortal soldiers would fall and then she would capture him once he had nothing more to give. All that remained was to provoke him, to pry open the scars of years spent suppressing grief, fury, and guilt, and shove him past the point of no return. And at last, she knew exactly how to do it.

"Just imagine that beast under my command...chained out at the castle gates like a dog on a leash." She muttered, earning a nod from the Captain.

But then something cracked. Something in her that called to the bond they once shared. The image of that little girl with long black hair who would visit her brother in the cell below the castle. She'd ask why he couldn't come out to play. And he'd tell her from the corner where he curled up alone.

"I'm not allowed. I might hurt you."

So she'd fetch a ball from her room and bring it to him, and they'd play through the bars of his prison. Once in the garden, she found a bird with an injured wing and brought it to him to nurse back to health. He kept it for three days before letting it fly away—

"You still prefer subduing him over just killing him?" The Captain's question snapped her from her memory. But it lingered, and she looked at her hands covered in smoky black markings that covered her fingers like soot. And suddenly some part of her wished she could stop it. But she couldn't. She wouldn't. It was that simple. She blinked, and the darkness overshadowed her once more, consuming the last bit of whatever was left of her soul. There was no way out.

"I think I do. I have more to gain that way," she said. "And thanks to you, I now know his weakness."

"What about the Shadow Woods? What if the Shadow wraiths do not welcome you, my queen?"

"They cannot banish a greater power than themselves." She nudged her horse forward. "And anyone who tries to stop me from entering will find out just how powerful I am."

At her unspoken command, the Captain's image flickered, fading as she released his presence and returned him to the work that defined his true purpose, far beyond her reach.

"Go now. You have a duty far greater than escorting me," she said. "Ensure that everything is ready for when I arrive."

52

INTO THE DARKNESS

Caramyn

Caramyn hardly remembered the walk through the castle doors and to her room in the tower. The soles of her feet ached with each step. Her muscles burned with each step up the stairs, threatening to give out with each leg put forward. The lack of sleep was dizzying, and the dark corridors blurred and twisted as she tried to blink away the throbbing in her head.

She fumbled in her gait and swayed with pure exhaustion, hardly aware of the footsteps behind her. Just when she felt she couldn't take another step, the prince's warm arms encompassed her, scooping her up against him and carrying her the rest of the way. She hadn't even realized he'd still been walking with her. Her weary head flopped against his chest, where she succumbed to the weight of her eyelids as the beat of his heart lulled her to sleep.

She awoke a few hours later, snug beneath warm blankets in her bed. The sound of a ringing tower bell outside summoned her, and she sprung to her feet to wash and get dressed. It would be a while before she could bathe again.

She scrubbed off the last of the salt from her skin and opened the wardrobe. This was no journey for delicate dresses, so she chose tall boots, a pair of form-fitting pants, and a long sleeve tunic tucked beneath a leather corset that she didn't remember being in the armoire before. Securing the clasp of her cloak, she scurried down to the courtyard in the purple haze of twilight, with Nocthar not far behind.

Eight horses stood, their riders standing at attention beside them as Asterious marched through their midst. He was back in his usual dark-colored princely attire, black armor, and black cloak.

He greeted his riders—the core four plus two of the scouts from the meeting, though Wryan was distanced from the rest. "Today we set out with one mission—to save this land from darkness from which I fear there is no return. You have been faithful and courageous and followed me to the deepest pits of hell. So I ask you to ride into the darkness one more time at my side, but I will not command it. And I will think no less of you should you decide not to. This is your final chance to decide."

One by one, they pledged their allegiance to the prince with a hand to their chest. "You have our strength and our loyalty, Prince Asterious." They each offered their oath, until it came to Wryan, who begrudgingly gestured his pledge and remained silent, as though he was waiting for something more as he glared from his post. Asterious then turned to face Caramyn, but he still spoke to the group. "Time is of the utmost importance, but before we set out, an apology is in order." He waved Wyran over and called his name, his voice darkening.

Wryan sauntered over, each step slow and unhurried, as his eyes cut into Caramyn with each step. He faced her, looking down ever so slightly, as he was not much taller.

"Ask her forgiveness." Asterious demanded. Just as Wryan opened his mouth, the prince added, his voice a tempered growl. "On your knees."

Wyran's cold stare flicked to the prince and then back to her in a way that made Caramyn shudder. As he lowered himself to kneel before her, he watched her with shifting eyes that made her feel like he would drive a knife in her back the next chance he got. "I'm sincerely regretful of my actions, Lady Caramyn. I made a grave mistake. And I ask for your forgiveness."

Caramyn glanced at Asterious for reassurance. He leaned in close and whispered to only her. "It is yours to give or withhold," he said. "He's only coming with us because I don't trust him anywhere else."

She drew a breath, prepared to say the words but never really having thought about whether she meant them or not. She wasn't quite sure that she'd ever extended grace to anyone before. "I will forgive you, Wryan," she said coldly. "But I will not easily forget."

Wryan stood to his feet as Asterious gave his approval. "Nor will I, Milady."

Asterious mounted his horse and everyone else followed. Caramyn had barely put a foot in the stirrup before he gave the orders. "All right then. No more pleasantries. We don't have a second more to waste. Move out."

The next day was a blur, steadily cantering across landscapes, pushing the horses to their limits alongside Asterious and his core four soldiers, Leejia, and the other scout, Starke. It wasn't lost on Caramyn how Wryan watched her, and how Asterious glared at him often. Caramyn clutched Frasya's tangled mane in her fingers, praying the mare would have the heart to forgive her for this arduous journey later. And with each passing hour, she worried Sinevia had already reached the Woods.

She often thought of how it would feel entering the Woods once more, to stand against its greatest threat yet, no longer burdened by the weight of her darkness but ready to use it as her strength.

The first night when they stopped to rest, she was still recovering from the exhausting strain so much traveling had put on her body, and she fell asleep without a word to anyone after they shared a small meal around a fire.

The second night, she finally felt more rested and lively, and she joined the group around the fire. Asterious had sent Wyran to gather firewood while he caught up on sleep Caramyn was sure he desperately needed. So, for the first time, she was alone with his soldiers and scouts, and was content to quietly listen to them joke and jeer amongst one another. But to her surprise, Leejia asked her a question, despite them having never spoken before.

"Caramyn, if I may, what led you to hide out in the Shadow Woods? How did such a place become your refuge when everyone knows the stories. Weren't you afraid?"

She lingered at the rim of her cup as she brought the drink to her lips. She took a sip, then answered. "I was afraid. But I was more afraid of the people outside of the Woods. I'd seen what they would do, and in comparison, the Shadows didn't seem so bad." She paused, staring at the fire flickering as she fought back painful memories. "But also...my mother told me the witch she sought to heal me in her womb lived deep within the Woods before it became the bridge between our realm and the Veil. So, it was the only place I knew to go. I ran straight there—almost by instinct. Like it was the only other place I had any connection to outside the cage that was my village." She glanced down at the ground in disbelief that she had shared something so personal with so many people at once. And in disbelief at how liberating it felt to say it all out loud.

When she glanced back up, the others leaned in, wearing focused expressions as they huddled beneath blankets and cloaks. Leejia straightened her broad shoulders and brushed back a loose strand of blonde hair from her single braid that fell to the unshaven side of her head. "You are braver than all of us put together. Don't be afraid to talk about what you've overcome."

Tyrios nodded, and Gariel and Riven followed suit.

"May we all be so fearless when we face the Woods again." It was Gariel who spoke, and then they clinked their pints together. A shy smile tugged at Caramyn's lips. For the first time, she could imagine what it felt like to have friends. And it felt like the comforting warmth of her fur cloak against her skin.

As the fire dwindled to embers, Wryan returned with water and doused it to completion. The men retreated to their scattered sleeping bags, but Leejia stood and placed a hand on Caramyn's shoulder.

"A kuhrissi does not fear the darkness, for the darkness is her protection. It covers her, so that her enemies cannot find her."

Caramyn looked up at the tall woman, startled. "How do you know that word?"

"I suppose Asterious hasn't had time to tell you I'm Silverean. I grew up in the Spines, but I left because I hate the cold…and the Frostlords." She chuckled with a shrug of her shoulders. "And then I realized the King below the mountains was even worse…so, I became one of his spies in hopes to infiltrate him from the inside."

"And you followed Asterious because you believe he might be able to restore the balance of magic to the land?"

"I followed him because I have no doubt of it." She patted Caramyn's shoulder, her sideways smirk growing as she walked to her sleeping spot without another word.

Then it was just Caramyn alone in the dark, the remains of the fire smoldering before her up to the stars that glittered above. She tilted her head back to look at them and noticed Nocthar's silhouette perched in a dead branch a few feet away, creating the perfect illustration of what Leejia had told her. His black feathers camouflaged him perfectly against the night sky, and if she were anyone else, she wouldn't have noticed him. Then her gaze adjusted, and she followed the faint light of the moon, which was nothing more than a waning sliver in the dark.

53
ONE HORSE

Asterious

He was supposed to be asleep, but instead he lay there listening as Caramyn spoke to his soldiers. He wondered what it might mean that Zera, Caramyn, and Leejia were so certain he could save this land. Because he wasn't so sure anymore. He couldn't even save his mother. How could he hope to save Evylere from his own sister when he was at the Blackheart's mercy? How could he hope to rule as a king when he was one slip away from becoming a monster forever?

He couldn't. And that's why he'd been struggling to admit to himself that he knew what he had to do if things didn't go as expected. If the weapon couldn't break his dark curse, it could end it another way. A single stab through the heart. That's all it would take. When its Light pierced his Shadows, his Blackheart should not survive it. But Caramyn would survive, and because of her, Evylere might just have a chance.

The next day the river awaited them. There was no time to travel the main roads leading to the south bridge. They would keep straight on, even if it meant forging their own path.

They woke before dawn so that they were at the river's edge with the first light. And they'd chosen the narrowest spot they could find. It was small but swift. Especially since the seasonal rain had deepened it since their last time crossing it when bringing Caramyn back to Vaerwynd.

"Hold your horses steady, and if they hesitate, encourage them. Do not force. Trust they'll take care of you, and they will." Asterious glanced back at his entourage as he stroked Alofreise's withers. Then he turned to face the rocky water, standing at the shallowest and narrowest point he could find. It flowed fast and clear along pebble-lined banks winding through tall, scattered pines that traced sections of its border.

Caramyn appeared beside him, her fingers latching around her mare's mane in reassurance, and she nodded. "I thought perhaps Alofreise would like a friend to go in with him...so he doesn't feel alone."

Asterious smiled. "I'm sure he would appreciate it." They urged the horses on together, and side by side they stepped into the river, splashing up icy water that seeped into their boots. The others followed, with the last scout's horse hesitating after dipping a hoof in.

"Keep him moving, Starke!" Leejia called as the animal balked beside hers.

Alofreise plunged chest-deep into the river. The current was stronger than expected. Asterious' muscles recoiled tight as the cold water struck his skin like needles.

He looked back just in time to see Starke's horse rearing in panic, throwing his rider into the river before bolting for the trees. Starke vanished downstream, swept away like driftwood.

"Keep going—I'll get him!" Asterious shouted to Caramyn as he turned into the current. His stallion swam hard, battering against rocks as they surged after the scout. When Starke slipped beneath the surface, Asterious dove, keeping hold of the reins as he caught the man by his shirt and hauled him to the saddle.

Ignoring the cold water's bite, he mounted again and dragged Starke up behind him, steering for the bank. The others rushed forward as they reached the shallows, Starke staggering free, teeth chattering.

"Lost a horse," he managed.

"Here." Riven rummaged through the saddle bags and tossed him a blanket. "This one stayed dry."

Caramyn dismounted and pressed Frasya's reins into Starke's hands. "You can ride Frasya the rest of the way. You need her warmth more than I do."

She looked up at the prince, soaked head to toe, sitting atop his stallion as steam rose from the wet animal into the crisp air. "I can ride with you."

The group was silent, and the prince knew what they must be thinking. He even noticed how Wryan glared at Caramyn for the mention. But he didn't have time to worry about it. She wasn't wrong about the warmth. Alofreise was the largest and strongest horse in the group. It would be easiest for him to be the one to carry two riders the rest of the way without slowing them down.

He'd managed to control himself with her between his legs before. This time should be no different.

He stretched out his hand for Caramyn and she grabbed it, swinging her leg over the seat of the saddle and settling in front of him. She pressed against him, and the warmth of her dry upper body covered his chest like a heavy blanket. He handed her the reins while he removed his gloves, and when he took them up again, she covered his hands with hers. For warmth, he told himself.

This time it shouldn't have been different. But it was, because he didn't hate her now. The loathing and mistrust she had once stirred up in him before was at least some form of barrier to his urges. But now there was no confusion to dampen the flames, and nothing standing in the way of his feral desire. He knew what he felt for her and there was not a semblance of doubt about it. And as they traveled on, he fought to fixate on every fallen leaf and drifting cloud, every bird chirping or woodpecker knocking. Every possible sensation besides the one of her hips nestled between his thighs, arousing the hardness in his center. Besides the kindling of a fire he wanted to let consume him entirely.

He was glad when she asked him a question, so he could keep his mind occupied with something other than wondering what her skin might taste like on his tongue. Only, he wished it might have been almost any other question than one that tugged at his already deepening worries.

"When we find this Shadowblood's sword, what exactly is your plan?" Caramyn shuddered from the cold, snuggling her face down into her own cloak.

"I free the Blade. It will override my curse of steel, and I will wield it. It will bring the powers of Light and Shadow back into balance under its command, and bind Shadow magic where it belongs—out of Sinevia or anyone else's reach."

"And if Sinevia does not yield?"

The prince allowed the question to linger in the silence for a moment before answering. "Don't think I haven't considered what it will mean if she is truly too far gone."

Caramyn reached over the rein, brushing his arm. "If it comes down to it, I will do it for you. I will not let you be faced with the choice to kill your own sister."

"I won't let you do anything on my behalf, especially that. I've thought this through," Asterious said, his voice low. "Either way, I will be damned. If the Blade cannot free Sinevia, I fear it won't be able to save me either. And if the only way to stop her is to kill her, and the only way to save you is to resist you forever—then I fear my curse is life itself."

Caramyn craned around in the saddle. "Don't you dare start talking like that. The Blade is going to be able to save you...and her." She tilted her head. "We'll find a way."

"How is it you always believe that?" He nuzzled his lips against her ear.

"Because it's what I've always done." Her hand slid down to his thigh, and she squeezed it gently, reassuring, cruel, and sensual. A touch that prodded him, drawing him to the flames as he imagined that hand sliding further up to caress the unbearable firmness pulsing between his legs.

"And that is why you are everything Evylere needs...everything *I* need. You have fought against the odds all your life and survived. You have *chosen* to survive. Magic or not, there is something more powerful in you than any of us. My impossible mystery, of Light and Shadow," he murmured.

The way her eyes shimmered at his words made her all the more magnetic. And if he didn't stop the horse, stop that bewitching, relentless motion of hers that coaxed his aching need, as the memory of bare body dripping wet in the sunlight bombarded his mind, every part of him was going to unravel there in the saddle, and he might very well take her in a moment of weakness—a moment of selfishness that would damn them all.

And that's when he ordered they stop for camp one last time. Just to let the horses rest. He knew it would delay another hour. But it was either that or succumb to his unquenchable thirst and risk becoming a beast forever.

54

INTO THE WOODS

Caramyn

It was a sensation she couldn't stop thinking about, the trace of him at her back even long after they'd dismounted. Her mind knew it was a wicked, fool's game to even entertain the idea of what it might feel like to entangle her body with Prince Asterious', but she couldn't stop playing nonetheless. Even despite the crushing certainty that it would always leave her the loser, empty and wanting.

After they'd rested a while, and mounted back up on their horses, Caramyn prepared once more to ignore the torture of feeling Asterious behind her, of his length pressed firm against her backside, hot and ever-present. She would have to stop talking to him so much, because she could hardly handle it when that velvet voice answered her against the back of her neck and sent a cruel warmth blooming through her.

She focused on Nocthar flying above, and on what it might be like to have wings. At least when the snow began to fall, its chilling beauty became something else to distract her as a thin layer of white coated the ground, a subtle contrast against the bleak grey clouds above.

And then, as the evening drew near, it came into view—the edge of the Shadow Woods. It lay miles into the distance, sprawling across infinite acres like a black hedge of white-tipped thorns. The dense trees jutted into the darkening sky with gnarled branches that might have been claws bursting from the smooth pure ground beneath it. And it beckoned, like an ominous threat and an old, familiar friend at the same time. Caramyn drew in a deep breath, unable to pry her gaze away.

"Are you alright?" Asterious leaned forward, his voice gentle.

"Yes," she mumbled. "It's just...it's strange to think that *that* was my home for five years. It was the only thing I knew—until it wasn't. A place that looks so hopeless from here, now that I've seen the beauty of what lies beyond. Now I don't know what home is anymore."

"Coming out of the fire doesn't mean we forget what forged us. This is still a part of you, just as much as the Lightborn lands, if you so choose."

Caramyn bit the inside of her lip, twisting her mouth as she thought. "The Shadow Woods will always be a part of me. A place I will protect as it protected me. And right now, it needs me...because an intruder lurks within—one even the Shadows can't seem to keep out."

She didn't need Nocthar to fly ahead and warn her. Somehow, just as she sensed the letter in the library and the prey in the Spires, she could sense the presence of Sinevia all on her own, even from here.

"Then what are we waiting for?" Asterious said. He commanded his men to follow as Caramyn dug her heels into the horse's flanks, sending him into the fastest gallop he could manage. He snorted with each breath as his hooves pounded across the fresh fallen snow, carrying the prince and the witch beneath the soaring shadow of Nocthar.

They slowed as they neared the foreboding forest's edge, where they dismounted, facing the entrance to the Woods. Dark tendrils of shadows curled along the snow-dusted forest floor, phantom wisps as they crept toward her feet. Eerie whispers and strange songs flowed from the depths of the swaying trees, beckoning her closer. It was a warning and a lure all on its own. And it was hers.

Caramyn tilted her head.

"I spent my whole life thinking that I was destined for darkness—that I could never do anything good. That my blood of Shadows would always outweigh the Light in me. But when I found the Shadowblood's letter, and then later when I saved Narahbi, it made me rethink everything. And I decided I was done letting others write my story," she said. "I still don't understand what I am, or why I exist. But I believe that, Shadow or Light, my destiny is my own."

She stared into the trees, the rest of everything fading away in the snowy silence. Then glanced down at her sleeve, where she could envision the black patterned veins beneath them as Zera's words breathed hope into her.

The darkness that marks you does not define you. What you do in spite of it, does.

She turned around to face the others. "This is as far as you all can go."

They looked at the prince, uncertainty written across their faces. He took a step back to place himself behind Caramyn. "Don't wait for orders from me to tell you otherwise. This is her domain, and we are to obey whatever she says."

Their confused faces told her they did not understand. They must've thought she would be able to shield them all. But they were wrong. She still didn't even know if she could convince the Shadows to permit Asterious—but they had before, hadn't they? When he first crossed to find her. Or maybe they had known if they tried to stop him, they might awaken something even worse. Either way, he was the only one who could come with her.

The Shadows hissed from the depths behind her, and she looked at them once more, reaching for her bow. "The Prince will go with me so that I can lead him through, but I can't protect all of you. If you decide to be brave and try to cross anyway, the Shadows will come for you. And I won't be around to put an arrow through you to spare you the misery."

Silent and bewildered, the group cautiously stepped back, a silent pledge to stay put at the forest's edge, though she secretly hoped Wyran might attempt to prove her wrong.

Asterious grabbed his stallion's reins.

"Leave the horse," Caramyn said. "I don't want anything to happen to Alofreise. I've never known the Shadows to hurt an animal, but the Woods are angry at Sinevia's presence. I don't know what they might do."

Asterious nodded, and turned the horse away.

Side by side, they entered the Woods. Nocthar fluttered from branch to branch, as if greeting each one with his return. They tread carefully, with Caramyn leading through every uneven spot, every low hanging branch, weaving through the maze of black trees like it was second nature. Each strip of bark against her fingertips, each frost-tipped bramble that she brushed aside, felt like a kiss from an old friend. And she felt a rhythm in her bones and a strange song in the wind, composed of the footsteps of a stranger never invited, one the Shadows did not welcome.

She walked with the prince at her side, guided by the thrum of darkness in her veins, desperate to drive out the threat to the place that had once been her refuge. But they had to find the Blade first. And this forest was vast. The trees stretched for miles, filling the landscape so far and wide it could take weeks to fully explore, especially if one did not know the farthest reaches that led to the Veil.

She called to her raven, and asked him to fly toward the Veil, and to spend as long as necessary searching for the Shadowblood's sword and for Sinevia. They'd continue to search the woods on foot for as long as they could—until nightfall would make it unsearchable.

"So how close have you ever gone to the Veil?" Asterious pushed aside a thorny branch from his face as he ducked underneath another.

Caramyn narrowed her eyes at a familiar cluster of trees in the distance, assuring herself they were heading in the right direction.

"I tried to see it once. I wanted to know what it looks like, to see if the rumors were true about it being unapproachable. I had to be less than a quarter mile away when the darkness came too unbearable even for me. I don't know if the Shadows would have killed me if I went closer, but something in me was too afraid to find out."

"How...encouraging. What did it look like?"

"Tell you and spoil all the fun?" Caramyn wrinkled her nose. "You'll get to find out firsthand soon enough."

The prince feigned a laugh, but the air was stiff between them. Fresh snow crunched beneath their boots as it deepened with the passing hours. As the woods began to darken, Caramyn held out a hand and stopped Asterious in his tracks. "Listen."

The sounds of wind wailing and unearthly whispers swirled around them, low at first, but then it grew. The branches swayed in a sinister dance as they carried the sound closer, growing until it felt almost tangible between the prince and the woman in the forest.

"The Shadows are hunting."

Asterious glanced around with a light shrug. "Should I be worried then?"

Caramyn shook her head. "I don't think so. It sounds distant. Just hope it isn't one of your men who tried to come looking for us."

The growl of the Shadows lingered in the distance, humming their eerie lullaby as night cast its cover over the forest. Caramyn was grateful for the snow, as it made the ground easy to navigate even without torchlight. She shuddered as a cold chill snaked its way down her spine and breathed a sigh of relief when the snow-covered roof of her cottage came into view, a bright white spot of hope in a maze of darkness.

"We'll have to resume our search in the morning. It's useless to be out here after dark. We'll wander blind all night." She knew her senses were strong, and that she could likely push through the night. But the midnight darkness fell so thick it was almost painful, like an oppressive force sucking away any hope that had existed during the day. And she feared it might just be enough to weaken Asterious and strengthen the darkness fighting to overtake him. Nocthar was already out searching. It would be unwise to press on through the despairing dark, too.

"My cottage isn't far. We'll be safe there for the night."

The prince nodded, gesturing for her to go forward. "Lead on." He never once questioned her or even asked for an explanation for anything she said. And something in her heart swelled at the thought that he trusted her completely.

55

THE COTTAGE

Caramyn

He followed her to the house, and when they reached the door, Asterious stopped, staring as though he'd seen a ghost.

"Are you alright?" Caramyn called.

"Yes," he stammered. "Just a strange sense of familiarity. Like I've been here before, as crazy as that sounds," he said as she pushed the wooden door open, the familiar scent of cedar and honey charging her senses.

It was too dark to even make out a hand in front of her face, but Caramyn navigated the room with ease, her feet following a path they'd learned through endless repetition. She hurried to a table in the corner, where she lit an assortment of candles, one by one, and then placed her bow across the table and her quiver in the corner. With the room now illuminated from the candle's soft glow, Asterious moved further in, his steps slow as he took in his surroundings.

He walked to her table by the shelf of endless jars, elixirs, and herbs. "Quite the apothecary."

Caramyn strode to the table, noticing the wilted leaves she'd never had a chance to dry. "You'd be surprised how many rare plants can be found here in the Woods—Here, smell." She opened a jar and placed it under his nose. "Willow Vein. One of my best sellers at Havenswood before people started getting suspicious."

The prince gagged and pushed the jar of powder away. "I'd be suspicious too if you tried to sell me that. That could kill a horse."

Caramyn tightened the lid with a laugh. "Despite the smell, it's the only cure this side of the river for Nerve Blight." She placed it back amongst her many other herbs and dried powders, thinking of the neurological illness caused by the bite of a fanged insect native to the forested mountains ranges.

"You no doubt saved countless lives." The prince walked to the window just above her bed, his hands folded behind his back as though he was afraid to accidentally touch something he wasn't supposed to.

"Maybe," she sighed. "But I took them, too. Mostly to spare them from the Shadows. But I'd be lying if I said sometimes it wasn't personal." Caramyn walked over to join him, noticing his fixation on the notch marks on the wall. Her heart dropped. She knew he'd ask. But he didn't. So she offered, because there were to be no further secrets between them. "I kept count of the men I killed."

The prince stared at the tallies, his face unreadable as heavy silence hung in the air like a wet towel. "One more and you would've made it to a hundred." He said matter-of-factly. She still couldn't tell what he was thinking, and it was turning her stomach to knots.

"That was supposed to be you," she said, watching the flicker of the candlelight cast a warm glow on half his face.

He turned his head, his gaze locking into hers. "Think of all the fun we would've missed out on." He smiled a taunting smile that lifted the weight from her heart and stole the air from her chest all at once. He was so handsome, so daringly, regally beautiful. And as they stood in one of the only places where she felt safe from the rest of the world, she realized she finally stood with the first person who'd ever made her feel the same way.

"Speaking of body counts," she said with a sly look. "How many women have you..." She glanced down at the bed, letting her gaze finish the awkward question for her.

"Well...none." The prince looked down as well, at the short space between their feet. He glanced back up, a darkness overshadowing the playful look in his eye. "I could never allow myself to get lost in that kind of passion. I couldn't risk a catastrophe for a few moments of pleasure."

"And that's why you can hardly stand to touch me." Caramyn blinked, a heaviness settling in the atmosphere. What kind of answer did she expect.

"When I touch you, I am nearly fractured at the seams. I fear I would bring down the world if we were to—" he straightened, a spark in his eye. "What about you? Did you ever have any fun with your trespassers before they met their untimely end?" The prince's teasing smirk returned.

Caramyn twisted her face into a sneer as she rolled her eyes. "Do you really think I would ever trust anyone enough for that?"

She chuckled with a head toss as she said it, but something in her ached at the truth in it. She yearned for intimacy—of both body and heart. As a woman, of course she felt natural desires for a type of satisfaction she'd never known. But she'd learn to push them out long ago. Pleasure, like love, was not necessary for survival.

So then why did she feel as though she would shatter without them now, as she looked at Asterious?

He smiled, his gaze flicking from her eyes to her lips, and stepped away from the bed—everything she wanted, right in front of her, yet so far from her reach.

"I should start the fire. These candles aren't doing much for warmth." Caramyn drifted past him to the hearth and set the wood kindling.

She felt his eyes on her, but his footsteps were everywhere else, as he paced around the room. "I still can't stop feeling like this is a place I've seen in my dreams." He swallowed, his eyes sweeping from her bookshelf and map scrolls to her wooden dining table. "No, not just a dream—a memory."

"When could you have possibly been here before?"

Asterious rubbed his forehead and looked up. "I remember staring at that thatched roof, hearing a woman sobbing. It's blurry but it's all coming back...bits and pieces. Yes—I remember...I was young, someone laid me on that table, af-ter..." he pointed, nearly breathless. "After...after my mother carried me through that door."

The room fell so silent it was almost tangible. Caramyn felt a chill, but it wasn't from the winter air. He stared at her, eyes haunted, and she stared back as the realization settled over her like the snow on the ground. And then he spoke again, confirming what she was thinking. "This was Zera's cottage. This was where she gave me the Blackheart."

"Then...it is because of Zera that we have found each other. And I'm starting to think we were always meant to." Caramyn shuddered. "Because my mother came her to ask her to save me, too. When I was supposed to die, as a Shadow-blood's child."

Asterious stepped toward her and brushed that same stubborn lock of hair from her face that he always did, somehow managing to avoid her skin, though she burned for the feeling of his touch. "Then does that make us bound by some saving magic?"

"I think it makes us bound by something," Caramyn whispered. "And it would explain why I've felt drawn to you since the day you carried me out of this forest."

"You feel it, too?" His voice was low "That incessant pull that never goes away?" He closed the distance between them, so that she could feel his breath on her skin. The desperation lingered between them, as though the air between them dared them to find each other.

Caramyn turned her face away, unable to face what she wanted to give into so badly. "Like an invisible string," she said.

He stood still as stone, but his eyes could not stop wandering her body, even as he finally said something, his voice low and breathy, like velvet night. "Do you know how dangerous this is? For me to be here alone with you right now."

She suddenly noticed there was no more space left to separate them. One nudge, one inhale, and their lips would meet. "I do," she breathed. "But dangerous doesn't scare me." She pressed her hands to his chest, looking up at him with pleading eyes, the growing fire in her concentrating in her core and pooling into a furnace between her thighs. "But the thought of losing you without even your touch to remember—that terrifies me. So please, I beg you, Asterious. Touch me."

Asterious took her hands in his, sliding his palms over her arms and up to her elbows, where he held her tenderly as he planted a kiss on her forehead. "I want you. More than anything, I want you, Cara. But it would mean damning us both."

"Then damn me."

He squeezed her arms in his grip like it would break him to let her go, his hands shaking. But then he did let go, and then he turned away and walked to the door with brash, hurried steps.

He reached for the doorknob, and Caramyn spat out the words without thinking. "The Shadows will kill you out there without me." She thought she saw him turn an ear toward her. "Don't you dare leave me here alone."

For a long stretch of silence that felt endless, she stared at his back, waiting for him to either turn the knob or argue. But he did neither.

He whipped around and stalked toward her without a word. Then he scooped up her face in his hands and pressed his mouth against hers like she was the last thing he would ever taste.

She tasted moonlight, pine, satin, and wine as his lips coaxed hers into parting, and she invited his tongue to dance with hers. Before she could tell what was happening, her own hands were reaching up, dragging her fingers through his hair, around his neck, and across the stubble that had grown during their time traveling.

He pressed her to him, the hardness between his legs firm and hot against her stomach. And she sighed with desire at the thought of feeling him. He spoke her name into her mouth, and she played with his breath, drinking in more of his taste, moaning as he covered her lips with his.

And then her back was against the wall, his heat closing in on every inch of her body. His hands slid down to her waist, but she grabbed one and guided it to the gap between her legs. He gripped her thigh, the pain of his grasp tantalizing. His kisses stole her breath as they drifted from her mouth to her neck, down to the opening of her shirt.

"We have to stop." He tore his mouth away from her just long enough to get the words out.

"Then stop," she said, though her eyes pleaded otherwise. He released a low growl as he gently sucked sections of her skin, a feral sound, almost inhuman. His muscles quaked against her as he tore down her sleeve to access her shoulder and collarbone. She shifted so that it fell even further.

Calloused hands scraped across the smooth skin of her breasts, giving gentle squeezes and teasing brushes. She groaned at the sensation, closing her eyes as she imagined what those hands—about what the rest of him—might feel like against the heat between her legs she could no longer ignore.

She reached for him in return, slipping her fingers beneath his shirt, tracing the map of old scars there, drifting lower with quiet intent. He recoiled as if struck, a sharp breath tearing from him. "I'm...I'm afraid. Afraid of what I could do to you," he said, silver eyes burning.

She stared at him for a breath or two, the absence of him already aching as her skin tingled in each place where his mouth had been. Gently, she took his face in her hands. "Don't feed the fear. Remember in the Spires? After you saved me—when you looked into my eyes, you changed back. The beast yielded. You were stronger than it. So, keep looking into my eyes now. Find what it was that you found then."

He hesitated, but then kissed her, and when he pulled away, his eyes locked with hers, slowing time itself. She could almost sense his every emotion, channeling through whatever unseen force was tethering them. She could even sense his heartbeat. It steadied. He breathed out the taut breath he'd drawn. His muscles relaxed, and she embraced him again, never taking her eyes off his.

Another hoarse and desperate rumble rose from Asterious' throat. "Are you sure you want this? If I cross the point of no return, you must promise me you'll run. Leave me here at the mercy of the Shadows."

"Yes." She nodded hungrily, brushing her lips against his. "I know it doesn't make any sense. But I want this. Because...because I want you, Asterious. And I'm tired of having to pretend that I don't." She pulled his face to hers, her fingertips raking across his thick midnight locks.

"Then have me. Before I break from the pain of needing you." He was burning hot. She could feel him aching with desire as he leaned his body into hers. She pulled apart the collar of his shirt so she could plant kisses on that muscular chest, covering each scar with the warmth of her lips.

She hadn't gotten far before he caught what clothing on her remained and tore it open, the fabric giving way beneath his hands as if he could no longer wait. His mouth found her neck again, lingering there before drifting downward in a slow trail of kisses, his hands firm at her hips as he guided her down onto the bed.

She fumbled at the buttons of his pants, undoing them with hurried fingers. When the barrier fell away, she paused, taken aback by every inch of him, before reaching out to trace him with tentative, reverent touches. He swore under his breath, his head tipping back on a strained groan, silver eyes flashing with a sharp, predatory gleam.

In a single, fluid motion he swept an arm around her, lifting her just enough to steal her balance before pinning her back against the wall. His other hand trapped her wrist above her head, firm and unyielding. The heat of his palm burned for a heartbeat—then roughened, his hold turning abrasive as claws unfurled in place of fingers, biting into the wood beside her wrist and locking her there.

Fear flickered through her, just for a heartbeat.

Until she met his gaze and held it. He growled through clenched teeth, as if wrestling something unseen, something vicious, inside his own mind. But then he steadied.

He Focused. On her.

On her eyes.

Those eyes that had so long been a mark of fear and hatred had now become a source of peace, the one thing that could pull him back from the edge, the only light capable of stopping his darkness before it swallowed him completely.

He released her wrist, only to send his hands exploring the rest of her. She shifted lower, and Asterious moved with her, following each breath like a loyal dog. He pulled his shirt over his head and leaned over her, his focused gaze never moving from her eyes. "I have to break this damn curse, because one day I want to be able to look at you—all of you."

Her chest heaved beneath him as she sank into the bed, letting herself melt into the weight of him. His hands explored her in deliberate, teasing movements, tracing the curves of her body, fingers lingering where her pulse quickened. He slid them down to her center, circling her nerves with lazy strokes before finding the depths of her. He lingered there with steady motions, and a low, sharp sound escaped her as shivers raced down her spine, the feeling of it all awakening new and beautiful sensations.

Her arms enveloped him, nails grazing his muscles as the gentle movements of his fingers continued to set her alight, while his other hand threaded through her hair, anchoring her against him.

He leaned close, forehead to forehead, lips hovering near hers, breathing mingling, silver eyes locked on hers. He withdrew, leaving her feeling empty, and then as his hands wandered along her body, a slick hardness pressed against her drenched center.

He groaned soft and low, hints of something feral in his voice. "Tell me if this is too much. Tell me before I can't stop."

"I don't want you to stop. Please," she whispered, the desire to feel him now becoming a need.

She pressed against him, back arching as he wrapped his arms around her, drawing her close. There was a sharp sting for a moment, a stretch that made her gasp, before a rush of warmth and pleasure spread through her, igniting every nerve.

He growled low, a mixture of frustration and desire, and she felt the tremor of his body beneath her. Each movement was stronger than the last, flashes of something wild lurking just beneath the surface. She shivered as the pressure building inside her released in waves, her hands clutching him as sensation pulsed through her.

With a sudden shift, he rolled onto his back, drawing her with him so she hovered above him, still pressed close. "I want you above me," he said between breaths. "In case something goes wrong...in case I'm not strong enough...you'll at least have a chance to run."

She nodded, pressing down into him, chasing the ache that had returned, letting it surge again. "I won't have to. You are strong enough," she whispered. "Because love does not make us weak."

Love.

She'd finally said it out loud.

And at this angle, looking down at him, she guided their rhythm, the heat between them rising with each movement. His hands roamed—sometimes gentle, sometimes claws—and she felt the growing intensity of his inner turmoil in every grip, every quiver.

His eyes squeezed shut for a moment, and when they opened, were framed by white hot lightning, looking through her, instead of at her. With no time to think, Caramyn leaned down, plunging her lips against his mouth. When she pulled back, his eyes followed, finding her again as they faded back to soft silver thunder. He reached up and squeezed beneath her jaw, tender and grounding, while she moved with him in a shared rhythm, lost in the sensation of his strength beneath her body. Then she found herself moving her hips more urgently, lifted and lowered by a need that had narrowed her world to nothing but him.

Suddenly the prince cried out with a sound that might've been a howl, her name spilling from his lips. He shivered against her, and a warm, surging energy flooded the space between them. Outside, the Shadows screamed their wailing song, and the candlelight flickered as a strange wind whispered through the room. She crested with him once more, their bodies rising and falling as one, fire sparking between them in the heart of darkness.

Spent from it all, Caramyn leaned down, planted a kiss on Asterious' swollen lips, and laid her head on his bare chest. She traced his scars—both flesh and Shadow—with her finger as his breathing slowed, and he reached an arm around her to stroke her hair. He pulled her to him, tucking her in the crook of his shoulder as he kissed her head and let his lips linger there.

"That was..." he began.

"Absolutely reckless?" Caramyn smiled.

"Hmm...reckless indeed."

"And yet, you didn't lose yourself," she said.

He chuckled softly with a relieved breath. "Oh, I lost myself. Just not in the way I expected."

She lifted her face to him, their lips meeting in an embrace before Asterious pulled away to whisper in her ear. "Caramyn of the Shadow Woods," he said softly, touching his forehead to hers. "You are both my ruin and my salvation. And I would have it no other way."

The fire in the hearth waned down to a flickering kindle, and the chill of the cold air finally settled on Caramyn's bare skin. She reached over to pull her pile of blankets and bedding across them both, burying her face into Asterious. She snuggled down into the mattress, entwining her legs with his beneath the blankets, treasuring the feeling of his strong body in this bed that for so long had only known hers.

She meant to say some words of devotion in return—to tell him she wanted to feel like this for the rest of her days, with him and only him, whatever the cost. But the candles' last light faded, and she was too tired and dazed to think. So, all she managed before her weary eyes closed to dream was, "And you, Prince Asterious, are mine."

A shiver woke her in the morning as dawn broke. She was on her side, her back nestled against Asterious, whose arms were wrapped around her as if he feared something would snatch her away in the night. She ducked deeper into the covers, wondering if what she remembered of last night had really happened, though their naked bodies pressed together like this was confirmation enough, and slight soreness between her legs made it all the more undeniable.

"Good morning." The rumble of Asterious' voice tickled the back of her neck. She rolled over to face him.

"Good morning." What else could she say? What could she possibly say to him after spending a night in the Shadow Woods entangled with him like nothing else mattered? After giving herself to him completely, all while his guard waited at the edge of the forest and his sister lurked within it, seeking its power for herself?

"How did you sleep?"

"Better than I have in a long time." He smiled, a lock of unruly hair sweeping across his forehead. "Far better than spending the night alone in chains, never knowing what emotions would be unleashed in my nightmares."

"You don't have to fear anymore," Caramyn whispered. "You were strong enough. You *are* strong enough."

"Only because of you, Cara."

She smirked softly. "Then I suppose you'll have to make sure you keep your eyes on me."

The prince's mouth curved into a smile. He closed his eyes and breathed deep, relaxed and free.

"There's a stream where we can wash up nearby before we set out." Caramyn sat up, despite every fiber of her yearning to stay in the warm, safe bed. But the intruder was still out there. And the Shadows were gathering. She could feel it. "Hopefully Nocthar has found something...anything."

The prince pushed himself upright, the covers sliding off him and revealing his perfectly muscular body. "Hopefully."

He stood and began to redress, and Caramyn looked at the shreds of her torn shirt and pants on the floor. Turning to her small wooden wardrobe by the bed, she rummaged through her clothing to find something new to wear.

"Sorry about that." Asterious muttered as he fastened his pants together. "I wasn't thinking."

"As you shouldn't have been. Because instead you were *feeling*." Caramyn shrugged with a playful curve in the corner of her mouth as she selected a black long-sleeve tunic. "I'd rather my clothing ripped to pieces than me."

The prince grunted, blinking those dark lashes as she left him with those words, and she proceeded to finish getting dressed. As she poked her head through the shirt collar, Asterious caught her eye, still sitting on the edge of the bed. Still staring at the floor as though his thoughts were holding him hostage.

She turned away, looking toward the small hearth where her kettle still hung. "I may have some oats and oil and whatever else that hasn't spoiled. Hopefully enough to make something warm to eat before we brave the rest of the Woods."

Asterious dressed in silence and then joined her at the hearth. But by the look on his face she wasn't convinced he'd finally settled whatever he warred with inside himself. It wasn't the time to ask him, but she only hoped he wasn't silently regretting everything—regretting *her.*

She shuffled to her herb shelf, just as the thought occurred to her, and swiped a jar of Moon thistle and Erri leaves—an effective contraceptive if taken within a day after the act. Regretful or not, the last thing she wanted to even consider was the possibility of it.

She turned around, and the look on Asterious' face as he stared at the burning kettle turned sour. "I can't believe I was so weak to give in. Last night, I knew better. I should've been stronger. If I'd have hurt you—"

"But you didn't." Caramyn set down the bowl she was carrying and strode over, placing her hands on his shoulders where he sat by the fire. "Don't you see? That was anything but weakness. It's not weakness to *feel.*"

Asterious looked up through locks of disarrayed hair, studying her eyes before speaking. "But what I feel," he paused, "is the fear that maybe this isn't real. You said it yourself—the pull we feel toward each other—it could just be from Zera's magic. What if we were just under the influence of some connection we don't understand. How can we even know what we truly feel for each other if magic is involved? What if it has manipulated us like it manipulates everything?"

"Damn the Shattered gods, Asterious. What are you saying?" Caramyn spat out the words in utter disbelief. "Did last night mean nothing to you? Are you really wanting to throw this away because you think it's just a trick of magic?

"I'm only saying that for now, until we know how this ends, we must deny ourselves any further affection. We should stay focused on the task at hand, and nothing more."

Something seethed inside of Caramyn. "Deny. Punish. That's what you've always done to yourself," she said. "And that's why you've begun to lose control. Stuffing it down only works for so long, until it finds a way out. Fear. Pain. Love. You can't push any of that down until it goes away. You can't ignore it. Eventually it will eat you alive. Trying to fight it is only making you weaker. To overcome a beast that preys on fear and pain, show it you're not afraid to feel anymore. Show it that you are not afraid to love and be loved, damn it."

"I am not meant to love you or anyone, Caramyn. You will *never* be safe with me if I can't rid myself of this curse. I may not lose myself with you. I may learn to control my fears and pain and whatever else. But sooner or later, I *will* have to kill again. And I would gladly kill a thousand men to protect you. But the moment I do, I will be lost forever. Along with my mind. And my love. And I cannot do that to you...*because* I love you."

Love.

The word from his lips rattled Caramyn to her innermost being.

"Fine. Deny me. And deny yourself. But next time warn me before you plan on breaking my heart, so maybe I can make an elixir to heal it in advance."

She ripped the kettle from the fire, refusing to give him another gaze, much less another word. And he didn't argue either, which made it hurt all the worse. But what made the pain even greater was that she knew he wasn't wrong.

So, she would still lead him through the Woods. She would still help him find the Blade to save the kingdom. And she would drive his sister out, even if she had to kill her. But she would not do it for him. She would do it for herself, and for a realm she would not see taken by misuse of her Shadows.

And after they each ate a small bowl of tasteless porridge in painful silence, they donned their cloaks and headed out into the Woods.

56
CONSIDER IT A DUTY

Asterious

He never should've let last night happen. He never should've done this to her.

Asterious followed Caramyn blindly through the thick of the trees, his thoughts echoing how beautiful she'd looked while unraveling beneath him in the candlelight. But now it was all drowned out by the wounded way she'd looked at him this morning, after he'd said the only terrible things he could think of to keep her from getting hurt far worse later.

They'd promise not to lie to each other. And he hadn't. All of it was truth. Cold, bitter, razor-sharp truth.

He trudged behind her, ignoring the ever-present hissing black fog threatening to nip at his ankles, as they headed deeper into the forest where he'd met this woman so many weeks ago. This woman who he never could have suspected would have brought his unfeeling heart to life.

And yet, he'd just broken it into pieces. Because it was all he could do to save her from the pain. Unless some miracle could save him, letting her love him would only end in tragedy one way or another. It would crush her either way, whether she would have to watch him become a monster forever—or end his own life in front of her.

The only hope was the Shadowblood's sword. If it couldn't save his black heart, at least he'd already done his part to spare hers...though that didn't change the fact that it was one of the most painful things he'd ever done. Far more painful than any blade that had ever left him bleeding.

Caramyn quickened her pace as the stream came into view, a narrow channel running through the forest like a vein.

Asterious was quiet, listening for the sound of birds to distract him from the thoughts that tormented him, but he realized there were no birdsongs this deep in the woods. The only sounds that filled this place were the whispering echoes from the Shadows haunting it.

Caramyn knelt at the stream, staring down in the trickling water as though she was captivated by something in her own head. Asterious waited for her to dip her hands in or lean over, but instead she straightened herself and looked over at him. Her eyelids fluttered, and she stuttered out a semblance of a word. "Asterious, I—"

The sound of flapping wings rushed overhead. The prince glanced up, squinting at the sun's glare off the frosted white branches. The raven had returned, soaring in figure eights, diving down just over their heads before swooping right back up to do it again, each movement brimming with urgency.

Caramyn leapt to her feet, never taking her eyes off the bird.

"Hide. Now." Her voice cut like stone.

The prince glanced around before he scrambled with Caramyn to find a place suitable enough to cover them in this maze of crooked tree trunks and twisting branches.

Distant hoofbeats and clanking armor closed in, their rhythm unsettling.

A Shadow curling at Caramyn's feet caught Asterious' attention. Snaking around the both of them, it coiled and curved through the trees. His eyes followed the winding black smoke against the white ground, settling on a massive fallen tree in the distance.

By the time he looked back, Caramyn had vanished, but her raven swept past him, leading him to the end of the fallen tree, a great dirt cradle from where the roots had once held. He slid down into the hollow space just as the footsteps passed right by the stream.

Asterious peeked through the gaps in the mossy cage of roots shielding him, hoping to catch a glimpse of what exactly they were hiding from. A small guard of men—dead men—marched through the snowy banks of the creek, their dead eyes as empty as the grave. Black metal armor glinted against the dullness of their decayed graying flesh as they moved in unison. Their steps appeared synchronized at first glance, but a closer look revealed the variation in their lifeless steps as they charged forward at the command of the one controlling them—a cloaked rider atop a nervous black horse that pranced behind them.

Asterious would recognize that regal silhouette anywhere. The jewel-encrusted horse head clasp on her cloak was enough of a giveaway on its own. But she pulled back her hood, lifting it over her obsidian crown, and with a quiet rage burning in her eyes, she scanned the area, searching desperately for something—or someone.

And beside her, atop a dark bay horse, was a man who was very much alive, marked by the ruddy color in his face and his eyes that scampered back and forth at his surroundings. And the familiar voice that pierced Asterious to the core as the rider slowed with a lift of his own cloak that made his features undeniable. Wryan.

Barring the confusion, the impossibility of it all, his greater worry was his soldiers, fearing Wryan might have done something to them. But he couldn't help them from here.

"This place is sending us in circles. We should've been at the Veil by now," Wyran hissed.

"Patience, Captain. I sense my brother's blood nearby. And even better." Sinevia lifted her chin with a wicked smile. "I sense his mate."

Mate?

His breath stuttered. It couldn't be. He'd considered it briefly but hadn't believed it could be possible—that he and Caramyn shared the rare bond of two souls intertwined before the Shattering itself.

But it would mean everything he'd felt, since the moment he saw her, was all real.

"Oh, she's here. And right by his side, no doubt." The sneer on Wyran's face told the prince all he needed to know. He'd told Sinevia about Caramyn, about everything.

Caramyn appeared beside him, sneaking in so quietly that he jolted at her presence. She moved like a wraith in this place. She knew every hiding spot, every fallen branch and dirt nook. But wherever she had been, he wondered if she had heard the same thing he did.

Mate.

He felt her body tighten next to him at the sight of Wryan glancing their way, and they both ducked down further.

"I have an idea," Caramyn whispered. "But you're not going to like it."

"What is it?"

"We never washed in the river. You still carry my scent." Her face was unreadable, void of emotion. "So, I suppose you can consider last night a duty, if nothing else. A necessity to mark you with my protection."

"Caramyn, that's not—"

"The Shadows won't hurt you, because they see you as part of me. You no longer need me with you to wander these woods." He was sure his expression must have betrayed his uneasiness as she continued. "I know these Woods and she does not. And whether she can manipulate Shadow magic with her spells does not change the fact that they are on my side. I'll lead her on a chase. It'll waste time and her Soldiers will expire. That will give you all the time you need to go find the Blade. Nocthar can lead you to it."

The thought made his stomach drop. She was his *mate*. And sending her into the hands of his enemies was something he could not bear to consider. Had she not heard the same thing? Was she pretending not to know? He couldn't bring up such a thing here and now. But neither could he express his devastation at her plan without doing so. "No...no, Caramyn. You want us to separate?"

"Why not? It's time we focus on the task at hand, remember?" Her amethyst eyes scorched as she turned his own words against him. She was always quite good at that.

Caramyn held her gaze on Wryan and Sinevia as they rode farther into the forest, the troops long ahead of them.

"It's too great a risk. This is my battle, not yours."

"It became my battle when Blackwynd blood crossed into these Woods."

She leapt up, her bow in hand, but Asterious grabbed her arm. "I won't try to stop you. I won't try to control you. But I want to make sure you understand that you'd damn better survive." He muttered, her face inches from hers.

She leaned in, her lips close—too close—as she cocked her head stubbornly. "I always do."

And then she was gone, like wind in the night.

Asterious whipped around at the shriek of surprise that came from Wryan, only to see Caramyn leap down from the treetops to land right in front of the horses, her fall softened by the Shadows around her. She looked up with cold eyes as the Shadows cleared, and the horses balked. "Did you get lost in my Woods, Wyran?"

Wryan was silent and went pale as a ghost. Sinevia stared at Caramyn for a long time, the air so tense Asterious could feel it from behind the tree stump.

"And just who are you?" Sinevia tilted her head, her unwavering gaze locked onto Caramyn. "Tell me like I don't already know."

Caramyn lifted her chin, but Asterious could see the way she subtly ran her fingers around her bowstring, the way she always fidgeted when she was nervous. "I am the Witch of these Woods. And you are a lost woman parading as Queen. The Veil's power will not truly give you what you seek."

"And how is it you know what I seek?" Sinevia laughed out the question, merely toying with her at this point.

"Because I once wanted it, too..." Caramyn's brow hardened, and she clenched her fists at her side. "You want vengeance. You want the world to mourn with you for what you've lost. And you want the power to make it happen."

Sinevia clapped her hands slowly, a low cackle escaping her red lips. "Beautifully put." She moved her hands, summoning Shadows from the most obscure corners of the forest, and sent them spiraling toward Caramyn, who made no effort to move, but instead stood her ground and watched the darkness come for her.

Asterious held his breath, gripping the edge of a root so hard it snapped. He could jump out now and let himself transform, driven by animalistic need to protect Caramyn and destroy these traitors, and kill every single one of them in less than ten heartbeats. But then he'd be trapped forever. Fully darkened by his curse until all that was left of him was a bloodthirsty, raging beast. One more kill was all it would take to imprison him forever.

He had to trust she knew what she was doing.

The Shadows collided into Caramyn, before breaking apart with a deathly whistle and falling away as if burned, slithering back to the depths from which Sinevia had called them. Relief flowed from Asterious in the form of an exhale. At least he knew even Sinevia couldn't turn the Shadows against Caramyn.

"Try again, *Queen*," Caramyn taunted her with a sideways smirk just before dodging an arrow fired from Wyran.

"Don't shoot her, you fool!" Sinevia reached across her horse and shot a burst of Shadow at Wyran, knocking his crossbow from his hands. By the time it hit the ground, Caramyn had once again disappeared, and Sinevia's fury roared at

Wyran and the Shadow Soldiers ahead. "Find that little bitch. If we have her, we have Asterious."

57

HEART OF THE VEIL

Asterious

The prince watched as his sister rode away, the footsteps of her undead guard still a haunting off-beat drumming in the distance. He seethed, wishing he'd ripped out Wyran's throat when he had the chance. But he had to focus. He thought of Caramyn as he felt the familiar knock of rage at his heart's door. Where once she was the very thing that sent him spiraling, now she was the only thing keeping him grounded. The icy snow on his hands as he climbed out of the hole shocked his system, snapping him out of his blinding fury.

He surveyed the treetops for the bird. A screeching caw rang out in the distance, and he followed it as fast as his feet would carry him across the mix of snapping leaves and crunching snow. The sound of his breathing became the only steady sound around him, each gasp a white puff of frosty morning air that sped up the longer he ran.

Left. Straight. Right. Over a log and through a thorn thicket. Right again.

371

His boots nearly slid on the frozen ground throughout the tight turns in this labyrinth of trees. Shadows danced around him, calling with their song carried on the branches, luring him, but he stayed fixated on the bird above.

With each footfall, he became increasingly disoriented. He knew not which way was right or left anymore. The Shadows' haze thickened, a deep dark smog slowly choking out his vision. He ran. He sprinted. He silently begged the damn bird to slow down. But he kept running.

The black and white forest blurred as he forced himself on, following only glimpses of black feathers flashing through the sunlight between branches. He could no longer hear the chirping birds or crackling leaves. His thoughts were void of words. Only visions. Visions of her. And of what he'd do to them if they hurt her. He could only stare, eyes locked onto black wings of hope darting through the trees.

The cold white ground disappeared beneath mist and shadow, a bleak thickness through which he waded, unharmed but not unaffected. The raven's call faded with each step, drowned out to the Shadow's aria. The clamoring echoes of the darkness grew maddening, an undeniable warning that he must be closer to the Veil than he'd ever imagined. Like shrill violins, like shrieking widows, like the sound of war and blood, their wails split his ears.

A weight burdened his shoulders, tearing and tugging at the healing wounds on his back like an unwelcome passenger—but an expected one—as he raced to the Veil. He gasped, the darkness so heavy it bound his very breath. He ran beneath the crushing weight, each step heavier than the last. His bones cried out in agony as they struggled beneath the weight his muscles failed to hold back. It was too much. Too much even for him. But not for a monster.

He could become it. There was no one around. No one's blood he could possibly shed. If he didn't, he would not survive the weight of this darkness. He would not reach the Shadowblood's Blade. He would not have the chance to break free of the curses that imprisoned him. And he would not see her again. His mate.

He thought of her eyes. Those bewitching, haunting violet pools of peace, where surely whole dimensions ended and others began. Those eyes that had stared down on him from above, as her touch coaxed his body and mind.

And then he found the strength to summon the demon he always fought so hard to hold back.

The dark fog clouding his vision gave way to the keen eyes of a predator, sharp and focused, so that he could once again see the black wings guiding him above. His fingers, curled into white-knuckled fists morphed into swooping razors rimmed with fur. And his veins glowed silver as his Light magic tamed the Shadow coursing wildly within him. Just enough. No further. The weight of the darkness tearing open his wounds became bearable. It was enough. And for the first time, he walked the line between man and beast, and did something he thought to be impossible—he commanded the curse within.

He prowled the earth with savage speed, somewhere between animal and human, every sense and strength heightened to withstand the weight of the Shadows' power. The wolf chasing the raven—to either his ruin or his salvation.

The smell of blood hit his senses, and he followed the scent to a dip in the forest floor where the Veil's darkness lingered like a wall of Shadow in the distance, blotting out what few shards of sunlight broke through the claw-like canopy above. Then he burst through a clearing, and the black bird swept up and soared out, lost somewhere in the black abyss. Asterious dug in his heels, scraping into the earth as he skidded to a stop to find himself standing amongst trickling streams of blood that pooled into crimson puddles on the white snowy ground.

He followed the blood paths, like red ivy veins claiming the forest floor. And there, even without his sharpened sight, he would've been able to see it clearly, but his wolf's sight enhanced it all the more. Lodged within a colossal ancient tree's twisting trunk—no doubt the very tree against which his father had slaughtered the last Shadowblood, still dripping with blood as fresh as the day he was killed—was a sword with a glinting black blade and a golden hilt etched with symbols. The Shadowblood's Blade, forged by Shadow magic and sealed in Lightborn blood.

The great tree stood taller than any other tree in the Woods, its thick roots mingled with the blood streams on the ground, and its branches formed an archway that stretched over and across the Veil as far as the eye could see, as if the single, sacred source of its power. As though this tree was the very doorway to Veil itself.

No—not a doorway. A heart.

Asterious shifted fully back to his human form, entirely at his own command, and stepped through the rivers of blood as his quivering hands reached for the hilt. He had to believe this time would be different, but he feared a fate worse than pain. What if he was not worthy or strong enough to remove the Blade? What if he'd come all this way for nothing, and he'd led everyone he cared about right into the hands of his sister?

His outstretched fingers touched the hilt. There was no searing pain, no stinging ache that coursed through his body. It called to him, in the same way that Caramyn called to him, through some unseen tether that pulled him to it. As if meant for him, and him alone.

He wrapped his hands around the handle and locked his feet in place beneath him as he prepared to dislodge the Blade. He expected resistance. But there was none. Not even a little. The blade loosened and slid out from the black bark with ease, yielding to his slightest effort to remove it.

A living, breathing weapon, he felt its essence overwhelm him with the whispers of the last Shadowblood's dying breaths. The blood dried up before his eyes, the last of it flowing into the roots of crimson veins leading into the base of the Veil. A force pulsed out from the Blade, sending a strange ripple through the air that quickly faded.

It had clearly broken at least one simple curse. But could it spare him from the other? He pulled down the collar of his coat, and his heart sank at the sight of his black creeping lines on his skin, still there, still one more stolen heartbeat away from claiming his fate forever.

Unchanged, with nothing left to keep him hoping.

And then the sound breached Asterious' senses. Boots crunching on the snow.

He turned to face it—Wryan, sword in hand and unfeeling amber eyes on the prince.

"You think I didn't expect you'd follow me." Asterious spat, looking up through the ruffled locks of hair above his brow.

"It makes no difference, Prince," he mocked the last word, a sly grin twisting across his face. "The fact is you brought me here. And now I know just where to bring Sinevia after I deal with you."

"You may have trained me, but you're a fool if you think you stand a chance against me, Wyran." The prince stepped forward, weighing the sword and silently relishing the feel of a blade in his hand after so long without. At least he knew one curse was broken.

"Oh, I'm not here to try to kill you," Wyran smirked. "We of course know that would be futile, anyway. But luckily, your sister has much more fulfilling plans for you." Ignoring Asterious' perplexed expression, he stepped closer, hand on the hilt of his own sword. "Besides, is that all I am to you, Asterious? Your trainer? Not the man who mentored you every step of the way after freeing you from your father's prison?"

"You manipulated me. You were no better than my father." Asterious snapped.

"No, Asterious. That's where you're wrong." Wryan shook his head, closing in. "I'm far greater than your father. Because I refuse to waste powerful resources when I see them. And I refuse to let someone who does stand in my way."

Then it dawned on Asterious all at once. "You—*you* killed the king. Not Sinevia."

"About time you figured it out." A darkness overshadowed Wyran's face as his mouth lifted into a smile, not a stitch of denial in his voice. "Your father was paranoid. And lazy. He dealt with you the easy way. Locking you away in that prison and throwing away the key. But you see, it's much more difficult to imprison the mind. To create a slave that doesn't even realize they are one." He grinned, touching the edge of his blade as he took another step forward.

"You think I'm your slave? You think you control me?" Asterious shifted, hands clenched on his sword, his world crumbling beneath his feet more and more with each word spoken.

"It was working rather well until that little whore came along and unshackled your mind." Wyran scoffed.

Trembling, Asterious spat, blood and power raging beneath his skin as the Shadows around them wailed. "You think Sinevia will reward you? She'll dispose of you as soon as you've outlived your usefulness."

"Like you did? The moment I turned on your little witch, I became nothing to you." Wryan closed the last bit of distance between them and swung, only to be met with sparks from Asterious' onyx blade.

"You were already working against me. All this time, long before I met Caramyn." Through clashing metal, the prince bared his teeth. "That's why you hated her. Because you knew she'd show me what I could not see. Because she would be able to lead me here before you could help Sinevia steal the Veil's power." Asterious tightened his grip on the hilt, the crossed blades locked in place as he held his ground against Wyran. "All I want to know is...why?"

Wyran deflected, pushing him away with the edge of his blade. "Someone has to improve upon what your father started," he hissed, coiling back like a viper waiting to strike. "And despite all the setbacks, I'd say the plan is still not totally ruined. You played right into it. You just led me right to the only thing capable of destroying you...and of opening the Veil." Wyran gestured to the great wall of unearthly shadow power behind him, as its smoky essence coiled and curled like a void of ghostly serpents. "And as an added bonus, you even brought leverage."

Asterious circled the glade opposite Wyran, every step measured, every muscle set for the next attack. "If you so much as think of touching Caramyn, I'll—"

"You'll what? Kill me? And therefore yourself? Then what?" Wyran's gaze hardened like the steel in his hand.

"I...I don't understand why you want any of this." Asterious squeezed his sword's hilt, his muscles taut with restraint. He wanted nothing more than to split Wyran in two and turn the snow crimson with his blood. "Why would you of all people want to open the Veil? What is it you're after?"

"Your Highness, with all due respect, I'm astonished that after all this time you still have not figured me out." Wyran sneered, cutting into Asterious with each word. "The Veil is not only a prison—it is a weapon. A sealed power so vast that even your father feared to name what lay beyond it. To squander it as a cage for magickind filth is weakness. Sinevia's power is just a means to an end. She'll raise me an army of the dead that she believes she controls. She will reduce you to a slave, no different from the rest of your kind. And with your Blade, I will have the power to unchain the Lightborn of my choosing from the Veil—not as citizens, not as allies, but as property. And in due time, alongside you and your sister, they will serve...or they will rot—at the feet of an Iron King." Wyran's voice crawled out like the haunting smoke of the Veil behind him.

Asterious faltered for words that wouldn't come, still unraveling everything, his feet seemingly frozen in place by invisible weights. Wyran stood before him now, merely a few feet away, within a blade's reach. "And thanks to that delightful ticking clock that is that heartbeat of yours, it's all entirely inevitable. It's simply a matter of time."

"You will *never* be King, you lying, fucking bastard," he growled, raw fury seething in his bones.

"Me? The bastard?" Wyran let out a cruel, wicked laugh as he closed the distance between them. "Poor Asterious...so starved and desperate for the acceptance of a father, that you overlooked all the warnings right in front of you." Wyran clicked his tongue. "You foolish, pathetic boy."

Something in Asterious snapped, and he surged forward, something far greater than rage rising in his veins. He swung the blade, and Wyran parried it with ease, that sinister smile still plastered on his face. Asterious called on that sliver of beastly power and shoved him backwards, swiping at him with the sword again before Wyran caught it in a cross-block.

"There it is. That brutish temper. Go ahead and let it take control." Wryan pulled back his blade with a chilling sound. "Make it so easy for Sinevia to make you her puppet, by killing me and becoming a mindless monster forever, leaving the fate of the kingdom—and your whore—in her hands. Whatever you choose to do, you lose."

Asterious lunged. A flurry of steel and sparks filled the darkness around them. The Woods echoed with the sound of cold clanging metal as their blades danced. Asterious knew he could kill Wyran easily with one stealthy dodge and a swift strike across the throat—and it took everything in him to keep reminding himself that Wyran wouldn't be worth the price.

Instead, he'd make him feel every bit of pain he'd caused him. Every bit of the torture he'd inflicted on his mind and body through the years. Every scar he'd convinced Asterious to take, he'd give him back.

His Light magic pulsed with each step, each breath. With invisible speed, he landed a well-placed slice across the side of his face. Wryan recoiled for a step as he wiped away the thin line of blood he seemed shocked to see, and then dove back in.

Asterious struck Wyran's sword, twisting his wrist so that he forced his arm back with it. Wyran yelped, and before he could even think to counter it, Asterious' blade was forcing his back again, scraping steel. He drove forward, his blade dipping down and across the back of Wyran's calf, drawing a stream of dark blood down his leg and a grisly cry from his lips.

"Pain is a tool." Asterious stated, recalling every time Wyran had spouted the words to him. "A necessary teacher."

He allowed Wyran the false hope of a block or two as he watched him limp toward him, playing on his desperation to hold him off here until Sinevia arrived.

He whirled around, flashing his sword up Wyran's ribs, flaying open the thin skin to expose the white stripes of bone. "Discipline—isn't that what you called it?"

Wyran howled in agony, but stubbornly tried to get in another hit, his movements crooked and crippled.

Asterious leapt back, and in the same breath, thrust his sword up into Wyran's outstretched arm, driving the blade through the flesh of his forearm like a spear.

His blood sprayed. He screamed out once more as his sword dropped to the snow, cold metal on frozen ground. Asterious pulled him toward him before he could drop to his knees, and as he looked into the man's amber eyes, his mind flooded with echoes of every twisted command, every degradation in the name of making him stronger that he'd ever wielded like a weapon over him. And he yanked him forward, bringing his face close to his.

"Whatever happens to me, it will be at my choosing. I want you to understand that you no longer have any power over me."

And with one last, unrestrained punch across his jaw, he tossed the bleeding, battered man against the trunk of the great tree that guarded the Veil.

And then he glanced down, smearing away the blood on the hilt of his sword. He focused on the markings, realizing they weren't just some decorative pattern. In the center of the carvings, there it was, with the same intricacy and delicate design—the exact same runic symbol Caramyn bore on her skin.

58

A MIRACLE

Caramyn

She leapt from each branch to the next one, nearly defying gravity, carried along by the Shadows and hidden in their mist. The queen rode below, only two remaining Shadow soldiers following behind her as they collapsed every few minutes, the magic sustaining them clearly exhausted, which meant the ones that had scattered with Wyran would be down soon, too.

"I know you're here, girl. Might as well show yourself," Sinevia called out with a sinister lilt.

Caramyn ignored her but climbed with purpose so that the branches would rustle with her movement. She wanted the queen to follow. Wasting her time was exactly the goal. She just needed to give Asterious enough time to find the Blade.

As she moved, flashes invaded her mind from a source she didn't recognize. Visions of the woman below chasing her. Images of her power, limitless and dark, held back by nothing to keep the balance. It distracted her, and her focus faded as she maneuvered through the woods.

"Perhaps the Shadows will not harm you, but that doesn't mean they won't betray your fears. Not when they have no choice."

She didn't understand it, but Sinevia had somehow become linked to her mind's eye. She sent visions of fire, visions of Asterious crying out in agony, deep scars bleeding from his back, and visions of her mother screaming as their home crumbled to ashes. She sent visions of Narahbi and Zera running from attackers in a frozen, empty tundra, and then visions of a black-eyed man gurgling on blood as he drove a sword through himself before the Veil.

The visions spun out of control in her head, coming one after another before she could determine memory from illusion and truth from lies, so horridly distracting and distorted that she couldn't move.

Sinevia waved a hand, uttering some incantation of old to draw all the Shadow wraiths to her. Caramyn felt their resistance from somewhere deep within her, but they succumbed to Sinevia's command. They had no choice but to obey.

The darkness surrounding Caramyn swirled like smoke before funneling toward the queen, abandoning Caramyn to the open treetops.

"Stop this!" Caramyn pleaded, the visions clawing at her sanity like ripping open barely healed wounds. "If you're powerful enough to do all this, what more do you want?"

"I want power that outweighs the fear of losing what I love. The power over life and death."

"But will it leave anything left for you to love?" Caramyn snapped, gritting her teeth as she fought to shake away the tormenting images in her head.

"I don't know," Sinevia cooed. "You tell me, Witch of the Shadow Woods. You're powerful, and yet you still seem to have lost your heart—and your sense—to love."

Powerful? She couldn't even master simple Spellbound magic and yet this Shadow queen spoke as though deep down she had a reason to revere her...maybe even fear her. What had her Seer abilities revealed that Caramyn could not see?

Caramyn laughed despite the pain in her mind. She would delay Sinevia as long as she could manage, no matter how deeply she cut. And as Sinevia filled her head with more horrific visions, she reached for her bow and took aim, desperate to end whatever game she was playing with her mind. Her Soldiers were all dead now. There was nothing to stop her.

The target was her upper arm, covered by no protection but the black sleeves of her elegant dress—nonlethal—and it would have been a perfect shot. But it flew right through her, as though she was no more than a ghost. Sinevia glanced up at her through an opening in the thick, dark branches. "Did you think I would really enter these Woods in flesh, unarmored, and unguarded?"

"How...how are you here then?"

"I'm very much here, girl. My mind. My power. But not my body. A Seer's greatest capabilities lie in illusion and transcendence—when one is willing to breach the limits."

"When one is willing to embrace forbidden magic, you mean," Caramyn shot back beneath her breath.

It made sense now, why the Shadows couldn't drive her out. She wasn't really there. No matter how real she looked, spoke and moved, it wasn't truly her. And that meant the real Sinevia...was somewhere else.

Perhaps still back in Felhold, safe on her throne. Perhaps standing right outside at the edge of the Woods. Or perhaps already at The Veil.

Suddenly she saw it flash before her mind. Another vision, brutal and unyielding. Asterious. Weak on his knees, trembling and covered in blood—Wyran's blood. He'd fought him, nearly to the death, with the Shadowblood's Blade, and now he was kneeling with it aimed toward himself, the tip of the sword hovering over his chest.

"No! Asterious!" She screamed his name into the nothingness of the forest around her, as if maybe by some miracle—if it wasn't just another illusion—he might hear her.

A wave of otherworldly force rippled through the air, and with it, a sharp pain reverberated in her chest. Had she felt it? Was that the moment Asterious had driven the Blade through his own heart? Was she too late to save him? Was any of it even real? She crouched over in pain, clinging to the branch from where she perched as Sinevia's laugh filled the space between them.

"So worried about my beastly little brother, aren't you?" Sinevia purred.

"It was just one of your visions—your lies..." Caramyn cried, tears welling as she pressed her hands to the sides of her face, trying to block out everything. It couldn't be real...it couldn't be...

But what if it was? What if she couldn't reach him in time. What if...what if...

"The thing about illusions, dear girl, is that they cannot manipulate the past. Only the future—because the future is not set. There are many paths it can take. I just have the power to show you the possibilities." Sinevia's stare could've pierced armor as she spoke, her voice like midnight. "What you saw may very well be Asterious' future if you do not stop him. Or, it may already be his past, because you failed to do it fast enough."

"You expect me to believe anything you're saying?" Caramyn cried, terrified that she was already too late. "You just want to trick me into leading you to him and to the Veil."

"I don't expect you to believe me. I don't care if you do. But if you don't, I will still find the Veil one way or another, eventually. But if you do," Sinevia continue softly, "you might still stand a chance at saving your prince."

"How?" Caramyn groaned through clenched teeth.

"Because if you simply show me where the Veil is—show me in your mind—I can take us there. Right now. In less than a heartbeat." Sinevia's smile sharpened. "And if Asterious really is there waiting with a sword aimed at his own heart, you may yet save him."

And if he's not...

Then it wouldn't matter. If Asterious was already gone, nothing would matter at all. He was supposed to be the rightful king. He was supposed to restore the balance of Light and Shadow and save its people. He wasn't supposed to die.

Just like he wasn't supposed to break her heart.

"Fine," Caramyn said, the word torn from her through the tears burning down her face. She dropped from the tree, boots crunching into the snow, and turned to face Sinevia, who watched her calmly from atop her black mare.

The queen slid down from her horse and extended her hand. "Lead me to the Veil."

The weight of the choice stung like ice in Caramyn's lungs. But the image would not leave her—of Asterious plunging that blade through his chest and bleeding out on the snow—and the choice became crystal clear.

She closed her eyes and reached for Sinevia's hand, picturing the path she'd taken so long ago out of sheer curiosity to the depths of the Woods where the Veil loomed. And in an instant, when her fingers touched Sinevia's open palm, the world unstitched.

Cold vanished. Sound collapsed. It felt as though her thoughts were being wrenched open, peeled back layer by layer, as Sinevia's will slid through her memories with ruthless precision. The path through the Woods blazed behind her eyes. The twisted roots, the narrowing dark, the heavy, suffocating pull in the air as the Veil drew near. Space folded inward, crushed, and remade around that single remembered place.

And for a breathless, agonizing instant, she was nowhere at all. Somewhere even the Shadows couldn't reach, caught between heartbeat and thought—all in the span of a blink.

And then she was there—feet slammed into solid ground again, winter air brushed her skin, and the overbearing weight of the Veil hung before her, presiding over a broken, blood-spattered Asterious—who stood staring down at the sword in his hands.

But he wasn't aiming it at himself. Instead, he held the length of it across both hands, the flat edge resting in one hand as his eyes stared down at the hilt in the other, as if deep in contemplation.

"Asterious, stop!" Caramyn ran to him, all other thoughts falling away into the bloodied snow beneath her feet. She didn't know if she'd left Sinevia standing behind her. She didn't care.

Asterious dropped the sword, the metal hitting the ground with a cold clang, and she ran straight into his empty arms, begging, pleading as her voice nearly caved in. "Don't you dare! Don't you dare!" She screamed, pounding her fists against his chest with each word. "You thought you could make me hate you, didn't you? That's why you pushed me away...so that I wouldn't try to stop you...but you're a damn idiot if you think I was going to let you do this."

"I—I wasn't." Asterious stuttered, "I mean, I did consider it...but how...how did you just—" He glanced at the space from where she'd just appeared, and Caramyn glanced back as well, expecting that Sinevia would be standing there. But she was nowhere to be found.

"Sinevia..." she said, eyes darting around the glade, "She's gone. She tricked me. She showed me a vision of you about to kill yourself with the Blade...So that I would show her how to get here—to save you." She spoke through hurried gasps, confused, ashamed, and paranoid that she'd just done something irreversible. "It was all an illusion."

"No. It wasn't." Asterious stuttered. "For a moment, I thought I might...I thought this land—thought *you*—would be much better off without me. And that at the very least I could be remembered as a man...instead of a monster."

Caramyn pulled back, hoping he could feel the heat of her glare. "Why would you ever think such awful things? We'll be monsters together. I don't care. Asterious, you freed me from the darkness of a prison I didn't know I was in. I *need* you...I..." the thought trembled its way from her lips. "I love you."

"I know," Asterious nodded, nearly shaking, tears shining in those steely eyes. "And I love you more than I ever even thought possible...which is why

I thought you were safest in a world without me in it. I thought my enemies would stop coming for you if I was gone…" Asterious choked out the words. "But then it occurred to me that was a fool's thinking. Because the enemies of this realm are more powerful than we realized." He placed a hand on either side of Caramyn's face and stared into her eyes, no longer with tenderness, but with a newly awakened fierceness as he steadied her between his hands. "But so are you."

Caramyn looked up at him, her brows drawn together in confusion as to what he meant by those last four words. He guided her gaze downward, pointing at the Shadowblood's sword lying in the snow between their feet.

"Look at those symbols, Caramyn. Look at the markings on your arm. They are the same." His voice rose with urgency, with confidence. "Caramyn…*you* are the Blade. Forged by Shadow and sealed in Lightborn blood. You are the impossible daughter of a Shadowblood and a Lightborn." He smiled. "Not a mystery. A miracle."

"What? No, it can't be. I don't understand." Caramyn stepped back, paranoid that Sinevia lingered somewhere unseen among them.

But Asterious was right—amongst other swirling symbols, the main sigil was the same as the one beneath her skin. Identical. And it made her shudder with overwhelm.

Asterious picked up the Blade. "You said it yourself, Caramyn—the darkness that guards the Light. The Shadow Woods have protected you all this time because *you* are the magic left behind by both Light and Shadow." Asterious' eyes flashed like lightning as he spoke. "The legend said whoever could bear the weight of its darkness—of its power—could free the Blade. I've seen your darkness Caramyn, and I'll bear it with you until the end of time."

Caramyn blinked as the words crawled from her in a whisper. "If it's true, then how do I stop this?" she stammered, more to herself than to him.

And then suddenly around them, the ground vibrated with the intensity of an earthquake. Asterious held her steady, fighting to keep them balanced as the snow cracked like stone, breaking apart like shards of ice as the ground below opened, the Veil's mist erratic and vicious.

From seemingly thin air, with arms outstretched, Sinevia materialized at the base of the Veil's great towering tree, chanting, muttering words in the ancient languages—words that Caramyn had come across in her readings but did not understand. Her tongue flowed freely, the incantation rolling from her scarlet lips, and an essence of dark power began to emerge from the Veil, toward her, ebbing and flowing toward her and back in an indecisive movement like the tide.

Bodies crawled from the earth, clawing their way up by their skeletal remains still clad in ancient Lightborn armor—the lifeless shells of those soldiers who fell here, battling Shadowbloods and drawing them to these Woods. They rose from the earth with groans and gasps, their eyes black voids of nothing, and marched with a crippled gait toward the queen, forming a protective circle around her.

With every fiber tensed, Caramyn looked on, her mind racing through a slew of ideas for what she could possibly do. If she was the Blade, why did she feel so helpless? How was she meant to stop this?

And then Sinevia's incantation stopped mid-word. The Veil flickered and the queen took a step back, something like fear—or perhaps disappointment—written in her serpent green eyes. The soldiers surrounding her stiffened. They breathed in horrific moans as though each breath was their dying one, and all at once they collapsed where they stood.

The queen wiped her hands on the long black skirt of her dress. "Well, well, well. How very strange. How very...unexpected." Her voice was wrought with dry, feigned surprise. "Something is already claiming the Veil's power...draining its essence like blood." She slowly turned around, as though the realization had crept up her shoulder while she spoke. "Or *someone.*"

Her eyes flicked straight to Caramyn and Asterious. She turned away from the Veil and stepped toward them, moving like satin, sleek and quiet. Asterious stepped in front of Caramyn, placing himself between them as he gripped the sword at his side.

"Brother." She looked at the prince with a wicked twitch of her lips. "It seems your darling 'Blade' is no more than a conduit. Her heart beats at the mercy of the Veil. And why? I do not know. But nor do I care. For as long as she breathes, the Veil's power is untouchable."

"Then there is nothing left for you to gain, Sister." Asterious said coldly. "Sinevia, this is not how I hoped to see you again. But it is unfortunately what I expected. Leave now. Renounce whatever pact you've made with the Shadows in exchange for their power. You are not a Shadowblood. You will never be able to wield their magic without corruption."

"You see, brother, that is where we differ. I do not care if my power comes with a price. You, however, expect the strength without the sacrifice. You want the crown without the blood."

"I've paid far more than my share in blood," Asterious said, his voice low with restrained fury. "The difference is that the cost of your power isn't yours alone. You're hurting innocent people."

"And you think you—a half-breed, bastard creature—belong on the throne?" Sinevia sneered.

"I belong to both worlds," Asterious said evenly. "And that is precisely why I can unite magickind and humans. You won't have to fear your own magic the way you did under our father." His gaze sharpened. "You're a gifted Seer, Sinevia. Imagine what you could do for the human court. I will restore the Lightborn court, and together we can bring the kingdoms back into balance. You could use your power for good."

"I *am* using it for good," Sinevia snapped. "The world needs order, and all other attempts to sustain it have failed. Magickind and humans have been given chance after chance at peace, and every time they've proven they don't want it." Her voice hardened. "You think you understand what's best for this realm? You know nothing, Asterious. You were caged as our father's slave. You know nothing of the world beyond those dungeon walls."

"I've seen enough of this world to know that I can't let it fall to you like this."

Sinevia raised her arms in surrender with a smirk. "Then kill me, Asterious. End it now. That's all you have to do."

The prince stared at her, unmoving. Caramyn watched him squeeze the hilt of the sword as if to seek some encouragement from the weight of it in his hand. She didn't know if perhaps that magic blade would be able to kill even the illusion of Sinevia, as her arrow could not. But even if it could, she knew well he would hesitate to kill his own sister, whether because he truly cared for her or because he feared it would be just enough to darken his heart forever. And Sinevia clearly knew it, too. Which is why she was prodding him, urging the beast to come out so that she could take him under her control. It had to be. Why else would she be wasting her time toying with him like this?

The queen lowered her arms with a shrug. "I'm disappointed but not sur-prised. Even with that indestructible beast inside you, you're still the weak little boy you've always been."

"Do you hear yourself, Sister?" Something in Asterious' voice cracked. "Do you see what you've become?"

"I see it clearly, dear Brother." Sinevia grinned.

Asterious leaned forward, growling through his teeth. "And what else do you see clearly? Do you remember what you promised me?"

Caramyn listened intently, remembering what he'd told her about their childhood promise, and wondering if this was the real reason Asterious was holding back—the frail hope of finding out what happened to his mother.

"Oh, I see what this is about. I did promise, didn't I? To show you your mother's untimely end. Are you sure you want to know what really happened?" Sinevia nodded, her crooked smile sending a wicked chill.

Before Asterious could answer, Caramyn leapt in. "Asterious, no. She's play-ing with your emotions. She wants you to see it so that you'll break. And then she can put you under her control."

Asterious stepped back, lowering his blade, and held his head high. "I will not break, Caramyn," he said. "You have shown me that I am at no one's mercy but yours. And because of you, I am finally strong enough to face what seeks to break me." He looked at her with eyes that pleaded beneath their steely armor. "And right now, I'm asking you to trust me."

And then something slid into her mind—not the sharp and invasive presence of Sinevia, but a calm, familiar warmth that she recognized as Asterious—somehow a shared thought carried across some unseen link. And that's when it occurred to her that this might be more than just a test of his strength and will. It was one last attempt to reach his sister, to draw her out of her darkness one last time, by the fragile echo of memory of a time before curses, crowns, and broken promises separated them.

"Your witch is clever," Sinevia mused. "But if you're so foolish as to think you can bear the burden you're asking for, I'd be a greater fool to refuse you. It's easier than provoking you, I suppose. Though I admit not quite as fun."

Caramyn watched as a tense silence stretched between them. She noticed the way Asterious gripped his sword, as if seeking its reassurance, before he yielded to his sister with a nod, The queen waved a hand, touched her fingers to Asterious' head, and he flinched. Caramyn drew a breath, every muscle in her body coiled and ready to spring as she watched each move Sinevia made. But something in that bond deep within her that linked her to Asterious' thoughts told her to wait. To let him have this.

And so she did.

59
CHILDHOOD MEMORIES

Asterious

"If you come to regret this, Asterious, don't blame me." Sinevia crooned. "The truth has been hidden from you for so long. But Father did always love hiding things." She stepped near the prince, whispering unknown words into his ear with a chilling softness in her voice. A void of black shrouded Asterious' vision, leaving nothing before him but empty, unending darkness.

"Asterious!" Caramyn's voice cut through the smog in his mind like chiming bells in a dream. Blinded, he called for her.

"She's gone, Brother. You are alone. Entirely alone. To finally face the truth. *Your* truth."

Asterious shifted and wavered, struggling to find his footing in a world that did not bend to reason or laws of nature. The space around him softened, dissolving into a vision woven from the mist of his deepest memories. Shapes stirred within it, glowing faintly like embers in the dark, their outlines slowly gathering form until figures long buried in the past stood before him once more, in the great throne room of Blackwynd Court.

He was brought before the King, his wounds fully healed, but now a weight in his young heart and a terrifying feeling that was gnawing its way outward.

"He survived your trial," his mother said proudly. "Now make him your heir."

Daemar sat back in his throne, his eyes wide with astonishment for a brief second or two, and then unreadable. "How can this be, Elysia? Unless something unholy has been involved. Something...magic." The King stood to his feet.

Elysia laid a hand on Asterious' shoulder. "Regardless of how, he is still your son."

A long silence darkened the air before Daemar finally spoke. "I will not claim a son who is tainted with magic. Prove to me that he healed of his own capability, and I will consider it."

"No," Asterious spoke, his legs trembling as he balled up his fingers into fists. "You won't. You won't do it, just as you won't stop lying to my mother, and giving her hope just to take it away. You will never accept me."

"Asterious, don't say anything. Be quiet, my love." Elysia leaned down to whisper her nervous warnings into his ear. But it was too late. The King's guards were moving already poised to seize them.

Daemar snapped his fingers. "Arrest them both. For treason by use of magic for unlawful purposes."

The guards closed in, Elysia locking her arms around her son protectively as she screamed at the King for mercy. "You cannot prove anything! Do not harm my son!"

Daemar watched from his throne, unmoved, as a guard ripped Asterious from his mother's grip. He fought them, kicking and punching, but when a guard struck his mother across the face with the edge of his knuckles, something greater than rage took hold of him. A bloodthirst, a fury like nothing else he'd ever felt. And then he was tearing open a guard with his claws, pulling out his innards with fangs, the acrid tang of blood in his mouth. The guards weren't strong enough to stop him, no matter how many of them swarmed and stabbed him. And the more they tried, the stronger he grew, feeding the darkness hungering within him as he ripped apart each one. He destroyed guard after guard as the King was ushered away out of the room. His mother's screams filled the air, horrified as she ran to him, clinging to the purest, wildest hope that she could stop him. She called his name, pleading through a voice shattered by tears and terror. "Asterious!" She gripped the fur on his shoulder from behind, begging, crying. "I'm sorry, my son! This is my fault! Asterious, please, you must stop!"

But in his unleashing, he whirled around and swiped her with his great claws, flinging her into a column that killed her instantly. She lay there, bleeding from where her head had met the column's edge, and the scent of her blood filled his nostrils among the rest. More guards came, and he killed them, too. Until he finally collapsed from exhaustion—from the toll the Blackheart's transformation had taken on his body—only to awaken wounded, with no memory of what happened except the dried blood beneath his fingernails, chained to the dungeon floor where he would spend the next fifteen years.

Something gave way and collapsed within Asterious. A suffocating emptiness in his chest that swallowed him whole, drawing breath from his lungs and dragging him under. He felt cold, and afraid, and weak. Nothing could have prepared him to see what he'd just been shown.

He wanted so fiercely to believe it was a lie—an illusion sent to rip open his deepest wounds—but he knew deep down that it was the truth he'd been avoiding all along. His greatest fear had been made real and undeniable from this point forward, seared into his mind forever. He would forever carry the pain, the shame, the guilt, and the grief of the horrifying truth that he had killed his own mother.

"He...he told me he'd imprisoned her somewhere far away..." Asterious' croaked out each word, through tears that ached as they fell.

"And he had no intention of ever telling you the truth, just as he had no intention of ever making you his heir." Sinevia's words were sharp, but she stopped, and a glimpse of that little girl that used to visit him in the cell broke through for a breath or two. "I saw them take you out of that room. That was the first time I learned you existed." She added, almost gently, almost like she cared.

He expected her to laugh at him, to meet his pain with sneers and taunts. But she only watched the tears he shed roll gently down the curve of his cheek. And something in her eyes shifted, like she longed to say something. Something softened, unfocused, as though she gazed at him through a memory instead of the broken man that stood before her. For a mere moment, her lips parted, words clearly there on the edge of being spoken.

He looked at her, hoping, praying she would say something that would give him any semblance of hope his sister was still there.

But she only tightened her jaw and looked away. And that quiet, intentional restraint cut more deeply than any cruel words she could've said.

He would forever carry the pain, the shame, the guilt, and the grief of the truth that he had killed his own mother. It would never soften, never loosen its hold on his heart. It would walk beside him in every choice he made, a hollow ache he could neither outrun nor forget. But he would not let it control him another day.

And then, just as he expected to look away to see Caramyn standing beside him in the glade, he was no longer at the Veil's glade, or even in the Woods. He was nowhere, and yet somewhere all at once—a void of nothingness, then back in the cell where his father imprisoned him all those years.

The revelation settled deep into his bones—he was still trapped in Sinevia's visions, locked within his own buried memories. And he could not find the way out.

60

RAVEN'S SIGHT

Caramyn

Caramyn watched Asterious and Sinevia in the snowy glade, a strange, silent moment between them as they faced each other, appearing more like broken siblings yearning to find peace with one another rather than two enemies fighting for a kingdom.

She kept a wary eye on the prince, refusing to feel comfortable leaving his mind vulnerable at the hands of his sister. He stared into nothingness, trance-like, his body still there but his mind very much somewhere else.

And she stood there, alone in a sense, left with only the scene around her to absorb— the Lightborn Prince and the dark Queen standing like statues, locked in their trance in the midst of a circle of corpses. And behind them, the great black void that was the Veil, churning and groaning as though it was angry it had been disturbed, as the massive tree that guarded it like a gate seemed to twist and sway. She studied it carefully, noticing the streaks of dried blood that ran down its bark and seeped into the base of its roots. And she noticed how the sigil on her arm bore a strong resemblance to the shape of the tree itself.

Then her eyes followed the twisting roots upward, the veiny lines reminding her of her own vine-like markings—the same one etched into the Shadowblood's Blade—and a shudder trickled down her spine. If she was the true weapon, what did that mean she had to do to wield herself? Where was her power, and how was she supposed to know how to access it?

And then, as her mind swarmed with these thoughts like a panicked flock of birds, her gaze snagged on the curves of the tree's trunk, tracing it with her eyes up midway to notice the ridges in the bark that were barely there, but clear enough to be seen by someone looking for them.

A vaguely familiar mark.

Not a mark. Not a rune. But a signature—one she swore she'd seen before, in coarse black ink at the bottom of a letter never meant to be found. Shaped with the same curving lines as the branching roots winding through her veins. A precise "M," formed in sweeping strokes like the outstretched wings of a raven—the seal of Morveth.

The chilling realization stole her breath as she considered that her father and Morveth were one and the same.

The Shadowblood who warned the Lightborn of their downfall was the very same who, at Daemar's command, sealed them behind the Veil. The same Shadowblood forced to bind all magic—even his own—away from the realm. The same Shadowblood whose mark lay hidden within her own.

And at last, she understood.

The prison was just a façade on the surface—a literal veil, hiding the truth deep within these vicious Woods—and guarding the Light locked behind it.

It *was* Morveth's last stand before his destruction—not against the Lightborn, but against Daemar, and those like him with truly darkened hearts, by sealing away *all* magic here to protect it from those who would seek to twist it for evil, locking it beyond reach in a world being stripped of Light.

Shadowbloods were never the enemies. They were never the real evil—they were the ones holding it back. The guardians of darkness. The balancers between

Light and Shadow. They bore the darkness where others could not. And since the Shattering, they had been driven into solitude, feared and reviled for the very power that defined them—just as she had been.

The world believed Shadowbloods and their power were a danger. But perhaps the true danger was in their absence.

The realization struck like mist lifting from her eyes, and it became all too clear what she was meant to do. She had spent so long believing her connection and immunity to the Shadows made her something less, something worse than even them. But now she was more sure than ever that it was her strength, guarding what little Light still burned within her.

As she watched Sinevia invade Asterious' mind with power never meant for her, Caramyn saw the future she would become if she failed. Sinevia was not born a monster. And neither was she.

She would guard her heart. She would resist. With power or without it. Even when the path forward wasn't clear. Even when it seemed too small to matter. Even when it felt futile or insignificant to fight back, she would not let the darkness win.

And as she looked back at Asterious, something in her understood where her next steps must lead, and what she must do in that moment.

The prince stood stiff, tensed, his back arched and his body trembling, tears pouring from his eyes. Helpless, unable to move. Unable to escape whatever horrors Sinevia was putting before him.

She knew he'd asked for this. But something was wrong. Sinevia had shown him the truth, and now she was not letting go. He'd shown her he was strong enough to tame the beast, and now she was going to try and awaken it by force. And as Asterious' body quaked and shivered, Caramyn reached for the sword in his hand.

Nocthar screeched above, battering his wings and circling with his warning call. And the moment she reached for the sword, he dove down in front of her as a crossbolt fired from somewhere in the Woods.

In a burst of black feathers, Nocthar dropped to the ground, his body pierced through by an arrow. Gone as quickly as one beat of his wings, he'd taken the shot meant for her without hesitation.

From the direction of the arrow, Wryan crawled out of the forest, his blood trailing across the shallow snow, just enough life remaining in him to have been lurking in the shadows, waiting for the moment to strike. He held the crossbolt tucked beneath his arm, dragging himself along the ground with the other before he collapsed from the effort.

Of course he'd found Asterious, and of course Asterious had no other choice but to leave him alive. But she was not bound to grant him the same mercy. And at the sight of her beloved raven, impaled, gasping and flailing at her feet, she drew her own arrow and stormed over to Wyran.

With the tip of her boot, she nudged the underside of his jaw, forcing him to look upward.

Wyran spat blood as he glanced past her at Asterious still trapped within Sinevia's trance. "Looks like the dog will not be able to save his bitch after all."

"Now I know why the Shadows let you get this far," Caramyn hissed, bow-string pulled taut and aimed at his head. "So I could put you down myself."

"You can end me, but you and your kind will always be remembered as the villains of the story." A cold smile crept across Wyran's pale lips.

"Perhaps, but you will never again have the chance to help rewrite it." She'd barely finished the words before she released the arrow. Directly into the space between his eyes.

She turned, ran, and dropped to her dying raven's side, overwhelmed at the disasters unfolding from every angle.

"No...no! Nocthar...no," she stammered through tears, pulling the gasping bird into her lap. His frantic breaths slowed. And she swore she could almost feel the small, waning patter of his heart. His movements stilled, as though her touch calmed him in his final moments. He turned his head, his glassy black eye reflecting the swirling void around them, and made an effort to curl his talons around her finger just before his body went limp.

She couldn't think straight. She couldn't see through the tears.

Her raven was dead. Her guardian, her watchdog, her very eyes. He'd guided her through every turn of the seasons for the past five years. He'd led her to fresh water, to prey, and warned her of danger more times than she could count. And now he'd given his life for hers in one final, ultimate act of loyalty.

And now failing the Shadows, leaving the Veil vulnerable, were no longer options. Nocthar's sacrifice would not be in vain. Some power in her was awakening, and she no longer feared the consequences of using it. And if Sinevia thought she could hold Asterious captive in his own mind and force him to succumb to his curse, she would face the wrath of the last Shadowblood. She would find a way to break him free before the beast did.

And that's when she noticed it. Nocthar's body in her lap became weightless. His night-black feathers faded like smoke, dissolving into the air as it coiled upward into nothing—into the Veil. She grasped at his vanishing form, desperate to keep him with her, but within mere seconds he had become mist, drifting past her, past Asterious and Sinevia, and toward the great Shadow abyss before them. Before his last feather fizzled out, she reached out in one last attempt to secure a piece of him.

The feather became a ribbon of shadow, wrapping itself around her hand as it twisted to reveal the faintest shimmering pulse of some amethyst and onyx magic for the length of a heartbeat before it snaked its way across her eyes and slithered down into the mark on her arm. And then she blinked.

"I created Nocthar," she whispered under her breath.

"You manifested your own instincts—your own power—the only way you knew how." Sinevia's voice caught her off guard. She leapt to her feet, wiping the tears away in a frenzy as the queen continued, walking toward her, talking to her, fully present, though Asterious still stood steps away, frozen in her snare. "That's how it happens. You don't realize the extent of your power until one day you do something you don't understand and there's no other explanation. And you realize, it's been there all along, bubbling up inside you like a pot boiling over…Until it spills out, and you realize you were never powerless at all. You just didn't know how to use it," Sinevia said. "You see, some of us are granted great power, and choose to waste it. And some of us are destined to take it, so that we can put it to proper use."

Caramyn, chilled by her words, flicked a desperate glance over at Asterious, his mind locked away somewhere she could not reach, while his body remained cemented in place. Then she whirled back to face the queen, who was tracing some pattern with her fingers, as if drawing runes in the air.

"Nothing in these Woods belongs to you," Caramyn growled. "Including Asterious. Let him go." The demand seethed out through her teeth. "You showed him what he asked to see…and he's shown you he cannot be controlled any longer! Release him!"

"Release him? And interrupt our lovely conversation here." Sinevia trilled, stepping closer. "We were just getting to the good part."

Suddenly cold, skeletal hands gripped Caramyn from behind. She glanced over her shoulder all too late to see a single resurrected Shadow soldier looming over her. The smell of rotting flesh and decay attacked her senses as much as it attacked her body, yanking each arm behind her so that she could not wriggle free from the grip of death that held her. And as she struggled, Sinevia closed the gap between them.

She stood inches before Caramyn now, the Veil groaning and rippling behind her, the Shadow wraiths wailing in protest around the border of the glade, where it seemed they could not enter. And even if they could, they'd be useless against an enemy already dead.

Sinevia lifted Caramyn's chin. She pinched the sides of Caramyn's face between her thumb and finger, digging the nails in as she stared straight into her eyes. "The last time I saw violets like those, I crushed them."

Caramyn ripped her face away with a snap of her teeth. "Your brother would prefer to save you," she said, "but I won't hesitate to kill you if you leave me no choice."

Sinevia seemed to ignore the threat. "Your power—your very life—is tethered to the Veil, to the last great source of Shadow magic. I don't even know how it's possible, but all that raw power is funneling straight to you." Sinevia reached forward, reaching a scarred finger towards her chest where she dragged it over Caramyn's heart. Her pulse thrummed so loudly in her ears it drowned out the hissing Shadows surrounding them. The queen purred, tapping her lips in thought until a devilish smile formed. "That fascinating truth has placed you in my way. And for that, you must be removed."

And that's when it struck Caramyn—the faintest glimmer of a falter in Sinevia's illusion. She'd flickered, off and on, as she spoke, almost unnoticeable. But just enough to let Caramyn know it was a drain on her power to maintain so many illusions at once—to summon a Shadow soldier long enough to restrain her, to hold Asterious in a trance from a distance, subjecting him to whatever horrible visions she was conjuring. And to still be here, talking to her.

She closed her eyes, reaching for her deepest instincts, for trust in her own power, drawing something through that Shadow link threaded through her blood.

And she became, for a moment, Nocthar. Only this time, she saw through the raven's eyes as though they were her own.

Her awareness tore loose from her body, rising into an omniscient vantage that showed her the scene with inhuman clarity, as if she were watching herself from across the veil of reality—herself restrained by a battle worn corpse, Sinevia standing before her, animating the creature, and Asterious, frozen in place with vacant eyes, the Shadowblood's Blade still clenched in his hand.

The sword in his grip did not belong to this world, but the realm of the Veil. It existed outside of Sinevia's design, bound to no single reality she could manipulate. Its edge could cleave through illusion as easily as it could through bone. Asterious believed it might save Sinevia, but Caramyn's Raven Sight revealed it could kill her—even here. It was not bound to curse or blessing, Light or Shadow—it commanded them.

The vision narrowed. Not on visible details, but on forces unseen with the mortal eye. She saw the forbidden magic animating the corpse soldier, how it moved not with muscle or any will, but like a puppet on a string pulled by Shadows stitched through sinew. And every so often, like the way Sinevia had flickered as she talked, the soldier's strength wavered for just a breath.

And she counted the seconds until it would happen again, like a steady rhythm as certain as a drum beat. One...two...three...falter. Sinevia would waver, and her soldier would falter. And the sword's power responded to her presence, as if reaching for her, tugging incessantly on something within her as a glowing essence of Light and Shadow intertwined around its gleaming blade.

Caramyn snapped back into herself and let the unforgiving seconds pass before the brief fracture in Sinevia's power flickered again.

One...two...three...

The death soldier's grip weakened, for less than a pulse. Caramyn drove her head backward, the crack of skull against rotting bone rattling in her ears and the pain of the impact turning her stomach. She twisted from its grasp as the thing staggered, and she did not give it time to recover.

As she ran toward Asterious, something snapped into place within her, like a soul finding its body. Her Sight caught glimpse of some string of essence, ethereal and sacred, that did not feel like magic, but more like a bond made manifest. A force that bound their fates. And she followed it, her heart beating out of her chest as Sinevia tailed her, cursing her name.

Six strides carried her to Asterious. He did not move when she reached him. He did not seem to hear her or see her.

But he would feel her.

Hope flared in her, that if she could just touch him, if she could just awaken him with the presence of that bond, he'd come back to her. His fingers were locked around the hilt of the Blade, knuckles bloodless, the weapon humming with restrained power. Caramyn grabbed his wrists and pried, her last hope literally locked within his hand.

She whispered, "Please, break free. I know you're strong enough."

Then Asterious looked up for the first time since Sinevia had taken his mind hostage. His eyes, one thunder grey, one silver, swept across the Veil and Sinevia charging toward them, something raging and lethal in her movements—and something sharp and glinting in her hand.

He released the sword to Caramyn just as Sinevia reached them. She raised the Blade above her head and swung, just as some piercing pain cut through her core, and when the edge came down on Sinevia, it shattered in a blinding explosion of light.

61

SHADOWBORN

Caramyn

The faint smell of smoke, ash, and burning wood filled her nostrils. The echo of flames crackled somewhere in the distance, as if on the other side of a wall. Asterious screamed her name, far away in a dream.

She was lying on the ground, surrounded by shattered pieces of black steel, looking up at the Veil. Shadows danced at the Veil's great tree and drew near to her, slithering up and around her arms, illuminating her Shadowblood veins. And in the midst of them stood a tall, menacing figure, with void-black eyes and inky veins like hers crawling across every inch of visible skin beneath his black mage's robe.

"Caramyn."

He called her name, his voice a gentle, comforting contrast to his sinister appearance.

"Caramyn, my child."

"Morveth?" She asked weakly, though the words weren't coming from her mouth, but rather from somewhere in her thoughts.

"Yes, my daughter." He inclined his head, dark eyes warm despite the shadows clinging to his form. *"Well done. The Blade is broken. It is the final proof that your power has awakened. It has released Shadows from their charge of protecting you, the last vessel of Shadow magic."* A faint smile touched his lips, pride softening his features. "And it has freed my bound form."

Caramyn stared at him, unable to look away, unable to respond, her jaw hanging open in disbelief and overwhelm.

"It was the only way to save you in your mother's womb," Morveth continued, lifting a hand toward the towering presence of the Veil. *"Your life is bound to it, and its life to yours. I never knew if the binding would hold—if you would even survive. And if you did, whether you would one day seek the truth."* His voice lowered. *"But I hoped. And now my soul knows that hope was not misplaced."*

"How?" Caramyn gasped, a subtle sting of pain rising in her stomach. "How is any of this possible? What about what Mother did to save me—when she sought out the witch?"

"The witch did nothing more than attempt a spell many have tried for centuries—and failed. By the time your mother reached her, your heart had already stopped. Shadowbloods were never meant to bear offspring. Our immortal blood is incompatible with creating new life." His expression darkened. *"But I could not let you die."*

"I'd been summoned to Felhold to discuss the celebration and talks of unity." He drew a slow breath. *"I fled Daemar's court once I learned of his true plans for the Order. I warned the Lightborn, abandoned the Shadowbloods and went into hiding—because I loved your mother, and I knew Daemar would use that against me. And he did. Eventually, he found me, and he promised he'd spare her if I would help him rid the world of magic. He didn't know she carried another life within her. And your mother never knew about the deal. I let her believe terrible things to protect her."*

Caramyn's chest tightened. She'd always believed the same. Always thought her father was a coward who'd left them to fend for themselves. And now he was standing before her in this dream-like state, a High Shadowblood who gave up the last of his power—and his reputation—just to save her.

"At the very moment your mother crossed the witch's threshold, I stood here before Daemar, raising the Veil and binding its power to the dying life within her womb—unbeknownst to all but me."

"It made me a traitor to so many, but a savior to you. And when Daemar tried to kill me—as I knew he would once the Veil was formed—I denied him the satisfaction." His gaze sharpened. *"I drove the sword through myself, trapping my soul within it so I could remain on this side of the Veil. So that one day, only when someone worthy of shouldering the darkness alongside you freed me, I could ensure the transfer of the last of my power to you in its fullness, when I knew that you wouldn't have to bear it alone. And when I was sure that you were ready to receive it."*

"What...what does this mean?"

"It means, my child, that you are the first and only Shadowborn, and the sole heir of a power capable of commanding both Light and Shadow. That is why Sinevia seeks your magic. Because none has ever been strong enough to raise an immortal army—until you, Caramyn Shadowborn."

The weight of it all pressed down on her. "What happens now?" she whispered through a lump in her throat, the pain beneath her ribs becoming more difficult to ignore. "What am I supposed to do? Will you help me learn what I am?"

A sadness touched his smile.

"I cannot. Not from here." He glanced toward the Veil, its presence humming softly. *"The Blade—my anchor to this realm—is broken, as it was always meant to be. The Veil is but a bridge between the living and the dead. I will pass beyond it, to the Realm of Souls, where all of us eventually must find our rest."* He met

her gaze one final time. *"My purpose here is fulfilled. And now yours has just begun."*

Morveth's apparition vanished as quickly as it came, leaving each word to echo in her mind as she fought to understand it all. And as her father's voice fell away, and power flooded her, weaving itself through her veins until, for a heartbeat, she felt them, then glimpsed—for a mere fraction of a moment—the shadowed tips of wings unfolding from her back.

All at once, the world crashed back into her.

The snow and cold air bit into her skin. The smoke-filled air burned her lungs. Wild amber flames consumed the edge of the glade, roaring through the branches as they burned through the forest. Asterious—his terrified eyes on hers, looking down at her, holding her in his arms.

And then the pain hit. White-hot and nauseating, radiating from her abdomen in violent waves. She looked down, breath hitching, and saw the dark ruby stain soaked through her clothes. Her shaking hand, when she pressed it to her stomach, came away slick and red. Too much blood. Far too much.

And then she remembered, all at once, in brutal fragments—the way Sinevia had charged toward her just as she'd lifted the Shadowblood sword. The way she'd plunged that cold dagger into Caramyn's body just as she brought down the Blade onto her. And the way she'd vanished when it shattered into pieces at her touch.

And now she lay here, bleeding out beneath a burning smog overtaking her Woods, her body slack across the Blackwynd Prince's lap as he pleaded with her not to die.

But his voice was somewhere she could not answer. And she was already drifting away from the sound of him, falling into the void of the Veil, where darkness and light waited as one.

62

TWO FAVORS IN ONE

Asterious

As his senses flooded back, the visions in his mind slipped away like ghosts, leaving him to face a reality just as horrifying—a burning forest, a broken blade, and his mate lifeless on the snow, an ominous tear forming in the Veil before them.

Nothing mattered. Not the smoke stinging his nostrils with each inhale of the smog and cinders. Not the wildfire, not the bloodied melting snow, not the blackened trees that seemed to bow to their dying queen. Nothing mattered but her.

If she was gone, let him die with her. Let him be damned to be a prowling mindless beast for all eternity. It would be far more merciful than a lifetime spent without his mate.

Sinevia had taken her from him and left him here to watch her fade. And with her had vanished a shard of the Blade—a sign that she was not defeated, but gone by choice with a relic she'd no doubt taken for dark purposes far more sinister than he could imagine.

He dropped to his knees and gathered her into his arms. There was no gasp of breath, no hint of life to be found in her limp body, and even as hellfire illuminated the forest around them, the entire world fell dark to Asterious.

"No," he whispered, a lump burning in his throat. "Cara, please..."

She clung to him with a feeble touch. Those dusky violet eyes fluttered shut over an emotion he could not decipher beyond pain and fear. His chest hollowed as he held her, watching a thin line of blood trickle from her mouth.

"No!"

Shadows snaked around them like vipers ready to strike, hissing and wailing their mournful song. As her life flickered, so did the cracks forming in the Veil, as though her fading soul was splitting it open. And now as it rippled with the weakening of her heartbeats, the arms of the Veil reached out, Shadows surrounding her like a mantle, coming for her, as if clawing at some desperate attempt to save itself by reclaiming her.

"You can't take her!" His desperate shouts turned to cries, through blinding tears that he could not swallow back. "You can't take her! You can't! You can't..."

He buried his face into her neck, nestling into her hair as though he could revive her with the anguish in his cries. And there he felt the faintest slip of breath graze his ear.

There was still some life left in her.

He clutched her hopelessly, rocking her back and forth on the ground as embers and Shadow danced around them. His howls overpowered the roaring flames, filling the Woods with desperate pleas to whatever gods or winds or ancient fates were listening. To save her. To save his mate.

And at his most hopeless, as he stared down at her, he noticed something peeking out from her pocket. It was the talisman Brenn had given her, and all at once Asterious remembered what he'd overheard him tell her on the ship.

Use this. I will come.

He clutched the charm, whispering the name, and prayed it would be enough.

Long moments followed filled with nothing but the agonizing crackling of fire and the sounds of the writhing Shadows within the Veil echoing their cries as they demanded their keeper.

Asterious watched Caramyn's chest, counting the seconds in between her feeble last breaths. He squeezed her cold hand, a tear falling onto her wound and mixing with the blood oozing from her stomach.

Footsteps made him jump, and the smallest bit of hope sprung up within him at the sight of Brenn walking toward them through the flames. He did not understand how it was possible for him to find them, or how he'd gotten here. But he didn't give a damn.

"Help her...please!" His voice cracked.

Brenn looked at Caramyn with gentle, pitied eyes, before addressing the prince. "I don't know what I can do for her." He crouched down beside Caramyn, placing a steady hand on her neck. Asterious watched, unable to blink as the warmth of her skin faded to a cold pallor despite the fire's glow.

"You're telling me there's *nothing* that can save her?" Asterious hit the ground with his fist so hard he thought the earth might crack beneath it. "Aren't you the healer who spoke so highly of your magic? What good is it if you can't save her?"

Brenn swallowed, his brow beginning to sweat as the flames drew dangerously near. He wouldn't look at Asterious. Shadows shifted around him, whispering, threatening to take Caramyn once and for all as the tear in the Veil grew wider.

He finally spoke. "Reviving someone from the brink of death...it just isn't done. And even if it could be, a life cannot be given without a life taken. Healing magic takes this very seriously."

"Use mine." Asterious spat.

"It means you'll die." Brenn glanced up at him.

"I don't care. Use it. Take my life and save Caramyn's. I gladly give it up for hers."

Brenn hesitated before looking back down at the dying girl. "This may not work the way you want it to, Asterious, I'm begging you to reconsider—"

"Fucking save her!" the prince roared.

Brenn nodded stiffly. "Very well," he said. "I...I need a vessel. Something forged to channel magic."

Asterious turned to glimpse his shreds of clothing lying nearby, immediately thinking of an object that could suffice. He scrambled to his feet, searching the torn shirt for his mother's ring. It was there, somehow undisturbed in the shirt pocket, thank the Shattered gods.

He couldn't work it out of the fabric fast enough, and held it up, breathless. "Will this work?"

Brenn studied the ring. "Is it enchanted already?"

"Yes, by Lightborn magic."

Brenn frowned. "I can't undo the enchantment. Is there anything else?"

"Damn it, Brenn!" Asterious threw the ring into the fire, glancing over once more at Caramyn's lifeless form. She had to be gone by now.

Then a glint of something caught his eye, the firelight reflecting off something in the ground beyond where they stood. The broken blade of the Shadowblood's sword. It had been strong enough to hold whatever power had exploded from it when it splintered into pieces. Surely it could channel a healing spell strong enough to pull Caramyn from the arms of death.

He rushed over, grabbing a fragment of the blade and sprinting back to Brenn. The fire should have swallowed them now, but the Shadows seemed to be slowing the flames as they prowled, circling in wait, to claim Caramyn the second she slipped from this world.

"This will work. It *has* to work." He held the shard up to Brenn's face, the reflection of his own eyes staring back at him in the obsidian blade.

Brenn reached out to take the broken piece, his fingers tense and his expression leery. "This is a Shadow relic. I don't know what catastrophe could ensue by channeling Light magic with a Shadow vessel. I know better than to dabble in something that may very well steal my soul in return."

Asterious' gaze hardened. "I'll damn your soul and my own a thousand times if it means saving hers. She is a Shadowblood. It will not corrupt her."

Brenn's eyes darkened. "I will try," he rasped. "But I warn you, I don't know what will happen."

"I don't care what happens to you or me," Asterious growled. "Just save her before it's too late!" He snatched the midnight shard from Brenn's grasp and placed it in Caramyn's open palm. "Now do what needs to be done! If it kills me and saves her, you'll have done the world two favors in one."

With a heavy sigh, Brenn stooped to slice Caramyn's open hand with the fragment, a line of bright crimson oozing from the cut. "Now yours. So that your life can flow to her through the connection the Blade creates," he said.

Asterious did as he instructed, hands trembling as he swiped the broken blade across his own palm. He gazed down at Caramyn, her eyes now closed as though she was sleeping. Still beautiful. His rose, wilting before him as he longed for nothing more than to see those striking eyes of amethyst once more, knowing that if—when—her eyes opened again, he would not be alive to see it. But it was a cruel price he would gladly pay.

Brenn placed the bloodied shard over Caramyn's heart, lifted his hands with a nod, and began an incantation. Words flowed from him, different from Sinevia's dark rune spells. Lighter, more poetic. More hopeful.

As though struggling against some invisible entity, Brenn fought to get out his words. A stream of light flowed forth from the broken blade, weakening as it stretched toward the wound in Asterious' palm, its glow dimming with the effort. The prince waited, expecting to feel the life pulled from him at any moment, but with bitter, aching disappointment, he felt nothing.

"Stop holding back, mage!" cried Asterious.

Brenn's eyes sharpened with coldness as he shot a threatening glare at the prince.

"I do this only for *her*. Not for you. *Never* for you."

With a shout that reverberated so loud it might split the Veil, Brenn opened his arms wide. He called the Shadows in his enchanted language, and they merged with the golden current of his healing Light magic, twisting and intertwining with renewed strength. Whatever repercussions could come of it, Asterious decided it couldn't be worse than letting Caramyn die.

The blinding glow of light coiled within the spiraling starkness of Shadows snaked from the blade, over Caramyn's heart, crawling like ivy up her arm and then Asterious'. As Brenn chanted harder, sweat now beading on his brow, a sudden crushing pain gripped Asterious' heart, tightening with relentless strength far more intense than even the pain he'd felt under Sinevia's curse.

Despite the agony, he stilled his quivering body by reassuring himself that the pain meant his life was now being transferred to Caramyn. The pressure in his chest grew suffocating, and his heartbeat thundered in his ears, slowing beneath the crushing sensation. And just as he felt he could no longer bear it, Caramyn's eyes flew open. Her chest rose as she dragged in a sharp, desperate breath, color blooming back into her face. And with the certainty of her survival seared into him at last, he finally let go.

63
BEYOND BLOOD OR VOW

Caramyn

Caramyn woke to Asterious looming over her, swaying weakly, his eyes pained and depleted. She bolted upright at the worrisome sight of him and the steady snaps of flames that sounded too close to ignore. She glanced down to where there was once a deep wound and the feeling of blood pooling in her lungs, but now there was only a scarlet stain on freshly healed skin, and a deep, steady breath in her chest. She winced from the sudden sting of a fresh wound on her palm.

She reached for Asterious, the marks of agony across his face now turned to those of relief. But then, the light in those silver-grey eyes dimmed as he fell forward into her arms.

The lifeless prince draped across her lap, heavy in her arms, as flames lapped at every corner. And there was Brenn in the midst of it all, somehow. She thought she had heard his voice earlier as she slipped in and out of consciousness. And now, that same voice was desperate, as he stood yelling to the blackened sky as Shadows swarmed like flocking birds.

"What's happening, Brenn?" Her voice quivered.

"I...I tried to heal you. The prince begged me to save you. But I fear what I may have done."

"What?" Something like unfettered rage stirred beneath Caramyn's skin, like she might explode any minute, and nothing could stop it. Like every small, unwelcome sound, or a single wrong word from Brenn, could release the fury building in her bones. "So you killed him...to save me?"

A strange, untamed strength took hold from somewhere within and worked its way outwards, like a fire igniting with nowhere to go. Black fire tinged with purple hues snaked its way down her arms and settled into burning orbs of black and violet flames in each hand. Behind her, flaming raven wings of blackfire unfurled, casting shadows that writhed like living smoke.

And every move, every breath, every thought, was driven by one thing—desire for vengeance upon the man who'd taken Asterious from her.

Her heart and hands ablaze with raw, unstoppable power, Caramyn lunged toward Brenn, feeling herself becoming something she didn't recognize. And it was only the sound of her name that stopped her.

"Caramyn."

She whirled around at the sound of Asterious' voice, her flaming wings folding, the amethyst flames still coiling up her wrists.

"You're alive?" She whispered.

Asterious nodded, his voice like low, calm thunder. "I'm still here."

She glanced back at Brenn, who still grasped at the sides of his head, shielding himself from her wrath. And suddenly, she realized how close she'd come to scorching him to death. "I'm...I'm sorry, Brenn. I didn't mean to...I don't know what happened to—"

"I think I do," Asterious said quietly, pain cutting through his composure. "And if I'm right, I'll beg your forgiveness until my last breath, Caramyn. Because this is something I never meant for you to carry." He lifted his shirt to reveal the silvery-black veins of the Blackheart curse—still there, but utterly transformed. No longer did they consume his entire torso, no longer did they claw inward toward his heart. Now they originated from a single point at the center of his spine, branching outward and up, jagged, wing-like veins blooming outward across the left half of his back and chest, as though reaching for something beyond his own body. The markings flowed down his left arm to his fingertips, no longer crawling towards his heart, but yearning outward. "You hold the balance. You took half of my darkness, and half of my Light."

Caramyn stared at him, then looked down at her own arm, the realization creeping in like the black veins that now covered it completely, her Shadowblood marking still there in the hollow of her elbow, but now woven into a new pattern that sprouted from a defined point rooted at the center of her spine. Crackling branches unfurled like twin wings, each arcing toward the other across her back and ribs, never quite touching. A pattern that mirrored Asterious' perfectly, and if they stood skin bare, side by side, it would've formed a symmetrical union of the black shimmering lines that met at the fanning tips.

Caramyn studied the flames in her hands, and the way they pulsed in time with her breath. Of course. A curse that preyed on deepest fears and emotion would not manifest the same way twice. Asterious' Blackheart was the wolf—strength, fortitude, endurance. Hers had become fire—survival, will, transformation. Something untamable.

She'd almost lost herself to it. And combined with the innate power of Shadow she carried in her blood, she shuddered to imagine how strong it could be.

I'm not a monster.

"A Blackheart?" Brenn shouted at Asterious, staggering between them. "I thought that was a myth." He stooped and grabbed the broken blade used to complete the spell and hurled it into the raging fire with a hoarse cry. "And yet you fractured it. Split a singular, deadly curse in two. That shouldn't be possible. There's no explanation for any of this unless—" He froze, something like horror dawning in his eyes. "Unless the curse recognized her as bound to you beyond blood or vow."

"Unless...she is my mate." Asterious looked at Caramyn through tear stains dried beneath blood and cinder, confirming the bond she'd felt—that she'd *seen*—between them. This prince who had once been no more than a stranger trespassing in these Woods, so fierce, regal, strong, and unshakeable, now stood before her in tattered, bruised, and broken, stripped of any armor but the truth. "The Blackheart no longer seeks a heart to claim. It reaches across us now—toward each other. And that means it will never stop reaching."

Caramyn noticed something like torment claiming his movements. Something like regret, uncertainty, and fear most of all. In his eyes, she saw everything she'd carried alone for years. Rage, grief, defiance, shame, and the ache of surviving when the world had demanded she break.

Did he know? Had he understood what it would mean when he'd asked Brenn to save her? How could he have known? If he had been dying, she would have done the same. Without hesitation. To watch one's mate die would bring the kind of desperation that made one, well, *reckless*.

Her heart had already been darkened by the world. The Blackheart had simply lit that dark heart afire. Not to destroy her, but to free her. To free *both* of them. To shape the pain into something purposeful. Something *good*.

She folded her wings behind her back. They vanished into smoke, and the violet flames died with them. The fire raging around them went up in a violent burst toward the sky before extinguishing, as if commanded by the same flames within her, leaving behind nothing but smoking tendrils and charred branches.

"I have nothing to forgive you for." Caramyn reached for the prince's cut hand. She pressed her palm to his and interlocked their fingers, mingling their blood. "I do not fear carrying darkness. We've been doing it all our lives. To carry it alone is the real curse. And we are no longer alone."

Asterious leaned forward, cupping her face in his hands. "I don't deserve to stand in your shadow, let alone at your side."

Caramyn faintly smiled at him, but something ominous swept over her as she stared at the rippling Veil in silence. It's abyss groaned and writhed as if beckoning her one last time, in either warning or in welcome, and it bothered her that she could not tell which. For a moment, she wondered what awaited beyond the great tree at its gate, and what it might've meant that the Veil had begun to split open as she was dying.

Asterious' voice pulled her from her spiral.

"We'll be back soon enough," he promised quietly. "But the road home calls us now."

"Yes," she sighed, a breath of relief as she flicked her gaze back to his face. "It does."

64
NOT OUT OF THE WOODS

Asterious

As the trio traversed back through the Woods, Asterious' thoughts weighted each step.

The Veil still stood. Sinevia was still queen. And in the furthest reaches of his mind, old scars had been torn open.

He knew the path to healing them would be a kind of torment all its own. But for now, he had all he cared to want. And as he watched the amethyst-eyed, fireborne woman walking ahead of him, leading them out of these Woods, he decided there was no kingdom he wouldn't let burn for her. She might have been a goddess of old, carrying herself with unshaken poise, new confidence blazing within her, ash and scorched shadow tracing her beautiful face like the memory of flames that had dared to burn her, and failed. Even the trees seemed to bow in her wake.

As they wound their way through the Woods with Brenn in tow, the only sound was frost splintering beneath their boots. There were no longer any traces of hissing Shadows or their chilling distant whispers, leaving the forest unnaturally still. A strange quiet had settled, a fragile peace that almost felt more dangerous than the Shadows' presence ever had.

Still, the unseen weight bore down on him of what had happened at the Veil. He'd been so sure—so foolishly sure—that once he had the Blade on his side, he would be able to reach Sinevia and pull her from the darkness that had ensnared her. Yet, she'd been unreachable, even as he'd offered her every chance to turn away from the Shadows.

"You did everything you could." Caramyn said softly, calming the storm raging through his mind. He hadn't even noticed that she'd stopped to wait for him to catch up.

The prince smiled weakly and looked ahead, the edge of the Woods a beacon of light in the distance. "Sinevia will come for you again. We must learn the extent of your power before she does." He clenched his jaw at the thought.

Sinevia didn't hesitate to stab Caramyn—didn't show an ounce of restraint at the thought of killing her.

There was no further room for grace. He couldn't keep lying to himself. He could no longer choose to see Sinevia as merely a victim of his father's cruelty, no longer only his misunderstood sister. She was an enemy who refused to yield, even when given the chance. And suddenly all of it—the magnitude of what lay ahead hit him like a gust of wind. "Before long, we'll need more allies to help oppose her...and we must begin spreading the truth of my identity to gain the people's trust."

Brenn's voice cut through the crunch of slush and dried leaves beneath their boots—surprising Asterious, given how long he'd lingered at the back of the line without a word. "I've heard talk of remaining Lightborn in hiding and secret druid councils that may be willing to accept the ascension of a half-Lightborn king—even if he is a Blackwynd. I'll spread the word and see if we can get them to organize."

"Thank you, Brenn." Caramyn nodded.

"Make no mistake, I don't do it for him." He jutted his chin toward Asterious. "I do it for magickind. For my family," he said. "And if this half-breed mutt prince is my best hope of seeing them again, then so be it."

Asterious glared at him, but his voice was hopeful and sure. "I cannot promise to restore everything lost—but I can promise to try." He turned away, resuming his forward pace toward the edge of the forest with Brenn and Caramyn trailing on either side. "Bring those that you find to Vaerwynd. We can build ally camps in the witchlands."

Brenn flicked his head in acknowledgement before straying from the path as the clear landscape ahead came into view through the lines of the trees ahead. "My horse awaits further down," he said. "If I find anyone willing, I'll do as you've asked. And Caramyn," he looked at her, his words landing softer. "It's been an honor."

Caramyn lifted a hand in farewell, dipping her head in a slight bow. A few shuddering breaths and trudging steps later, Brenn had already put a wide stretch of forest between them, their paths, and their destinies, quietly diverging among the trees.

"You trusted him enough to tell him all that?" Caramyn blinked, lining her steps with Asterious'.

"I'm not sure I have much of a choice. He already knows everything else. Besides, I'm sure you'll burn him to a crisp if he tries to double-cross us." Asterious laughed. "Don't worry. I'm sure we haven't seen the last of him."

Caramyn wrinkled her nose. "What makes you think I'm worried about whether or not we see him again?"

"You kept his talisman, didn't you?" Asterious teased as Caramyn shook her head without response.

Their steps quickened as the edge of the Woods greeted them. The last light of ember sunset dwindled through the branches and guided them towards the silhouette of a small camp where Leejia, Starke, Tyrios, Gariel, and Riven awaited them. They met them with tears and embraces and tale of how Wyran managed to slip into the Woods, despite their efforts to stop him.

"It was as if the Shadows wanted him for some unknown purpose, drawing him in while casting us out." Leejia explained.

"The Shadows have a way of making people think they're in control." Caramyn uttered. "Wyran was just a willing pawn in a much bigger game."

"As we all seem to be at some point or another..." Asterious stared into the stretch of open land before them, the looming Bleak Wilderness waiting to be traversed before the next snowfall. "For now, we return to Vaerwynd Court to regain our strength. We're going to need it for whatever lies ahead."

Alofreise nudged his hand, and he gave the stallion an affectionate pat before mounting, Caramyn settling behind him in the saddle. Together, they all set out for home, back to the forbidden witchlands, leaving the Shadow Woods and all that it held behind.

65
FOR NOW AND FOREVER

Caramyn

It had been days since they'd returned. Vaerwynd castle was buzzing with life, as a new hope had sprung within the court as the account of what happened in the Shadow Woods spread, but also a sense of unspoken fear, for now the Shadowborn lived and breathed within their walls.

Frostlight would begin in a few weeks. Asterious assured her even Sinevia wouldn't disregard Evylere's largest and oldest celebration shared by magickind and human alike if she wanted to maintain her influence over the people. Felhold and the rest of the kingdom would be busy with the season's preparations, and it would give her some time to become more familiar with her power.

But Caramyn hadn't left her room, for fear of losing control of herself once again. Whenever she thought too long or too hard about even the slightest frustration, flames flickered at her fingertips like ash-tipped amethyst. She suppressed thoughts of how fiercely she missed the feeling of Asterious' body against hers, and how she saw him each night in her dreams, and the embarrassment she felt knowing the prince likely could feel the strength of her desire through their bond.

At sunset, she stood at the window of her room watching snow flurries dust the withered garden below.

Her room.

A knock at the door made her turn.

"Come in," she said gently.

"You have a gift," cooed Azell, peeking her head in through the door. "If you want it."

Caramyn lifted her chin in curiosity as Azell entered and placed a long box across her bed. With a mischievous smile, the maid exited without another word.

Caramyn peeked beneath the lid with slow, careful movements.

There within the box lay a ballgown—sleeveless—glittering like the night sky and accented with fabric rosettes and intricate vines of lilac and wisteria. Quite possibly the most beautiful piece of clothing she'd ever seen. She picked it up by the corseted bodice to examine the delicate beadwork closer. And beneath it, she found a handwritten note.

> *I know you prefer personal deliveries, but I'm afraid if I'd taken the pleasure of bringing it to you myself, I wouldn't be able to experience the full brunt of your rejection, if you decide to leave me standing in an empty ballroom—as I so rightfully deserve. But if you still want that dance for your birthday, consider it yours.*

With a blush that left her cheeks heated, Caramyn smiled. Azell returned soon enough to help her into the fitted strapless bodice, smoothing out the thick satin skirts that bloomed from beneath the corset and flowed to the floor, and doing her hair into an intricate half-up, half down style that left her loose brown waves tumbling down her back.

With a deep breath, Caramyn counted the steps down the stairs, focusing on keeping her emotions in check as she made her way to the grand ballroom. Just before entering, she stood at the half-open door, remembering where she had once lingered in the darkness in awe at the beauty of the empty ballroom on the other side and yearned for a moment like this. Finally, still clinging to her breath, she pushed the door open, and walked through.

The ballroom was now bathed with lively warmth, even though night had fallen. Starlight shimmered through the snow-sprinkled glass ceiling, creating refractions of light that seemed to fragile and celestial for this world. Through the ivy curling up the walls and the ornate pillars gleamed a radiance that felt all too much like magic. The white floor glittered from the kiss of moonlight above, and in the center of it, within the arcs of the crescent moon emblem, waited Asterious.

He stood, dressed in a regal uniform of midnight and silver that made those eyes of steel and thunder steal her breath as he held them fixed on her.

"You came," he said.

"It's almost like something just won't let me stay away." Caramyn smirked, glancing down at her arm at the black patterns that mirrored his. "And you do still owe me that dance." Her voice was light, but inwardly, she still carried the fear of what might happen if she let too much emotion shine through.

Asterious held out his hand. "I'll dance with you until every last star falls if that's what you want."

She stepped forward to take it. He pulled her closer and began to sway gently. Her body tingled at the soft sensation of his hands holding her, guiding her footsteps through a dream, moving as one. She let herself fall into it, swept into each movement as the sweet music filled the air in a language all its own.

"Don't be afraid of it—of yourself." Asterious leaned in, his lips grazing ear as he spoke. "It was you who showed me that sometimes the only way to control the power within...is to let go."

"But what if I can't stop myself from going too far?" Caramyn whispered. "I could destroy everything."

"The alternative is destroying yourself. And I won't let you do that." Asterious' voice was like velvet. "You showed me how to break free, Cara. And I will be here with you through it to help you do the same. Because I love you."

Caramyn beamed, her fear melting away as she stared into those rolling thunderclouds that pierced through her like lightning.

She could fight against the darkness raging within her, but she stood no chance against the fierce longing she felt, or against the deep love for him—her *mate*—that claimed her whole. And when Asterious touched his lips to hers, she surrendered herself into his arms.

He breathed against her, the faintest hint of a beastly purr buried in his words. "You, little mystery, are finally *mine*."

His hands found the small of her back, and a sigh slipped from her lips. She gripped his midnight hair, raking her fingers across it as his mouth wandered from hers and down her neck and chest. With tender movements, his fingers carefully teased the lace at her back, and Caramyn reached for him, sliding her hands beneath his shirt, eventually trailing from his stomach to the hard length below. He pushed himself against her as though he could merge himself with her where they stood. But then he pulled away for just a pulse, and Caramyn knew he must've sensed her emotions overwhelming her through their bond.

"We should take things slow," he whispered. "Until you're stronger...only as much as you feel ready."

"As much as I want you," Caramyn muttered softly, "I agree." She slid her hand out from beneath his belt and back up along his abdomen, tracing the branching scars with her fingers, still yearning to feel him to the fullest, but knowing her heart, her mind, and her power, were not yet ready. To entwine herself with her mate, and the literal other half of her heart, while still learning the depths of the power that bound them, terrified her and enthralled her all at once. "Just hold me for now."

"For now, and forever." Asterious breathed into her hair before drawing back to meet her gaze. "Just keep your eyes on me."

About the Author

To keep up with my current works and be the first to hear about new releases and special reader opportunities, follow me on social media @authorvalelane or sign up for my newsletter at authorvalelane.com
Be sure to follow along for updates about the next book in the Shadowblood Duet series and check out my other series:

THE SHADOWBLOOD DUET

FROM TORMENTED TIDES *Trilogy*